Oxfordshi...

To renew:

Hilary Boyd ... ...fordshire g... ...ries ... a small
cancer charity before becoming an author. She has written
twelve books, including *Thursdays in the Park*, her debut novel,
which sold more than half a million copies and was an inter-
national bestseller.

By the same author

Thursdays in the Park
Tangled Lives
When You Walked Back into My Life
A Most Desirable Marriage
Meet Me on the Beach
The Lavender House
A Perfect Husband
The Anniversary
The Lie
The Affair
The Hidden Truth

The Escape

HILARY BOYD

PENGUIN BOOKS

PENGUIN BOOKS

UK | USA | Canada | Ireland | Australia
India | New Zealand | South Africa

Penguin Books is part of the Penguin Random House group of companies
whose addresses can be found at global.penguinrandomhouse.com.

First published 2023

001

Copyright © Hilary Boyd, 2023

The moral right of the author has been asserted

Set in 12.5/14.75pt Garamond MT Std
Typeset by Jouve (UK), Milton Keynes
Printed and bound in Great Britain by Clays Ltd, Elcograf S.p.A.

The authorized representative in the EEA is Penguin Random House Ireland,
Morrison Chambers, 32 Nassau Street, Dublin D02 YH68

A CIP catalogue record for this book is available from the British Library

ISBN: 978-1-405-95223-1

www.greenpenguin.co.uk

'My dad had limitations. That's what my good-hearted mom always told us. He had limitations, but he meant no harm. It was kind of her to say, but he did do harm.'

Gillian Flynn

Prologue

Walthamstow, 10 December

Dearest Bel,

I'm so sorry to be writing this. I know what I've done will shock you to the core, but I felt I had no choice. Things have been hell recently, for both of us. But you're so much better at handling it than me. I've been feeling as if my head would burst. I know the restaurant is history. And I know I've been in denial about the situation. But recently it's begun to sink in that my lifelong dream for 83 is over. You've known for some time, of course. For me, realizing this was the last straw.

Something crazy has happened to me, Bel. I hoped you would never find out about this – I'm not proud of it – but back during lockdown I started dropping in on Trinny sometimes when I went for my run. (As you know, she lives near the park.) It was just sex at first. I like her, obviously, we all do, but I was really just being incredibly selfish and sounding off at what was a difficult time for us all. Then two weeks ago she told me she was four months pregnant. (Christ, even writing this is painful, as I know how I treated you in the past, faced with the same situation, and how devastating it was for you when things didn't work out back then.) Anyway, Trinny wants to go back to her family – who live in south-west France, as you may remember. And it seemed like the ideal opportunity for a new start. So I've gone with her. I know what I said about being a father again, but somehow this feels different — maybe it's my age. I can get work there easily, I imagine.

I realize you will hate me for this. And I deserve everything you throw at me. But neither of us has been particularly happy for a long while now, Bel. I partly blame my obsession with the restaurant — I haven't been easy to live with, or very nice to you at times because of it, and I truly apologize for that. Things just seemed to fizzle out between us, didn't they? Maybe working together, and the financial strain of 83, killed it for us, I don't know . . . Anyway, sell the place, take what's left. I relinquish my share of the flat and the business.

I wish you all the very best in your life, Bel. I will remember what we once had with love and great fondness.

And so, goodbye.
Louis xxx

As Bel sat, letter in hand, on the dusty step leading down to the street from their Walthamstow flat, emotions surged through her body, like a typhoon hurling everything about in its path. Shock, disbelief, excruciating hurt and contempt vied for pole position. But it was pure, uncontaminated rage that won out. Her whole being seemed electrified by it, to such a degree that she was catapulted upright, swinging the hand holding the letter round so hard in the narrow hallway that it hit the wall with brute force and she screamed. But instead of nursing her bruised hand to her chest, she ignored the pain. Instead Bel, who had never screamed in her life, just screamed some more, and louder. Unembarrassed, barely herself, she flopped over, knees bent, back arched, hands balled into fists, and allowed the sound to pour unfettered from her open mouth: an ear-shattering, visceral howl of agony.

No one heard, the blare of the London traffic drowning her out. If anyone did hear, like most city dwellers they would barely have registered it – just someone messing about. Finally she ran out of steam, the noise weakening with every breath until it was just a breathless squeak.

The letter was still in her right fist, crumpled into an angry wad, Louis's small writing fractured by the heavy creases in the paper. But she unfolded it, smoothed out the single sheet with shaky fingers as she tried to get her breath back.

What shocked her almost more than his words, on this second reading, was his unwavering air of complacency. Yes, she'd hate him, he was saying, *But, hey, it is what it is.* They hadn't been happy, after all. And what's a guy to do, given this wonderful opportunity to dump all responsibility for the collapse of his business – plus his partner of nearly fifteen years, of course – and walk off into the sunset with 83's pouty French waitress, their baby and a brand new life?

Their baby . . . That was a step too far. Bel could not deal with that particular agony right now.

PART ONE

I

March, three months later

'Didn't sleep a wink,' Bel's father complained, blinking at her.

She'd got up early – as she'd been doing every day since moving back to her childhood flat in late January – so she could make her breakfast in peace, potter around, do some chores and listen to the radio for a couple of hours on her own, before her father emerged from his lair. The vast quantities of wine or whisky he consumed on a nightly basis tended to knock him out till gone ten most mornings. But Dennis had beaten her to it today, and was already ensconced at the table in the kitchen reading the *Telegraph*, a cup of coffee cradled in one hand.

'Our Spanish friend was stamping around into the wee hours,' her father went on. 'I was of a mind to go up and give him what for, but I couldn't be arsed.' The 'friend' in question was a very polite banker in his fifties, who was clearly an insomniac, his slippered feet shushing back and forth across the parquet floor in the flat above Dennis's room on the rare nights he was in town. Bel had been summoned to listen on one occasion. The sound was barely audible – but she appreciated it was hard to ignore once you'd begun to notice.

'Poor you,' she said lightly. It didn't do to get too involved or this popular bellyache could gather momentum very quickly. Like the one about the boots and the buggy the Argentinian family on the ground floor left cluttering the hall, or the fact that the owners of the top flat rented to Airbnb customers every summer.

She went over and pulled a mug from the cupboard. 'Is the coffee still hot?'

'I'd make some more, if I were you.' She felt his eyes on her back as she did so, watching, always watching, or so it seemed to her. 'So what are you up to later? I can hardly bear the excitement of my own day.' He accompanied his words with a jaundiced snort.

Bel had observed, since she'd been back living with her father, that life for him and his age group had never quite returned to normal, post-pandemic. The bridge club, for example, had still not re-formed. The wine club had lost Petroc, its driving force, to the virus. And her father's social life generally had suffered, routines lost, with ongoing anxiety from those of his friends who remained. For someone who had always been sociable and busy, the losses had left a big gap. It was clear Dennis was bored and had too much empty time on his hands.

'I've still got paperwork to finish,' she said, with an inward sigh. The flat and restaurant premises in Walthamstow had sold quickly. A young entrepreneur who planned to open another in a chain of vape stores had taken swift advantage of Bel's misfortune. She was left with nothing, the negative equity and defaulted mortgage payments – which Louis had hidden from her for months – eating up the sale money and

8

more, her life with Louis dismantled amid a humiliating pile of baffling online meetings and paperwork.

Her father, much to his quite reasonable irritation, had felt obliged to shell out a substantial sum to cover the shortfall. The loan, he'd grudgingly agreed, she and Louis would repay gradually, over time – an arrangement of which she'd informed Louis in France via email, although he had not chosen to respond. So Bel had had little option but to move in with her father again – although that part Dennis seemed to be enjoying.

Her father harrumphed. 'Well, you can make me some breakfast before you start, then. And not one of those nancy poached eggs you're so fond of. I need a proper full-fat fry-up this morning, bacon and the works, after the night I've had.'

Since her arrival back in the large West London flat where she'd grown up – and spent much of her thirties, indeed, following her devastating accident – Bel had taken over the cooking in a vain attempt to improve the appalling diet her father favoured: anything fried, sausage rolls, tinned soup, cake, and vast quantities of cheese and crackers, not a vegetable or piece of fruit in sight. Her efforts, though, met with such regular complaints that she might not have bothered if cooking hadn't been such a pleasure for her – particularly baking, when she tended to lose herself delightfully in the absorbing manipulation of the dough. 'We don't have any bacon,' she said.

'Christ, girl.' He rolled his eyes. 'What are you trying to do to me? I'm seventy-eight years old, pushing eighty. If I can't eat as much bacon as I like at this stage in my life, then when the hell can I?' Dennis Carnegie was thickset and of medium height, shorter than Bel. With his fleshy nose, smallish eyes, high forehead and mane of hair – originally black from his Italian grandmother, now white – people said he resembled the actor, Dustin Hoffman. And, like Hoffman, when he chose, Dennis had an easy, seductive charm and a quick wit. Women flirted with him, men wanted to hang out with him.

Ignoring his tetchiness, she said, 'True. If you die, you die, I suppose.'

Her father seemed to find this funny, his face breaking into a grin. 'That's the spirit. You'll get some for tomorrow, then, eh?'

'If you give me some food money, I will,' she said. It was agony having to ask for every penny, only to watch Dennis pore over the supermarket receipt and query every purchase. 'I loathe anchovies. Why did you buy anchovies?' he would grumble. Or 'One pound seventy for four rolls of toilet paper? Daylight bloody robbery.'

Bel made him fried eggs and fried bread, all of it squelching with grease so she wouldn't face any more complaints. For herself, she poured some muesli and chopped a banana on top.

Eyeing her as he munched, Dennis swallowed, then asked, 'Trying to lose weight?'

Bel winced. She had put on weight since Louis's defection, no longer rushed off her feet all day, or the recipient of her partner's elegant cooking. For a while, she found herself giving in to supermarket ready meals, or anything that required the minimum effort or thought. Plus chocolate . . . and biscuits. Sometimes a whole bar in one sitting, or an entire packet of Bourbons, eaten standing furtively at the kitchen counter, shovelling one after another into her mouth as if to fill the void. The sugar produced a guilty haze for a blissful hour or so, before the crashing low sent her reeling.

'Your mother always had such a perfect figure,' Dennis commented, with a wistful smile. 'I'm not sure who you take after. There's no one like you on my side of the family. And Agnes's lot were all like her: dark and petite and pretty. I loved the way your mum looked.'

Her cheeks burned with shame. Bel would willingly accept she could never be described as 'petite' but she didn't consider herself big either. Just tall, with an athletic build, her weight gain only moderate. She didn't respond, the muesli turning to sawdust in her mouth.

Dennis, perhaps realizing he'd offended her, reached across the table and laid his palm against her face for a second. 'You have the most beautiful violet eyes, though, sweetheart. Just like my own dear ma.' Leaning back, he added, 'Your generation are bigger on the whole, of course. Better nutrition in childhood, I imagine.'

'OK, Dad,' Bel cut in softly.

Dennis eyed her balefully. 'I was only saying. You go on about healthy eating, but it's not me who's carrying the extra pounds.'

Which was uncomfortably true. Unable to bear his scrutiny any longer, she got up and took her bowl to the sink, putting it down with deliberate care, as if it were her own heart. 'I'm going for a walk,' she said, feeling like a child again. She was being over-sensitive. She knew he didn't mean it. Knew he probably wasn't even aware of the effect he had on her.

Outside, the streets were still quite empty so early. It was a bright March Monday, and soon the gloomy red-brick West London square would be hectic with children, buggies, harassed parents on the way to school or people hurrying to work – the Tube station was only two hundred yards from Dennis's front door, on the busy main road.

A jogger almost collided with her as she stepped onto the pavement from the flat entrance, then swerved round her, giving her a wide berth as she began walking away from the roar of traffic – rising up, twenty-four/seven, from Earls Court Road like an insatiable beast – towards Holland Park via the quieter streets. She'd been walking a lot in recent weeks. Not in a conscious effort to get fit or lose the weight her father had mentioned, but because it went some way to soothing her jittery mind, gave her a temporary break from the constant anxiety about her future, the oppressive gloom of the flat and the brooding presence of her bored father. Sometimes she felt so isolated, it was as if she and her dad were the only people left alive in the whole world. *This is my life now*, she told herself, as she entered the high, wrought-iron gates of the park. But she struggled to find the positives in that statement.

'So, how's the job-hunting coming along?' Later that morning, the Zoom face of Krishna, the accountant who'd dealt with their restaurant business for years and had become a friend, peered at Bel with her usual fast-blinking, distracted expression, her dark hair in a disordered ponytail, her brown eyes rimmed grey with tiredness. She had four children under ten and a husband who worked most of every week in Marseille. *She has every right to be tired*, Bel thought.

They had been in regular touch since the debacle last December, and on many occasions returned to prod at the bruise that was Louis de Courcy. Krishna was kind, but tough with Bel. It was all about financial security in her book.

'I've got an interview tomorrow morning,' Bel replied, with more enthusiasm than she felt. 'A sort of bar-restaurant place on Kensington High Street, wanting a front-of-house. Not sure it's really my scene but I'll give it a go.' In fact, she was worried about her age. Would a trendy establishment like that — industrial-style decor, neon signage, a young crowd by the look of its Tripadvisor reviews — want a woman of fifty-seven? She doubted it. Plus her CV made her seem overqualified. She had virtually run her father's wine-importing business, then managed all the front-of-house side of 83. She was willing to do any work for the time being, though, that would get her out of the flat and give her some cash, even if it wasn't what she was used to, or paid badly. *They're probably looking for someone less than half my age*, she thought.

Krishna nodded encouragingly. 'At least you can stay on with your father. You don't have to worry about rent.'

'True,' Bel agreed, not mentioning the emotional price she felt she was paying in lieu. An independent woman, reduced to creeping home to her ageing father because she didn't have a bean to her name? It wasn't something to be proud of.

'You have your property in Cornwall, of course. What's the situation with the sitting tenant, these days? Prices out of London are still really strong.' Krishna cocked an eyebrow. 'It would free up some cash.'

Property? Bel couldn't help a smile. It made the house her mother, Agnes, had left her sound so grand. *More of a shack, really.* Situated in a small village on the not-so-trendy south-west coast, near Penzance, it was a tiny stone one-and-a-half up, one down that had belonged to Bel's grandmother before Agnes. But her mother had a kind heart, and as a favour to the then vicar had allowed Lenny Bright, a vulnerable young man, to move in, rent free. It was meant to be temporary, until he was found accommodation by Social Services. But Lenny had stayed on these past forty years.

'The cottage is yours,' Agnes had said to her twenty-two-year-old daughter, not long before she died. 'I haven't been there in years, I'm afraid. I know the community help Lenny with repairs and such – they never ask me for money – but you should go and check it out. Be kind to him, won't you? It's your inheritance, but it's his home for now.'

At the time, the last thing on Bel's mind, as her mother lay dying of a rare form of kidney cancer, was a cottage in Cornwall that she only vaguely remembered visiting during a few summers when she was young. Since then, the family had always been to some swanky villa in Tuscany or the South of France – Dennis had never considered Cornwall a proper holiday. But the year after Agnes's death, she'd made the long trek down to the south-west, not sure what she would find.

She was hijacked before she even got to the cottage door by Patsy, the nearest neighbour, whom she remembered her mother talking about – a tanned hippie, in her thirties, with straggling pink hair and an arm full of woven bracelets. Then she'd been introduced to an anxious committee, made up of Andrew, the vicar, Wayne, the landlord of the village pub, and others with whom she'd never got to grips. They guided her quickly into Patsy's house, where she was sat down with a strong cup of coffee and asked to listen.

Basically, they told her, Lenny loved the house. He was happy and settled for the first time in his life. And if Bel could see her way clear to leaving him there, just a bit longer, they would look after the house, and Lenny. They accepted it was irregular, they knew it couldn't go on for ever, but unless she was desperate for the money and wanted to sell, would she consider leaving Lenny in situ until such time as she did? Between them they would cover any costs and get help from Social Services.

At the time, she'd been on her way to Chamonix, to a job cooking in a large chalet, and a winter doing what she loved best: skiing. She'd had no desire to turf out the man she saw as her mother's tenant, and she hadn't needed the money. She was young and carefree, dying to leave the country and her father's oppressive grief. And in the years that followed, she hadn't even considered changing the long-standing arrangement her mother had made ... Or reneging on Agnes's exhortation to be kind. Even when she was desperate for the money, how could she live with herself if she threw a vulnerable man like Lenny out on the streets? Her cottage had been his home for decades.

Bel roused herself from the memories. 'Lenny's still there.' She knew she had no intention of selling her mother's rundown shack, anyway. Not now, however broke she was. 'Don't worry, Krishna, I'll find a job,' she assured her friend. And, as the distant screams of a small child made Krishna frown and give an apologetic shrug, Bel thanked her and ended the call.

2

'Looking forward to this. I love roast chicken,' her father said later, rubbing his hands together with glee. While she prepared supper he regaled her with an amusing anecdote from his past, when he'd thrown a glass of Sauvignon over some 'rude cove's' monogrammed Jermyn Street shirt when they were on a wine-tasting weekend in the Dordogne. 'Lucky it wasn't red,' he said, chortling at the memory.

Now he stood, tumbler of whisky clinking with ice in hand, propped against the counter of the scuzzy eighties kitchen – varnished brown units, mottled fake-marble surfaces, cream Smeg fridge-freezer, gold-coloured taps – watching her every move, as usual. 'Should you be cooking chicken with butter?' he asked, peering over her shoulder. 'Won't it burn on the skin?'

Bel laughed. 'When did you last cook a chicken, Dad?'

He gave her a friendly nudge. 'Fair play. I suppose Louis taught you to do it like that.'

'It's just a recipe. I do have a mind of my own,' she replied, trying unsuccessfully to keep a lid on her irritation at him breathing down her neck all the time.

Dennis stood back, eyeing her as if her mind were actually displayed on her body for him to assess. 'Hmm. I'd say you've always been quite easily influenced, no?'

When Bel did not reply, he went on, 'I mean look at Louis. You rushed into his arms as if he was the last man on the planet, when it was perfectly clear he was a chancer and only after your money.' He spoke in a light, conversational tone, as if he were passing the time of day, not delivering a killer punch to Bel's already punctured psyche.

Her breath caught in her throat. Wiping her hands on a piece of kitchen towel with careful deliberation, although her heart was pumping wildly against her ribs, she turned to him. His small, dark eyes were alight. *It's not true*, she thought. *He doesn't mean it.* Swallowing hard, she said, as coolly as she could, 'Thanks, Dad. Good to have that clarified.'

Dennis was not fooled. Raising an eyebrow, he went on, 'Well, face it, Bella. He bled you dry, then legged it as soon as a better offer presented itself.'

The 'better offer' swam, unwelcome, before her eyes. The girl – because she was hardly more than that in Bel's opinion, although probably in her late twenties – was languorous and bordering on lazy in the restaurant, but she was also very pretty with her pouty smile and faltering English, and was always a hit with the customers.

Bel could not imagine, though, what the pair talked about when they weren't having sex. Because unless Trinny had a plate in both hands she was permanently staring at her phone. Otherwise it would be tucked sexily into her back pocket over her full bottom. She seemed to know almost nothing about culinary matters and had scant interest in finding out more, her sole fascination being Instagram influencers and TikTok stars. Louis only ever talked about food, in all its forms. *What is he doing with her?* Bel asked herself, feeling jealousy tearing at her stomach, like a chainsaw, as she opened the oven door and slammed in the chicken. The answer was depressingly obvious.

'What do you want me to say?' she asked softly, pushing past her father to get salad from the fridge. The door of the Smeg was wonky and had to be secured at the side with a piece of silver duct tape, which had to be replaced every week or so. In that second, it seemed like the most important thing in the world to smooth the tape down exactly, with no air bubbles.

Her father, behind her, had gone silent. 'God, I can't say anything to you, these days, sweetheart, without you taking offence,' he said eventually, sounding hurt. 'It's not very nice for me having someone around who's always in a bad mood, you know.'

She turned, stung. She was trying so hard.

'It's not *my* fault you're in this mess,' Dennis went on. 'You shouldn't take it out on me, when all I've done is support you, given you a home . . . bailed you out to the tune of tens of thousands.'

Bel took a shaky breath. She didn't know how to react. He was right: he had offered the financial help she'd badly needed, which she was determined, somehow, to pay back as soon as possible – she absolutely hated owing him. And he was right that she was upset a lot of the time. But he seemed unaware of – and unabashed by – the casually critical things that came out of his mouth.

As she shook the salad into a bowl and retrieved some

peas from the freezer, she watched her father wander unsteadily to take his place at the kitchen table. *He's old . . . he's drunk*, she told herself, heart softening. It was true. His face was flushed and sweating, the broken veins standing out on his nose and cheeks – although Bel considered him still reasonably fit for his age, given his total disregard for his health.

'Let's not fall out, Dad,' she said soothingly, splashing water into the pan with the peas.

Dennis looked up, surprised. 'Fall out?'

'Look, I'm really grateful to you for rescuing me, you know I am. And I'm sorry I'm often in a bate. Obviously things aren't great for me at the moment. Finding a job and somewhere to live isn't easy under my current circumstances.'

Her words were conciliatory, and Dennis nodded his approval. 'There's a roof over your head, food to eat, cash when you need it. Stop fretting, girl. You have a full-time job looking after your old dad, now.' He patted her shoulder. 'You know I love you being here, even if you are a bit sulky at times.'

She forced a creditable laugh, but inside her guts curdled. 'You're quite capable of looking after yourself,' she said brightly.

Dennis shook his head. 'This knackered old body isn't what it used to be, sweetheart. I wake every morning with a twinge here, a wee ache there . . . It's proper shite getting old.' He took another gulp of wine. 'Your mother was the lucky one. She went too soon, of course, but she avoided all this crap.'

Bel was mindful of the long months of painful, time-consuming treatment, the agony her mother had suffered so stoically as the cancer moved to her bones. 'She had her fair share of crap, Dad.'

Dennis frowned. 'Yes, but it was easier for her. She was stalwart, good at coping. I'm not.'

Good at hiding how much pain she was in, more like, Bel thought, but didn't say.

'You'll never find another job at your age, will you? Not one you actually want to do,' she heard her father muse. And, despite the potential truth in his words, it made her want to scream. Instead she opened the oven door, rearing back as a gust of smoke from the old, dirty oven engulfed her, and pulled out the chicken to baste.

3

'Take a seat,' said Brad, the wiry, man-bunned manager of Grind the following morning, indicating the wooden ladderback chair across the small café table. He smiled a welcome, but looked distracted, constantly flicking his eyes to his laptop screen.

Bel sat down nervously. She hadn't known what to wear. *Is a dress too formal, too fuddy-duddy?* she'd asked herself, rifling through the contents of the mahogany wardrobe in her dingy, cream-painted bedroom. Settling on jeans and a navy cotton shirt, she still felt like the man's grandmother.

'Umm, so . . . we're looking for someone who can be a personality, someone the punters relate to as they step through the door.' He paused, checked his screen again. It was as if he was memorizing a script and had forgotten his lines. Then his eyes focused on her again. 'But we also need someone who can keep a sharp eye on the other staff, the smooth running of the floor. See when things are going slow, punters getting impatient, et cetera.'

She nodded, gave him her most winning smile. 'I can do that.'

He gave her a long look. 'You said in your CV you've had your own place? Well, this is a chain. We have to do things the way the head honchos decree. No going off-piste.'

'That wouldn't be a problem for me,' she said firmly.

He nodded slowly, then told her how much she would be paid. It seemed fine to Bel. Any potential salary sounded like heaven to her right now, even if the hours would be long, the music loud, the clientele rowdy and young, a far cry from the sedate white tablecloths and culinary reverence of 83.

Brad sat back in his chair, muttering something about the other staff, the pressure, the new chef – Bel got the impression his heart wasn't really in any of it. 'Right. Well, thanks for coming in. We'll be in touch.'

A pretty twenty-something with fluttery waist-length blonde hair and an oversized denim jacket pushed past Bel as she left. Glancing through the plate-glass café window, Bel noticed the manager visibly perk up. She knew she hadn't got the job.

On her way home, Bel called Tally de Courcy, Louis's twenty-five-year-old daughter, who lived across town in a small flat behind the huge Tesco near Lewisham station. Bel adored her 'virtual-stepdaughter', as Tally sometimes referred to herself – a sly dig at her father for not marrying Bel. And Bel had been rewarded with the girl's obvious love for encouraging Louis to bond with Tally as a stubborn, wary teenager.

'How's it going?' she asked. 'Any news from the Front?'

Tally exhaled wearily. 'Yeah, I spoke to him last night. He sounded like he was being overheard. Sort of shifty? Honestly, I've got no idea what's going on down there.'

Louis had not only left Bel in the lurch. He'd also run

out on his daughter without a proper explanation. Bel had had the Letter, Tally only a brief text, which said, *I'm going away for a while, Tally. Don't worry about me. Be in touch soon to explain. Love you so much, xxx.* No mention of Trinny or the baby or that he was leaving the country. When Bel commented on the pregnancy, assuming Tally would know, the girl had been devastated.

'It's probably not as much fun as he hoped it would be,' Bel said.

'He hasn't even got a job yet. He says it's because he can't speak French.'

'Shoulda thought of that,' Bel muttered to herself, waspishly. But she didn't want to wind Tally up. 'Hope we can meet soon, have a big hug,' she said instead, knowing how busy her stepdaughter always was, overworked and driven hard in her human-resources job for a large multinational in Canary Wharf. She didn't need this long-distance drama with her father.

'Let's fix a Saturday in April. I need to get the end-of-quarter stuff done and this grisly team-bonding weekend out of the way first,' Tally said. 'Picnic in the park in the spring sunshine?'

'Perfect. Can't wait, sweetheart. Throw me some dates and we'll make a plan.'

As she turned off the main road and approached the flat, her phone rang. 'Aunt P' flashed up on the screen. 'Bel, are you there?' Aunt Phyllis asked. 'You'll laugh, dear. I'm standing on the patio in the sunshine wi' a towel round my shoulders and foils in my hair, waiting for my roots to cook. So I thought I'd give you a bell. Next door's cat's gawping at me as if I've lost my mind.' She chuckled, sounding full of spirit, as usual.

Bel laughed. She adored her aunt, who was small and feisty, like her father, although there the resemblance ended. Phyllis was the kindest and funniest of women, with a huge heart. Her Glaswegian accent was still strong but her father had ironed his out to fit in with the wine world's public-school, signet-ring, red-cords and MCC-silk-tie brigade. Bel rarely saw her, as Phyllis still lived in Glasgow, but she checked in regularly for a catch-up. On the subject of Louis, her aunt had been philosophical. 'He's a charmer, but his first love will always be his kitchen,' she'd croaked, having run out of breath from roundly cursing him to hell and back for his defection. 'You'll find someone who suits you better.' Bel had smiled at this implausible scenario.

Now Bel, instead of going up the steps to the main door of the block, veered quickly away and kept walking round the square. She couldn't risk speaking to her aunt while she was in the flat: her father would have a conniption if he knew. Dennis hated Phyllis – for reasons lost in the mists of time – and hadn't spoken to her in more than twenty years. And her father, Bel had discovered, loved to eavesdrop.

The other morning she'd been on the phone to Flo, one of the waitresses from 83 who, like Krishna, had become a friend over the years, when she'd heard a noise. Opening her bedroom door, she'd found her father skulking outside, breathing heavily. 'What are you doing, Dad?' she'd asked.

Dennis jumped and looked sheepish. 'Wasn't sure where you were, sweetheart,' he said. 'Who are you talking to?'

'A friend,' she said, and closed her door gently but firmly, listening for the sound of his slippers scuffing back along the hall's black and white geometric tiles.

'So is the old eejit behaving himself?' Phyllis asked now.

'Oh, just the usual.'

'That's a no, then,' her aunt replied.

Bel chuckled. 'He does his best.' But the laughter made her chin wobble and tears prick behind her eyes. 'I don't know how serious he is, but he's making noises about me staying and looking after him.'

From the safety of the Walthamstow flat she'd shared with Louis, Bel had managed to distance herself from her father, only taking a third of the calls that poured in daily and going over to Earls Court every couple of weeks. When they had connected, though, she'd gleaned that he was still busy, socially engaged and leading a full life. The pandemic had changed all that.

Being able to observe him more closely now, she was noticing a frailer version of her father, one who seemed to have lost a lot of his pugnacious vitality. It worried her and made her sad.

'Grief, you canna do that, dear,' her aunt responded briskly. 'It'd kill you . . . or you'd murder him. You can always come and stay wi' us if you canna stand it any longer. It's no' grand, but we can always find room for my favourite niece.'

'Thanks, Aunt Phyllis. Such a kind thought.' But Phyllis lived in a small terraced cottage in a suburb to the north-west of the city with her retired son, Rory, and two lively, incredibly badly behaved Irish setters. With all the cabinets of commemorative china her aunt collected, her cousin's indexed boxes of comics, and the dogs, there was hardly room to breathe. She paused to blow her nose. 'I just think Dad hasn't been the same since that bad bout of Covid, which he didn't believe in until he got it, of course. He doesn't seem to have got up to speed again yet.'

Her aunt snorted. 'The man's fit as a butcher's dog. He'll see us all in our graves. Pay no attention to his fretting. He'll be winding you up.' She spoke brusquely, as if she didn't want to hear that her brother might be weak or ill. She pretended she didn't care about Dennis, but Bel knew she did and was probably scared that he might die before they'd had a chance to be reconciled.

Cutting their chat short – aware of her aunt probably freezing on the patio, despite the sunshine – Bel walked back round the gardens, still smiling from her chat. But when she opened the door to the flat, her father's voice brought her abruptly back to earth.

'Where have you been?' Dennis was standing in the hall, arms akimbo, his white hair long and swept back from his high forehead, dressed in the now habitual jeans and grey T-shirt, the flat always boiling as he insisted on turning the heating up to the max. 'You can't have been walking all this time! You've been bloody hours.' His voice was sharp and heavy with anxiety.

'Sorry. I went for the interview, remember?'

Ignoring her reply, Dennis went on, 'I saw you, walking

27

round the square just now. Who were you talking to? Why didn't you come inside?'

'I'm back, Dad. It's OK,' Bel said, running a soothing hand down her father's arm, then moving past him, not wanting him to see her face, knowing how hard it was for her to hide things from him.

Dennis followed her down the hallway. 'Did you get the job?' He'd made it quite clear he thought she was mad even to apply for it when they'd talked earlier.

'Nope, don't think so.' She turned to him as she reached her bedroom door and tried to change the focus of the conversation. 'You should get some fresh air, Dad. It'd do you good. I'll come out with you, if you like. You never take any exercise.' In fact, he never did anything much these days, except scan the paper, do the crossword, peruse wine articles – frequently snorting with derision at what he read – and follow her about.

Dismissing her suggestion with a wave of his hand, Dennis narrowed his eyes. 'Who *were* you talking to, Bella?' he repeated, his voice light but insistent. Bel felt herself flush, pressing away a small flinch in her gut at his tone.

Taking a deep breath, she was surprised at the ease with which she constructed a lie. 'Just a catch-up with Mouna. You remember Mouna from school?' She hadn't actually talked to her old friend in a while, but they emailed regularly, and she remembered her father had had a soft spot for the charming Lebanese girl.

Dennis frowned as if he didn't want to believe her, but his expression cleared. 'How is she?'

'OK, I think. She's back in Lebanon with her mum. Her father died in the first wave of the virus.'

Her father harrumphed. 'I was worried you were talking to that shite chef again.' His expression had relaxed somewhat, but Bel was still on her guard. 'The one who emptied your bank account, remember? Drove away in your van with the French totty and banjaxed your life. That one,' he warned, wagging a finger at her.

Like I need reminding, she thought, twitching as she recalled herself running hopelessly around the backstreets of Walthamstow in the December drizzle, looking for the red Berlingo the day after Louis disappeared. And Hari, the middle-aged owner of the Malaysian café next to 83, taking her arm and pulling her to a halt, asking her why she was upset.

As soon as Bel was alone in her room, the door firmly shut, resisting a sudden urge to lock it against her father, she shook her head at herself, bewildered. *What's wrong with me? I'm a grown woman and I have to lie to my father because* . . . because what? Was she actually scared of him? Scared of telling him she was in touch with her only and much-loved aunt? She tried to dismiss the notion. *He's frail and nearly eighty, for God's sake.*

But thinking back, as she sat huddled on her bed, she knew she'd been conscious of a tension around her father her whole life, of always being on her guard, even when she was small. It was the sense, from an early age, of her father's perpetually simmering anger, hidden beneath the surface, much of the time, with charm and conviviality. His moods could turn on a penny, smiles morphing into sudden flashes of sarcastic rage, during which Bel would hold her breath as she watched her mother shrink and cower in defensive silence.

She was familiar with Dennis's tales of his own childhood, which were lurid although, according to Aunt Phyllis, grossly exaggerated. Brought up in a Glasgow tenement in the forties and fifties by a violent father – out of work and traumatized by his experiences in the war – and a mother too worn down by circumstance to help, Dennis was always at pains to remind Bel of how lucky she was to have the cosy existence he'd struggled so hard, through thick and thin, to provide. Her admiration – genuine, to a degree – was a necessary coda to all these stories.

But she remembered, too, the warmth and strength of her father's rare embraces – he was not a man much given to physical contact – and how entertaining and fun he was capable of being. As long as she and her mother danced to his tune, and Agnes had made sure that they did, things remained mostly on an even keel at home. It was just the prickling insecurity that hovered like a miasma around her all the time they were together. And the moment – always unpredictable – when Bel felt the air shift . . .

It's not the same now, she insisted to herself. *He's just cranky from the after-effects of the pandemic.* She could hardly blame him.

4

Bel noticed the arrival of spring on her daily walks as pale green began to shadow the winter branches, like mist, and vibrant butter-yellow clumps of daffodils and frothy pink camellias decorated the paths in Kensington Gardens. The air took on a kinder note. She'd sent out twenty email-CVs and been for two more interviews: a front-of-house in a busy Notting Hill wine bar with a huge garden, and an assistant-manager post in a gastro-pub chain in Bayswater. In both places she'd been treated kindly, but she felt – rightly or wrongly – it was the polite, pitying sort of kindness. The sort that silently queried, *Why on earth would we employ someone of her age here?* The problem, she knew, was finding somewhere to work within reasonable range of the flat where she wasn't up against a million eager, cheap millennials and Zoomers. It was not proving easy to get a job at managerial level – paying well enough – even though hospitality was crying out for staff.

Today, a beautiful spring morning, was her fifty-eighth birthday. Up and dressed early, she wore jeans and a raspberry lambswool polo-neck Louis had given her for her birthday a few years back. She washed her face, but put on no make-up. Her skin was creamy – the sort that tans golden in the sun – and relatively unlined for her age, the eyelashes and brows above her violet eyes a pale corn colour, matching her thick, wavy hair, which was now past her shoulders and contained in a ponytail most days. There was only the odd strand of grey, which had annoyed Louis, whose dark hair was rapidly losing its colour. 'I'm younger than you,' he'd often teased.

Rubbing moisturizer into her cheeks, she asked herself, *Has Louis remembered?* Her mind flew back to her birthday last year, when he'd made her a beautiful *Sachertorte*, her name piped across the top. He wasn't much of a pastry chef and he'd been particularly pleased with himself at the success of the cake. *Does he miss me?* He'd claimed they hadn't been 'particularly happy for a long while' in the infamous letter, but that wasn't what Bel remembered. She would have been the first to admit that they'd been busy and hadn't had a great deal of leisure time for each other. And Louis had drunk too much during the pandemic, with nothing to occupy himself. But she felt they'd been good together, supported and made each other laugh, hadn't they?

As she pulled a brush through her long hair, she tortured herself with the image of Louis waking in his new home in the south-west of France . . . *Wasn't it Carcassonne Trinny said she came from?* Terracotta tiles on the floor, a wrought-iron bed with embroidered white cotton sheets, blue-painted wooden shutters open at the window, allowing in the warm Mediterranean sun . . . his fingers running up Trinny's luscious young thigh. Bel could see the flame in his dark eyes as he kissed her full lips, remembered the way he would hold his breath when he was about to come. It was like a porn movie on a continuous loop, from which she was unable to drag her eyes.

Every inch of herself, in that moment, wanted none of this to have happened. She longed just to be back in Walthamstow, in their sparsely furnished flat, the restaurant buzzing below, Louis manic and fired up with today's menu ideas . . . things to do, people to talk to, the hours of the day flashing past until sleep overtook her. It had not been perfect, but it had been a full, engaged life, with a man she had truly loved. She frowned at herself in the bathroom mirror, then forced a grin, which started wan, but became genuine after a second as her tragic expression made her laugh.

Tossing her ponytail and straightening her jumper, she squared her shoulders determinedly: she had her meeting with Flo to look forward to this morning. Her bare feet were cold on the hallway tiles as she crept past her father's bedroom towards the kitchen – she didn't want to wake him and risk her good mood being ruined by his potentially bad one.

But as she drew level with Dennis's door, it flew open. He wore his frayed plaid dressing gown open over a pair of grey joggers and a vest, his hair flopping around his sleepy face, upon which was a warm smile.

'Thought I'd beat you to it and get some celebratory breakfast going,' he said. 'But you're up already.' Patting her shoulder, he pecked her lightly on the cheek. 'Happy birthday, Bella.'

Bel found she was chuffed. Her father had always been a bit haphazard when it came to birthdays, seldom managing a card, mostly just a late present, not wrapped, which would appear at some random time in a supermarket bag, almost as an afterthought. And this year there was hardly much to celebrate, from her point of view. But now he linked his arm in hers and pulled her towards the kitchen.

'Right, so I think it's not the day for that muesli nonsense,' he said, winking at her. 'I'm doing my special scrambled eggs, OK?'

She laughed. 'That'd be lovely, Dad.'

'You sit down. I'll sort it.'

Bel knew this meant a lot of bumbling about, faffing over how many eggs, finding the right bowl in which to beat them and his favourite pan, cursing the bread knife as he hacked from the loaf huge slabs that wouldn't fit in the toaster. But neither of them was in a hurry, and it was nice to be treated for a change.

'Shall I do the coffee?' she suggested, making to rise from her chair.

Dennis, in the process of beating the eggs, wagged a dripping fork at her. 'Nope, sit. I'm on it – as the youth of today would say.'

It was, as she'd predicted, a long old process, entailing a fair bit of huffing and puffing and even more profanities. But in between, her father whistled under his breath, and shot her the occasional smile that seemed oddly mischievous, as if he had some surprise up his sleeve.

'That was delicious,' she said, when they'd eaten the eggs – stirred to her father's exacting standards: no milk – blasphemy – touch of Tabasco, salt and pepper, plenty of butter, soft but cooked through.

Dennis, across the table, beamed. 'That's not your only treat, girl.'

34

Bel raised an enquiring eyebrow, a little taken aback by her father's current mood of indulgence towards her – it made her uneasy, and she waited for the moment, so familiar from the past, that might cause his humour to tip.

'Stay there,' he said, wiping his chin – which sported a fuzz of white bristles that morning – and getting to his feet.

A minute later he was back, a square box under one arm. It was old, about the size of two egg boxes laid side by side, and covered with faded burgundy leather, worn and scuffed around the tarnished metal lock. Bel recognized it immediately.

Dennis, sweeping the butter dish and her coffee cup to the side with one hand, placed the box carefully in front of her. 'For you.'

'Mum's,' Bel whispered.

He sat down close to her. 'Go on,' he urged, as she slowly ran her fingers over the surface of the box. 'Open it.'

The inside was lined with padded, now yellowing, cream satin, small, billowed cushions fitting each section and protecting the jewellery inside. Lifting a cushion, Bel pulled out a heavy gold-link bracelet and held it in her palm. The gold was cold, but the smoothness between her fingers brought her straight back to her mother's side. Agnes had always worn it, even when she was really sick. In those final weeks it had hung loosely on her wrist, which had shrunk to the size of a child's. Bel felt her heart contract as her father's hand brushed her own.

'I know it's been a long time. Agnes left it all to you in her will, of course – it's not like I was going to be wearing her jewellery.' He gave a sad laugh. 'I just couldn't part with it at first. And then I forgot I still had it. I've kept her wedding ring – I hope you don't mind? The rest is yours.'

Bel could only nod and smile her gratitude. Words wouldn't come. Never a materialistic person, and frozen out at the time by her father's intense grief – as if he were the only person affected – she had been reluctant even to mention her mother's name in the months after she had died. She wouldn't have dared either to ask her father about her possessions. Instead she'd swallowed her heart-break as best she could and concentrated on pursuing her passion for skiing and the Alps, for dear Bruno. But it surprised her now that the jewellery appeared untouched, just as her mother had left it, all these decades later, that her father still cherished the ring her mother had worn. Because she couldn't remember witnessing, when Agnes was alive, the overwhelming love he always claimed after her death.

What Bel recalled, growing up, was an uncomfortable feeling that her father thought her mother a bit simple and regularly quite irritating. There was never any sign of respect for her opinions or desires. As a child, Bel didn't question it. They were her parents. It was her norm. Dennis treated Bel much the same, anyway. Following some slight or show of temper, her mother would say, 'It's just his manner. He doesn't mean anything by it.' Closing the box, Bel felt her mouth twitch as she realized that she, too, said the same thing to herself whenever her father was snippy: *He doesn't mean it.*

'What are you smiling about?' Dennis queried.

'Oh, nothing.' She thought quickly, feeling his eyes on

her, suspicious, suddenly. 'Just remembering Mum, and how I always knew where she was in the flat because I could hear the bracelet jangling.'

Dennis sat back, mollified, and clearly satisfied that his surprise had hit the mark. 'She would approve, you know, our beloved daughter back home with me like this. She always said family was the most important thing.' Bel's tough old dad looked almost tearful.

Bel winced. She wasn't sure how to react to this emotional version of her father, whose cynical nature seemed to allow very little to touch his heart. Confused, it was a moment before she registered what he had said.

'I won't stay for ever, Dad, I promise,' she said, making a joke of it. 'I'll be out of your hair soon and you won't have to put up with your grumpy daughter ruining your days.'

She expected a caustic comment in return, but her father just looked baffled. 'Where would you go?' he asked, plaintively.

'Oh, I don't know. It won't be yet. I'm just saying, you don't have to put up with me for ever.' She was trying for jaunty but knew she sounded slightly desperate.

Dennis's face clouded. 'Seems daft, you paying exorbitant rent on a squalid place in the boondocks – which is all you'll be able to afford on a waitress's meagre salary, I imagine. What's wrong with living here?' He seemed perturbed. 'Listen, I'm not gagging for the money you owe me. You being you, I know I'll get it back eventually. And I'm getting used to you and your moods,' he added, with a wink.

Bel sighed inwardly at the dismal picture he was painting of her future employment prospects. 'Nothing's wrong with it, Dad,' she said. 'I just value my independence, that's all.' She managed a grin she hoped was a bit mischievous. 'You taught me that, remember? I'm sure you wouldn't approve of me sponging off you for the rest of my life.'

Dennis did not respond to the grin. Instead he cocked an eyebrow. 'Independence is all very fine, but how are you going to pay for it, eh?' He shook an admonishing finger at her as if she were soft in the head. 'I'd take advantage of me and my millions while you can, girl. And make sure I last as long as possible. I'm leaving everything to Glasgow City Mission when I go.'

Glasgow City Mission. Bel didn't know whether to take him seriously or not. She was familiar with the charity, which her father always cited as having helped the Carnegies out of a deep hole when his father couldn't work because of mental-health problems. 'It's a worthy cause,' she said honestly. She didn't want to think of him dead, anyway.

Dennis gave her a curious look. 'Shocked you, have I? I thought you knew.'

'You can leave your money to whoever you like, Dad.'

'Ah, but you'd rather I left it to you, no?' He grinned slyly.

Ignoring his jibe, she rose, picking up the box. 'Listen, thanks for Mum's jewellery. It means a lot.'

'You'll look after it? I don't want some eejit getting his hands on it.'

She stopped and gave him a quizzical look. 'What "eejit" is that, Dad?'

Dennis tapped the side of his nose. 'The one you were talking to as you paced round the square the other day?'

He chuckled triumphantly. 'I may be old but I'm not stupid. I saw your face . . . Mouna, my arse.'

Bel, weary and once again out-manoeuvred, could find no retort. She didn't even bother to deny it. 'I'm off to the park. I'll pick up some food on the way home.'

Her father looked like the cat who'd got the cream as he waved her off with a dismissive flick of his hand and turned to pick up the newspaper.

5

Flo handed Bel coffee in a takeaway cup, and a white cardboard box tied with thick red string, in which nestled a vast cupcake piled with swirly pink icing and glittery hearts. 'Happy birthday, darlin'.' Flo was tall and skinny, in her late thirties, with a neat Afro wrapped today in a colourful wool scarf. She was wearing frayed jeans and a fake-fur jacket.

They were sitting on a bench beside the lake in Victoria Park, East London. A gaggle of Canada geese were shuffling about on the muddy grass of the bank, a nervous toddler eyeing them, but not letting go of his mother's hand. The park was not busy on this chilly Friday, but there was intermittent sun, and both women turned up their faces to receive the transitory spring warmth.

Thanking her and laughing at the beauty and size of it, Bel took a moment to divide the cake into two with the wooden knife in the bottom of the box and hand one half to Flo on a paper napkin, licking the delicious sweetness off her fingers before diving in. She felt her heart lift at seeing her friend again. Yes, Bel had been her employer, but they'd had a warm friendship, too, right from the off, nearly fifteen years ago now.

'So how's it going with your dad?' Flo asked, after they'd got past the first mouthful. She had been circumspect when Bel had told her, months ago now, about Louis's flight, saying little, perhaps because she'd known what was going on with Trinny. Bel didn't hold that against her. It was not Flo's secret to divulge.

Bel pulled a face. 'Oh, you know. Moving back to live with your parents is seldom a plan.'

'Ha! I never left. We drive each other nuts but it works somehow. And I literally don't know what I'd do if it was just me and Henry. Mum cooks up a storm every day and Dad's a star with the homework and all the football stuff.' Flo was a single parent, Henry her ten-year-old son.

For a moment Bel imagined the bustling home full of three generations – one of the households that politicians had slyly criticized in the past for spreading Covid – and envied Flo. 'Have you found work yet?'

'I signed on with a cleaning agency. It gives me more flexibility. I do as much work as I want, mostly private houses, some offices. It'll do for now.' She laughed. 'You know me, I love to clean!'

Bel rolled her eyes, laughing too. It had been a running joke at 83, how spotless Flo always made the place.

'You?' Flo was asking.

Bel shook her head. 'I've had a few interviews, but nothing so far. I'll get something soon, I'm sure.' Her tone was upbeat, but she worried one of the barriers to her getting the jobs she wanted was her confidence: it was at rock-bottom. Any prospective employer would pick up on that. 'I think I baffle them. I'm too old and not hip enough for the West London crowd . . . Might have to lower my sights.'

'You're not too old,' Flo said kindly. Then, after a moment's thought, she added, 'You know what? You should take off, try somewhere new, out of the city. Everyone's doing it.'

Bel nodded, thinking of Glasgow and Aunt Phyllis. 'I'm not sure ... Dad's pretty keen I stay with him.'

Flo frowned. 'Oh, right. He needs your help now? That's different, then.'

'No, no, he's fine, thank goodness. I just think he likes me being there.'

Peering closely at her and maybe gleaning something from her expression, Flo said softly, 'If that works for you.'

Flo knew something of Bel's tricky relationship with her father, and the tacit understanding brought tears to Bel's eyes. She tried to swallow them, but they were on a mission. Before she knew it, Flo had wrapped her in her arms, giving her the best hug she'd received in a long time. She rocked back and forth with Bel, holding her tight, saying not a word.

When Bel finally pulled back, embarrassed by her display of emotion, she said very quietly, almost to herself, 'I'd really love to take off.' She took a large gulp of air. 'Anywhere. I'd love to go anywhere.' And she knew, as she said it, it was the absolute truth.

As if the universe was responding to her heartfelt wish, when Bel got back to the flat and checked her emails on her laptop – which she'd set up on top of the mahogany bureau by the window in her bedroom – she found one from Bruno Carli. Bel corresponded only sporadically with the man she should have married back in her twenties. Since those days, he'd been through a marriage and a divorce and had two grown-up sons, one of whom helped him run his small hotel in Chamonix.

Bel and Bruno had been obsessive skiers, both in love with the mountains, the slopes and runs, the dangers and challenges, every breath they took of the crystal-clear air . . . and each other. They'd wanted to make skiing their career, open a ski school when they could raise the money. But life, as Bel knew, didn't always work out the way you planned. Bruno was calm and kind and strong in his square-shouldered, blue-eyed beauty. She trusted him with her life. But when she was airlifted back to London with extensive injuries, things became too complex for the relationship to survive.

'Don't go out,' he'd said to her, that February morning, the day of the accident, as if he'd had a premonition of what was about to happen. 'The weather is wrong, you might get stuck.'

She had kissed him, stroked her finger gently down his cheek and watched his eyelids flutter with pleasure. The tiny flat they rented on the outskirts of town was all new pine and no furniture, but the views across the valley were spectacular. 'I'll be back by lunchtime. The weather should hold till then.' She pulled herself up, pushing off the thick French duvet and gave him a quick kiss on the lips. Bruno had a shift at the hotel till three so he couldn't join her, but she wasn't going to waste the chance of a morning on the slopes in the sunshine. Dinner prep for the ten clients she cooked for in the chalet in town could be sorted this afternoon – she had it down to a fine art.

As it turned out, it wasn't the weather that caused Bel to fall. Her ski hit the tip of a thick branch buried in the powdery snow and she crashed headlong into a pine tree. Even now, thinking about it, she had no memory of what happened afterwards, but she felt – to this very day – the sudden fierce jolt shooting up her leg as her left ski made contact, the lurching lack of control, the pine looming huge and dark, silhouetted against the brilliant sun. She'd had no time even to be afraid. Then, nothing, until she woke in the French hospital with a shattered pelvis, a spiral fracture of her left tibia and fibula and worrying concussion. Bruno had been by her side every moment he could, until her father had brought her home.

Dennis had not liked Bruno one little bit. *He's a Swiss waiter, for God's sake, Bella.* So, when she returned home – first to the Hammersmith Hospital, then to convalesce in Earls Court – Dennis did not pass on the phone calls Bruno made from a freezing Chamonix call box, no mobiles in those days, or sneaked from the manager's office in the hotel where he worked. Or the letters he wrote. Facts she found out when Bruno eventually scrimped and saved enough for a flight to London to visit her. But by then they seemed to be living in different worlds. His tanned, robust fitness seemed too vibrant, too much at odds with the pale weak shadow Bel had become.

By the time she had emerged from the haze of painkillers and recovered some control over her life, Bruno had pretty much given up. Although she had taken her father to task for hiding Bruno's letters, refusing his phone calls, making it so hard for them to keep in touch, she later wondered if it had made any difference. She might never ski again – it was a while before she could even walk unaided. Their world, hers and Bruno's, was the mountains, the snow, a sporty, carefree life on the slopes.

'Bon anniversaire!'

Bel read in Bruno's email. He always remembered her birthday.

How is your life these days? I am going good.

His spoken English was fluent, but written, it always sounded a little odd.

The hotel is busy again. Dario stays with me. Lukas now lives in Berne with his Karin. I am to be a grandfather in the fall! Come visit soon, Bella, if your restaurant make time. Bring Louis. Stay as long as you like – as my guests, of course. Bisous, Bruno xxx

Bel smiled. She had not been on skis since the accident, but her bones had eventually healed well. She knew she could be strong and fit again, if she put in the work. *Shall I go over there when I can afford it? Spend some time with him?* Find out how she felt at being in that environment again. She gave an involuntary gasp as she mentally inhaled the cold freshness of the mountains, saw the evening sun shadow the smooth sweep of snow crystals a metallic blue. *Might I still find him attractive?* she wondered mischievously, as she heard the ping of her mobile and opened a lovely birthday WhatsApp from Tally with impressively exploding fireworks and floating balloons.

Preparing supper that night, Bel had a spring in her step. She remembered the feeling of panic, the day Louis deserted her, that she was suddenly alone in the world. But she was wrong. She had Tally and Flo and Mouna, Bruno, even her father. They all cared for her and had left her loving messages. Nothing from Louis, but she knew he wouldn't dare.

She called up a compilation of Mozart arias on Louis's HomePod mini – which he'd left behind, even though it was his favourite toy – while she cooked tomato and chilli pasta. Her father loved opera. She didn't rise when he peered into the pan and told her not to forget he loathed parsley. She even laughed at one of his bad Boris jokes.

Bel had not yet replied to Bruno's email. But his words blew gently around her, a beckoning waft of crisp mountain air, whose trail she could follow, she told herself, if she so wished. She refused to think through the ramifications of such a trip. Because if she did, she knew she would come across the solid barrier of her lack of funds and her father's now firm grip on her life.

After supper, Bel even agreed to play backgammon with Dennis. They were currently engaged in their third game of the evening, the board resting on a low rosewood table between the two armchairs in front of the gas log fire in the sitting room. Bel's left cheek was uncomfortably warm, but she didn't want to complain and ruin her father's mellow mood – perhaps brought on by her own lift of spirits. *I've been so touchy recently*, she thought, as she waited for her father to make his move. *It can't be easy for him.*

Dennis loved backgammon and would normally have spent every Friday with his friend Reg, locked in their weekly tournament. Reg was an excellent player whom Dennis was forced to respect because he often lost to him. But Reg had not been well for a while now. He had COPD and was terrified of getting a chest infection. As a result he was reluctant to venture out of his Chelsea basement, despite Dennis's frequent blandishments.

Her father sucked his teeth theatrically as Bel moved her checkers. She glanced up at him, not knowing if he was pointing out a genuinely foolish move or just winding her up. She was fairly average at the game and he often got frustrated with her. But he also liked to win. Now he grinned wickedly and said nothing, grabbing his dice cup and shaking the two die within vigorously, spilling them with a soft clunk onto the leather board. After a long moment of consideration, he moved his own pieces, raising his eyebrows in challenge.

'The surgery texted *again* this morning, bullying me to get a poxy booster, even though I never had any of the original jabs to boost,' he said, as he waited for her to play. 'Clearly their system's on the blink. I'm living proof, of course, that it was all a pointless waste of time.'

Bel nodded, mentally rolling her eyes. Her father seemed to consider himself some kind of hero for being a rabid antivaxxer.

'I kept telling them, didn't I? But they wouldn't listen.

Why would I be pumped full of shite just to tick boxes for some programme created by a government you wouldn't trust to put the rubbish out?'

'OK, Dad. Heard it all before,' she said mildly.

But he was on a roll. 'Bastards. They should have let me be and used their energy to bully the poor fools too weak to refuse.' He took an angry swig from his glass of whisky.

'Fools like me, you mean.'

Dennis sighed. 'I've said it before, Bella. You're easily led.'

This time the familiar insult washed over her head. It was as if, living with her father, she was acquiring a sort of insult fatigue, ceasing to hear, or maybe to care, when he put her down.

'Get a move on,' her father nagged benignly.

Bel held the dice cup absently as she stared at her father across the table. 'Would Mum have refused the vaccine, do you think?'

Dennis snorted dismissively, as if he thought Bel was using her mother to reprimand him.

'It's not a loaded question,' she said, shaking the die slowly but still not throwing. 'I'm not worried you'll get struck down and end up in ICU on a ventilator any more.' She shrugged with apparent nonchalance, although her assertion was not entirely true. She did worry, in general, about his health, because he was old and wheezy and never did any exercise. 'I was just wondering what Mum would have made of this strange world we've been living in.'

Her father seemed lost in thought for a moment. Then he said, 'She was a gentle soul, your mother. Honest and kind as the day is long.' He paused. When he spoke again, though, Bel noticed his voice had acquired an edge of contempt. 'But Agnes wouldn't say boo to a goose. I'm sure she'd have been the first in line to do whatever that scumbag crew told her.'

She was surprised at his tone. Normally Dennis disappeared into a haze of sentimental nostalgia when talking about her mother.

Indignation spiked on Agnes's behalf as she watched him wander unsteadily to the built-in bookcase that ran along the wall beside the fireplace and pour a hefty slug of whisky into his glass from the crystal decanter he kept there on a silver tray. When he was seated again, she said, 'Mum wasn't weak.'

Dennis frowned in puzzlement. 'I didn't say she was.'

Breath short in her chest, Bel found herself blurting out, 'She wasn't weak, Dad. She was just very nervous. I think you scared her and that's why she ended up not being able to say boo to a goose.' Trembling from her unthinking audacity – she had never said such a thing in her life before – she blinked at her father. He was staring at her, with an odd smile. For a moment she couldn't decide whether he was upset or not.

Dennis carefully set his glass on the crested wine-company coaster he kept on the table by his chair. Cocking his head to one side, eyes narrowed, he regarded her sardonically. '"Scared"?' The word hissed towards her, like steam from a kettle.

Heart pounding, Bel hesitated. *Back down*, the voice in her head insisted. Dennis's cold gaze was still fixed on her face and she felt her cheeks flush scarlet. 'I . . . I . . .' She couldn't say it. Couldn't say that she saw how defeated her mother sometimes looked, how Agnes would flinch, eyes blinking, like a frightened rabbit's, as Dennis berated her about something entirely trivial. How Agnes made a small strangled sigh when she heard her husband's key in the lock, immediately patting her hair and smoothing her dress, glancing nervously around to see if anything was awry. Bel, as a child, had taken it as normal. *He doesn't mean it* . . .

Suddenly thrusting his face closer to hers, dark eyes small with fury, the board skewing, checkers sliding as he half rose, leaning heavily across the table, her father jabbed a finger towards her face and whispered, 'Impertinent little bitch. How dare you even suggest I would intimidate your beautiful mother?'

Bel gasped. But her father hadn't finished. He leaned even closer, trapping her in the high-backed chair, until his nose was almost touching hers, his panting old-man breath on her skin, sour with whisky. 'Have some bloody respect,' he spat, before falling back onto the faded chintz, grabbing his glass and swallowing the contents in a single gulp, eyes closed.

Sitting there, stunned, Bel tried to get her breath, pressing her hand to her chest to stop her heart jumping out of her body. Then, gingerly, worried that any sudden move might set her father off again, she stumbled to her feet and, without another word, walked quietly across the room towards the door.

'Bella!' Her father's voice rang out behind her, making her jump. It was a command, not an apology, and she kept moving. 'Bella, come back here!' As she reached the corridor, she thought she could detect a tinge of regret as he repeated her name for the third time, but now she was hurrying, gasping, tears choking in her throat, desperate not to make a sound until she reached the safety of her bedroom, where she locked the door and threw herself onto the bed, like a humiliated child.

Crawling into bed later – without cleaning her teeth, washing her face or peeing, because she didn't know if he would be standing silently outside her door – Bel waited. *Will he come and apologize?* All her senses were primed for the sound of his slippers scuffing on the tiles. *Please don't come,* she begged silently. And the flat remained silent and still.

6

Bel woke later than usual, tired and jumpy from a fitful sleep. Dressing slowly, reluctant to start the new day and face her father, she found her heart beating uncomfortably fast as soon as she stuck her nose outside her bedroom. The place was silent. Her father, she hoped, was still sound asleep. He had consumed more than enough whisky before their spat, and God knew how much he had drunk after she had gone to bed.

She crept along to the kitchen, where she turned on the light. The kettle sounded like the start of the Third World War in the quiet early-morning flat, and she winced, certain it would wake her father – he would already be in a bad mood from his hangover. *I am not going to apologize*, she decided staunchly. But her curdling guts told her otherwise as she waited in trepidation for the inevitable confrontation.

As she sipped her coffee and glanced through yesterday's newspaper, her attention was caught by a movement in the corridor. She looked up, preparing herself, but was surprised to see a woman standing framed in the doorway.

'Oh, hi,' Bel said, confused.

The woman grinned. 'Just off,' she said, as she bent to pull on a pair of black suede ankle boots she'd left just inside the kitchen. She must have been about Bel's age, slim, with dyed black hair pulled into an untidy knot on top of her head and a pale face, made paler in contrast to the heavy black lashes fixed to her upper lids. She wore a frilly white blouse that showed off ample cleavage under a black leather jacket and a knee-length black skirt. 'I'm Pauline, by the way,' she added, when she straightened, her face flushed from the effort.

'Bel,' Bel said, stretching out her hand in welcome. She had no idea who the woman was, appearing at the kitchen door at that hour of the morning.

Pauline moved forward and they clasped hands. 'Nice to meet you,' she said, with a smile, but offering no explanation.

'Umm, do you want a coffee or anything?' Bel asked. 'I've just made some.'

Pauline shook her head. 'Should get going. I have to be at the office later and I can't go in like this.' She laughed without any apparent embarrassment. 'Bye, then,' she said, hefting a capacious leather bag onto her shoulder, which had been hanging on the back of a kitchen chair, unnoticed by Bel.

Bel frowned. But before she'd had a chance to think, Pauline was back, her hand clutching a pile of letters, which she placed on the table, in front of Bel. 'Didn't want to tread on them,' she said, with a grin.

Then she was gone again, the front door closing quietly behind her.

Bemused, Bel thought back. *He's never mentioned a Pauline.* He'd had various women friends over the years since

Agnes had died. None had stayed the course, but then he'd never appeared keen they should.

Marcia, a wine buyer at Waitrose, was the most long-standing. Bel had liked her, with her bubbly red curls and snorting laugh, her ridiculous heels. Two years into the relationship, however, when Marcia was spending most of her time at the flat and Bel had assumed she would actually move in, she had suddenly stopped coming. When Bel – still living at home after her accident – asked her father what had happened, he refused to comment. 'None of your business, girl,' he'd said. So Bel never knew who had dumped whom although, looking back, she suspected her father had lost his temper with Marcia once too often, or said something demeaning, and she had decided to quit.

Now the uncomfortable certainty that Pauline had come round for a night of sex made Bel shudder with distaste. She knew it was unfair. Dennis had every right to do as he pleased. But she couldn't help unfortunate images of her ageing father *in flagrante* with Pauline flashing before her eyes. In spite of Bel considering herself mature and broad-minded, and even though her father had been single since his forties – and she hadn't heard a thing last night – she wished she had never encountered his woman friend.

So absorbed was Bel in her thoughts, she didn't imme-diately notice him standing in the doorway, stock still, as if waiting for permission to enter. When she looked up, he gave her a decidedly sheepish nod, then scuffed into the kitchen, head lowered. He was dressed in his day clothes – T-shirt, jeans, slippers – and had shaved, but his face looked pinched and tired. Still processing her encounter with Pauline, Bel almost forgot the row they'd had last night. But now, seeing the shifty glance he shot her as he reached for the coffee pot and held his hand to the glass to test its warmth, she realized that he had not.

'So, I met Pauline this morning,' Bel jumped in, trying to keep her voice cool. 'She seems nice.'

Dennis raised one eyebrow at her, as if trying to gauge what she was thinking. 'She is. Very.' He put the coffee pot down, disappointed. It must have been only lukewarm. 'Not someone I'd take to dinner, obviously,' he added, by way of explanation.

'Meaning?' Bel asked, with feigned innocence, although she knew perfectly well what he meant.

Her father smiled as he turned and went over to the kettle, which he filled and switched on silently. Bel waited. For the next few minutes Dennis fussed over the cafetière, emptying the grounds from the coffee she'd made earlier and swilling out the jug, then sloppily spooning more into the base, pouring on the boiled water and fixing the plunger in place. He came back to the table with his favourite white bone-china cup – the saucer lost or broken long ago – and sat down with a grunt. 'There are women you take to dinner, sweetheart, and there are women you take to bed,' he said matter-of-factly. 'And occasionally there is a woman with whom you do both – your dear mother being an example.' He paused to press the plunger on his coffee. 'Pauline's a dear. I'm very fond of her. But I doubt I'll be inviting her to meet my friends or share a cosy supper at Wilton's.'

Prickling with disgust, Bel stared at him.

'Don't look at me like that. A chap has his needs . . . not that we're allowed to say that, these days, of course.'

When Bel didn't reply, worried she would start shouting at her father and mindful of what had happened over back-gammon last night, he went on, 'Take Louis, for instance. Doesn't his behaviour with that French piece entirely prove my point?'

His thoughtless use of Louis as an example broke Bel. 'Dad, stop it, please,' she begged. 'You sound like some Neanderthal who drags women from the cave by their hair. This is just bluster. You don't really believe what you're saying.' She reached across the table and patted his hand. 'You're not like that.' By insisting on her father's integrity, Bel wanted to make it true.

Dennis blinked, clearly surprised to have the wind taken out of his sails.

'Mum would roll in her grave if she heard you say those things,' Bel added, mustering a wan smile, aware she was using her father's own tactics to bring him round, remind-ing him of the bond that would always bind them.

Her father looked momentarily irritated, then gave in to a chastened laugh. 'Your mother had a tongue on her whenever I stepped too far over the line. I always knew when to hold up my hands.' He eyed Bel intently. 'You remind me of her in that respect, sweetheart. You may be a pushover with the likes of Louis, but you know funda-mentally what's what.'

Bel wasn't sure if she should take that as a compliment or as yet another reminder of her father's ability to damn with faint praise.

Conversation clearly over, as far as Dennis was concerned, he sat up straighter, rubbing his hands together in anticipation. 'Shall we get some breakfast on? I could eat a horse.'

Bel rose from her seat and obediently went to fetch bacon from the fridge, feeling flattened by the recent skirmish. She loved her father, wanted desperately to respect him, but sometimes it was just too hard. She had a sudden vision of these moments being played out endlessly between them, like a song on repeat. Over and over for years to come, until one of them died. *I must reply to Bruno's email*, she thought, as the rashers began to sizzle in the frying pan.

7

A week later, Bel found she had a job. She had given up expecting a front-of-house managerial post in the trendy West London venues she'd previously approached, and settled for a counter job in a sandwich shop on North End Road, behind Fulham Broadway – she'd seen it advertised in the window on one of her meandering walks and, on the spur of the moment, seized upon it. The place was run by Vinny, a harassed-looking Irishman in his sixties, Bel calculated, who welcomed her with open arms.

'Thank Christ,' he said, mopping his sweaty face with a stained tea towel when she agreed to start the following day. 'I've been on my knees since Lorraine fucked off.'

Bel had no idea who Lorraine was, and didn't ask. It was part-time: seven thirty until four, Tuesday to Friday, paying the minimum wage, but in cash, and there would be no late nights, no pressure. She felt she had to do something other than sit around annoying her father. It would give her a chance to get her hand in again, time to look for something more suitable, and get her out of the flat. She could even give her father some of her meagre earnings – however embarrassingly small – show him her intentions concerning the debt were honourable since currently she had no overheads. *How hard can making sandwiches and coffee be?* she asked herself, as she walked home, feeling a small sense of achievement in getting herself out into the world again.

Her reply to Bruno had been measured. She hadn't wanted to admit she didn't have the money even for a plane ticket. He would probably offer to buy one for her, and that would be embarrassing and inappropriate, since they hadn't seen each other in decades, only emailed two or three times a year. She'd finished her note with 'I'd love to come over and visit soon. Just got some stuff to sort out first. Looking forward to seeing you again, Bruno. x' But the surge of optimism she'd felt when she'd first read his message now seemed equally far away.

As it turned out, making sandwiches at high speed, under impatient customers' laser stares, was extremely stressful. Bel considered herself an efficient person. But each punter wanted little tweaks here and there. In that first week, at busy times, she could feel the queue collectively twitching and holding its breath as she stumbled through the orders.

'I said no butter with that.'

'Wanted it toasted.'

'Is that decaf?'

'You forgot the pickle.'

Vinny did most of the coffees, but Bel had occasionally to pitch in too, and the machine was like a teasing, malevolent beast whenever she approached it.

Vinny hardly spoke to her, but kept up a stream of Blarney banter for his customers' benefit, which, along with the radio blaring generic pop and shouty ads, the barked orders and being on her feet all day, meant that by four o'clock she was barely able to breathe.

The wad of cash her boss pressed into her hands on that first Friday, though, fleetingly made her heart swell. And just having a job, no matter the stress involved, gave her life a pattern, a purpose it had lacked since the recent debacle. But she hoped she would soon find other options.

On the days she wasn't at the sandwich shop, she returned to her passion, baking, to fill the otherwise empty hours. But her first attempt – a simple farmhouse loaf, which she could normally have done with both hands tied behind her back – was dismal.

'What's that supposed to be?' her father asked, wrinkling his nose as she tipped the solid, sunken offering into her gloved hand. Then, seeing her face, he added quickly, 'Oh, bread. Great. Well done, sweetheart.' Bel held her breath with the humiliation. She hadn't even really enjoyed the process. The oven was so unreliable, the kitchen itself so dark, grungy and dysfunctional, her father always hovering in the background. The dough, she was sure, had sensed it was a non-starter from the off.

'Bit of a disaster,' she admitted to her father, downcast. It had seemed ridiculously important that the loaf was a success. *It's what I'm good at.* 'I used to do all the bread for the restaurant, you know, in the beginning.'

'I'm sure it was good,' her father said, his tone placatory.

'It was. But it wasn't economic, we decided. And the kitchen was small. Baking takes up a lot of room.'

Her father tapped his nose slyly. 'Mr Chef wanting his domain all to himself, eh?' Before she had a chance to defend her ex-partner, he just patted her arm and wandered away.

This warm, sunny April Saturday, she had arranged to meet her stepdaughter at Hyde Park Corner for a picnic lunch in the park, and she couldn't wait. There was a coffee stall at Speaker's Corner, and Bel had promised to bring sandwiches, Tally something sweet for dessert.

'What are you doing?' Her father was suddenly by her side as she spread slices of brown bread with butter – she was making egg mayo and watercress, others with cucumber, both of which she knew Tally loved. Louis tended to complicate things on the rare picnics they enjoyed. He'd insist on complex ingredients, like buttermilk chicken, dill salsa, pickled cabbage, chilli, sumac, that sort of thing. He would take hours and it could end up as a bit of a drama, although the result was delicious. Bel preferred to keep it simple.

She looked up from her task. 'I'm meeting Tally for a picnic lunch.'

Her father put his head on one side. 'Louis's daughter? Why are you seeing her?'

'Because I'm very fond of her,' Bel answered simply.

Dennis looked disapproving. 'After what he did to you? I'm surprised you want anything to do with his family.'

'Tally is my family too,' she stated. Part of her was quite nervous about seeing her stepdaughter. However angry she was with Louis, she desperately wanted to maintain her relationship with Tally. She hoped Louis's behaviour wouldn't drive a wedge between them. But she also knew how important it was for Tally to remain close to her father. Maybe they could eventually find a way through the current mess that worked for them all. Not that she could imagine she would ever want to have anything to do with Louis.

'How long will you be gone?' her father asked querulously.

'We're meeting at twelve. Should be back by three-ish? I've got my phone, Dad. You can always ring if you need anything.'

'Where are you meeting?'

'Hyde Park.'

After a long pause, her father, still hovering at her elbow as she spooned egg mayonnaise onto the bread, said, 'I don't think you should go. You'll get dragged into that bastard's business again. She's probably only seeing you because he's told her to.' He pursed his lips in distaste. 'He wants something, believe me . . . Money, at a guess.'

Bel stopped what she was doing and turned to stare at him in disbelief. 'Thanks, Dad. Good to know that's all I'm worth.' She took a steadying breath.

Dennis cocked his head, apparently unashamed. 'Just saying . . . You have a soft heart, sweetheart, when it comes to Louis.'

Unable to contain her frustration yet knowing she must or she would never make it through the front door, Bel bit her lip, not daring to answer in case she shouted. As she reached for the bread knife to slice the sandwiches in half, she felt his hand grip her arm, just above the elbow. 'Watch out, that's all.'

She pulled away. 'Shall I make you a sandwich too?' she suggested, wanting to distract him.

He didn't acknowledge her offer, just gave an irritated sigh and padded sullenly out of the kitchen.

Bel quickly wrapped the food in greaseproof paper and laid it in a plastic box. She found some kitchen roll and a couple of apples and shoved it all into an old canvas bag from one of the supermarkets. She felt twitchy, itching to be gone. *He can't stop me*, she told herself, feeling foolish for even thinking he might.

Bel was just passing Kensington Palace, at least twenty minutes' walk from her destination, when her father rang.

'What's up, Dad?' she asked, repressing a sigh.

'The boiler's making funny noises.'

'What sort of noises?'

'It's a whooshing sound. Really loud. I'm worried.'

'It always makes that noise. It's just firing up.'

'Are you sure? Could you come back and check? I don't want to be blown up.' He gave a mirthless laugh.

'I don't know the first thing about boilers.'

'I still think you should be here,' he insisted.

'I'm not coming home right now, Dad. I'm meeting Tally. If you're really worried, ring down for Riggs. He knows how everything works.' Riggs – first name, Martin, but he preferred plain Riggs to Mr Riggs or Martin – was the slightly creepy, shaven-headed, fifty-something ex-army caretaker for the block, who resided in the basement.

Her father harrumphed. 'The lazy sod never answers his mobile.'

'No, well, keep trying, if you're worried. I'll be back later.'

'I hope for your sake there's nothing wrong,' he said, before clicking off.

She hoped so too. She knew her father was winding her up, but she couldn't suppress a sudden flash: coming back to see smoke issuing from the first-floor window. She dismissed the image and laughed at herself, determined to enjoy her time with Tally.

Bel wrapped Tally in the warmest of hugs. It was so good to see her. The sunshine was bright, the park at its sparkling spring best, and there were lots of people milling about, strolling along the wide avenues and lounging in groups on the grass.

'So, Mum's got a new guy,' Tally dropped into the conversation once they'd been settled for a while on a quiet bench on one of the narrower paths, lined with shrubs and spring blooms, behind the bandstand. Bel's sandwiches and apples lay on the wooden slats alongside Tally's tin of home-made chocolate chip cookies, and a latte each that they'd bought from the mobile food truck. 'Jeff. He's a hedgie, holed up in Monaco for most of the year – for obvious reasons. Mum says he's so rich he makes her teeth ache.'

Bel laughed as Tally pulled a face, tossing her glossy rope of dark hair over her shoulder. She was a beauty, with her green, sea-glass eyes and the flawless, olive-gold complexion from her mother Nadia's Anglo-Indian background. Dressed in a pretty red cotton maxi dress, oversized Fair

Isle cardigan and clumpy Nike trainers, her slim figure drew the eye of almost every male who passed the bench – not that Tally seemed to notice. She'd had a few boyfriends over the years, but she didn't seem the sort who needed a man constantly by her side.

They hadn't talked about Louis yet, sticking instead to safer subjects, such as Bel's sandwich-queen nightmares, Tally's crazy workload, the great quality of the pop-up coffee, the gorgeous warmth of the day.

'Jeff's insisting on taking Mum to Monaco on his posh yacht, for an extended stay. Which is not a plan. Mum gets seasick crossing wet grass.'

Bel grinned. 'She turned him down?' She was loving every minute of her stepdaughter's company.

'God, no! She's way too smitten. Says she's going to take Boots' entire stock of Kwells with her. But it won't end well, I'm telling you. Whenever she's popped them in the past, she's fallen asleep for, like, literally days.'

They chatted on, enjoying their lunch and the lovely spring air. Bel knew she should bring up the proverbial elephant, but she didn't want to ruin things. In the end, a silence fell, and both women knew what the other was thinking.

'Have you heard from him?' Bel asked.

Tally licked a smear of chocolate off her thumb. 'Last week. But we ended up having a row. He was complaining that he still hasn't found a job because the French are all xenophobes. And Trinny's mum – whose house they're living in – can't stand him, apparently.' She sighed. 'I hate the way Dad says things are hard for him and sort of makes out he doesn't know how it came to this.' She gave a wry grin. 'So I got annoyed and said he should bloody stop moaning and start to own his life and the mess he's made of it, instead of pretending he'd had no hand in it, which didn't go down well, of course.'

'Oh dear. Did you make it up with him?'

'Not really,' Tally said quietly. 'He wants me to visit in the summer. But the baby's due next month and he says there isn't a bedroom for me. Like I really want to spend my meagre holiday allowance on one of those hard French sofa things, baby screaming all night, the bossy mother-in-law hammer and tongs with my dad.'

She was making light of it, as was her wont, but Bel could tell Tally was quite reasonably upset by the situation. 'Will you go?'

'I'll never see him if I don't, will I? He's obviously skint – another of his beefs – so he won't be able to afford to come home any time soon.'

Bel's heart contracted. It still seemed impossible that Louis, the man she'd loved, had wrought such havoc on so many lives almost singlehanded. 'What news of Trinny?' she asked, although she didn't really want to know.

'No idea,' Tally said primly, but Bel could tell it hurt.

'You must be feeling a bit abandoned, sweetheart . . . First your dad legging it, then your mum sailing off into the sunset with this hedge-fund bloke.'

Tally managed a weak smile. 'Glad I've still got you.' She sniffed and turned away.

'Come here,' Bel said, shuffling along the bench, pushing the remains of their lunch into the canvas bag at her feet and putting her arms around her stepdaughter. They sat together like that for a long time. *It's not just Tally who needs a hug*, Bel thought.

'I keep banging on about me. But are you OK, apart from the grisly job obviously?' Tally asked eventually, as they let each other go.

'I'm fine,' Bel said firmly.

'And your dad?'

'He's fine, too.' *No need to burden Tally with my mess.* 'As soon as I have enough money, I'll get my own place.'

There was a silence.

Clearly unconvinced by her stepmother's narrative – she knew something of Bel's problems with her father in the past – Tally said, 'You could come and live with me if things get really bad. It'll be the sofa, I'm afraid, but it's quite a big one – better than Dad's, I expect. I'm at the office for most of the day, anyway.'

Bel was really touched, knowing how small the flat was. 'That's very kind. Thank you. But I'd never impose.'

'Or we could run away, like everyone else. Hitch a ride on Jeff's yacht, get off at St Tropez and hit the beach!' She gave Bel a playful nudge. 'Could be fun, no?'

Bel laughed. 'Sounds good to me!' She paused, feeling suddenly wistful. 'I had this boyfriend once . . . well, more than a "boyfriend". Bruno and I hoped to get married until the accident I told you about. Anyway, we've been in touch, and he suggested I go over for a visit to Chamonix. He runs a hotel there.' She took a breath. 'When I get the wherewithal, I might take him up on his offer. You can come with me. It's beautiful there.'

Tally's face fell and she eyed Bel suspiciously. 'Hmm, is he married?'

'Bruno? No, divorced. Why?'

'Well, you're single now. Suppose you end up getting together? I can't cope with you deserting me, too.' She adopted a mock-tragic expression.

Bel's eyes widened at the idea. 'I think we're jumping the gun here, sweetheart. I haven't seen him in nearly thirty years. He's probably got a beer belly and no hair,' she joked, knowing it was far more likely Bruno had remained svelte and tanned, his blue eyes just as bright, his hair silvered, perhaps, but still plentiful and thick. She wondered, for a fleeting second, what it would be like to see him again. Whether there'd be even the faintest shadow of what they'd felt for each other in their twenties after all this time.

She shook the thought away. Glancing at her watch, she saw it was gone three. The day had flown. She didn't dare look at her phone, lying in the bottom of the bag, where she was sure there would already be fifty irate messages from her father. 'I ought to get going.'

'Really? I was hoping we could do a bit of a walk. It's such a lovely day.'

'Dad gets antsy if I'm gone too long.'

Tally cocked an eyebrow but said nothing as they collected their bits and pieces together. Bel felt she owed her an explanation. 'He's getting old. I think he's come to rely on me rather a lot since I moved back in,' she said.

Tally paused in her packing. Her leather daypack dangling from one hand, she stared at Bel. 'You could still get your own place, though, if you wanted to . . . couldn't you?'

A small chill passed up Bel's neck, making her shiver. 'Of course. God, yes, absolutely.' Her tone was high and artificial. She could see from Tally's face that she'd heard it too. And Bel knew, despite fantasies to the contrary, that she wasn't going anywhere. Part of her was beginning to accept that. Another part was not.

Her stepdaughter didn't question her further. 'Listen, if you're walking, I'll come with you across the park, get the Tube from Notting Hill.'

8

When Bel got home, her father was nowhere to be seen. 'Dad ... Dad?' she called out. But he didn't answer and she felt a small contraction in her gut. '*Dad* . . .' He wasn't in the sitting room or the kitchen and his bedroom door was open, the room empty. She clicked on his mobile number but heard the phone ringing loudly from the side table beside her father's armchair in the sitting room. *Where would he have gone?* she wondered, knowing this must be some ploy of his to pay her back for her lunch with Tally: he had barely been out of the flat since her arrival, except to wander the corridors of the building, looking for anything out of place about which he could complain to the managing agents. *He can go out if he wants, without consulting me*, she told herself. Although it was clear the same rules did not apply to her.

It was nearly nine o'clock when Bel finally heard her father's key in the front door. She'd been getting increasingly anxious as the hours went by and there was still no message, no sign of him. Riggs, she ascertained by a trip to the basement, had not seen him. She'd even resorted to ringing his best friend, Reg, whose number she had found in his unlocked phone.

'He's probably gone to his club,' Reg said.

'I think he cancelled his sub during the pandemic.'

'Oh, did he?' He sounded vague and unengaged, so Bel thanked him and clicked off.

Now keen not to show she'd been fretting, Bel took a deep, calming breath as she waited for him to appear. Dennis sauntered into the sitting room. He was properly dressed for a change, in dark cords, a slightly crumpled blue shirt and his old tweed jacket.

'Hi, Dad,' Bel said nonchalantly, looking up from her book.

'Hi, sweetheart,' her father said, grinning foolishly. She immediately realized he was drunk. In spite of this, he wandered over to the whisky decanter on the bookshelf and poured a large measure for himself. Then he flopped down into his armchair, his breath expelled in the usual old-man groan.

Bel waited. She wasn't going to ask him where he'd been. 'Good day?' she enquired eventually, when he remained silent. He looked exhausted, she thought.

Dennis started, as if he hadn't realized she was there. 'If you call listening to old Gerry Seymour pontificating about his stellar career good,' he mumbled sourly. Gerry was one of his wine buddies from way back, someone with whom he had always been fiercely competitive. She remembered him from when she'd worked for her father and had always rather liked him.

She laughed. 'Both been at the Malbec, have you?'

'A tatty Rioja, unfortunately,' her father slurred. 'Nasty back taste and no body.' He winked at her. 'Losing his touch, I fear.'

71

Gerry lived in a flat off Gloucester Road – not far – which was clearly where they'd been holed up. 'Must have been more than one bottle,' she ventured.

Dennis gave her a sly glance. 'I seem to recall a rather more palatable little Bordeaux at some stage of the afternoon.'

Bel found she was relieved at the impromptu outing, despite the state of her father. He'd got himself dressed up, for whatever ulterior motive, and gone to spend time with a colleague – even if he didn't much care for him. It was a start.

A minute later, her father was on his feet. Grabbing his startled daughter by the hand, he dragged her upright and took her in his arms, beginning to waltz around the furniture, humming loudly the tune of Shostakovich's Second Waltz – a tune Bel knew from childhood as one of her mother's favourites.

Her father danced very well, his posture upright, his guiding hand on her back light but confident as he trod the box step, Bel's feet, after a moment, settling into his rhythm. She couldn't help laughing as he escorted her, still humming loudly and keeping perfect time, out into the corridor and across the black and white tiled floor, faster and faster, executing a smooth, sweeping turn at her bedroom door and setting off again, almost at a gallop, the box step going to pot as they neared the front of the flat.

Once back in the sitting room, he dropped Bel as if she'd burned him, and fell into his chair, breathing heavily but with a broad smile. 'Jesus Christ,' he gasped, reaching for his whisky and gulping the remains as if it were water. He viewed Bel through half-closed lids. 'Life in the old dog, eh?'

Bel, also out of breath, flopped into the other chair. Laughing and brushing her hair out of her eyes, she nodded. 'No question, Dad.' But almost before she'd finished, her father's eyes had closed completely and he was out cold.

Later, after she'd struggled to haul his dead weight to his bedroom – Dennis grunting and complaining every step of the way – she sank under her own duvet. Tonight reminded her of times when she was small and he'd come home in a cheerful mood. He would stride over to the record player and draw a disc from its sleeve with a flourish, dust it gently with his shirted forearm, then slot it onto the turntable, bending so he could be at eye level to set the stylus exactly in the groove as the vinyl began to spin.

Then, music filling the room, he would pick up young Bel in his arms, swirling her round and round, singing at the top of his voice, until she was giggling uncontrollably and too dizzy to speak. Her mother – relaxed for once – would watch, smiling and clapping. Bel sighed in the darkness, remembering those rare moments of happiness. *Was Dad a bit tipsy back then, too?* she wondered, as she slid into a deep sleep.

Bel paid for their moment of fun. Dennis emerged from his bedroom late in the morning, like a bear from hibernation: scratchy, growling and still half asleep.

Bumping into his daughter in the corridor, Dennis

started, then stared Bel up and down with a heavy frown, as if seeing her for the first time. 'Christ, girl, why do you wear those awful clothes all the time? A woman should look pretty – like a woman, not some genderless lump.' He spoke in a harsh whine that drove through her like a table saw. He looked away as if the very sight of her offended him.

Bel was shocked. However much she knew his remark came from a banging head and throbbing liver, it still hurt. She was in jeans, as usual, and a T-shirt and, OK, it couldn't be called a specifically feminine outfit, or in any way 'pretty', but there was no one to see her today. 'That's a bit mean, Dad.'

He looked as if the energy needed to answer back had deserted him because he shook his head wearily and began to move off down the corridor.

'The dancing was fun,' Bel called after him, not so much to curry favour – although she wasn't above that – but because it was true and she wanted him to know that she wasn't always in a bad mood.

Her father turned sharply. 'Dancing?'

'Last night, you and me . . .'

He frowned in concentration. Then he chuckled weakly. 'Good one, sweetheart. You had me going there for a moment.'

'No, seriously, Dad. You came back from Gerry's, remember, and started waltzing me round the room and down the corridor, humming Mum's favourite Shostakovich.'

Dennis stared at her, blinking his tired eyes. 'Dancing . . .'

'Don't worry. I think you'd had a lot to drink.'

74

He shrugged. 'I'm sure it'll come back to me.'

'It was fun,' she said brightly, hiding her concern.

He gave her a vague wave and turned away, muttering, 'Good. That's good.'

Bel retreated to her room. The incident had made her forget, temporarily, her father's cutting remark about her appearance. But now, as she caught sight of herself in the mirror beside the cupboard, it came back to her with full force. She stared at her reflection. What she saw was a tall figure with a square set to her shoulders, perhaps a little too much weight around the hips, but potentially an attractive woman with her large violet eyes and corn-coloured hair, straight nose and full mouth. As she gazed into the mirror, though, she also saw what her father had noted: the sad sheen that shrouded the woman in drabness – invisibility, in fact.

She felt herself falling into a strange trance, unable to drag her eyes away from an image she had no desire to acknowledge. It was very quiet in the room, but her body seemed to be vibrating, a strange sensation tickling up through her gut. It wasn't fear. It wasn't despair. It was, she slowly became aware, the tender shoots of rebellion.

She'd thought she was resigned to her fate – or had at least gradually come to accept that her life, her future, was there with her father. But those two cruel words, 'genderless lump' – although perhaps technically no worse than others that had gone before – somehow pierced her to the core. *If I live with Dad much longer,* she thought, *I'll be so crushed, so humiliated, that I'll never be able to escape.*

She laid her palms against her closed eyes and turned from the mirror. When she opened them again, her gaze immediately fell on her mother's burgundy leather jewellery box, sitting on the top of the bureau. It seemed almost to be glowing, as if it was calling to her.

Picking it up and carrying it over to the bed, she opened the lid and began to take out the contents, laying them on the duvet. It was a mishmash of good pieces – the favourite gold-link bracelet, diamond drop earrings, a string of pearls (the clasp broken), an emerald-studded eternity ring – and junk jewellery, beads and bangles she remembered her mother wearing on holiday. At the bottom was a square red box with scalloped gold scrolling round the outside. Bel thought it must contain Agnes's watch. Along with the bracelet, she had worn it every day.

Opening the box, Bel gazed at it, wrapped neatly around the display collar as if new. It was gold, heavy black Roman numerals decorating the round white face, on which was inscribed 'Cartier' in bold capitals, and 'Paris' in smaller script beneath the upside-down IV. The strap was dark brown and looked, to Bel, like crocodile. It was worn along the edges, curved to her mother's wrist shape, creased where the buckle had sat.

She smoothed it on her palm. Her mother had been a neat, pretty woman who – unlike Bel – had cared a lot about her appearance. She was always so perfectly turned out and this watch, with its understated elegance, epitomized her classic taste. *I'll never wear it*, Bel thought regretfully. She was sad that – as her father took cruel pleasure in pointing out – she would never manage such style or grace.

But clasping the watch in her hand, trying somehow to find her mother's essence therein, she was suddenly struck by a thought that made her eyes widen. *Could I?* Her father's fierce injunction rang in Bel's ears, not to let some imaginary 'eejit', born of his suspicious mind, get his hands on her mother's jewellery. But this watch was *hers*. It always had been, although her father had kept it back from her for decades. She held it to her cheek for a second, felt the smooth warmth of the gold against her skin, like her mother's kiss. 'Thanks, Mum,' she whispered, replacing the watch in the box and closing the lid.

A moment later, she was on her laptop, searching prices for vintage Cartier watches with box.

9

The following morning Bel was carrying a basket of washing she'd collected from her father's bedroom to the small utility room when her phone rang in her back pocket. She frowned at the screen, wondering for a moment who Patsy was, although the name was saved in her contacts. Then she remembered.

'Hi, Patsy.' Bel rarely spoke to the woman who lived next door to her mother's Cornish cottage. There was no need. The village seemed collectively to sort out any maintenance problems for Lenny, the tacit agreement that Bel would let him stay long since accepted by everyone. Now she waited to hear the reason for the call.

'How are you?' Patsy began.

'I'm OK,' Bel replied cautiously. It was a hard question to answer these days.

'Good. It's just I did ring you at the end of last year, but you didn't pick up or call me back. So Rhian Parry, the vicar, wrote to you . . .' She paused. 'I'm not sure if you've heard? Lenny died, sadly, in early December, from Covid.'

Bel was taken aback. 'Oh, no. I'm so sorry.' She thought about what Patsy had just said. 'You rang me?'

'Yes, a couple of times . . . He died on the tenth, so it must have been soon after that. Then Rhian sent you a letter and the order of service for his funeral – it was only a few of us from the village.'

Four months ago. The tenth of December, Bel thought. It was etched on her memory: the date at the top of Louis's 'Dear John' letter. She couldn't remember any calls from Patsy around that time, but she'd been so discombobulated and crazy. 'Things were a bit chaotic back then,' she explained. 'I never got the vicar's letter, though. I've been living in my father's flat since January. Maybe it got lost in the mail redirection.'

'Maybe,' Patsy agreed. 'Rhian sent it to the Walthamstow address you gave us. Anyway, that's how things stand. I just wondered what your plans might be, and if there's anything you want us to do to the place. So far we've left it as it was.'

Bel was trying to take in that her cottage was now empty. 'Umm . . . Goodness, Patsy, I don't know. This has come as a bit of a surprise. I'll have to think about it.'

'No hurry,' Patsy replied calmly. 'You'd be very welcome to stay with us if you want to check the place out.'

'I'd love to come down,' Bel said, at the same time remembering all that might stand in her way: money, her father, Vinny's sandwiches . . . But she would find a way. The thought of a visit to Cornwall made her heart beat a little faster. *Just a week off . . .*

'I've got my granddaughter living here,' Patsy was saying, 'but she's young, won't hurt her to bunk on the sofa for a few nights.'

Bel thanked her and heard her begin her goodbyes. 'Before you go, Patsy, what sort of state is the cottage in?'

'Hmm, not a pretty sight, I'm afraid. Lenny wasn't the tidiest of men.' She laughed softly, perhaps at some memory of her friend. 'But nothing a bit of house clearance couldn't sort out, I suppose. Depends what your plans are.'

'Right. Thanks. I'll be in touch when I've had a think.'

They said goodbye, and Bel continued along the corridor to the utility room to put the washing on. Her mind was buzzing. *The house is free*, she kept repeating to herself. She didn't know exactly what the implications were for her. But she knew they were significant.

Her father was in the sitting room at his desk, fiddling with the clip at the top of a pile of what looked like bills, when she told him what Patsy had said, adding, 'I never got the letter. It must have been lost in the post.'

Dennis didn't reply, didn't look at her.

'Dad? Did you hear what I just said? Lenny Bright died.'

He turned in his chair. 'Oh? Did he?' He wouldn't meet her eye and feigned interest in the bulldog clip again.

Bel stared at him. 'Did you know?' She was suddenly sure, from his shifty look, that he did.

'I think there might have been something . . . a letter . . . I meant to give it to you, but I must have forgotten.' He flashed an apologetic smile. 'Brain can be a bit fuzzy, these days.'

'Wait. So you opened the letter the vicar sent me about Lenny?'

Her father threw his hands into the air. 'I really can't remember, sweetheart. I might have opened it thinking it was for me. Easy to do.'

'Where is it, Dad? Where's the letter?' Bel was trying not to make more of this than she needed to. But it was hard not to be irritated, and suspicious of her father with-holding something so important to her.

'Oh, I don't know. It's months ago now. Why do you need it, anyway? You know he's dead.'

'Please,' she said, with admirable restraint. 'Can you look for it? Maybe it's in the desk drawer. It's where you put most of your post.'

With clear reluctance, Dennis turned back to his desk. He seemed flustered, which only served to make Bel more certain that this was deliberate. Muttering under his breath, he made a show of leafing through piles of paper in the various drawers in the knee-hole desk. After a few minutes of heavy breathing in the silent room, he finally came up with a brown A4 envelope and waved it casually at Bel. 'This might be it.'

Bel took it from him. There was a typed Royal Mail redirection sticker across her previous address, but 'Isobel Carnegie' was written in bold black marker pen above the label. Hard to miss.

'I meant to give it to you,' Dennis repeated stubbornly.

Bel did not reply as she took the letter back to her room. She sat on the bed and lifted the already-torn flap, drawing out a typed letter clipped to a funeral order of service. On the back was a photograph of a smiling man with sparse hair, a round face and uneven teeth, probably in his forties at the time of the snap. His expression was full of joy. Beneath it she read:

LENNY BRIGHT
14 SEPTEMBER 1953–10 DECEMBER 2021
NOW WITH GOD

Bel turned back to the letter:

Dear Ms Carnegie,

I thought you might like to see the attached.

Your extraordinary contribution to Lenny's life and wellbeing is without precedent. He was always so grateful.

Lenny was a wonderful man and we all loved him. He will be sadly missed by the whole community.

Your cottage, as Patsy will have told you, now lies empty. But, rest assured, we will continue to keep an eye until you decide your next move.

Look forward to meeting you, when you have time to venture down this far again.

With warmest wishes,
Rhian Parry

Rev. Rhian Parry
Vicar of St Saviour's Parish Church, Penruthyn, Cornwall
administrator@StSaviourschurch.org.uk

Bel stared at the photograph of Lenny, but her thoughts were centred on her mother. It was Agnes's kindness for which thanks were due, not Bel's. She had merely followed her mother's instructions, but had done nothing proactive for Lenny – she'd only met the man for a fleeting, slightly awkward handshake all those years ago. Yes, she had let him live in her cottage, but she hadn't wanted to live there herself, and she hadn't needed the money then.

There had been a moment, she remembered, when Louis had suggested she was being foolish, letting an obvious financial asset go to waste. But there was no chance she would have turfed Lenny out, even if the cottage had been much more valuable than its probable dilapidation indicated. It was one of the rare occasions when she'd stood up to Louis, because she knew that if she'd gone ahead and done such a cruel thing, the money would only have been sucked into the bottomless maw of 83. *I'll go down as soon as I can arrange it*, she told herself now. Her spirits spiralled upwards at the prospect.

Later, when she and her father were having lunch in the kitchen, Dennis still seemed defensive about Rhian Parry's letter, although Bel hadn't mentioned it again, her mind taken up with thoughts of her newly vacated inheritance.

'You must know how easy it is to open someone else's mail by mistake,' he said, as he munched his ham sandwich.

Bel nodded. 'I've done it myself, occasionally.'

Her father looked relieved. 'It wouldn't have made any difference to you, knowing sooner, anyway,' he said complacently.

She was suddenly on the alert. 'How do you mean?'

'Well, I imagine it's a worthless wreck after all these years of neglect.' He chuckled drily. 'It wasn't up to much in the first place.' When Bel didn't reply, he added, 'It's not as if you're going to live there. So, no harm done, eh?'

He was eyeing her intently. She said nothing, although she was well aware of his motivation for not giving her the letter. *He doesn't want me to have money . . . choices.* The knowledge should have made her angry. But it only made her scared. *He doesn't want me to leave.*

10

A week later Bel walked across the park to Burlington Arcade, off Piccadilly, her mother's watch in her bag. She had tidied up for the occasion, digging out a navy dress with large white buttons down the front, pleased to discover it still fitted her, despite pulling a bit at the waist. With some basic make-up, hair pulled up behind her head with a tortoiseshell clip and her red wool jacket against the chilly morning, she was ready. It was only eight, and her appointment was not till ten fifteen, but she'd crept out of the flat before her father was awake – she didn't want an inquisition.

She felt almost furtive as she entered the dark, high stone arch of the arcade, fortified with a coffee from the stall at Hyde Park Corner where Tally had bought takeaways for them both a couple of weeks ago. She'd told her stepdaughter what she was planning, and Tally had suggested the watch exchange where she was now headed. Tally's mother had used them in the past, apparently, and had given her a contact name: Nathan Riker.

Bel rang the bell at the small, glass-fronted shop, feeling like a character from a Charles Dickens novel. A man opened the door – almost Dickensian himself in a sober, tailored suit and tie, around fifty, with tortoiseshell-framed glasses above tidy features and smoothed-back dark hair.

'Miss Carnegie?' He bowed formally, then ushered her inside and through a narrow door into the back of the empty shop. She inhaled a soft whiff of aftershave as he indicated a leather Juliet chair for her, set in front of his shiny walnut desk. He offered her a cup of coffee, which she declined.

Bel felt unaccountably nervous as she retrieved her mother's watch box from her bag and laid it in front of Mr Riker. *Supposing he laughs in my face*, she thought. Because, in the days since Patsy's phone call and finally reading the vicar's letter, she realized she'd begun to set a lot of store on the outcome of this morning's business.

Nathan Riker took his time. He drew a brass loupe from his suit pocket and slid his index finger into the hole, brought the magnifying glass to his eye and the watch to the glass with his other hand. For what seemed an age, he turned it this way and that, took off the back with a small tool lying on his desk to check the movement, fiddled with the black-tipped crown, Bel holding her breath the while. Then he turned to his laptop and typed in the serial number from the back.

Finally, he looked up and gave her a satisfied smile. 'I do love Cartier,' he pronounced. 'I gather you don't have papers?'

Bel shook her head.

'Shame. But at least there's the box.' He looked thoughtful. 'Is this in part-exchange, or are you looking to sell?'

'Sell, please.'

There was a long pause. 'Right, well, let's see. This is a Vendôme, of course. It's in fair condition, bit of wear and tear. Made, according to the serial number, in nineteen seventy-six, which gives it some age.'

Bel nodded, trying not to let her impatience show.

Mr Riker, however, was not in a hurry. 'We take twenty per cent commission,' he went on, his smooth vowels reassuring. He looked at her questioningly, and she nodded.

'After commission, I could offer you . . . three thousand eight hundred pounds today?'

Bel took a deep breath. She was trying to look as if she were weighing up the sum, but her heart was bursting in her chest. She'd hoped for two or two and a half, tops. She supposed the watch, if she'd been hard-nosed and taken the time and trouble to shop around, could possibly fetch more than Mr Riker was offering, but she didn't care.

She drew herself up in her chair, unsure if bartering was the done thing in the hallowed halls of Burlington Arcade, but it was worth a try. 'Could you go to four?' *Don't ask, don't get* had been her father's favourite mantra, drummed into her since she was very small.

The watch dealer did not look surprised. He smiled, in fact, as if her boldness amused him. 'Very well, Miss Carnegie,' he said, after a moment. 'A round four it is.' He reached across the shiny desk to shake her hand, his grip firm. 'If you give me your bank details, I'll have the money transferred into your account within the next forty-eight hours.'

Bel might easily have hugged him, although she restrained herself. Her voice weak with relief, she thanked him and waited while the paperwork was completed, heart thumping. Once outside in the sunshine again, she took a huge gulp of air, almost skipping home. Four thousand pounds! It was life-changing – certainly in the short term. *I can give some to Dad, keep enough for some sort of plan*, she told herself joyfully, texting the news to Tally as she walked.

Hooray! Tally texted back. *But if you move to France, I'll follow you. Be warned.* A string of heart emojis followed.

Bel laughed when she read it. *Not leaving the country. Promise xxx*, she texted back. Because she already knew where she wanted to be, even if she didn't know how she would manage to leave her father, or what she would do when she got there.

When she opened the door to the flat, she immediately heard her name barked. Her father's voice came from the sitting room.

She entered, finding him still in his dressing gown, on his haunches, old photographs spread out around him on the rug. A battered cardboard box, whence the photos must have come, was tipped over the arm of his chair.

On seeing Bel, Dennis raised an eyebrow. 'Ooh, get you. To what do we owe this sudden sartorial upgrade?' His expression darkened. 'Been out cavorting with that new fella of yours, eh?'

'For God's sake, Dad, I don't have a "fella". How many times do I have to tell you?' She had hoped to make it to her bedroom unseen and change back into the clothes her father despised before she could be questioned. 'What are you doing with all those photos?'

Dennis wasn't to be so easily diverted. Grunting and

wincing, he drew up one knee, and, leaning heavily on it with both hands, managed to lever himself upright, where he stood, breathless, eyeing her. 'Where have you been, then?'

The debate had been raging in Bel's head ever since she'd decided to sell her mother's watch: *Should I tell Dad?* Her instinct, for obvious reasons, was that she should not. But it felt wrong, somehow, going behind his back. Even if the watch was legally hers, didn't he have the right to know she'd sold it? But she flinched inwardly at the thought of how he would react to what she'd done. She inhaled, on the verge of telling him the truth. But courage failed her. 'I met a friend for coffee.' Nathan Riker wasn't exactly a friend, and she'd refused his offer of coffee, but still.

'Which friend?'

'No one you know.' She turned to go.

'A man friend, I assume, from the coy expression on your face,' her father challenged, following her as she walked from the room.

'Yes, he is a man.'

'Aha! I knew it,' Bel heard, as her father skipped round her and stood blocking her way in the corridor, hands on his hips. 'You've been up to no good, Bella. It's written all over your face.'

Bel said nothing, jaw clenched. She sensed glee in her father's hectoring.

'You're not going anywhere until you tell me the truth.'

His voice had turned icy cold and she felt a shiver run up the back of her neck, a small but familiar shaft of dread around her heart. The money soon to be dropped into her account, though, seemed to give her new agency, made her care just a little bit less. 'What are you going to do, Dad? Wrestle me to the ground until I confess?' she asked, with a thin smile.

Preparing to push past him, Bel didn't see it coming. Face suddenly flushed puce with rage at her uncharacteristic challenge, her father's hand whipped across her cheek with a loud crack, which seemed to echo in the still air of the dark, high-ceilinged hall.

Bel's breath was knocked from her body. She stared blankly at her father for a second. He stood motionless, eyelids fluttering rapidly.

'Bella . . .' His voice was barely above a whisper, and she thought she saw fear in his eyes.

He reached out for her, but she was gone, stumbling down the corridor, barely able to breathe.

11

Time stopped.

Weakened and winged by the endless drip-drip of insults, put-downs and casual sniping, her father's sudden explosion of violence seemed to tear a hole right through Bel. She sensed her very essence draining away in the days that followed . . . and became almost lifeless.

While still functioning like an automaton on a practical day-to-day level – she went to work, cooked and cleaned as always, changed the sheets, smiled when required – inside Bel existed in a numb darkness. True to his word, Nathan Riker had deposited the four thousand pounds into her account. But it sat there untouched, barely considered. Cornwall no longer featured in her thoughts. She'd made no specific resolve to go or not to go, just stopped thinking about it . . . or anything beyond the mundane decisions required of her. *Pick up Dad's medication from the surgery. Get sausages for supper.*

Her father had not apologized for the vicious slap. Neither had Bel mentioned it. They had carried on entirely as usual. If he was sheepish in the immediate aftermath, she didn't notice. If his normal teasing routine resumed or not, she didn't notice that either.

And so the first week passed. Then the second. Bel remained cocooned in her lifeless state, where no thoughts troubled her. There was no pain, no anguish, no questions to ask of herself or her father. That would have been far too difficult.

Today was the beginning of the third week. It was a beautiful Sunday at the beginning of May – although Bel was unaware of the blueness of the sky, the bright spring sunshine, the smell of new growth scenting the air.

She was cooking lunch, going through the motions with a joint of pork and roast potatoes, cabbage and apple sauce, her father lurking around her, like a heavy mist, as usual. But Bel had no agency any more. If he wanted to be there, he could.

Dennis's eyes sparkled as he sniffed the meaty aroma coming from the kitchen.

'Roast pork,' he said, with an enthusiastic hand rub. 'The perfect excuse to bring out that classy little Merlot I've been saving for a rainy day.'

Bel dutifully nodded, barely paying attention.

The meal went down well for once, Dennis muttering the occasional 'Delicious' between mouthfuls. Not that Bel cared. She ate mechanically, half listening to her father's one-sided chatter from across the kitchen table.

'Those old photos I found the other day,' she heard him say, as he finished his pork and set down his knife and fork. 'You were such a cheeky wee thing back then. There are some great ones of you and your mum in that Italian castle place we went to near Pisa. I'm putting them in an album. I'll show you after lunch.'

'OK.'

Raising her head, she realized he was watching her closely. 'Your mother's death must have hit you hard, sweetheart.'

Bel was nonplussed. *Now?* she thought wearily. 'Of course it did,' she said dully.

Dennis nodded, seemingly unaware of – or unwilling to acknowledge – Bel's persistent, enervated mood. 'So maybe it's what caused you to lose that cheekiness, the spark you can see so clearly in the snaps,' he mused, almost contemplatively.

It took her a moment to understand what he'd said through the miasma that clotted her brain. Her heart, by rights, should have been broken by her father's clear disappointment in his only daughter. But she was not aware of hurt. Dennis's judgement chimed too closely with Bel's own. He was right. There was no spark left in her.

Not even trying to find a response, she rose in silence to fetch the dessert from the fridge, serving the fruit salad in the cut-glass bowl her mother had always used for the purpose – it brought an approving smile to Dennis's face. She handed him his portion and pushed the cream jug across the kitchen table.

'Thanks,' her father said. Then he peered into his bowl and frowned. Without saying a word, he began to pick out with his fingers all the raspberries mixed in with the other fruit, placing the offending berries, dripping, on his cloth mat.

'What are you doing?' Bel asked.

Dennis's face, when he looked up, was pruny with distaste. 'I hate raspberries in fruit salad, you know that.' He spoke matter-of-factly.

Not true. Only a week ago, and two weeks before that, Bel had given him fruit salad with raspberries and he'd eaten the lot.

It was such a small thing, utterly insignificant compared to the more serious transgressions her father had perpetrated over the months since she'd taken up residence. He wasn't even angry. The air remained quite still.

But as she watched him, Bel was conscious of a sudden sharp twinge, deep inside her. Something small and tight and long-held seemed to burst open, with the loud crack of damaged masonry, detonating the foggy darkness in her head, like dynamite in a pit.

Recently so insentient, her body began cranking fiercely to life, her system flooding with adrenalin, making her buzz and shake. She gasped, clutching her chest – it felt so real, so violent – and shot to her feet. Her father, munching happily on his doctored fruit salad, cream rimming his lips, didn't even look up.

She laid her napkin carefully on the table and, with trembling legs, walked from the room. Behind her she heard her father's surprised cry, 'Bella? Where are you going?'

For reasons Bel didn't even try to explain, his ill-mannered pickiness over the blameless raspberries had been the catalyst – the last grain of sand to tip the scale. It trumped even his insults and the slap, stripping away her forbearance, like paper from a damp wall. It dragged her back to life. *I cannot . . . I* will *not take it any more*, she heard herself say as she closed her bedroom door.

Fired up, finally, as if her body-batteries had been plugged in and given a super-boost, she felt manic, almost too alive, her nerve endings tingling as if she'd just emerged from a freezing sea. She needed to make a plan, right now, before the power failed again. Reaching for her phone, she dialled Patsy Wornum's number in Cornwall.

'You're planning to stay in the cottage?' Patsy sounded doubtful when Bel outlined her idea.

'You think I shouldn't?' Bel asked.

'Hmm. I suppose it depends what you're prepared to put up with.' She laughed, a deep, throaty chuckle. 'To be truthful, it's a shambles in there, love. We did our best, but Lenny was a bit of a hoarder – to say the least. And, as I told you before, not the tidiest of men. I wouldn't think it'd be much of a holiday for you.'

'I'm sure it'll be fine,' Bel said uncertainly. In her mind, she'd envisaged a shabby, none-too-clean and somewhat rickety interior. Not what she was used to, but still manageable. Patsy was pricking that bubble.

'How long are you planning on being here?' Patsy was asking.

'Umm, not sure. A week, maybe?'

'OK. Well, if you're really serious, there's no way you can sleep on that mattress. It's a million years old and rank.' Bel heard her sip something and swallow. 'There's a bedding shop in Penzance. I can send you the link.' Another sip. 'I'll lend you a duvet and sheets if you're only here for a short time. Or, as I said before, you'd be most welcome at ours.'

'You're very kind,' Bel said, 'but I'd like to be in the cottage, if possible.'

'Up to you, love. I'd get going on a new mattress and pillows, then. It'd be a queen size for that base. And you'll need the leccy turned on. Social Services stopped paying when Lenny died.'

Bel thanked her again and told her she'd be in touch about dates. Then she sat in the quiet of the bedroom and brainstormed her future. She could take the train to Penzance in the middle of May – two weeks from now – giving her time to sort out her father. She'd bring her bike – currently stored in the basement – and the absolute minimum of clothes. *It's just a short break from Dad*, she told herself, knowing she risked upsetting Vinny at the sandwich shop so soon after he'd employed her. She hesitated as she booked her train ticket, aware of the very tiniest pinprick of an idea settling in the back of her mind . . . But still big enough for her to plump for an open return.

It's my inheritance, she told herself, feeling guilty, almost furtive, as she paid for the ticket from Paddington on the train app. *The longer the place is left empty, the more it'll deteriorate*. She felt, ridiculously, that she needed a cast-iron excuse to leave her father – even if her stay in Cornwall was brief.

A little daunted by her conversation with Patsy about the condition of the cottage, but still determined, Bel found the bed shop online and made an order. Delivery was scheduled for five days' time, which information she sent to her neighbour. Then she contacted the utilities company.

Finally laying aside her laptop, Bel rested back against

the wall and let out a slow breath. She could feel a buzz of excitement in her gut. *What will I find down there?* There was also the small matter of her father.

Now, though, she was too tired to think. It was only four in the afternoon, but she lay down, pulling the duvet tight round her neck, and closed her eyes.

The kitchen, when Bel emerged from her nap later that evening, was exactly as she'd left it, the debris from lunch scattering the surfaces. Her father was nowhere to be seen. She went through to the sitting room and found him asleep in his chair, a shouty presenter she recognized from *Antiques Roadshow* on the screen. She smiled, knowing what he would be saying if he was awake. Dennis liked watching television only in order to deliver a running commentary. 'What the hell is that female wearing?' and 'The fella's a moron. Shouldn't be allowed on TV,' and 'Bloody mumbling. Can't understand a word anyone says.' It drove Bel mad.

Now she stood looking down on him. She was dying to wake him, tell him of her plan, but she knew he would be groggy and irascible when roused, after all those glasses of red wine and too much roast meat. She decided she would wait until she heard from Patsy that her mattress had been delivered – wait until all her ducks were in a row and her trip watertight. She didn't want there to be any chance of her father talking her out of it.

By the following week, Bel was all set. Patsy had confirmed Lenny's old mattress had been disposed of, Bel's new one safely delivered. Her ticket was scheduled for a week on Tuesday and she'd begged her boss at the sandwich shop for a week off.

Vinny had clutched his head dramatically and dragged the names of all the Holy Family through an agitated rant – as if they could help him with his egg mayonnaise and tuna. 'I thought you were too old to be a fuckin' snowflake,' he told her, adding ominously, 'so don't be expecting your job to be here when you get back.' Bel thought she'd take her chances.

Now all she had to do was tell her father, a prospect that made her gut clench, her heart bang in her chest. Dennis had been particularly grouchy in the last few days. He complained his back was playing up, a disc in his lower spine worn down and causing him occasional pain. Bel sympathized, but could do little to help.

'Dad, I need to tell you something,' Bel began tentatively, as she cleared away yet another bacon breakfast, surreptitiously patting the back pocket of her jeans, in which she'd squashed a thick envelope.

He was sitting at the table, the newspaper open in front of him, his reading glasses perched on his nose, still in his dressing gown, white stubble shadowing his chin. He did not respond. Bel turned off the tap, set the frying pan on the draining-board and turned to face him. 'Dad?'

He glanced up with a smile. 'What?'

'I'm going to Cornwall.'

'Cornwall?' Dennis looked surprised. 'To the shack?'

She nodded, waiting for him fully to take in what she'd said.

'It's a ruin, no? That fella won't have looked after it.'

'I don't know. That's what I need to find out.'

His eyes narrowed. 'And you want some money, I assume, to pay for the trip?' There was a certain amount of glee in his anticipation of her request.

'No, I'm OK, thank you.'

'You are?' He looked put out. 'How come? Sandwiches paying more than I thought?'

The question she'd dreaded. *He has no right to ask.* 'Don't worry about it, Dad,' she said quietly, heart in her mouth.

There was a long pause, during which her father eyed her with growing suspicion. Then he shook his head as if dismissing something.

Bel found she was holding her breath as she waited for the penny to drop. Because she knew it very soon would.

'Wait a minute . . . not your mother's jewellery,' Dennis finally said, his voice fallen to a disbelieving whisper.

She saw no point in lying. 'Her watch, yes.' She paused, heart fluttering. 'I'd never have worn it.'

Outrage sparked in his eyes as he jumped out of his chair. 'The Cartier? You sold your mother's Cartier?' He eyed her furiously, breathing hard. Bel could see the rage building, watched him clench his fists by his side, perhaps to prevent himself lunging at her. 'You scheming bitch,' he growled. Angry spittle formed in the corners of his mouth. 'I gave you her things in good faith. *I entrusted them to you.*'

Trembling, she straightened her shoulders. 'The watch was mine, Dad. Mum would have wanted me to use it to look after the cottage. She loved that place.'

'Ha!' Dennis scoffed, stepping back and uncrossing his arms. 'That's your justification for pawning your dead mother's jewels?' He was wheezing noisily now, his face suffused a dark pink, his stocky frame still powerful and threatening. 'How much?' he barked, a small sneer appearing on his lips. '*How much?* Not nearly enough, I'm sure. You've got that sort of face. The sort that makes people think they can rip you off.' He shook his head, like a wet dog. 'You make me sick.'

Bel took this opportunity to drag the envelope out of her back pocket and hold it out to him. 'There's fifteen hundred in there. It's not much, I know, but I don't want you to think I've forgotten the debt we owe you.' She had supplemented a portion of the watch money with cash from the sandwich shop.

Dennis eyed the packet charily, as if she were offering him blood money. He made no move to take it. So Bel laid it gently on the table. But it seemed to have taken the wind out of his sails.

When next her father spoke, his tone was indignant, rather than angry. 'So what am I supposed to do while you're gallivanting in Cornwall? Maria's buggered off back to Portugal. Who'll do for me?' Maria was Dennis's cleaner – sullen and pretty useless, in Bel's opinion, but she loved laundry – who had gone back to her home town after the pandemic to be with her extended family.

'That's what I wanted to talk to you about. I can find someone to come in if you like,' she said, in a conciliatory tone, twisting her fingers together in front of her, just dying to get away from him.

He huffed indignantly. 'You don't give a toss about me, do you?' He clutched his back theatrically, just to remind her – although it hadn't bothered him just now, when he'd sprung to his feet with the speed of a much younger man. 'I take you in when you're on your uppers, look after you, but as soon as it suits, you're off without so much as a by-your-leave.' He turned away. 'What a bloody fool I've been.'

Bel sighed inwardly, then mustered a soothing reply from the tattered remnants of her patience. 'Of course I appreciate all you've done for me, Dad. You know I do,' she said, not for the first time. 'But it's only for a few days. We can find someone else to do your laundry while I'm gone.'

She watched her father stop in his tracks. He spun round slowly. 'Is that all I mean to you? An old man who needs his smalls washed?' His voice cracked. 'Did it never occur to you I might be lonely, rattling around on my own with no one to talk to and nowhere to go since that sodding pandemic wrecked my social life?'

Suddenly ashamed, although she knew her father was a past master at pulling her heartstrings, she repeated, less certainly this time, 'It's only for a few days, Dad.'

Silence.

He shook his head, tiredly puffing out his cheeks. 'Oh, do what you like, Bella. It's not as if I have any say in the matter.' With that, he picked up his reading glasses from the table – leaving the money where Bel had dropped it – and shuffled out of the room.

She waited till she heard his bedroom door close, then scooted along the corridor and shut herself in her room. *I will not cry*, she told herself. *I won't let him get to me.* But she was trembling. Guilt vied with desperation as she wondered if she really was being thoughtless, leaving him alone. *It's not for long*, she insisted to herself, staring out onto the communal gardens from her window. *Maybe a break is all I need.* The small seeds of a more permanent freedom were shrivelling in the hot air of her father's emotional blackmail.

'Cornwall!' Tally exclaimed, when Bel phoned her a couple of days later. 'Great idea.'

'It's only for a week.'

'Yeah, but it'll be amazing to have fresh sea air, some different wallpaper to stare at.'

'Not sure there's any of that in the cottage. It'll probably be so manky I'll turn tail and be back in the smoke by the weekend.'

'Listen, Bel. Take a proper holiday,' Tally said firmly. 'Even if your place is gross – and it sounds like it might be – I'm sure there are spots where you can camp out. You've got the beach, the sea, and it's almost nice weather. Send pics, make me jealous.'

Bel laughed. 'Will do.' She fiddled with a thread coming loose on the seam of her jeans. She wanted to confide in her stepdaughter about her fears over leaving her father alone. But Tally was speaking.

'Sorry, Bel. There's a work call coming in I'd better take. Listen, have a wonderful trip.'

'Yeah, talk soon.' Having said goodbye to Tally, she continued to sit on her bed, thoughts racing round her head. It was Friday and she was leaving in four days. Her father had been a nightmare since she'd told him her Cornwall plan. He'd barely left her side for a single minute, following her about, knocking on her door at all times of the day and night with concerns about how he would cope when she was gone.

'I can't carry stuff home from the shop with my back,' he'd say. So she had set him up with online shopping from the local supermarket – he was perfectly competent on the computer. 'The washing machine isn't working properly.' She checked and it was fine. 'How do you make that spaghetti sauce with the tomatoes I like?' She'd made a batch and put it into the freezer, along with single portions of macaroni cheese and shepherd's pie. And 'I don't know how I'm going to manage without you,' delivered over and over in a mournful tone, until she began to believe him. She'd offered to find someone to come in and help, but he'd stubbornly refused. She was beginning to wonder if the trip was even worth the hassle.

Now, as if her thoughts had summoned him up, she heard a loud knocking and her father's voice urgently calling her name. Sighing, she got off the bed and went to open the door. 'What's up, Dad?'

Dennis was bent over, clutching his back, his face pale. 'My sodding back's gone. I can't stand upright,' he gasped, almost falling into Bel's arms. Letting him lean heavily on her, she took his arm and helped him shuffle slowly along the corridor and onto his bed, gently lifting his legs until he was lying flat.

Her father was sweating, panting, his dark eyes creased with pain.

'I'll get you some ibuprofen. She hurried to the box in the kitchen where Dennis kept all his medication, her heart frozen in despair. *NO*, she wailed silently. *No, no, no!*

By the evening it was quite clear that her father couldn't cope on his own. His pain appeared genuine, even though Bel knew he wasn't above exaggerating the problem for his own ends. He seemed barely able to get out of bed for a pee, let alone make himself anything to eat. Bel was beside herself. Pauline had been round again the night before and God knew what she and her father had got up to. Would he be sufficiently improved by the time she was due to depart in a few days? And even if his back was better, it didn't seem right to leave him in such a vulnerable state.

On Saturday morning – after a sleepless night – she waited for him to wake so she could assess the situation. She made him a strong coffee and a piece of toast and marmalade and took it through to the bedroom. Dennis was sitting up in bed, reading the *Spectator* in the bright beam of the bedside spotlight. Bel put down the toast and coffee and went to open the heavy curtains to the bright spring morning.

'How are you, Dad?'

Pulling off his reading glasses, he let out a long sigh. 'Hardly slept a wink. Every time I turn over, it nearly kills me.'

'I'm so sorry. But you've got Holly coming at ten. She'll sort you out.'

Dennis smiled as he reached for his coffee. He loved his physio. She had a dark, bouncy ponytail and a wide smile, and bossed him about with a combination of Nanny-knows-best and irresistible flattery.

Bel hovered while her father ate his toast. Neither of them had an answer to the question burning on her tongue: 'Will you be better by Tuesday?' *A lot can happen in three days*, she kept telling herself. But her courage was waning fast: the trip appeared doomed.

Holly stood in the corridor with Bel. Her father's door was shut, but the physiotherapist spoke in a low voice nonetheless. 'He's pulled a muscle in his lumbar spine. Nothing too serious, this area's often caused him grief in the past, but the spasms must be painful. I've done what I can. Now he's got to mobilize his back, not lie in bed all day. I've sent him exercises on email.' She grinned. 'Probably won't do them, of course.'

'So he should get up and start doing things?'

'Absolutely. Just walking about for short periods – the stretches will help. Paracetamol every four hours.' She stuffed a rolled-up towel into her sports bag and hoisted it onto her shoulder. 'I'll be back on Wednesday.'

'Thanks, Holly. See you then,' Bel said, wondering if she would as she thanked the physio and showed her to the door.

'I can't go,' she said to Tally, when she rang her that evening. 'I'll feel terrible if I do.' Her father had been up and about since Holly's visit – Bel had insisted. Apart from a fair amount of grunting and groaning he was clearly a lot better. But whenever Bel asked him how he was, he would pull a face and groan, 'Shite.' She had no way of assessing the degree of his pain, of course, and was still unsure of the extent to which he might be laying it on thick for her benefit.

'Wait a minute,' her stepdaughter said. 'You say he's up and about, and you're not going till Tuesday. He'll be fine by then, won't he?'

'Probably not,' Bel said gloomily. 'And even if he is, he'll pretend he isn't. I'll just worry.'

She thought she detected a tinge of frustration in Tally's sigh. 'Isn't there someone you could arrange to drop in every day, check on him?'

'No,' Bel said, without thinking.

'What about the porter guy? You could ask him to swing by, maybe do the odd bit of shopping.'

'Riggs? He's too weird.' Bel knew she was being stubborn, but she didn't feel as if she deserved to get away any more.

Tally laughed. 'Right. Well, that rules him out, then.'

'It was stupid, thinking I could just go off like this. He obviously needs me.'

'Best to give up then, eh? Just settle down and accept your fate as a long-term carer for your dad.' Tally's tone was solemn, mimicking Bel's.

'I'll go another time.'

'When he needs you less?'

The silence between them was like a tug-of-war. Bel, despite resisting, knew Tally was right. Her father would only ever need her more. It was now or never.

'What about Flo?' Tally interrupted her thoughts. 'You said she was doing shit cleaning jobs. Maybe a couple of weeks grappling with your dad would be light relief. He's got the money, you say.'

Would she? Bel wondered.

'You could ask her,' Tally suggested, when Bel didn't reply.

'Dad's so racist. He'll probably give her a hard time. That wouldn't be fair on her.'

'Bel!' Tally almost shouted. 'For God's sake.'

'OK, OK! I'll ring her.'

'Blimey, it's like coaxing a frightened cat out of a tree.'

'Flo, the waitress?' her father asked on Monday morning. 'I told you I don't want anyone here.'

'I'm going to Cornwall tomorrow. You keep saying you can't manage without me,' Bel reminded him.

'Like I need some idiot stranger fussing over me.' He dragged his eyes from the morning programme he was watching.

'Flo's in no way an idiot or a stranger. You met her lots of times at 83. You always said you liked her.'

'I don't want her,' he stated bluntly, turning back to the television.

Bel, frantically channelling Tally, stood her ground. 'She could help with the shopping, do a bit of cleaning, cook for you, all the things I do . . . And Flo makes a fantastic curry.' She knew this because Flo had once cooked a Jamaican curry chicken – served with fried plantain, coconut rice and beans (which Flo called 'peas') – for her, Louis and the rest of the staff one night when 83 was closed between Christmas and New Year. Bel could still remember its deliciousness.

Bel saw Dennis's ears prick up at the carrot she was so shamelessly dangling. Her father adored curry. He didn't reply – probably not wishing to give her the satisfaction of capitulating so soon – but she could tell he was thinking about it. She left him to mull it over. Even if he rejected the idea of Flo, she felt she was off the hook. She had found someone to help him. It was up to him if he wanted to avail himself of the offer.

Later, she texted Tally: *Flo on board. Dad cantankerous. At least I tried. Off to Cornwall in the morning. THANK YOU! xxx*

Her father, whose back was noticeably better, except when he realized Bel was watching, barely spoke to her the next day, as she prepared to leave. Flo had come over the previous evening for Bel to go through everything with her. She'd picked up a key and some cash for the next ten days, agreeing to come in for three hours a day until Bel returned.

'You've saved my life,' she said to Bel, beaming as she tucked the key and the money into her purse. 'One more rich client with attitude and I might have stabbed someone.'

'That's Dad you're describing, I'm afraid,' Bel said. 'He's probably worse than all of them put together.'

Flo looked if she thought Bel was joking, then saw she wasn't. 'I'm sure I'll cope,' she said, with a reassuring smile.

'If, or should I say *when* he's rude, or racist, or sexist or any of the other "ists" he favours, I apologize in advance,' Bel said. 'He's probably nastier to me than anyone else, if it's any consolation. He doesn't mean it.' *There I go again*, she thought, wincing. Even if her father didn't mean it, he should know better than to indulge his baser instincts so casually.

Flo raised an eyebrow but said nothing.

And when Dennis was introduced to Flo, he'd been at his charming best. She'd asked about his back and he'd thrown one hand into the air with a flourish. 'Takes more than a pulled muscle to bring Dennis Carnegie down,' he'd said gamely, an almost flirtatious look in his eye as he smiled at Flo. Bel hoped her friend would survive.

Now her father stood in the hall, arms folded resentfully, and watched in silence as she dragged her backpack to the front door. Her packing was minimal: she'd bike to the station and then from Penzance at the other end so she couldn't carry much.

'OK, Dad, I'm off,' Bel said, straightening after zipping her phone into the front pocket of her pack. 'I'll ring when I get there, if there's a decent signal.' She leaned forward and pecked his cheek. 'I hope you have a good time with Flo. She's a gem.'

Mouth pursed and an eyebrow raised, he eyed her coolly. 'Safe journey,' he mumbled, and turned away. Bel tried not to feel hurt. She would have liked a hug. Or to have been able to share her excitement – and nervousness – about her trip. But Dennis had stonewalled her since the moment she'd said she was going away.

Riggs was waiting in the basement. 'I did the tyres. Back one was flat as a pancake,' he told her, as he pushed the bike into the lift and propped it against the wall. He was smiling that discomfiting smile of his, but Bel was grateful and told him so. 'Going far?' he queried.

'Cornwall for a few days. A friend's coming in to help Dennis while I'm away. Flo Liverpool. She's got a key.'

He held the lift door back with one arm. 'I'll keep an eye.'

She thanked him again, and emerged onto the pavement, leaning on the handlebars and letting out a huge sigh of relief . . . as if she'd just escaped from a long spell in a dark, airless dungeon.

The journey to Paddington station was hairy and she took it slowly. Bel was an experienced cyclist: she'd spent many hours circling the paths of Epping Forest with Louis and on her own when she lived in Walthamstow. But her backpack, although not huge, was heavy enough, threatening to unbalance her, and being out in the traffic of Central London for the first time in months was unnerving.

It wasn't until the train was easing slowly out of the station – bike and case stowed, reserved seat located, tuna sandwich, crisps, apple and water in the bag at her feet – that she allowed herself to relax a little, and finally breathe more easily. Over the last few days she had felt as if she was balancing on a knife edge. She'd never been quite certain – even with Flo's help – that she would actually get away.

Now, she leaned back in her seat and closed her eyes, hardly able to believe she was on this train, heading out of London . . . It seemed much more significant than just a few days in Cornwall. She thought of a line from *Winnie-the-Pooh* that her mum often used to quote to her when Bel was small and reluctant to socialize: '"You can't stay in your corner of the Forest waiting for others to come to you," sweetheart.' *I'm coming out of my corner, Mum*, Bel thought, as the carriage swayed gently and she drifted off into an exhausted doze.

PART TWO

13

As the train snaked west, pottering along the south coast – the views across the sea spectacular as they passed through Dawlish and later Plymouth, Saltash, Par – Bel began to feel a quiet excitement brewing in her belly. She mapped her bike route from Penzance on her phone – it seemed straightforward enough, a pleasant half-hour ride along the A394 – although the nearer she got to her destination, the darker and more threatening the May clouds became. By the time the train drew into the station, the carriage windows were spattered and blurry with heavy rain.

Bel smiled to herself as she wheeled her bike along the platform and towards the turnstile. *Just my luck.* She wore her anorak, but her backpack was old and probably not very waterproof, neither were her jeans. But, despite the weather, she breathed in the clean Cornish air and felt it zing through her body, like a tonic.

She almost missed Patsy. It wasn't till she heard someone tentatively call her name that Bel, focused on manoeuvring her bike through the turnstile, spun round and spotted the cardboard sign with her name in bold marker-pen capitals – torn from the side of a box, by the look of it. A tanned older woman, small and wiry, dressed in a denim shirt and off-white cargo shorts, battered Birkenstocks, her grey hair in two short, untidy plaits, was holding it. Patsy was grinning at her. Coming over, she said, 'It is you, right?'

When Bel nodded, also smiling, Patsy offered a hand across the bicycle, her grip firm and welcoming. Bel was amazed her neighbour was there. She'd told Patsy when her train was arriving because she had asked, but she hadn't expected to be met.

'Let me take something,' Patsy said, grabbing the carrier-bag resting on the handlebars. It contained the remains of Bel's picnic, a book, a newspaper and various bits and bobs she couldn't cram into the backpack.

'Will the bike fit in your car?'

'Not a problem. Dora's outside.'

Bel had no idea who this was, but she was thrown by Patsy's sudden appearance and didn't ask as she followed her outside into the rain.

Dora, it turned out, was an old, pale green Volkswagen camper van with a cream roof, which Patsy had parked in one of the line of empty disabled bays right outside the station. She shot Bel a defiant glance. 'I'm not disabled yet, thank goodness, but Dora's pretty long in the tooth and not up to much, these days.'

Bel laughed. 'She looks just fine to me.'

Patsy slid open the side door, revealing a see-through plastic storage box, a purple yoga mat, a crate of what looked like tins of tomatoes and a pair of muddy walking boots. She pushed all this aside and Bel hefted the bike into the space, then threw in her pack. Patsy pulled the door shut.

Once they were on the road, Bel let out a long, slow

breath. 'Oh, my goodness, thanks so much for picking me up, Patsy. You didn't have to.'

Patsy shot her a glance, her dark eyes full of amusement. 'I never do anything I don't want to, love. Not these days.'

'You're lucky,' Bel said, without thinking.

Eyes on the road, Patsy replied, 'Takes practice,' then added, 'Your mattress and pillows arrived. Although I can't imagine you'll want to sleep there.'

'I'm sure I'll be fine.'

Patsy laughed. 'Stubborn like your mother.'

'You knew Mum quite well, then?' Bel asked.

'She came down for a few summers when you were too small to remember. Agnes loved it here. But your father . . .'

Bel waited, but Patsy didn't go on. 'I never thought of her as stubborn,' she said quietly.

'Maybe not as a general rule. But when it came to letting Lenny stay in the cottage . . .' Patsy glanced across at her. 'Put it this way. Your father was dead set against the idea.' She chuckled. 'But she got her way.'

Bel felt a small shaft of pleasure at the thought of her mother standing up to her father for once. She wanted to ask more, but the van was turning right off the main road and Patsy announced, 'Nearly there.' They began winding their way along the narrow lane, downhill towards the village. Then, rounding a corner, the sea suddenly came into view on the horizon. Bel gasped. The afternoon sun had broken through the clouds, illuminating the grey water with an almost biblical shaft of sunlight.

Patsy slowed down. 'Welcome to our magic place.'

As the two women got out of the van, Patsy held out her hand with a flourish towards the building next to her own. 'Yours,' she said simply.

Bel stared at the cottage in silence. The last time she'd seen it, the house had belonged to Lenny – to all intents and purposes. Now she looked at it through different eyes. It seemed smaller than she remembered – a square, white-painted stone building with a slate roof nestling behind the hedge, small casement windows and a bottle-green front door – but also solid, reassuring . . . welcoming. And, as Patsy pointed out, *hers*.

Later, Bel took the single Yale key Patsy handed her. 'It's quite stiff. Lenny never locked up.' They were sitting in Patsy's kitchen, where she'd insisted on giving Bel a cup of tea. Bel was grateful, but she was on tenterhooks, dying to go and check out the inside of her cottage, which was divided from Patsy's home, a former Wesleyan chapel built of dark yellow stone, by a low shed. Patsy's kitchen was cosy and Bel was tired from the journey and all the emotions attending her escape. It would have been easy to sit there, accept Patsy's offer of a bed, and attack the cottage in the morning. Now she was there, though, her fingers itched to open the door to the place her mother – and her grandmother before her – had loved.

'Shall I come and show you where everything is?' Patsy offered.

Bel, not wanting to offend her neighbour, hesitated. 'I think I'll just go in on my own first . . .' She stopped, not knowing how to explain without sounding strange. But Patsy nodded: she seemed to understand.

Bel jiggled the key in the lock for a few moments before it gave, the cast-iron thumb latch cold and wet, resistant to her grasp. She realized she was holding her breath as she finally pushed open the green wood door and stepped onto the trodden-down coir mat inside.

What greeted her was the chilly smell of stale human habitation. Old fat, sweaty upholstery, festering rugs, trapped woodsmoke, cold ashes, stone walls, drains. Unable to prevent herself from recoiling slightly, she held firm, inhaling carefully through her mouth.

Looking round the small living space, she saw to the left an ancient solid-fuel, once-cream Rayburn, the square tops scraped and caked. Resting on the edge of the stove was an old-style aluminium kettle, dulled from wear and spotted with brown burn near the base; the knob from the lid was missing. The grey melamine counter top – scorched in places – ran beside the stove and round the sink, supporting a small fridge from a previous era and a cup stand with three green and yellow petrol-station mugs still dangling from the prongs. Two rickety plain-pine cupboards fitted underneath the worktop, and one sat above.

The dusty air caught at her throat and made her cough as she checked out the sitting area to her right. Here she found a large, deep armchair in what must have once been a chintz cover – she wondered if it dated back to her mother – now so faded and stained it was hard to tell what it would have looked like new. The only other furniture was an oblong, varnished coffee table, ringed with cup marks, and a wooden kitchen chair, on which balanced a very old television and video recorder. A tatty square of brown, swirly-patterned carpet partially covered the stone floor beneath the armchair.

But what unsettled Bel most was that around the periphery of the room stood high, chaotic stacks of what looked like newspapers, magazines, videos without their boxes, bulging plastic bags, laundry baskets full of glass jars, bottles and plant pots. She let out a low groan. Patsy had mentioned Lenny was a hoarder, but this was extreme. Much worse than she could ever have imagined, despite Patsy's warning. Bel felt a spike of weary disappointment forming in her gut but determinedly pressed it away.

Straight ahead was the door onto the tiny, paved garden at the rear. She opened it. One previously white moulded plastic chair stood there, the seat pooled with brackish green water, and a rusty whirlybird washing-stand. Grass and weeds had grown up in the cracks between the mossy paving stones, and the crumbling wooden fence looked to be on its last legs. Standing there, quite still, for a long moment, she felt the soft evening air on her cheek, the sun fading over the rooftops to her left, and tried to still her anxiety, not focus on the appalling state of the house behind her.

Taking a deep breath of fresh air, Bel went back inside and ventured up the steep staircase. She glanced into the bathroom at the head of the stairs and pulled a face. No toilet seat, the pan stained dark below water level. The retro-pink bath was hung with a mildewed shower curtain, and a hand-held shower attachment lay in the bath, the fixture that had held it to the wall clearly snapped off. Dots of black mould decorated the grout between the tiles, and many of the blue-grey linoleum floor tiles were curling at the edges.

Heart sinking still further, she continued along the small landing and into the bedroom, where the metal bed frame supported a startlingly bright white mattress, still in its plastic wrapping and so out of place in the dull, grimy chaos.

A pine chest of drawers stood along the far wall, an old-fashioned brown-wood nightstand with a cupboard beneath squeezed into the near side. *Patsy must have cleared this room*, Bel realized, struck, yet again, by her neighbour's thoughtfulness: there was no sign of Lenny and his mess on the nightstand or in any of the drawers.

She sat down heavily on the slippery mattress cover and took a quiet breath, thinking back to what Patsy had said about her mother. She'd never been told that Agnes often brought her here when she was little. There were only a couple of brief visits she remembered, when she was older, probably around eight. *Did Dad come too?* She couldn't imagine her father's restless personality confined in this cramped space.

Closing her eyes, she evoked the presence of her small self in this very room, cuddled securely in her mother's arms. She remembered her scent – of Imperial Leather soap and cold cream, rose-scented talcum powder – her soft voice, the way she used to brush butterfly kisses along Bel's cheek, her lips warm and so gentle. And as she sat there, the walls seemed to wrap comfortingly around her, holding her close, exuding Agnes's kindness and Lenny's innocent spirit in a place that generations of women had loved. Tears formed behind her eyelids and she let them flow.

The buzzing of a message on her mobile brought her back to reality. *Dad*, she thought, with a resigned sigh, as she pulled the phone from her back pocket. She'd texted to say she'd arrived, but it wasn't from him.

Got duvet and sheets etc, if you need them x, Patsy's message told her.

Bel smiled. Her neighbour's kind offer somehow tipped the balance. Until this minute, she hadn't known if she could hack staying in the cottage among all the smells and grime. But now she knew she'd give it a go. *Nothing some Flash and a bit of elbow grease won't cure.*

Coming over, she texted back.

Patsy was stirring something in a wide frying pan on the stove when Bel walked in. A girl was sitting at the kitchen table, headphones on, school books and a laptop open in front of her. She had long brown hair across her shoulders, a pale face, and was still in her white uniform shirt and green school blazer. Patsy's granddaughter, Bel presumed. She glanced up with large dark eyes and Bel thought she detected wariness in them.

Patsy turned, waving a wooden spatula at the girl. 'Bel, meet Jaz.'

Jaz gave her a nod and a shy half-smile, then lowered her gaze to her computer again.

Patsy was eyeing her questioningly. 'So?'

'Thanks so much for the bedding offer. There's no way my backpack would've fitted my own sheets. Also, could

I possibly nick some cleaning products tonight? Obviously I'll replace them.' She smiled nervously. 'I think I might give it a go.'

Her neighbour's eyebrows shot up. 'OK. Made of sterner stuff than I thought, then.' She grinned. 'Have some supper with us, and I'll help you do the bed.'

'It was unbelievably kind of you, clearing out the bedroom, Patsy,' Bel said, when they were seated at the table, Jaz's homework swept to one end. Her neighbour had cooked a warm, melting risotto, buttery and glistening, with broad beans, peas and baby leeks, sprinkled generously with parsley and fresh Parmesan. Bel thought she'd never eaten anything so delicious in her whole life – and that included Louis's much-vaunted version of the dish. She was surprised to find that bringing her ex-partner to mind did not have the power to upset her tonight.

'Oh, I got the boys to do that.' Patsy pushed the large wooden salad bowl across the table to Bel. 'Lettuce from the garden. Broad beans and leeks, too. Couldn't be bothered with peas this year – all that podding for such small return.'

Bel gave a contented sigh as she helped herself. 'It's all amazing. Thank you,' she said. 'So who are the boys?'

Her neighbour chuckled. 'Shouldn't call them boys, really. They're both grown men in their forties, although they don't always behave as such.' She helped herself to some salad and offered the bowl to her granddaughter, who frowned. Then, perhaps knowing she wouldn't win this particular battle with her grandmother, she took a small quantity, reluctantly, of the lettuce leaves. 'JJ and

Micky. Burnouts from the city who are surfing themselves back to health . . . or so they claim.' Munching in silence for a moment, she added, 'They're good lads. Turn their hand to anything without moaning, which is great for me. They were so helpful when Lenny was ill, came in twice a day to feed him and that old stove, give him a wash and some company.'

Bel was trying to picture the two men Patsy described and failing. 'Are they a couple?'

Patsy roared with laughter. 'Blimey, there's a thought!'

Bel's remark even raised a smile from the almost silent Jaz.

'You can meet them tomorrow, decide for yourself, unless the surf's up on the north shore, of course.'

It was late into the night when Bel, completely done in, threw down her cloth and cleaning spray, wiping sweat from her brow. Patsy had helped with the bed, then left Bel to her own devices, insisting she come over, even in the middle of the night, if it all got too much. 'Door's always open,' she said.

Bel had attacked the bathroom first. She'd scrubbed the toilet bowl to within an inch of its life, although it was still rimed with ancient limescale she couldn't chip off and very cold to sit on without a seat. She ripped down the mildewed shower curtain, scrubbed the bath and the basin and washed the stained blue lino. The toilet flushed, the taps ran cold water, as she hadn't lit the Rayburn yet. That, she decided, was a job for the morning when she had her wits about her.

Patsy had explained about vents and flues, spin wheels

and ash cans, given her a quick tutorial on how to light the thing – there were still logs and kindling in the lean-to beside the porch – but she hadn't really taken any of it in. Patsy even offered to light it for her the first time, but she had stupidly refused, embarrassed at how much her neighbour had already done to help.

Bel climbed under the chilly duvet around two in the morning, wishing she'd accepted Patsy's offer of her stove-lighting skills. She had on her sweatshirt and joggers, the temperature of the May night having dropped considerably. The thick stone walls of the house had clearly lost any residual warmth over the months since Lenny had died: the warmth a home accumulates from daily human habitation.

She chided herself for being so stubborn and feeling she must cope with everything alone as she pulled the duvet round her, shivering with tiredness, remembering how hard Tally had had to work to persuade her to ring Flo. It had been a revelation, since meeting Patsy, how easily she helped Bel without the usual fuss and martyrdom both her father and Louis had always displayed.

Earlier in the evening she'd finally rung her father, because he hadn't responded to any of her texts.

'Hi,' he'd said, when he picked up, his tone distant and irritable. 'I'm watching something.'

'Oh, OK. I was just checking in to find out how you are.'

'I'm fine,' he said.

'Right,' she said, lingering just a moment longer in the hope he might enquire about how things were going for her. 'I'll leave you to it, then.'

'Night,' Dennis said, clicking off before she'd had time even to say goodbye.

Bel had stared at her phone resignedly, angry with herself for expecting more, for worrying about him at all. *If that's the way you want to play it . . .*

But now, finally warming up in her strange new bed, she inhaled a long breath. *I don't have to deal with Dad right now. I don't have to do anything I don't want to for the next few days.* The fact that she was no longer in the gloomy London flat, her father prowling the corridor outside her room, was almost too much for her tired brain to take in.

14

Bel was woken by the early morning light – there were no blinds or curtains at the bedroom window – and a cascade of birdsong. For a moment she was completely disoriented. Her sleep, when she'd finally managed to settle on the firm new mattress, with the unfamiliar smells and the country silence, had been short, but incredibly deep. She lay on her back, blinking in the bright coastal dawn. *I'm really here*, she thought, with a smile. Then she remembered where 'here' was. *The seaside.* She sat bolt upright, tossed away the duvet and set her feet on the chilly wood floor.

Minutes later, teeth brushed and face sluiced with cold water, she was in her red swimsuit, her shorts and sweatshirt pulled over it, rubber flip-flops on her feet. She grabbed the beach towel Patsy had lent her, gulped a glass of water and walked out into the stunning spring morning. Glancing up at her neighbour's house, she saw that the curtains were still closed, so she shut her front door softly, then turned down the narrow lane towards the beach.

She walked for five minutes, past other silent cottages and their spring-flowering front gardens, the small, now empty car park, the closed wooden beach café, the lifeguard's hut, and went down the gritty hard onto the sand, where she stood and sucked in the sea air, filling her lungs with the salty freshness until it almost made her dizzy.

The sea was glistening and calm in the sunshine, the sky a pale azure, dotted here and there with fluffy children's clouds. A couple of dog-walkers were already pacing the sands, but otherwise she had the small bay to herself. She clicked off a few photos to send to Tally later, then quickly shed her outer garments before she lost her nerve.

Running to the water's edge, she felt the cold, stinging rush between her toes, the sand falling away around her feet as the wave retreated. Shivering in pleasant anticipation, her arms clasped around her body, she stepped in deeper. The soft early-morning breeze caressed her, lifting her hair off her face. When the waves reached her thighs, she held her breath and splashed icy salt water up over her body, gasping as the cold hit the warm flesh of her arms and chest. After another second of hesitation, she held her breath and dived head first into the sea.

It was heavenly. Bel was a good swimmer, courtesy of stringent lessons in the Kensington baths, which her father had insisted upon, and all those Mediterranean villas with sparkling aquamarine pools where she'd spent so many hours as a lonely only child that her skin had turned soft and pruny. Now, she powered through the water, feeling her tired city muscles – so unused to any exercise beyond stamping the concrete pavements – resisting initially, then slowly locating the muscle-memory that allowed her freestyle stroke to flow. By the time she reached the end of the bay she was breathless and wheezing, but wanting to shout for joy. Every bit of the strife about her trip was temporarily washed away in those short minutes. *It's all been worth it*, she thought, as she ran her palms across her face and hair to clear the salt drips.

Climbing the hill back to the village later, legs shaky from the unaccustomed exercise, flip-flops rubbing between her toes – she couldn't remember the last time she'd worn them – she realized she was starving. The dreaded stove was still not lit and she had no supplies, so she continued on past her cottage and up the lane, where she'd noticed a café the previous day, picnic tables dotting the sloping grass outside. It was open early, unlike the beach café, and already a couple of men, one with a grey hoody pulled over his face, were sitting hunched in sleepy silence, nursing coffees in reusable takeaway cups, open cardboard boxes containing what looked like breakfast rolls on the slatted table between them.

Bel went inside.

'Hiya,' said the heavily tanned, auburn-ponytailed woman behind the counter, giving Bel a cheery smile. 'Patsy's neighbour, right?'

Taken aback, Bel nodded.

The woman laughed. 'Saw you arrive yesterday. Not much escapes us round here, I'm afraid. Martine,' she added, by way of introduction, reaching a hand across the high top of the counter display, which contained the likes of brownies and millionaire's shortbread, cheese scones and muffins in various flavours.

'Bel.' She shook the proffered hand.

They had a very British chat about the sunshine, the calmness of the sea, the coldness of Bel's swim, the beauty of the place, before Martine, fingers moving like lightning on the till computer, took her order.

The two guys were still slumped at their table when Bel went outside with her black coffee and a bacon sandwich. But the one with the hoody perked up when he saw her, pushing his hood off his face. He stared at her for a second, then smiled as she walked past. 'Morning,' he said.

'Hi,' she said, disarmed by his arresting grin.

His friend also looked up. *Are these Patsy's 'boys'?* She'd told Bel they lived in two mobile homes parked in the corner of the field on the headland, next to the beach café. She hovered for a moment, clutching her breakfast. In London she would never have dreamed of striking up a conversation so impulsively with two men in a café. But the warm sunshine, her exhilarating swim, the sheer fact of having jumped all the hurdles to be there – even surviving a night in the grungy cottage – made her bold.

'Are you, umm . . .' She searched her brain for the names Patsy had mentioned and drew a blank – she'd been so tired last night. So she started her sentence again. 'Are you Patsy's surfer friends?'

Both men laughed. 'That'd be us,' said the blond one. His hair was bleached almost white, a riot of curls framing his face, like a Raphael angel. He was slim, with round, girlish blue eyes, his bleached lashes giving him an almost startled expression.

'I'm Bel, her neighbour.'

'Saw you swimming,' he said. 'Micky, by the way.' He tapped his chest. 'And JJ,' he added, indicating his handsome, broad-shouldered friend.

'Join us,' JJ said, shuffling his bottom along the bench which he sat astride, his tanned legs muscled beneath his faded orange Bermudas.

Bel didn't hesitate. 'I can't thank you enough for sorting the bedroom out,' she said, when she'd settled at the table and opened her sandwich box. Her stomach was rumbling and she took a large bite of the seeded brown bread, filled with buttery streaky bacon, crisp around the edges.

'Good, huh?' Micky asked, smiling as he watched her eat. 'Martine's famous for them.'

JJ was watching her too, his gaze steady from dark brown eyes, lightened with small flecks of gold. His hair shone blue-black in the sunshine and straight to just below his ears, his tawny skin a marked contrast to Micky's ruddy, freckled fairness. 'You actually slept there?' he asked, slightly incredulous. His accent was from the south-east, not quite Estuary, but a refined version of it – the accent she often heard among younger Londoners. Micky spoke with the flatter vowels of a Midlander.

Bel swallowed her mouthful. 'I did clean up a bit.'

JJ tipped his head back and drained the last drops of coffee into his mouth but didn't comment.

'You staying long?' Micky asked.

'A couple of weeks, maybe.' In her mind her trip, in the planning stages, had started as just a few days, then become a week, then ten days – which was what she'd told Flo. Now it seemed to have stretched again.

Micky's blue eyes widened. 'Bit grim in there, no? Get rid of that gross chair, if I were you. And the carpet. You'll not want to take fleas back home.' He cast a quick glance at his friend. 'We'll help, if you like.'

Fleas? Bel blanched. 'Could you?'

'Sure. Stick it all in Dora and take it to the dump.'

'You won't have anything to sit on,' JJ pointed out seriously. He was obviously the quieter, more thoughtful of the two, Micky bouncing them both along with his easy charm.

'I know I'm bonkers. I just needed to get out of London.'

They nodded emphatically.

'We came for a couple of weeks two years ago,' JJ said, with a satisfied grin.

'Didn't you have jobs and stuff?'

'We quit,' Micky said simply. She waited for him to go on, but he seemed intent on finishing his roll instead.

For a moment there was silence at the table.

'Was it hard adjusting?' Bel asked. She knew it was mad to think she could live here in that tumbledown place with a dwindling float of cash and no job. But they seemed to have done it.

'It was like breathing properly for the first time in years,' JJ said softly.

Bel thought she knew exactly what he meant.

'We're sort of self-confessed surfer dudes now,' Micky declared. 'And handymen. No job too small, that's us. Although we like a challenge.'

'And the sea. We like that too,' JJ added whimsically.

When she'd finished her breakfast, Bel strolled back to the cottage. She met Jaz in the lane, on her way to school, with what looked like a cripplingly heavy daypack hoisted on one shoulder, her long hair neatly plaited down her back.

'Hey, Jaz,' Bel said, as she passed. 'Have a good day.'

Jaz gave her a shy smile in return. 'Doubt it,' she muttered, rolling her eyes melodramatically.

Bel wondered what the story was. The girl – Patsy had said she was nearly sixteen and in the middle of GCSEs – seemed very settled with her grandmother.

Entering the cottage, she was assailed by acrid fustiness again and wrinkled her nose. *It isn't just the chair*, she thought, eyeing the vast accumulation of junk lining the room. Leaning against the counter, she sent a couple of the photos she'd taken on the beach to Tally with a message that read, *This should make you jealous! All good. Love you xxx*

Then, knowing it was stupid to put it off any longer, she laid her phone down and stared hard at the Rayburn. She felt like such a useless townie, never having lit a woodburner in her life. But there wasn't much call for the skill in a London flat. Now she was worried she'd do something daft and set the whole place alight.

The cast-iron grate was cold and dusty, ashes swirling into the air and spilling everywhere as she yanked off the front. But Patsy had said to leave a layer of ash, so she set balled-up newspaper from one of the piles and kindling on it. There were no firelighters, but she reckoned they couldn't be essential – people had been lighting fires without them for centuries, hadn't they?

The fire smoked alarmingly and seemed reluctant to

catch. She'd opened the chimney vent and the spin wheel on the front, but had to put more matches to the paper as she watched anxiously for a proper flame. Finally the paper and kindling flared, flames leaping up inside the stove. She threw in a couple of split logs, closed the door and breathed a cautious sigh of relief. *Fingers crossed*, she thought. Her skin felt tight, hair stiff from the sun and salt water – not unpleasantly so, but it would be good if the Rayburn actually worked and the water was warm enough for a shower later.

Turning from the now-crackling stove, she wondered what she should do next. She was at a bit of a loss, unable to settle. It felt so strange, being in this place: technically it was hers but it still felt like Lenny's, with nowhere to sit. She had no plan for the day, other than making a start on sorting out the cottage. Despite her beach swim this morning, she didn't feel exactly in holiday mode.

I should get a house clearance team to empty the place, she thought. That was the logical thing to do, although she knew it would cost money she didn't have. And what was she clearing it for? To sell, was the obvious answer. *I could certainly do with the money* – to pay her father back for a start, even if he wasn't shouting for it. But her whole being balked at the idea of saying goodbye to her mother's beloved cottage.

As Bel stood there, quite still in the silent room, she was aware of a powerful longing pressing around her heart to make these stone walls her home. Get rid of the junk and the smell, warm the rooms and fill them with her own cosy stuff. She had always yearned to fashion her

134

space to her own taste – not be constrained by the men in her life, as had always been the case in the past. *I could do that here*, she thought wistfully. *I could make it into a lovely spot to live.* But her ageing father intruded into her thoughts. Reaching for her phone with a deep sigh, she pressed on Flo's number.

'He's not too bad, physically,' Flo replied, to Bel's query. 'The physio came this morning and his back's really improving. I've done the washing and stuff, made him a big pot of curry he can heat up.' She paused. 'But he seems a bit low. Complains he's lonely. I'm only here for a few hours so I can't do much to cheer him up.'

Flo's words pierced Bel to the heart.

'He keeps asking when you're coming home, even though you've only just left.'

Bel sighed. 'Thanks, Flo. I'm so grateful to you for stepping in.'

'God, listen, darlin', this job's a doddle compared to picking up used condoms off the bedroom floor and wiping dog shit from the furniture.'

Bel groaned. 'You shouldn't be doing that.'

'Not like the 83 days, that's for sure. I think I'm over this cleaning lark. I'll find a decent job over the summer, even if it means working evenings again.'

'Let me know if you need a reference.'

They said goodbye to each other, Bel struggling with renewed guilt. She was sure her father was lonely. But it upset her that he was articulating it to Flo – knowing, perhaps, it would get back to her. *Is he being manipulative?* she wondered, then felt ashamed that she was dismissing his

probably genuine complaint because it was too uncomfortable to acknowledge.

A knock at the door made her jump. JJ was outside,
dark head bent to accommodate the low porch.

'Micky'll be along in a minute,' he said, as he stepped
into the cottage, where he immediately began fanning his
hand in front of his face. Bel realized the air was thick
with smoke pouring from the stove. Smiling, he said, 'No
point fighting with a wood-burner. It'll always win.'

Bel laughed. 'I thought I'd got the bloody thing going.'
She lifted the cracked Bakelite door catch and pulled open
the firebox, whence issued even more choking smoke,
making them both rear back.

'Shall I fix it?'

'Just show me, can you? I want to do it myself.'

Raising an eyebrow, JJ looked amused. Once again she
was struck by his looks. *He's beautiful*, she thought, his
tawny skin smooth from the sun and sea, the expression
in his flecked eyes one of confidence and calm.

Kneeling beside her on the stone floor, he picked up a
forked cast-iron tool from a wooden box hanging on the
wall – which also contained a shovel, a soft brush and a
stiff wire brush – and raked the charred remains of logs,
kindling and half-burned paper, into the metal bucket Bel
had used to carry wood from the store by the porch. 'OK,'
he said, turning to her when the grate was clear. 'I think
there was too much old ash in it.'

His large hands rested on the Rayburn's metal rail. 'You
have to start again.' He rose to his feet. 'Twirlies are the
way forward.'

'But Patsy said to leave a layer of ash,' Bel protested, having no idea what a twirly was.

'Normally, that's true. But ol' Ray here is obviously in need of a fresh start.'

'Him and me both,' Bel found herself saying, catching the hint of bitterness in her voice and regretting it.

JJ gave her a steady look. 'Want to talk about it?'

'No,' she said quickly, feeling the heat creep up her cheeks. But, under his gaze, she found herself beginning to speak anyway. 'I'm just . . . I'm not in a great place at the moment. Our restaurant . . . My father . . .' She stopped, embarrassed, unable to untangle the mess that was her life in one easy sentence.

JJ, meanwhile, had grabbed a handful of newspapers off a pile near the door and was busy opening a single sheet on the worktop, folding one corner into the middle, then rolling up the page till it was a long tube, which he then twisted into a loose knot. 'Ta-dah!' He handed it to her. 'It's way better than scrunched-up paper. Bury a couple of fire-lighters under a few of them, kindling on top, and Bob's your uncle.'

Head bent as he began on another, he asked, 'Has something happened to your dad, then?'

Bel sighed. 'No. He's fine. It's just I'm living with him at the moment . . . long story . . . and I needed a break, if I'm honest.' She took a sheet of newspaper and, standing side by side at the counter with JJ, attempted her own twirly.

'Tricky, is he?'

She laughed. 'You could say that.'

'Why are you living with him?' His question was gentle and she found she wasn't offended by his curiosity.

'Because my partner ran off and our restaurant went bust.'

'You're a chef?'

'No, he is.'

JJ thought about this for a moment. 'OK. That sounds a bit rubbish.'

His ability to sum up her situation with such phlegmatic understatement made her laugh.

'It certainly is. It's as if I never left home and I'm a child again.' As she said it, tears pricked behind her eyes. She bit her lip, trying not to cry. But her efforts were useless, the last twenty-four hours finally taking their toll. 'Sorry. I'm so sorry.'

She felt his arm go round her shoulders. 'Hey, cry if you like. I'm cool with it.' He gave her a reassuring squeeze. 'We all go through shit.'

Bel inhaled slowly, wanting so badly to get herself under control. Another deep breath, another bitten lip and she was almost there. She smiled wanly up at JJ. 'Thanks, you're very kind.'

'One thing I've learned since I dropped out of my allotted future: life is about more than a fancy salary, a cool apartment and a pretty girlfriend.'

'It is?'

'Sure.' He thought for a second. 'It's a wave with a clean break all the way to shore, salt drying on your lips, a waft of Martine's bacon sarnie on the morning air, waking to the sound of the sea, a beer with friends round the firepit . . .' He took his arm from her shoulders and went back to his folding task, apparently unembarrassed by his almost poetic description of what moved him.

Micky chose that moment to poke his head through the open casement window by the front door, his eyes crossed, an evil grin widening his mouth. 'Albert Steptoe, at your service,' he announced, imitating the sitcom rag-and-bone man to a T.

Bel felt a sort of wrench as she turned to greet Micky. Talking to JJ had felt surprisingly comforting.

Patsy appeared as Bel and the two men lugged out the festering armchair, the square of carpet, along with the antiquated television and video recorder and two bulging laundry baskets clanking with glass and flower-pots. She waved aloft a sandwich bag containing four firelighters in one hand, a light bulb in the other – the one in the bedroom had blown, they'd discovered, when they were making the bed.

'You're all invited for supper tonight,' she said. 'I'm making *the pie*.'

There was a whoop from Micky, as he staggered down the path with the television in his arms, a thumbs-up and a broad grin from JJ.

'Jaz won't touch it, of course,' Patsy told Bel. 'Those little fishy faces poking up to the sky freak her out. She can have pasta.'

Bel, mindful that she still hadn't bought any food, lit the stove, or even found out where the nearest shop might be, gladly accepted the invitation, vowing to buy the best bottle of wine she could afford for her kind friend that afternoon. She had no idea what 'the pie' was – except that it involved fish – but if Patsy's risotto was anything to go by, they were in for a treat.

By the time the two men had climbed into Dora and driven off, Bel was left in an almost empty room. The stone square exposed beneath the discarded carpet now shone darker and smoother than the rest of the floor – it had lain there for so long. Only the wooden kitchen chair, previously supporting the television, and the bordering mound of newspapers remained.

As she stared, a movement caught her eye. She spun round, feeling a spurt of alarm, thinking a rat might be emerging from the heaps. A large ginger cat was standing just inside the door, absolutely still and on the alert. Its right front leg was missing, the fur closed over the area as if it had always been that way. Bel smiled and held out her hand. 'Hey, there,' she said softly. She'd always wanted a cat, but Louis had said they jumped on surfaces and were unhygienic. The cat crept towards her warily – seemingly unaffected by the missing limb – and sniffed her, whiskers twitching. She wondered if it had been a visitor in Lenny's time. Its coat was smooth and soft. *Obviously well fed*, she thought, as she stroked around its ears.

It wandered off, slinking round the paper – probably detecting all sorts of tempting scents of mice – and she turned back to the stove, a proud heap of twirlies now at her disposal. 'Take two,' she muttered to herself, as she unhitched the firebox door and began to follow JJ's instructions. This time, though, the stove took it upon itself to behave and the fire, when she checked an hour later, was glowing in what looked like a satisfactory manner, the thermostat on the right-hand door creeping slowly round to where Patsy had said it should be. Bel patted one of the lids affectionately. Ray, it seemed, was now a vital part of her life and she wanted to keep him sweet.

15

'Is this a good time?' Bel asked her father. She had called just before going over to Patsy's for supper and could hear the tinkle of *The One Show*'s incidental music in the background.

Her father laughed, but Bel wasn't sure if it was at what she'd said or at something on the television. 'Maybe I'll call back tomorrow,' she suggested.

'No, no, sweetie, it's good to hear from you,' Dennis said, sounding to Bel unusually mellow. *Probably already downed a glass or two*, she thought. 'Tell me about the hovel.'

'Well, it's quite hovel-like. But some friends helped me clear out the worst bits. I even managed to light the Rayburn.'

'Friends?' her father queried. 'Not that hippie female from next door?' He coughed. 'She never liked me.'

'Her name's Patsy, Dad. And, yes, she's been brilliant.'

'Still got pink hair?'

'No, it's grey now.'

Dennis harrumphed. 'So you're having fun?'

Bel looked for an edge to his question, but could detect none. 'I am. It's gorgeous here. I had a swim and a bacon sandwich this morning. The water was freezing – you wouldn't have liked it.'

He laughed. 'Well, I'm really missing you, girl. Place is

horribly quiet without you. Don't get too comfortable, I'm counting the days till you get back.'

'Are you having Flo's curry tonight?' she asked quickly.

'I am. Looking forward to it. She's a great cook. Better than you.'

'Thanks, Dad.' She was sure he was just teasing, but she twitched, nonetheless. 'OK, well, I'll let you get on with your evening,' she added.

There was a long silence. 'Dad?'

When he spoke again he sounded almost choked. 'You won't leave me, will you, Bella? Please . . . don't leave me all alone again. I know I can be a bit of a nuisance sometimes, but I love having you around. It's changed my life.'

She held her breath. 'Of course I won't leave you, Dad,' she heard herself say. She couldn't bear the despair in his voice.

'You're not there with that man of yours, are you?' he asked plaintively.

'Dad, please . . . *I haven't got a man.*'

He took a while to reply. 'I love you, Bella,' he said quietly. 'You do know that, don't you?'

Dennis very rarely said those words and Bel was taken aback.

'I love you too, Dad.'

After she'd said goodbye, she stood in the silent cottage and let out a weary sigh. Her father had been nice to her that evening. A bit maudlin, but he'd seemed happy to talk, after the recent rift over her trip away. It was harder to remember his dark side when she was at a distance and no longer under constant hectoring. Harder still to stand

143

back when he was behaving well. *I've just promised I won't leave him*, she reminded herself, torn and confused by the conversation.

Outside she heard the arrival of the two men at the chapel next door and knew she had to go. But first she went into the back garden and pulled some delicate pink blooms from a straggly rose bush by the fence, pricking her fingers as she wrestled the stalks from the plant – there were no scissors in the kitchen drawer – and burying her nose in the sweet, almost spicy freshness, which reminded her of her mother. It was all she could think of to take Patsy tonight – small recompense for all her kindness – but she vowed she would remedy that as soon as she made it to a shop tomorrow. She'd intended to go out earlier, but she'd lain down for what was supposed to be a short nap and slept for nearly three hours.

Micky nudged Jaz as Patsy set the glorious pie on the kitchen table. It was baked in a round blue-rimmed enamel dish, mustardy, garlicky steam wisping from the pie whistle in the centre of the glossy golden crust. He pronged his two fingers towards the sardine heads poking comically up through the pastry, then swivelled and pointed them at Jaz. 'They're looking at you,' he said, in a sinister voice.

Jaz yelped in mock alarm and covered her eyes, her cheeks flushing. It was clear to Bel, sitting opposite with JJ, that the teenager had a bit of a crush on Micky and his cherub charm – which he seemed in no hurry to dispel.

Patsy, dressed in an orange cotton *kurta* over faded jeans, feet bare on the stone floor, took up a large knife and ceremoniously slid it into the pastry. Her weather-beaten face was sweating, but her dark eyes were alive with pleasure. 'Couldn't get pilchards today. Had to settle for sardines.'

They watched in hungry anticipation as she doled out portions of the dish with a pie slice. Inside were chopped hard-boiled eggs and tiny new potatoes, a rich sea of bacon lardons fried with onion, garlic, fennel, parsley and tomatoes surrounding the upright fish. For a second, Bel wished Louis was there. Although she knew if he was he would be bending Patsy's ear to extract the exact details of the recipe for the mouth-watering dish. A big bowl of lettuce – fresh from the garden and dressed with lemon and olive oil – was the only accompaniment.

There were groans and exclamations of appreciation round the table, followed by a reverent silence in the warm kitchen as everyone concentrated on their delicious food – except Jaz, of course, who was picking unenthusiastically at her bowl of butter and cheese spaghetti.

'So what does JJ stand for?' Bel asked, after the pie had been dispatched and Micky had cleared the plates. Patsy was dishing up stewed rhubarb in blue pottery bowls, a tub of Cornish vanilla ice cream doing the rounds.

'It's grim. I don't tell people, in case they decide to use it.'

'I'll say if you don't,' Micky threatened, to general laughter.

Giving his friend a dirty look, JJ turned to face Bel. She couldn't help being amused by his apparent distress. 'Jonjo,' he said dully.

'Like the jockey.'

JJ sighed. 'Yeah, yeah, like the bloody jockey.'

'Everyone always says that,' Micky told her, with a grin.

'When I was ten, I decided to call myself JJ instead. I refused to answer to anything else until everyone gave in.'

'I don't see what's wrong with Jonjo,' Bel said honestly. 'You're Irish, then?'

'My father is. My mother's Hong Kong Chinese.' He smiled at her. 'It could have been Wing or Fung or Chong, not that either Irish or Chinese played particularly well at Moorcroft High.'

'Were you teased?' Jaz asked, ears pricking up.

'Nothing I couldn't handle. Boys are just mean if you're different.'

'So are girls,' Jaz said, with feeling.

Bel caught the fleeting look of anxiety in the teenager's eye, but Patsy appeared not to notice. It was strange, she'd barely been in the village for twenty-four hours, yet already she cared about these people as if she'd known them for years. She felt oddly at home, her father and the Earls Court flat existing in another universe.

'So, did Lenny's spirit leave with his beloved chair?' Patsy asked Bel, seemingly in all seriousness. 'I certainly felt him strongly last night.'

'You did?'

Jaz sighed resignedly. 'Nonna sees ghosts all over the place.'

'Well, that's because there *are* ghosts all over the place, young lady. I hope the poor man is transitioning well.'

Transitioning? Bel thought of the modern use of the

word and quickly dismissed the prospect of Lenny wanting to identify as a woman.

'He didn't have a negative bone in his body,' Patsy mused, to no one in particular. 'I can't see him getting trapped in the lower realms, myself.' She turned to JJ. 'Can you?'

'Totally not. It was only the chair that held his imprint. Now it's gone, he should be free. I hope he is.'

Bel glanced sideways at him to see if he was joking. But he didn't seem to be. Micky, on the other hand, was grinning broadly.

'You'll be laughing on the other side of your face when you die and find yourself earth-bound,' Patsy, noticing his grin, retorted. 'Don't come crying to me when you can't move to a higher dimension or meet your spiritual guide.'

Micky didn't look remotely worried. 'I'll tell on you to Rhian,' he teased.

Drawing herself up, Patsy said, 'I don't think the vicar would disagree with anything I've just said.'

'Hmm. Not so sure about that.'

Ignoring him, Patsy turned to Bel. 'Rhian will be back on Thursday. She's been visiting her old mum in Plymouth, who's got dementia.' Bel watched as her face lit up, her eyes sparkling. 'I can't wait for you to meet her.'

Bel nodded her agreement, feeling suddenly a bit disoriented. It was as if she had been transported to another dimension, sitting at the large red Formica table with solid pale-wood legs – probably from the fifties – among her new friends in this strange kitchen, the wooden chapel beams above her strung with drying herbs, the air warm

147

with cooking scents, listening to talk of ghosts and the afterlife. But the dimension seemed familiar to her, one that she felt she'd inhabited many times before.

When Bel got back to the cottage at the end of the evening, the stove was still quietly glowing. She stood for a moment and wondered about Lenny, took a moment to see if she, like Patsy, could feel his presence. A nominal Christian, long since lapsed, she liked the notion of Lenny's spirit being free. He sounded like a special person. But there was nothing except warmth and quietness inside the thick stone walls and she felt a little foolish. JJ had offered to show her how to bank down the Rayburn for the night, but she'd thanked him and said she would manage. She filled the fire-box with logs and left it at that. *If it goes out, it goes out*, she thought, as she poured water into one of the two tumblers she'd found in the cupboard and went upstairs to bed.

The next morning was as beautiful as the previous one. Bel was down on the sand by six thirty and stepping through the cold surf with laughing anticipation, shivering as she went. There was a chilly breeze today and she knew getting out would be harder. But as soon as she was submerged in the salt waves, she forgot that the water was cold, stretched out her arms and kicked her legs with the utmost pleasure. It felt as if her limbs were almost thanking her for the effort as she pulled strongly towards the far end of the beach, adrenalin surging through her body.

Half an hour later, towel wrapped round her waist, grey sweatshirt on, she made her way back up the concrete hard. As she reached the lane leading to the village, she heard her name called and turned to see JJ waving at her from the steps of his van on the headland at the far side of the beach café. 'Coffee?' he called, lifting his arm as he mimed drinking.

She waved back, giving him a thumbs-up.

'Come round by the path,' JJ instructed, pointing.

Bel walked behind the café along what she thought must be the coastal path. It was narrowed by spring foliage and uneven underfoot. On the other side of a thick bank of bramble bushes – bent inland from the continual offshore wind – and to the left of the path stood his silver and black motor-home. A surfboard in a blue neoprene cover and what looked, to Bel's inexperienced eye, like a paddleboard were propped against the back. There was no sign of Micky's van, which Patsy said was normally parked alongside.

JJ was standing in the open doorway, grinning. 'Thought you might like a warming Americano.' As she walked towards him, he glanced at the towel around her waist. 'You should invest in a dry robe, you know, if you're going to swim every day. They have some acid green ones on sale at the Co-op on the main road at the moment.'

'Dry robe?'

He laughed, standing back to usher her inside.

Bel climbed the rickety step and entered the van's interior. To the right she saw a small sofa and drop-down table. To the left, at the driver's end of the van, there was a double bed with a yellow duvet, and a tiny closet she assumed to be a toilet/shower room. The kitchen, complete with two gas hobs, a microwave and a small fridge, was in the middle. It didn't feel as claustrophobic as Bel had expected, although the pastel blue, green and pink floral pattern on the upholstery did not seem like JJ's taste. He kept the place immaculately. Even his two wetsuits – one short, one long – hung just inside the door.

'Small but perfectly formed,' JJ said, as he watched her take in her surroundings.

Bel smiled, feeling self-conscious with her bare legs and damp swimsuit, hair plastered to her head. The space meant she and JJ were close enough for her to smell the eucalyptus scent of his shower gel and she found it oddly disturbing. 'It's great,' she said, as JJ selected a coffee pod and slotted it into a serious-looking machine.

'Black? This baby froths milk if I ask it nicely.'

'Black is fine,' she said.

'Sit.' He waved a hand towards the pastel sofa.

'I'll make the seat wet, I'm afraid.'

'You can change, if you want.' He pointed to the closet door.

She shook her head regretfully. 'I came ill-prepared. I've got nothing to change into.'

He smiled. 'Gotta get the robe.' Turning, he pulled a supermarket bag from the top of a mesh tube hanging on the wall above the sink and handed it to her.

She sat down, the bag under her soggy towel. JJ lounged against the wall – there was barely room for two on the sofa – as they both sipped the delicious black coffee. 'Where's Micky?'

'Off putting up shelves for one of his mum's friends. In

Penzance.' His gold-flecked eyes rested on her for a moment. 'We're not joined at the hip, you know.'

It seemed important for him to tell her this, although she wasn't sure why. There was a brief silence between them. It didn't feel awkward to Bel – JJ seemed uncommonly laid-back – but his masculine beauty made it hard for her not to stare.

'What did you do in London?' she asked, wanting to dispel her thoughts.

From the look on JJ's face it seemed he was reluctant to answer, but knew he must. 'I was an events organizer for super-rich Americans, for my sins. People who wanted a VIP experience in the UK.' It was clear he was reciting from a much-repeated script. 'So, for instance, I'd arrange a private tour of the Royal Mews, or a day test-driving everything from a go-kart to a Lamborghini, or a last-minute dinner at Gordon Ramsay's impossible-to-get-into gaff, that sort of thing.' He gave an apologetic shrug. 'I had a lot of fun – checking out five-star hotels around the world, for instance. Doing stuff, going places I'd never be able to afford otherwise. But after a while it became a tad depressing. Those no-shit rich people are never satisfied. Nothing's ever special enough.'

The job seemed such a strange one for her new friend. 'I can't really imagine you all spruced and suited and kowtowing to the jet set,' she said, with a smile. *Although he's charming enough*, she thought. 'Did you always do that sort of work?'

JJ put his cup on the side and slid down the wall onto his haunches, his eyes now level with Bel's. He gazed at her silently, not answering her question. 'You have unusually pale eyelashes,' he said. 'Like Micky's, but his are sun-bleached, of course.'

Bel blinked and, annoyingly, found herself blushing.

'Sorry. That sounded a bit personal. It wasn't meant to.' He rose to his feet again. 'Anything to avoid talking about my other life. This one is all I have right now.' He seemed almost defiant.

She, too, got up, reminding herself she hardly knew this man. But right from the start their exchanges had felt more direct than she would have expected from a new acquaintance.

'Have I frightened you off?' JJ asked, looking anxious that he'd offended her.

Bel laughed. 'Not at all.' But she was suddenly keen to be out of the confined space of the motor-home and put some distance between her and JJ. His presence was having a strange effect on her.

Inhaling the cool sea air with some relief, she walked back up the lane. Her damp swimsuit was making her shiver, although the morning air had warmed and the breeze had dropped. Entering the house, she cast an apprehensive glance towards the Rayburn, which, miraculously, had managed to retain just enough hot ashes overnight for her to rekindle the fire earlier. *Still alive.* She patted one of the lids with a satisfied smile as she heard her mobile vibrate on the counter top.

'Hi, Bel,' Tally said, her voice heavy. 'Can you talk?'

'Of course.'

'Dad's been on. Trinny's had the baby. A boy.' Tally fell silent and then Bel heard a muffled sob. 'I'm sorry. I didn't mean to cry. It's just he sounded so made up about it. Kept saying how amazing he is and how beautiful, how much he loves him . . . Told me how fantastic it is having a *son*.' Another sob. 'I just found it really hard.'

'Oh, sweetheart. I'm sure you did. He's your father.'

'I'm not five, Bel, I'm twenty-five. How can I be jealous of an innocent little baby?' She sounded furious with herself.

Bel didn't reply at once. She was dealing with a mix of emotions but she didn't want to acknowledge any of them. Instead she felt angry on Tally's behalf at Louis's insensitivity towards his daughter. This was a baby Tally had found out about just a few months ago, the mother a woman barely older than Tally herself whom she'd met only briefly at 83.

'I know it's silly,' Tally was saying. 'And I know he does love me. But he didn't love me enough to be around much when I was small. It was only when you came on the scene that he started making an effort.' Bel heard Tally exhale loudly. 'He sounded so in love with Apollinaire.'

'Apollinaire? Quite a mouthful.' Bel now felt the bite of jealousy she'd tried so hard to hold off, as she imagined him cradling another woman's baby. Renewed pain, too, at her own loss, the familiar knowledge, so long accepted in the shadows of her mind, that she would never hold her own child in her arms.

When she'd found out she was pregnant, a few years after they'd got together, Louis had folded her in a hug with real tenderness. Gazing at her sadly with his dark eyes, he'd said, 'I'm so sorry, Bel. You know I don't want more children. I did warn you. I was very, very clear.'

Torn, shocked by a pregnancy she'd never thought would happen, she'd held her palm to her belly. 'I know you did. But that was in the abstract. This is real. This is *our baby*, Louis.'

He'd continued to hold her, but his expression clouded. 'You're, what, forty-three? That could be dangerous for both you and the baby, couldn't it? And suppose there's something wrong with it?'

Desperate not to acknowledge what he was implying, she'd insisted tearfully, 'Lots of women have healthy babies in their forties, these days.'

He'd sighed and led her over to the sofa, sat her down as if she were an invalid. Waving one hand around, the other clutched over hers, he went on, 'This place, it's small, on the main road, and with all those stairs, it'd be chaos, a nightmare, with a small child and a buggy.' When she didn't reply, he added, 'How would we cope? We both work twenty-four/seven.'

She'd been too confused to offer a coherent argument. Stumbling over her words, she said, 'People work with kids, they manage . . .'

Louis, at his most reasonable, nodded slowly. 'True. Although I'm sure it's hell.' Then he paused. 'But, fine, maybe, if those people really want children. *I just couldn't handle the responsibility of being a father again.*' Another pause. 'I can't do it.'

Tears streaming down her face, she'd insisted, 'But you *are* a father again, Louis. I'm carrying your baby, *our baby*, right now.'

'It's not a baby, Bel,' he replied, with the patience of a

parent correcting his ignorant offspring. 'It's a minute embryo. You can't be more than a few weeks gone. You had your period on my birthday.' Which he remembered, maybe, because they'd both wanted to make love.

Then he folded her in his arms again. 'Don't cry. Please. You know how much I love you. I just can't do this. Not even for you.'

The word 'abortion' had not been mentioned until the following day.

With huge reluctance and misgivings, Bel had booked the appointment at the clinic – mostly to stop Louis's relentless nagging – although she never believed in her heart of hearts that she could go through with it. In fact, she was considering the possibility of having the baby on her own, if Louis remained steadfast in his refusal to be a father again.

What would have happened to their relationship if she'd kept the baby or gone ahead with the termination against her will, though, was never tested. She miscarried three days before she was due at the clinic – a surprisingly simple, sharply painful, devastating expulsion one summer evening, just after service had finished. In the agonizing aftermath, Louis was the kindest and most solicitous he had ever been. She even began to believe that he was genuinely sad the baby had been lost.

Tally's voice brought her back to the present. 'They can always call him Olli . . . or Polli,' her stepdaughter was saying now, in an attempt at humour she clearly didn't feel.

'I'm certain your dad was exactly the same when you were born, Tally. He won't have told you, because that's

Louis for you, but I'm sure he absolutely adored you then, and still does, of course.'

Tally ignored her reassurances. 'He's really keen I go down over the summer.'

'Well, it might help to meet the baby. He's probably very sweet. And he is your half-brother.'

'I know, I know.' She sniffed. 'Do you think I'm a horrible person for being jealous?'

'God, no. My own feelings are much more horrible than yours, I assure you.'

'Sorry, Bel. I didn't think,' Tally said. 'Are you OK?'

'I'm fine. But your father's dealt with the whole thing in such a crap way. It's not surprising we're smarting. Don't beat yourself up about it. Your reaction is entirely normal.'

'I don't know what I'd do without you, Bel,' she said, in a small voice.

Her stepdaughter's words were so heartfelt, Bel wanted to hug her.

'How's Cornwall?'

They chatted on for a while, putting behind them the painful conversation they'd just had, until the usual demands of her work made Tally hurry off.

Bel sighed. *Apollinaire: Louis's baby.* It seemed so unreal she was almost unable to take it in. His eager acceptance of Trinny's baby was in such stark contrast to the fight he'd put up when she'd told him she was pregnant. *It's a long time ago*, she told herself now, in an attempt to mitigate the ache. But it was only a few months since she and Louis had been working at the restaurant and living together above it, her life path with him firmly set out before her.

Despite the financial problems with 83 – exacerbated considerably by the pandemic – she'd had no inkling of the eruption waiting to blow her world apart.

Shaking herself free of her thoughts, she went upstairs to shower. *I'll take the bike and explore*, she thought. *Find the Co-op, buy some basic provisions, something nice for Patsy, maybe even run to a famous dry robe.*

Patsy seemed to take it for granted that Bel would eat with them every night, but she felt awkward accepting her neighbour's hospitality without contributing, and looked forward to being able to return the favour properly if, at some point, her kitchen became a bit more functional. *Even if it's just a sandwich and salad supper on the beach*, she decided, casting a guilty thought Vinny's way as she remembered slathering white sliced with margarine and rubbery ham.

As she stepped over the lip of the pink bath, Bel had to accept that the cottage still felt quite strange, but she was getting used to the newspaper stacks and the cold porcelain toilet rim. They seemed like a small price to pay for the kindness she'd met with, the sense of home the village engendered. Even three-legged Zid, the cat, named after Zinedine Zidane, according to Patsy, by the previous vicar – who'd been as obsessed with football as he was with God – had popped in again that morning and actually deigned to sit on her lap for a couple of minutes.

Louis is my past, she told herself firmly, holding the shower attachment aloft and dousing herself in lukewarm water. *Leave him, his girlfriend and his baby to history.*

16

Toiling up the lane through the village to the main road on her bike – dismayed at how her thighs screamed at the effort – she stopped at the junction. She'd come from Penzance station, to the west, so she decided now to go straight across, diving into the twisting lanes on the north side of the A394. She was nervous. Riding the London streets seemed like child's play compared to the pretty, quiet, deceptively empty lanes, where a car, van or even a huge, belching tractor could career round the corner and straight into her path without the slightest warning. But after a while she began to relax a little. The sun had come out, the hedges and verges vibrant with spring green and dotted with yellow, cornflower blue and white flowers, blossoms lighting up the trees. It was peaceful and beautiful.

She rode slowly through a couple of villages and got lost in the back doubles, coming round on herself a number of times. But it didn't matter. She wasn't in a hurry to be anywhere this morning. When she finally came out onto the main road again, and turned for what she hoped was home, she spied a farm shop, a sign reading 'Fresh Local Fruit and Veg' in scrawled chalk, and pulled into the small gravel lay-by.

I'll buy fruit, she thought, *and something special to take to Patsy's this evening*. Even though her kitchen was a mess, she could still put together a fresh salad to add to Patsy's supper.

There were empty crates piled against the wall of the large wooden hut, the lane leading past the shop giving onto open fields. Leaning her bike next to the crates, she stepped, sweating from her ride, onto the rickety wooden platform. It was open at the front, displays on the right-hand side of brown onions, leeks propped tall like soldiers, smooth-skinned squash, green-topped bunches of slim carrots, globe artichokes, knots of thick asparagus. To the left were apples and pears, oranges, satsumas, punnets of golden apricots, juicy strawberries, a tray of pink rhubarb stalks, like the ones Patsy had served stewed last night. Bel hovered, her mouth watering. Compared to the supermarket in Earls Court Road, this was food wonderland.

Inside, the wooden planks creaking loudly with her every step, Bel was confronted by the deliciously earthy smell of fruit. It was coming from the gnarled, misshapen beef tomatoes in shades of dark red, yellow and green, cherry and plum varieties still on the vine and luscious-looking pink heirlooms, cradled in blue tissue-lined boxes along the wall. There was the tang of goat's cheese on the air, the sweet scent of apple juice, the yeasty smell of fresh-baked bread and the aromatic hint of herbs, bunched neatly beside trays of crisp lettuces and watercress.

Bel was in heaven. She felt heady with delight at the goodies on display. One of the things that she and Louis had always bonded over was the importance of the very best and freshest ingredients. She just wished she had a functioning kitchen in which to prepare them. Obviously Lenny had never cooked. There was only a grease-blackened frying pan, a small aluminium pot and a sad array of utensils in the cupboard. *I've got to remedy that*, she thought enthusiastically, feeling the cooking muscle — bruised in the flat by the appalling state of the kitchen and her father's sneering — begin to awaken and flex itself deep in her gut. Then she remembered with a jolt that she might only be in Cornwall for a short time.

'Hello, there.' A voice pushed her thoughts to the back of her mind.

Bel looked towards the far wall of the hut and saw someone emerging from a room behind — the shop was much bigger than she'd first thought. 'Hi,' she said, smiling.

The woman was in her fifties, Bel assessed, with unkempt, greying hair wisping to her shoulders around a strong, lined face, handsome without make-up. She was dressed in a blue smock over jeans, worn white plimsolls on her feet. Bel noticed the multiple silver rings on her square, tanned fingers as she wrapped a glass jar of honey in a brown-paper bag and set it aside. 'This place is amazing,' she said.

The woman smiled. 'It's not mine, but I'm glad you like it.' Her voice was rough and gravelly as if she smoked. 'You're staying around here?'

'In the village. My house is next to Patsy Wornum's.' Bel was sure the woman would know her neighbour.

A fleeting frown crossed her face. 'You're . . .'

'Bel Carnegie. I own the cottage Lenny Bright lived in.'

The frown disappeared. 'Oh, right. Good to meet the phantom landlady at last,' she said, smiling. 'Brigid.' She held out her hand.

'Who owns this place?' Bel asked, as they shook hands.

'Mr Ajax.' She lowered her voice. 'First name's Ron, but he likes to be called Mr Ajax at all times. So I do.' She rolled her eyes at Bel. 'Those fields behind are his. All the tomatoes, lettuces, asparagus – a large proportion of what you see around you, in fact – is grown here.'

'That's brilliant.'

'It is,' Brigid conceded. 'Mr A's a bit of a grumpy old goat, but he does an incredible job.'

After a blissful quarter of an hour wandering around the shop, Bel had chosen her purchases. She was in the process of paying for a crusty dark rye loaf and a wedge of Cornish Kern cheese for herself, with a selection of beef and heritage tomatoes and watercress for tonight's salad, two fat bundles of asparagus and a good bottle of red wine for Patsy, when a handwritten card propped next to the till caught her eye. Written in thick blue felt tip, it said:

WANTED – sales assistant. Mornings 8–12 p.m.,
Monday–Thursday. Must be able to add up!
Enquire at till.

As she read it, something odd happened around Bel's heart, which made her breath catch in her throat. Pointing at the notice, she said, 'Add up?'

Brigid laughed and indicated the compact black machine on the table in front of her. 'It's old-school, like the owner. Doesn't add up. Only takes the final sum and prints a receipt.'

A young couple in matching lime-green anoraks carrying walking poles creaked into the shed, interrupting them. The man asked Brigid if she did coffees. When she said no, and directed them down the road to Martine's, they wandered out again.

'I've told Mr A there's a huge profit in coffee,' she said, when they'd gone. 'But he says it's too complicated, and he's probably right.'

Bel's heart, during this exchange, had not settled down. *I can add up*, she was thinking. In fact, she'd always been excellent at mental arithmetic – even Vinny had commented on her skill. Not maths so much, she'd never really got to grips with equations and geometry. But she could calculate a column of figures in her head quicker than everyone she knew – it had stood her in good stead when she was front-of-house for 83. Now, breathing in the earthy smell of the hut until her lungs were full of it, she was certain she wanted that job more than anything else in the world.

'Umm . . .'

Brigid waited, eyebrows raised for her to continue.

'Umm, I . . .' She got no further.

In the silence that followed, Brigid pushed her brown bags across the table for Bel to put in her backpack.

'I'd love the job,' Bel blurted out, flustered and red-faced, to the obvious surprise of the other woman.

'You would? It doesn't pay much. Minimum wage. And Mr Ajax is grumpy, as I've said. Have you done this sort of work before?'

Bel shook her head, panic seizing her guts until she wanted to bend over and ease the pain. 'But I'm really quick at arithmetic.'

Brigid took this in, but still looked uncertain. 'So you're staying for a while?'

The breath Bel had been holding was involuntarily expelled in a whoosh. 'Oh, God, I don't know. I want to, but the cottage is a mess, and I have my father back in London waiting for me to come home.' The words tumbled out of her mouth. 'If I do stay, I'll need a job . . . and I love this place.'

'Right,' Brigid said slowly, clearly thinking Bel was a little unhinged. 'Well, if I give you my number, you can ring when you've decided.'

'What if someone else comes along and wants the job?'

Brigid shrugged. 'Up to Mr Ajax. But we do need someone. Lena's gone back to Poland to have her baby.'

Bel watched as Brigid scribbled a mobile number on a piece of paper torn from the small pad on which she'd totted up a customer's bill and handed it to her.

Bel took it, picking up her loaded backpack. 'Thanks.' She wanted to say she'd be in touch. She wanted to throw caution to the winds and apply for the job. Above all, she wanted desperately to make a decision that she knew she didn't yet have the guts to make.

When Bel arrived home, still buzzing from, and ruffled by, her impulsive enquiry about a job at a farm shop she'd just set foot in, the front door was ajar. She assumed it must be Patsy, but walked in to find Micky reclining in a wide, rusty-orange armchair behind Lenny's ringed coffee table, eyes closed. The chair looked modern, but not new, Scandinavian in design, a double wing-backed bucket chair with padded, buttoned upholstery, the pale wooden legs emerging from the base in an A line, pitted as if a dog had chewed them.

Micky jerked awake, mumbling something incomprehensible and jumped to his feet, as if he'd been caught out doing something he shouldn't.

Bel raised her eyebrows. 'What's this?'

'Oh my God, Bel. This,' he held out his hand like a compère introducing his next guest, 'is called an angel chair.' He pointed to the two wings by way of explanation. 'And it's the most insanely comfortable chair I've ever sat in. I'd be tempted to keep it myself if I had room in the van.' He pulled Bel forward by the sleeve of her T-shirt. 'Come,' he urged. 'Sit, have a go.'

Laughing, Bel complied. Despite its stylish appearance, it was roomy and squashy, the back high enough to support her head and reclining at just the right angle. 'Wow,' she said. 'It's gorgeous. Definitely from the angels.' She looked up at Micky. 'Where did you find it?'

Micky grinned. 'Mum's garage. She's a hoarder, my dear mother. The place is rammed to the ceiling with furniture from the big house we had outside Newquay. Everything's just rotting in there, but she won't get rid of it.'

'I'll pay her for it, of course.'

He shook his head vehemently. 'She'd never take your money. See it as a loan, not that she'll want it back. By the time you return it, the space in the garage will have been filled with some other piece she'll never use again.'

Bel got up and hugged him. 'Thanks, Micky. Thank you

so much. I can't believe you did that . . . went off and found me a chair.' She was so touched by his kindness.

'Oh, I was going over there anyway. Doing some stuff for one of Mum's mates. Thought I'd have a rummage, see what I could come up with. You can't stay here with nothing to sit on.' He appeared almost embarrassed by her thanks. 'Where have you been?' he asked.

'I biked around the area, then found the farm shop. What an amazing place.'

'I suppose,' Micky looked surprised at her enthusiasm, 'if you're prepared to take out a mortgage for every carrot. I stick to the Co-op.'

It had been expensive, he was right. She reminded herself she was on a budget and couldn't get carried away in future. *In future . . .*

I almost applied for a job there. The words hovered on her tongue but she didn't let them loose. Micky would only ask questions – as Brigid had done – that she couldn't answer. Or, also like Brigid, think she'd gone nuts.

He was looking around the room. 'You know, you could make something of this place, if you got rid of these piles of crap and did a paint job. The stove still does its thing and I could probably source better kitchen units.' He went over and leaned against the Rayburn rail, arms crossed. 'You can cook fantastic stuff in these old ovens. I've done work for a lady over near Helston and she bakes buns and cakes to die for in hers.'

They contemplated the Rayburn in silence for a moment. 'I'm a bit nervous of it, to be honest. I've never had a wood-burner before. I keep expecting it to blow up in my face.'

His cherubic face broke into a broad grin. 'The worst this old guy ever does is go out,' he said. 'You cook?'

'Baking's my thing, when I'm in the mood.'

He waited for her to go on, but she didn't feel like expanding on how that mood might come about. To change the focus, she asked, 'JJ said you were putting up shelves this morning? Are you a carpenter?'

'I wouldn't go that far, but I do love it. Better than being a systems analyst, that's for sure.'

Bel wasn't entirely clear what a systems analyst was, but she was aware JJ hadn't wanted to talk about his past much, so she didn't ask Micky. She'd look it up later.

'Patsy keeps telling us we have to live in the moment,' he went on. 'JJ pays more attention to her instructive ramblings than I do, but I feel my stressful city life was just a stepping stone to this one.'

'Do you earn enough, though?' It was something she'd wondered about, from a personal perspective. 'You both seem to do things for nothing.' She indicated the chair with a smile, although she'd pressed cash into a reluctant JJ's hand for the removal of Lenny's armchair and the rest.

'That's different.' He brushed off the implied altruism. 'I got paid for the shelves, for instance, and we charge for all the handyman stuff we do.' He shrugged. 'Our lifestyle isn't expensive, obviously.'

When Micky had gone, Bel went over to the stove and checked out the dial on the right-hand door. There was a bake knob you could turn if you wanted the oven hotter instead of just running the water heater, and she wondered if she should try it out with something simple, like biscuits. But she didn't have a baking sheet or a mixing bowl or a rolling pin. She couldn't justify spending her limited cash on stuff she might not use past the end of next week.

Later, asparagus bundles, tomato salad – in a scuffed Pyrex bowl because that was all she could find in Lenny's cupboards – and wine in hand, she walked the short distance to her neighbour's house. Knocking and receiving no reply, she pushed open the door to the kitchen, to be greeted by Patsy and a small, round woman with a dark bob, in jeans and a paisley shirt, dancing wildly, arms waving, and singing at the top of their voices the chorus of the Abba hit, 'Chiquitita'. They sang of the sun shining above them, about having no time for grieving, about singing a new song. They weren't quite Agnetha and Anni-Frid, but Bel noticed some impressive harmonies as she stood there smiling, watching the two women dance so joyously.

Jaz was sitting in her homework spot, presumably revising, at one end of the Formica table, her headphones on against the racket. She looked up when she saw Bel and rolled her eyes, although Bel thought she detected a tinge of amusement in the teenager's gaze.

When Patsy saw her, she stopped singing, breathless and clutching her sides. The other woman also fell silent, looking a bit sheepish.

'Just having a moment,' Patsy said, laughing. 'This is Rhian.' Then she turned to her friend. 'Rhian, this is Bel, Lenny's saviour.'

Rhian's face broke into a warm smile as she held out her hand. 'Welcome. I'm so pleased to meet you.' Her soft Welsh accent had the stretched and stressed vowels, the glide from high to low. 'Maybe not the most dignified introduction to the local vicar,' she added, wiping her forehead with the back of her hand and rumpling her fringe back into place.

Patsy had told her that the vicar and Zid, the cat, lived in the functional eighties-build behind the church, which sat a couple of lanes up from Patsy's chapel, on top of the hill. The old vicarage – creepy Victorian Gothic Revival, apparently – had burned down in the seventies.

'Oh, I loved it,' Bel insisted. 'I want more!' She wanted to sing too – she loved singing.

'Supper's nearly ready,' Patsy demurred. 'The cabaret will have to wait.' She seemed momentarily disconcerted, giving Bel a searching glance. 'Off the table,' she said, to her granddaughter.

Rhian jumped to and laid the table, obviously very familiar with the kitchen, while Patsy retrieved a bowl of what looked like cucumber raita from the fridge and two jars, one of lime pickle, the other of mango chutney, then proceeded to chop a lime into quarters. The earthenware dish of curried potatoes and cauliflower that she placed in the centre of the table smelt divinely of garlic and ginger, turmeric and chilli, the vegetables flecked with black mustard seeds and sprinkled with chopped coriander. Waving a saucepan of fluffy white rice in Bel's direction, a serving spoon in her other hand, Patsy urged, 'Dig in.'

Bel sighed with pleasure as all the tastes mingled in her

mouth. The potatoes were perfectly soft, the cauliflower still a little crisp, the accompanying raita soothing the hit of fiery chilli and lime on her tongue. 'You'd give my ex a run for his money, Patsy,' she said. 'And he's a talented chef.'

Patsy shook her head. 'Pulling something out of the earth and cooking it that minute is what makes the difference.'

Rhian leaned across and gave her friend's hand a squeeze. 'Yes, the cook's got absolutely nothing to do with this gorgeous meal, of course.'

Patsy gave her a sidelong glance, her mouth twitching in a delighted smile, which broadened into a grin when Jaz added, through a mouthful, 'It's really yummy, Nonna.'

Bel did not stay late. She left after she'd helped Patsy clear up and stack the dishwasher, tired not only from her morning's swim and bike ride but the mental exertion of taking in her new surroundings and meeting so many new people. But what tired her most was the ongoing uncertainty about her future. She realized, as she climbed into bed, that she hadn't called her father that day and felt a wave of guilt. He hadn't rung her, either, which was almost unheard of. She was too sleepy to get out of bed and do it now – she was sure he would still be up, whisky glass in hand, muttering obscenities at the television. She fell asleep thinking not of him, though: her mind was buzzing instead with the wonderful people and tastes and smells and sights ... possibilities ... that currently filled her senses. *Patsy and Rhian*, she mused as she closed her eyes, *are in love*.

17

'So you'll definitely be home Saturday week,' her father told her – didn't ask - when he finally called her back after several left messages. It was early on Friday afternoon before they spoke. 'Because you know what Sunday is.'

Bel did know.

'I thought we'd go to the grave. Lay some flowers, have a chat with your dear mum. Then we can get a good plate of beef and Yorkshire at the Hawk, if Joey hasn't died of the plague.'

She was silent, overwhelmed by the prospect, not just of visiting her mother's grave but of sensing the gloomy walls of her childhood flat closing in on her again, smelling the decay in the fabric of the place, the fear of being confined again in the same space as her teasing father. A frisson of anxiety prickled across her skin, making her shiver. He was ordering her about, as usual, calling the shots, like a prison guard beckoning her inside a cell.

'Bella?'

'Yeah, OK, Dad. That would be nice.' She knew as she spoke that she was being played. Her father never visited her mother's grave. Never even mentioned the day she had died in any of the years Bel had been with Louis. But now he was carefully reeling her in, using her dead mother to bring her back to the fold. *I just gave in*, she thought. *Without a single word of protest, I gave in*.

'I imagine you're sick of the hovel by now, anyway. Be glad to be back in your own cosy bed,' Dennis was saying, his mood upbeat. 'You should get rid of the place ASAP, sweetheart. Agnes only kept it for sentimental reasons, because her mother grew up there, apparently, in misty-eyed poverty and despair, some such crap. It'll never be anything but a dump.' His tone was sarcastic and patronizing. Then he chuckled. 'Backgammon board awaits. Reg still refuses to get better enough to come out of his lair.'

Backgammon. Bel ran into the word as if it was a brick wall. She was finding it hard to breathe. The fear as her father's face pressed close to hers, the rage in his eyes, the rank smell of spirits on his breath was so real it could have been happening right here, right now, in the Cornish stone cottage.

She got up from the new chair and started pacing the small living room. Time seemed to stop. Then she felt herself taking in an involuntary gasp of air. It seemed to gust right through her body, as if someone had opened wide a portal in a storm. It was cold and cleansing, but the sheer force of it made her burn. Bel felt her cheeks flush, her heart hammer. *I cannot go back next week*. The sentence fell into place in her mind like the last turn of a Rubik's Cube.

She heard her father call her name, waiting for her to reply.

'Dad . . .' She wasn't sure how to say it, now the moment had come, but the words had to be said. 'Listen, I know I just said I'd be back next week. But, in truth, I'd prefer to stay here for a while. It's such a long way and so expensive to come just for a few days, even though it would have been great to visit Mum.'

There was a blank silence.

Trembling from her own words, Bel ploughed on: 'The house needs a lot doing to it and I ought to get it sorted before the whole place falls down.'

Another silence.

'You're not coming home?' Her father's voice was pinched and shrill.

'Not right now. I'm sorry.' She didn't go on, sensing cold beads of sweat breaking out on her forehead.

'There's something you're not telling me,' Dennis muttered suspiciously. 'I can hear it in your voice. What's going on down there?'

Bel sensed his anger bubbling up, but reminded herself that she wasn't in the flat, and he wasn't there in front of her, breathing into her face. *I don't need to be afraid.* 'I love it here,' she said simply. 'That's all that's going on.'

Her father gave a sardonic snort. 'Ha! It's a man, isn't it? This fella you've been stalking. I knew it. What other reason could you have for claiming to love that rat-hole?'

Bel sighed and repeated, for the umpteenth time, 'There's no man, Dad.'

'Don't lie. I can always tell.' He spoke softly, but it was clear his paranoia was escalating. She shuddered as she imagined the furious look in his dark eyes, sending up a grateful prayer to the universe that she was three hundred miles away. 'You promised you'd *never leave me.* You said it, Bella.' Her father was pleading piteously with her now. 'Only the other day you *promised me.*'

'Dad, calm down, please,' she begged, feeling the guilt slicing at her gut. *I did say that.*

Neither spoke, the connection seeming to hum with tension.

'Well, don't come crying to me, girl, when this latest piece of shite lets you down and you don't have a roof over your head.' She heard a wheezy intake of breath.

'Dad, listen –'

He cut her off with a venomous hiss. 'Ungrateful bitch.' Then the line went dead.

Thoroughly shaken, Bel sat down again and buried her face in her hands.

'Bel?' JJ's voice startled her. He was standing in the doorway, large frame looming. 'Has something happened?'

'No. Nothing, I'm fine,' Bel blurted out, embarrassed and trying in vain to compose herself.

Raising his eyebrows, he echoed softly, 'Nothing?'

Bel didn't contradict him this time.

He approached the chair tentatively. After a moment's hesitation, he reached down and took her arm, easing her gently to her feet and pulling her close against his broad chest in a warm hug. Bel, unable to resist, clung to him as she hadn't clung to anyone in a very long time.

Between trembling breaths, she poured out her conversation with her father. JJ listened, gradually letting go of her, but never taking his eyes off her face. He guided her back into the chair. 'Wow,' he said. 'What father calls his daughter a bitch?'

'Oh, he's done it before.'

'And that's OK?'

Seeing the shock on JJ's face, she realized how much she'd normalized her father's behaviour over the years. Even now, she almost said, *He doesn't mean it.* But she stopped herself. 'No,' she said quietly. 'No, it's not OK.'

He took a step back, hands pushed into the pockets of his hoody. 'Don't feel guilty,' he said, although she hadn't spoken.

'How can I not? He's my father and he's old. You can walk away from a partner if you don't like how they behave, but it's way more difficult to dump your own flesh and blood.'

JJ seemed to be considering this. 'True. But that doesn't give him the right to abuse you.'

'It's not really "abuse",' she said quickly, needing what she said to be true.

He raised his eyebrows, said nothing.

'So why are you here?' she asked, with more asperity than she intended.

He didn't seem to notice her tone. 'Just a thought,' he replied, with a smile. 'The sea's flat as a pancake. No joy surfing. I wondered if you fancied a paddleboard this evening. High tide's at five forty, and it would have to be a bit later so we can get down on the sand.'

Bel had mentioned to JJ over supper that she'd never been on a paddleboard, although she'd done a few stints at surf school when she was much younger – on family holidays in Spain and Brittany – and loved it. But at this precise moment she felt so exhausted she didn't think she could drag herself to the front door. She blew out her cheeks. 'I probably won't even be able to get on the board, let alone paddle the bloody thing.'

'Won't know unless you try.' He straightened up, grinning, taking her prevarication for assent. 'Great. See you down there at six thirty?'

After JJ had gone Bel crept up to bed. She didn't want to think about her father, but her mind seemed overwhelmed by him, as if he were a rampaging virus. She realized she actually felt scared. *What will he do?* she found herself asking, as if the man wielded some malign power over her. She knew she was being ridiculous. *He's just someone who likes to get his own way*, she assured herself. But his anger felt more potent than that, his anguished cry sounding as if it came from physical pain, not mere peevish outrage. As if a limb was being torn from its socket. *You promised you'd never leave me* . . . Bel cringed and pulled the duvet tighter around her head for comfort.

But her heart was still beating nineteen to the dozen beneath the stuffy confines of the bedding. *Damned if I do and damned if I don't*, she thought. Which was worse? The guilt that was now tearing at her gut, like scavengers at a corpse, or being shut up with her father indefinitely? There seemed no third option. After a while, tiredness overtook her and she fell into a heavy doze. When she woke, it was just after six. Jumping out of bed, foggy from her nap, she pulled on her swimsuit and hustled her things into a bag, throwing a couple of logs into the stove as she passed. Then she stumbled through the village and down the path to the beach.

As Bel walked, her mind was blank. She was still slightly in shock that she'd stood up to her father, refused to buckle to his demands. But even telling him part of the reason why she wanted to stay in Cornwall – that she loved it – had produced such a violent reaction she was still bruised by it. She dreaded to think what might happen if she told Dennis the other, equally valid, reason why she didn't want to go back: that she couldn't live with him again.

Jumping down onto the sand, she gasped. The evening was utterly still. Nothing moved. The sea, high up the beach, was like sheet-glass, waves breaking almost apologetically in the quiet, the upside-down image of the rocks attached seamlessly to the real thing without flaw. Sunset was at least a couple of hours away, but the sun was low and hazy in the sky, hiding coyly behind strands of cirrus cloud, casting a soft sheen on the water. It was breath-stoppingly beautiful.

There was almost nobody else on the beach, with the tide so high. She saw JJ perched on a rock at the bottom of the steep steps cut out of the cliff face – which Bel had so far avoided, preferring the smooth slope of the hard. There were two boards – one blue, one white – and two paddles on the sand at his feet. His wetsuit was pulled down to his waist, leaving his tanned, muscled chest bare, his blue-black hair tucked behind his ears. He looked almost sculpted as he gazed, silent and motionless, out to sea.

'Hi,' she said softly, reluctant to break into his contemplation.

JJ turned at the sound of her voice, smiling and leaping

to his feet. 'I wondered if you'd come,' he said. 'How are you feeling?'

'Bit dazed, if I'm honest. Wrangling a paddleboard might be the perfect antidote.'

He laughed, his dark eyes lighting up. 'You'll be fine.'

The water was cold as they waded in with the boards, which seemed very bulky and cumbersome to Bel. She shivered, wishing she had a wetsuit. JJ showed her how to attach the ankle lead. 'Very important always to wear this,' he said seriously. 'If you fall off and lose your board, you might not be strong enough to swim back to shore without it.'

Bel nodded obediently. She was dying to get on now, and watched impatiently as JJ pointed to the handle in the centre. 'Lay your paddle across the board and put your knees either side of the handle.' He demonstrated, hopping onto the board with ease. 'OK.' He indicated that she should try as he slid off and stood in the water, steadying her board with one hand.

Taking a deep breath, Bel leaned over, pressing on the shaft of the paddle and lifting one knee. The board wobbled violently and, despite JJ's hold, skittered away. He pulled it back and she tried again, laughing with embarrassment. This time she managed to mount, feeling the board knobbly and hard beneath her bare knees. Crouched over and tense, she tried to get her balance, on the verge of slipping sideways, but JJ reached over and put a hand on her back to steady her.

Red-faced with effort and aware of her bare thighs, pale after years of no sun, her bottom ill-concealed by her

177

thin swimsuit, she was rigid, helpless, ridiculous, stuck on all fours. 'I can't straighten up – I'll fall in,' she gasped, letting out a strangled laugh.

'Breathe,' he encouraged. 'Sit back slowly, get a feel for the board.'

Her old knees creaked in protest as she sat back gingerly on her haunches, paddle in hand. But the board seemed to comply and she gave a small sigh of relief. When she looked at JJ, he was smiling reassuringly.

'Great. Now put the paddle into the water . . . No, the blade goes the other way round, curve to the back. Watch this.' He jumped onto his board and began to move forward, dipping his paddle in straight by the nose of the board, as if he was spearing a fish, bringing it back to his feet, doing it again on the other side.

Bel tried to copy his expert movements. She was good at taking instruction, and felt herself begin to glide slowly, hesitantly through the water – although the paddle change nearly unseated her each time. Her stroke was choppy and awkward, but it still felt exhilarating. *I was strong and sporty once*, she reminded herself, recalling her years on the slopes of Chamonix with Bruno, and sensed her body agreeing, her muscles sparking up, waking to the challenge.

Nervous still, she paddled in JJ's wake along the bay. He was standing now and she wanted to stand too – the knobbles on the board were hurting her knees. She called, and he turned his board and came back to her side.

He knelt down again and showed her how to come into standing. He made it look so easy. 'Lean on the paddle again. Put your feet exactly where your knees are.'

Bel managed to pull up one knee. But the other, on the side where she'd had her accident all those years ago, was stiffer. She struggled to drag her foot to sit square on the board, lost her balance, and splashed heavily into the water. The cold was initially a shock, but as her head broke the surface of the still water she found she was grinning. *Not so bad*, she thought. Then another thought struck her. *How do I get back on the bloody thing?* The water was deeper here, the board, with her feet on the sand, at waist level. She'd never have the leverage.

JJ jumped off his board, laying the paddle along its length. 'Ready?' he asked. Without waiting for an answer, she could feel his body close behind her, lifting her between his large hands as if she weighed no more than a pound of butter, until she was on top of the board again. She felt slightly hysterical, flopping down and giggling like a schoolgirl. 'Sorry . . . thanks,' she gasped. 'I'm a bit hopeless at this.'

'On the contrary,' JJ said, as he mounted his board again. 'You're doing brilliantly.'

On the third go, Bel managed to stand. Now she breathed in, back straight, knees slightly bent as JJ instructed, getting a feel for the board's balance beneath her feet, and began to relax. The knots of tension engendered by her conversation with her father gradually melted away in the soft evening air. They paddled the width of the bay and back a couple of times, watching the sun slowly sink in the sky, enjoying the cool breeze that had got up and was ruffling the water. It was so peaceful, only the gentle swish of their blades as they glided towards the rocks at the far end of the beach. For Bel, nothing else seemed to exist beyond this moment.

'Come to mine for a drink?' JJ suggested later, as they pulled their boards up the beach in the dying light. 'I've got wine and a firepit.'

Bel, collapsed on the sand, felt as if every muscle in her body had been violently hammered. But she was elated by her success on the board, intoxicated by the sea air, the workout, the sheer beauty of her surroundings. 'I'd love to, if I ever walk again.'

They sat side by side on the scrubby headland, in front of his van, on blue folding canvas chairs. JJ had lit the logs in the firepit, which were smoking and crackling as the wood caught. He handed her a Duralex tumbler of red wine and placed a big bowl of crisps on the upturned crate between them.

'You're not expected at Patsy's tonight?' he asked.

'She had to go to Jaz's school for some sort of meeting. They were planning to get a burger afterwards.'

The sun was now a hazy circle of burning orange-gold as it began to dip beneath the horizon. Bel was mesmerized.

Neither spoke for a while as they sipped their drinks.

'That was amazing,' Bel said quietly. 'Thank you so much. I loved every minute.' Her tired body, now wrapped in her sweatshirt, shorts and a blanket JJ had pulled from a drawer beneath the bed, was warm and tingling, her mind floating across the sea. She couldn't remember enjoying a moment so much in a long time.

They talked until the sky was dark, the sand grey, the sea black. JJ told her about the area, some of the characters in the village, his surfing adventures on the north shore. Much of what he said went over her head: she was too drowsy with the wine to concentrate.

'Are Patsy and Rhian an item?' Bel ventured, as she watched JJ riddling the logs and setting fresh ones on the glowing ash pile in the firepit.

He looked up. 'You noticed?'

'Hard not to.'

'Patsy says they don't have sex.'

'OK . . .'

'Rhian calls them "romantic asexuals".' He grinned. 'It's a thing, apparently.' He sat down again and picked up his glass. 'Patsy says she's too old for the sex lark and Rhian just never fancied it with men or women, but they really seem to love each other.'

'I could see that,' Bel replied. 'I suppose not having sex makes it less complicated for Rhian, as a vicar. The Church might take a dim view.'

JJ was staring off across the sea. 'Funny thing, sexuality.' He turned to her. 'Micky's been known to swing both ways. Whereas me . . .' He paused.

Bel's heart jumped. The dark was intimate, the firelight seductive. She'd been enjoying JJ's proximity all evening, his hands on her waist, hoisting her onto the board earlier, the salty, sweaty, rubbery smell of his skin, released from the wetsuit, the rugged outdoorsy ease with which he'd humped the boards up from the beach and lit the fire. But he was nearly fifteen years her junior. She felt she could only admire his beauty from afar.

JJ put his glass on the crate. He got up, then sank to his haunches in front of her chair, placing his palms on her bare knees. 'In fact, I'd really like to kiss you,' he said, the pale-gold flecks in his irises caught by the flames so that his eyes seemed actually to dance. He sounded so serious, it might have made her laugh, if she hadn't been so taken aback. 'Would that be something you'd consider?'

The question was put in an almost comically direct way, but JJ seemed calm and in control. It was nothing like any experience Bel had ever had. But she was in no condition to examine her options, suffering as she was from sensory overload at the end of a totally surreal day. All she knew – regardless of the consequences – was that she'd like nothing better in the whole wide world right now than for JJ to kiss her.

Placing her hands over his on her knees, she smiled. There was a second where they just stared at each other in the semi-darkness, then JJ rose, lifting her with him till they were both standing, and pulled her into his arms. Bel closed her eyes as his lips met hers. His kiss was gentle but confident, his body strong as he pressed against her. She found herself almost crying out with the tingling pleasure of it.

A second later, the strong beam of vehicle lights strobed across where they stood. Bel heard JJ groan softly.

'Micky,' he said, releasing her with a frustrated grin. 'Timing's never been his thing.'

Both began to laugh.

'Hey, guys.' Micky climbed from his van, swinging his outstretched arms like windmills and yawning loudly. 'What have I missed?' He wandered over, eyeing the wine bottle, the dying fire, the empty crisps bowl.

Bel wasn't sure if he'd seen them kiss. She was embarrassed now, slightly flustered, the spell broken. But JJ didn't seem fazed. 'I've got another bottle,' he offered his friend.

'Think I'll get home,' Bel said, not quite able to meet JJ's eye. She turned to Micky. 'JJ got me up on the paddleboard this evening. It was brilliant.'

Micky, head on one side, was staring at her with an amused look in his blue eyes, which made her blush. She hoped the darkness hid the worst.

'She was great,' JJ put in. 'Like a pro.'

'Listen, thanks for a wonderful time,' she said.

He pulled her into another embrace, this one short and friendly. 'Let's do it again.' His look, as he smiled into her eyes, gave his comment a double entendre, which Bel didn't fail to note.

As she walked up the lane, her phone torch lighting the way in the dense country darkness, Bel's head was spinning. *What just happened?* She laughed to herself as she pushed open the door of the cottage, which was pleasantly warm from the dying Rayburn. *It doesn't get much more romantic,* she thought, as she threw down her beach bag and climbed the narrow stairs to bed, *than a clifftop kiss by firelight on a warm spring evening with a beautiful man.* She would consider the consequences in the morning.

18

Heavy rain outside the open casement window woke Bel. She lay on her back, staring up at the undulations and cracks in the dirty-white plaster of the ceiling and the peeling brown patch in the corner where water must have seeped in from a loose roof slate in the past.

In the grey dawn light, lying alone, the magic of being footloose and fancy-free suddenly seemed a little unsettling and precarious. It was all very well falling in love with the romanticism of a Cornish village and a broken-down stone cottage, kindly neighbours, a farm shop from her fantasies and a dark-eyed, handsome surfer. She'd been here less than a week. This could be one giant all-encompassing delusion.

Events of the previous day began to float back to her, but her clifftop kiss, however delightful at the time, now appeared to be a potential cause for awkwardness. She hoped she hadn't ruined her friendship with JJ and Micky for that casual moment of pleasure.

Sitting up, Bel felt her head reel with the after-effects of too much red wine, her stomach muscles screaming in protest. All that balancing on the paddleboard had done for her lax, ill-prepared abdominals. Once upright, her thighs joined the throng of complainants, her knees too. It was as if she'd turned ninety overnight. Groaning and in need of a strong coffee – which she did not yet have in the cottage – she threw on her jeans and sweatshirt. She wanted to get to the café before the surfers.

Anorak pulled over her hair, she hurried up the lane. There was no one about, bar one damp dog-walker buried in a massive Barbour duster coat and a wide-brimmed hat. Bel ordered a coffee from Martine, who'd just opened, then scuttled home. She would eat the seeded rye with Kern, and slice one of Brigid's juicy, misshapen beef tomatoes for breakfast.

'Dad and I had a falling-out yesterday,' Bel explained, when she called Flo later. 'He hung up on me, told me never to darken his door again.' She was making light of it, although recalling the conversation still upset her.

'I've just left,' Flo replied. 'But he was properly on one today. Ranting about how ungrateful you were, et cetera, et cetera. It was kind of embarrassing.'

Bel winced. 'I've tried to call him, but he's not picking up.'

'He doesn't want me to come in any more. Said I was a "sop to your conscience" and he doesn't need me.'

'Right,' Bel said, after a minute. 'Well, his decision, I suppose. He wasn't rude, was he?'

'I didn't take it personally,' Flo replied carefully. 'Listen, I owe you. I've only done half the days you paid me for.'

'Keep it. You've earned every penny.'

Flo thanked her. 'Let him cool off, Bel. He's your dad. It's not like he's actually going to cut you off, never speak to you again.'

'Is that what he said?' Bel asked anxiously.

'He said it, but I'm sure he didn't mean it.'

Bel knew her father certainly had meant it in the moment. But his moods were traditionally up and down, like Tower Bridge. He would eventually relent, she was certain, even given the example of Aunt Phyllis's two decades of exile. But if he was refusing to speak to her now . . . She felt a little spurt of rebellion. *Don't come crying to me, girl*, he'd said. Well, maybe she should take him at his word this time, instead of making excuses for what he might have meant to say. If he didn't want her back . . .

Inhaling deeply, she went and sat down in the orange chair, tried to put her muddled thoughts in order. Was it such a foolish idea that she stay in Cornwall a while longer, possibly begin to consider a life here, in this village, with these people? Take the job in the farm shop until she could find something with better pay, do the place up . . . *live here*. She felt as if she were tugging against an invisible but nonetheless Herculean cord that bound her to her father. *I'm here, though*, she told herself, with a small thread of pride. *I managed to walk away, even if it was only meant to be for a few days.*

She began to delineate in her mind all the reasons why she might not be able to do what her heart cried out for: *The place is a terrible mess. I could be imagining how much I love it here, after so short a time. Maybe I'll find it hard to survive financially – and there's the debt. Winter is probably grim. I'll be alone. Dad will kick off.* Despite forcing herself to dwell on the downsides, though, Bel was aware of only a mild nervousness at the prospect. Her heart was thumping, she realized. But from excitement, not fear.

Now, she turned her attention to the alternative: the

city, the flat, her father . . . maybe for the rest of her life. Her gut roiled and clenched in solid rejection.

For a long time, Bel sat in the quiet room, turning it all over in her mind. And gradually her roller-coaster thoughts began to ease off, settling like tea leaves in a pot, until she had her answer. It wasn't solid or definitive yet. It still seemed like a hopeful breath of air wafting around her head. But she was setting her intentions. *I will stay . . . for a while at least.* The words felt so portentous, she almost laughed at herself. *It's just a cottage in Cornwall.* But it seemed like so much more than that to Bel.

Make a plan, she decided, straightening her back. Eyeing the ring of rubbish that surrounded her, almost like a theatrical set, she shuddered, imagining, not for the first time, the bugs and other wildlife contained therein. Then her gaze travelled to the rickety kitchen and her new resolve began to slide. Was this madness? Was it really worth it, to put her meagre resources into the cottage, when her father's weathervane moods might summon her at any moment, on any pretext . . . possibly one she couldn't ignore?

But the sun took that second to send a bright shaft of spring through the window, falling warmly on Bel where she sat. It seemed like a message. She felt her seesaw spirits lift, her heart soar. *No, I can do this*, she thought, brushing aside the darkness with an imaginary sweep of her hand.

Her brain began to kick into gear. *If I stay, I must work.* The cash wouldn't last long once she'd spent money on kitchen equipment, a new toilet seat, fixing the shower, a paint job, kitchen cabinets, bedding – Patsy would need hers back at some stage. And that was just the basics. Plus she had to consider the day-to-day expenses of utilities, logs, food, paying her father back. She knew she could live cheaply but 'cheaply' didn't mean 'free'.

Bel regretted, now, not keeping the stuff from the Walthamstow flat. But her father had said he didn't have room and she couldn't afford to store it. So she'd spent long, dreary hours selling some of Louis's more high-end kitchen equipment, the oak dining-table, his Eames armchair and more on eBay – giving all the proceeds to her father – and asked the Salvation Army to take the rest. At the time, she'd been in such despair as to be unable to think ahead, even to the next meal, let alone what she might need in the future.

'So you want the job?' Brigid asked doubtfully, when Bel rang the number she'd been given. 'I'll have to talk to Mr A. He'll be back in a minute. Maybe you should come in.' She gave a husky laugh. 'You haven't met him yet, of course.'

It sounded like a friendly warning to Bel, but she wasn't put off. 'Thanks, I'll see you later.'

Bel had nothing tidy to wear. Her meagre supply of clothes had all been worn multiple times – she hadn't yet availed herself of Patsy's offer to use her washing machine. Jeans and a T-shirt would have to do. It had stopped raining, sunshine dodging the clouds in fitful bursts, but there was still a stiff wind as she set out on her bike.

Turning north on the lane, she cast a quick glance towards the headland. She could usually see the tops of

JJ and Micky's vans above the line of the bramble hedge, but not today. *Surf must be up*, she decided. The two men would no doubt have been woken by a pre-dawn ping on their WTW (Where's The Wave?) app, and were currently shivering in the cold sea somewhere, hitched to their boards, waiting for what they hoped might be the best wave of their lives. Remembering JJ's kiss, she cringed. *That was stupid*, she thought, with regret. *He'll probably avoid me now.*

When she walked across the creaking farm-shop boards, inhaling the delicious aromas she remembered with such pleasure, the place appeared empty, except for a customer poring over the cheeses in the cold cabinet in the smaller area to the right of the main room. Bel couldn't see Brigid, but she wandered over to the till, then jumped as she noticed a man seated on a wooden chair by the opening to the back room, quietly drinking a cup of tea.

'Mr Ajax?' Bel asked nervously.

The man looked amused and sat up straighter. 'He's in there,' he said, jerking his thumb over his shoulder.

'Sorry.' She hovered uncomfortably, not sure what to do.

'Ron?' he called. 'Someone to see you.'

Bel shot him a grateful glance as she heard a peremptory shout, 'In here.'

The owner of the shop was in his sixties, Bel calculated. Bald, except for a wispy tonsure around his ears, he was of medium height, a paunch pushing out the tartan flannel shirt he wore over baggy jeans – both faded and shabby. His expression was ferrety as his small, beady eyes sized up Bel from behind his over-large gold-rimmed spectacles. Brigid had warned her that Mr Ajax was grumpy, but she was surprised that a man with his unwelcoming, chary exterior could create such a lusciously inviting shop.

He was checking a pile of invoices with a calculator on the worktop in the kitchen area – which, to Bel's surprise, was fitted with impressive, professional-looking stainless-steel counters and a sink, a large, industrial oven. The room was shiny clean and almost empty, but for various boxes of produce stacked on the floor in the corner.

He stopped what he was doing with a sigh. 'Yes?'

'I've come about the job,' Bel said.

Mr Ajax raised an eyebrow. 'You're the one who claims to be good at adding up?'

'I *am* good at it,' she replied steadily.

He almost smiled. 'Brigid seemed to think you weren't sure if you were staying down here?' His accent had the soft burr of the West Country.

'I wasn't, when I spoke to her. But I am now.'

'Right. Because I don't want to train someone up, just to have them take off a few weeks later.'

'I won't.' She knew she sounded more convincing than she felt.

'Customer!' the man drinking tea called through.

Mr Ajax shot her a challenging look. 'OK, let's see what you're made of,' he said, as he shooed her through to the till, beside which the woman who'd been at the chill cabinet had plonked a full basket of groceries. 'The prices should be on all the items,' he told her. 'You need to weigh the produce on the scales.' He pointed to a digital scale with a flat metal plate and display screen with fruit and veg images, like the one Bel recognized from supermarkets. 'Just tot it up, I'll deal with the rest.'

The man on the chair was looking on with interest. He was tall and lean, long legs – encased in dark cords – sticking out and crossed at the ankle above frayed leather boots. His tanned, handsome face was framed by a mass of brown curls – greying and chaotic – keen grey-green eyes curious as he watched her.

Who is he? Bel wondered, wishing he would stop staring as she set to with her task.

It was easy, she found, despite her nerves. She relished totting up the eleven prices she'd listed on the pad, using the pencil Mr Ajax provided, with lightning speed.

He was apologizing to the customer – who was clearly a regular. 'She's never done this before,' he told her, his tone slightly patronizing.

But the woman shrugged. 'That was quicker than usual,' she commented.

'Ah, but is it correct?' Mr Ajax asked, clearly sceptical as he snatched the pad. It seemed to Bel that he wanted her to fail.

He checked the figures slowly. 'Hmm. OK, fine . . .'

After the customer had left, the man on the chair piped up: 'Who needs those nasty modern computer things when you've got your very own human calculator, eh, Ron?'

Mr Ajax almost chuckled. As he turned to Bel, his expression became suspicious again. 'Brigid said you've no experience?'

'Not in a shop, no. But I used to run a restaurant.'

He frowned. 'Why do you want this job, then?

Restaurants are crying out for staff and I'm only paying ten pounds an hour.'

'I like it here,' she said simply. 'I think it's a wonderful place.'

Her words came from the heart, she wasn't trying to flatter him, but she saw a flush of pleasure colour his pallid cheeks.

'I'll second that,' said the man on the chair.

Mr Ajax exhaled loudly, but seemed to hesitate for the longest time. 'OK. Monday to Thursday, eight to twelve, ten pounds an hour. Cash in hand. Start a week on Monday?'

She nodded and grinned. 'Thank you.' She reached out her hand to shake his dry, gnarled one. Then she turned to the other man. 'Bel Carnegie.'

'Harris,' said the man. 'David Harrison, a.k.a. Harris.' He smiled warmly at her as he also took her hand. 'That was impressive.'

She gave a relieved laugh. 'Not really. Comes naturally.'

He rose to his feet. 'Right. Well, now the show's over, I suppose I'd better get back to work,' he said, rolling his shoulders up and round in a circle as if his back was stiff. 'Looks like I'll see you next week,' he said to Bel, then took his mug through to the kitchen, where Bel heard the tap running.

'Wildlife artist,' Mr Ajax commented softly. 'Quite famous in these parts.'

Bel said goodbye to her new boss and cycled away, triumphant, her heart lifting with every rotation of the pedals. *Forty pounds a day for four days means one hundred and sixty pounds a week . . . cash in hand.* It wouldn't make her rich, but it would pay for the basics and give her time to fix up the cottage, feel her way in the strange new life that was blooming all around her, like the spring flowers peppering the verge and hedgerows along the road.

When she got home, she would message Vinny at the sandwich shop and apologize, explain that she wasn't coming back.

19

'Hi, Dad. Please give me a ring. I need to know you're OK.' Bel delivered the message – virtually the same as the previous five or six – in a monotone, with little hope that she would hear back. They hadn't spoken since the row – which was only two days ago, admittedly – but she knew Flo was no longer going in.

She hated the silence between them. However tricky her father was, she didn't want a situation to develop in which hostilities escalated, laid down roots in his paranoid brain, and they lost contact. Her worry about him hovered, always there, like the gulls gliding through the blue May sky above her. Short of returning to London, though, there was little she could do if he refused to call her back. Shaking off her concerns, she went upstairs for a quick shower. She'd had an amazing swim earlier and needed to get rid of the salt stiffening her hair: she was due back at Patsy's soon for Sunday lunch, which she'd helped her neighbour prepare, picking and scrubbing the carrots, peeling the potatoes, washing the lettuce, laying the table, although Patsy had insisted she didn't need any help.

Will JJ be there? she wondered, as she soaped her body under the lukewarm water, which seemed all the Rayburn could manage. She hadn't seen him since Friday night.

Please don't let it be awkward between us. The last thing she needed was for a distance to grow up between her and her new-found friends over a silly moment in the warm spring night.

In the event, JJ clasped her to his broad chest with unashamed warmth, her hair wet against his cheek. 'Mm, you smell nice,' he said, into her ear. She knew she was blushing as she pulled away, but the others in the kitchen – Patsy, Rhian, Micky and Jaz – were too busy talking loudly over each other and laughing about the strange shapes of Patsy's baby carrots to pay any heed. JJ smoothed his hand down her back before letting her go, and she felt a shiver of pleasure run through her. *This is ridiculous*, she told herself sternly, but couldn't help enjoying it.

'So, I've got a job,' she told the table, as they settled down to the succulent slow-cooked lamb – Patsy had got up at seven that morning to put it on. She served the meat shredded and melt-in-the-mouth, accompanied by mountains of smooth olive-oil mash dotted with chives, the crooked carrots and pools of rich brown gravy. 'At Mr Ajax's farm shop, four mornings a week.'

Micky clapped. 'Congratulations! But how the hell did you get under the Ajax wire so quickly?'

Patsy smiled at Bel's confusion. 'The suspicious old sod's famous for scrutinizing his workforce's CVs for weeks on end before he makes a decision . . . even though he pays rubbish and doesn't actually need a rocket scientist to tot up a few lettuces.'

'He did test me. Made me add up a customer's shopping.'

'Cheeky bugger,' Patsy said. 'Just because he's too mean

to invest in a proper computerized system like everyone else on the planet.'

'So you passed,' JJ said. 'Respect. He'd never hire me.'

'Or me,' Jaz put in, almost proudly.

'I think it helped that his friend Harris was there and egging him on.'

'David Harrison's drawings of birds are amazing,' Rhian, still in her dog-collar from morning service, commented. 'He's seen locally as a bit of an eccentric,' she went on, round face flushed from the warmth of the kitchen, 'but I like him. He lives down the lane behind the farm shop and keeps himself to himself, comes in sometimes for a bit of company . . . even if it is only grumpy Ron's.'

'Rumour has it Brigid and Harris were getting down and dirty during lockdown,' Micky stated, with a grin.

JJ gave a throaty laugh. 'No secrets in this town, eh?'

'Paddleboard later?' JJ asked, as the party broke up and Micky took off to play snooker with his mate in Falmouth.

Bel hesitated. 'Not sure my stomach muscles have recovered from last time.'

'Swim, then?'

She'd been aware all through lunch of his body heat, his muscled thigh in cotton shorts so close to hers on the wooden bench at Patsy's kitchen table. Now JJ was staring at her with those eyes of his. Even the vague threat of being the subject of salacious rumour in the village was not, she found, as she stared back, enough to deter her. 'Love to,' she conceded.

Her mobile – which she'd left in the cottage, as there didn't seem such a need to have it pinned to her in Cornwall – was ringing as she opened the front door. *Dad*, she thought, racing to catch the call before he rang off.

'You're not going to believe this!' Tally's agitated voice declared, without even a hello. 'Dad's just rung in a terrible state. He says he and Trinny have split up! They were having a set-to the other night, apparently, and she told him he might not be Apollinaire's father.'

'*What?*'

'I know. I'm sort of struggling with it.'

Bel was shocked. She couldn't help feeling a pang of sympathy for Louis. 'What does she mean, "might"?'

'Seems she told him she was having it off with this other guy at the same time as Dad.'

'So the baby might still be Louis's,' Bel said. 'I reckon she's just winding him up. It's the biggest stick a woman can hold over a man when they want to hurt them . . . *He's not yours.*'

'Dad believed her, though.'

'What's he going to do about it?'

'No idea.' Tally sighed. 'And just when I was beginning to get used to the idea of a baby brother . . .'

Why did he need to involve Tally at this stage? Bel thought, irate, her sympathy for Louis evaporating as she heard the concern in her stepdaughter's voice. 'Listen, sweetheart. I'm sure it's a storm in a teacup. He'll ring tomorrow and say it was all a stupid mistake.'

'You think so? He seemed to think she was deadly serious.'

'Yes, but people often say things they don't mean in the heat of the moment. Trinny might just have been winding him up because they had a fight.' She didn't add that Louis had a tendency to overdramatize things, from a missing napkin to a slightly too thick sauce. On a good day, his passionate intensity was part of his charm and charisma. It was what had attracted Bel in the first place – that and his dark good looks – when they'd first met at one of her father's wine-tasting weekends.

Tally did not reply immediately. Then she said, 'You know what, Bel? It'd be just great not to have to worry about my bloody father for once.'

'Oh my God, Tally, I'm so with you on that,' Bel said, her reply heartfelt.

After she'd said goodbye, Bel found herself shaking her head from side to side as if to dislodge a wasp from her hair. *Not my problem*, she told herself firmly.

JJ's freestyle was splashy, but he was strong and quickly outstripped Bel as they ploughed across the bay and out to sea. Her stroke was much more efficient than his, but she wasn't yet fit enough even to think of keeping up. When they finally left the water and ran breathless up the sand, her body was trembling with the effort.

She plonked herself down on a rock by the steps and let out a shaky breath, drawing her towel around her shoulders and wishing she'd biked up to the Co-op and bought that bloody dry robe. It wasn't cold, but the sun was low in the sky, the heat of the day waning fast.

'Come to the van,' JJ said, also breathing heavily as he hovered over her. 'It's warm and I've got wine.'

'It's warm at mine, too, now,' she said, with a proud grin. 'But no wine.'

JJ considered this. 'OK, well, I could fetch a bottle. More room at yours.'

Bel took great pleasure in making JJ some cheese on toast in the stove. It was the first thing she'd ever cooked in the Rayburn. Scrubbing the simmer plate with the wire brush in the box by the door, she laid the rye bread slices directly on the heat and shut the lid. A few seconds later, she opened the lid and flipped the bread. Then she layered the toast with Mr Ajax's sliced tomatoes and Kern cheese and put them into the top oven for five minutes. It could have gone horribly wrong, but the toast was crisp, the gooey cheese melted and bubbling beautifully. She found two small tea plates in the cupboard and handed JJ his snack as he perched on the counter top, his long, bare legs swinging, while she curled up in the orange chair.

While she'd been changing into dry clothes and preparing the snack, Bel had been in a state of tingling anticipation. On the walk up to the cottage JJ, having collected a bottle of red from his van, had put his arm around her shoulders and pulled her to his side, asking, 'Would you like another kiss tonight?' It was, she thought, the same direct tone he might use were he offering her, for instance, a lift to the station.

Tickled, she'd replied in the spirit of the question. 'I'm quite old.'

He raised an eyebrow. 'Definitely not relevant. And not answering my question.'

'OK. Well, yes, then. I would like that.'

Then they'd kept walking and had not mentioned it again.

But now, meal dispatched and half the bottle of wine consumed, the room snug and cosy, intimate from the stove's glow and lack of much other lighting, JJ jumped down from the counter top and came over to where Bel sat.

'Scoosh over,' he said, and squashed his tall frame alongside hers, putting his arm around her and easing her legs over his thighs. Bel's heart fluttered at his closeness but he made no attempt to kiss her.

'Do you have family?' she asked, to defuse the yammering his warm salty maleness had set off through her body.

'Sure. My parents live near Limoges in a large, crumbly house which leaks everywhere. Their hopeless retirement project, but they love it – at least, Dad does.'

She laughed. 'So you don't see them much?'

'Nah. We chat on FaceTime, but they don't approve of my lifestyle. Dad's always making fifties-style comments along the lines of "Why don't you cut your hair and get a proper job?"'

'Better than calling you a bitch, I suppose,' she said drily.

There was a moment's silence before JJ turned and laid his palm to her cheek, gazing at her. 'That was really rough on you.'

'I'm fine,' she said softly.

He stared at her for another long second. 'OK, so this is the kissing bit.'

She felt a bubble of laughter rise in her chest, quickly quashed by his lips reaching down to meet hers. His kisses were soft, lazy almost, but effective: they stirred up a desire long missing from her world. *Why not?* she asked herself, as she felt his hand snake up beneath her sweatshirt and find her bare breast.

'Very nice,' JJ declared, leaning back a little and staring at her approvingly after they'd been kissing for a while. Bel's body was on fire, she was hot and trembling in his arms. 'Take it to the next level?'

She gulped and nodded.

'Not sure this chair is ideal,' he added, with a grin. Then, tracing a finger across her brow, he said, 'You've got the most spectacular eyes, you know.'

Embarrassed, she laughed. 'You, too.' His dark ones, she could see, were currently sparked up and glinting with desire. *Oh my God, oh my God. Am I really going to have sex with this beautiful man?*

She didn't have time to think before JJ was lifting her out of the chair and pushing her gently in the direction of the stairs.

Much later, Bel let out a wobbly sigh and lay back on the pillow. They both had stupid grins on their faces.

JJ was nodding slowly, although she hadn't spoken. 'That was pretty amazing.'

'I'm afraid I'm a bit rusty,' she said.

'I don't do this often either. But who's counting?'

Who indeed? she thought, suddenly a bit overwhelmed to find herself in this bed in her very own cottage with a gorgeous surfer.

They lay for a moment in contented silence.

'Do you want me to push off?' He brushed his shiny black hair off his face.

'You're welcome to stay, if you like.' She was too sleepy and too satiated to make that sort of decision. And it looked as if JJ was too.

'At least I won't annoy you by leaving the loo seat up,' he joked, as they settled down to sleep. 'Must do something about that, by the way,' she heard him mutter, then wasn't conscious of anything else until the birds woke her in the morning.

Patsy smiled knowingly at Bel when she bumped into her coming back from coffee and an egg bap with JJ at Martine's. Micky had just picked him up – on the way to a day's gardening for a couple in nearby Goldsithney – but her neighbour must have seen them coming out of the cottage together earlier, noted JJ's arm around Bel's shoulders as they crossed the lane.

Bel smiled back. She might have blushed, but she was feeling so good today. And not embarrassed, she was surprised to find.

'Cuppa?' Patsy offered.

When they were seated on the wooden bench, each with a cup of green tea, in her neighbour's tiny front garden, surrounded by pots planted with ivy and ferns, pretty blue forget-me-nots, purple sage and yellow anemone, Patsy said, 'He's OK, JJ. Not the most focused of men, but he's got a good heart. And he's learning stuff about his spirit he needed to know, which is important.'

Bel nodded, although she wasn't quite sure what she meant. Patsy had a way of talking that assumed some mystical, arcane knowledge to which no one else was privy.

'But don't go losing your heart to him,' she added. Her tone was light, but the warning clear.

'It's not like that,' Bel said, not really sure what it was like. Fancying JJ had taken her by surprise. Sex with him was warm, sensuous and unpressured . . . fun. But she was not about to start worrying about where the relationship – if you could even call it that – was going. The last thing she needed right now was the complication of another man in her life. She had a quick thought about Louis. *I hope he's sorted things out*, she thought, *for Tally's sake, at least.*

20

It came as a surprise to Bel as she woke on Tuesday morning to realize that it was only a week since she'd left London. It seemed like a couple of lifetimes. So much had happened. Not just mentally, but physically too, her body coming alive with the sunshine and fresh sea air, the swimming and paddleboarding . . . sex with JJ. But what particularly astonished her was the number of people she'd met in that short space of time and come to value already as friends, albeit recent ones. Her brain felt so crowded with these novel experiences that she barely had time to consider her old life. Even her dad – who still refused to speak to her – had slipped a little in her consciousness. She still rang him every day, left messages, only to receive a deafening silence in return.

Today, she jumped out of bed with eager anticipation. She had agreed a sum with Micky the previous day – good use, she decided, of her precious and ever-dwindling stash of cash – for him and JJ to help her remove the putrid piles of newspaper. They were coming at eight, Patsy having kindly offered Dora to transport the rubbish.

It was a filthy job. The three of them humped the paper to the van in wads, shaking off the spiders, beetles and mouse droppings that fell out as soon as the stack was broken up. The paper, once the air got at it, properly stank and Bel found herself running to the van holding her breath, her burden damp and foetid in her arms.

They worked in silence, only stopping to high five once the last armload had been squeezed in, the door pulled shut. Then they took off to the dump where they carried out the process in reverse. It took hours and they were all exhausted by the time the task was finished. Bel was relieved to find she did not feel awkward being around JJ. The other night seemed to have done nothing to dent their easy friendship. And if Micky knew what had been going on, he gave no sign.

When Bel entered the cottage later, it was already transformed. She spent the rest of the day scrubbing the newly exposed stone floor and walls, throwing open the windows, polishing the glass. By supper time, the house – suddenly a lot bigger without the rubbish – smelt primarily of pine from the spray cleaner and woodsmoke. Bel collapsed into her orange chair and breathed it in with the utmost relief.

Paint next, she thought, as she closed her eyes, *and kitchen stuff*. Even just making toast for JJ the other night had reminded her of how important her kitchen was to her. Tomorrow she would take the bus and see what she could find in Penzance's pound stores. She might even price up kitchen cabinets, although the cost was no doubt prohibitive right now. *Open shelves?* She liked the idea. Her phone went off on the counter and she opened her eyes. Zid had jumped in at the window and was sniffing about, but he scuttled under the chair at the loud ringtone.

'Evening, Bella,' her father said, his tone genial.

'Dad!' She found she was incredibly relieved to hear his voice at last.

'How's the hovel?' He chuckled quietly.

He's had one too many and forgotten he shouldn't be speaking to me, she thought, smiling to herself. 'It's good, thanks. Not quite so hovel-like now. I've chucked a lot of stuff away.' She paused. 'So how are you?'

'I'm just as bloody bored and lonely as when you left,' he said merrily.

'Sorry to hear that.' Bel didn't know what to say, where to start in telling him about her new life. She wasn't sure her father would want to hear it, anyway.

'Are you coming home, then?' His voice lost some of its humour and Bel felt a small chill pass through her.

'Not yet,' she said brightly, holding her breath. Quickly changing the subject, she asked, 'So have you seen Reg?' As she spoke, she wondered what she normally talked about with her father. He never seemed interested in her life unless it directly impacted his own. But now that he wasn't asking her what was for supper or carping about something she'd done, or bought, or forgotten to do or buy and there were no television programmes or neighbours or Louis to trash, it was hard to know what to say. She certainly wasn't going to tell him about her job at the farm shop.

There was a loud snort. 'Lazy old bugger finally got off his arse and came over on Friday.'

'Is he better, then?' Bel asked, knowing Reg suffered from quite serious chest problems.

'Oh, I don't know. The fella coughs all the time, but

then he always did. And he's still banging on about the virus, still wearing a mask in the street.'

'Not everyone's as brazen as you, Dad,' she said teasingly.

Which made Dennis laugh. '"Brazen" is it? You sound in a good mood, girl. Sun, sea and sex improving your spirits, eh?'

Bel twitched at her father's sixth sense. Was her night with JJ apparent in her voice? Then she realized it was just his paranoia that she'd shacked up with some undesirable in Cornwall. *Not so far off the mark*, she thought, with a smile. *He definitely wouldn't approve of JJ.*

Before she had a chance to deny it, her father, capricious to the last, was saying, 'I've had a thought, sweetheart. If the mountain won't come to Muhammad . . . I'll visit you. See what all the fuss is about.'

Bel held her breath. 'It's a long way, Dad,' she stammered. *Please, no.*

'About time I took the Jag out for a spin,' he went on, as if she hadn't spoken. 'We haven't been anywhere since before the plague.' Her father drove a much-loved XKR coupé in racing green, which he'd owned for at least fifteen years.

'It's a good six hours, and that doesn't include stops.' But as Bel spoke, she knew her words were falling on deaf ears. When her father made up his mind, it was impossible to shift him.

'Are you trying to put me off, girl?' her father asked, mild suspicion back in his voice.

She forced a laugh. 'Of course not. I'm just thinking it'd be good to wait, come in a month or so, when I've got the cottage a bit more sorted and I know the area better.' *Maybe he'll have forgotten about the trip by then*, she thought optimistically.

'Don't fret about the state of the hovel. I certainly won't be staying there. You can find me a billet close by . . . maybe the pub. I remember liking the landlord, although the fella's probably long dead. Is it still pink?'

'Yes, still pink,' she muttered distractedly. Bel had not yet ventured into the Queen Bess, the three-hundred-year-old coaching inn that dominated the entrance to the village. Logan, the current landlord, was apparently a good friend of Patsy's – along with the rest of the village, it seemed.

'Right, well, sounds like a plan, girl. Something to look forward to,' her father went on. 'I'm so sick of these four walls.'

Bel heard her father give a small sigh, then a loud sniff. 'Dad?'

'I do miss you, Bella,' he said, his voice tremulous.

'I'll talk to Logan at the pub and find out when he's got a room free,' she said, sensing his mood was sinking. 'We can go swimming and eat pasties, do some exploring. It'll be fun.' She found herself gabbling brightly, suggesting a plan that would bring about the result she most dreaded: her father back in her life. But she couldn't stop herself. He sounded so sad. 'I'll see you very soon, Dad.'

After they'd said goodbye and Bel was sitting in panicked silence, she felt a softness against her bare leg that made her jump. Zid was weaving in and out of her calves as she sat, bare feet cold on the stone. She patted her lap and he leaped onto it, allowing her to stroke his back, behind his ears, under his chin, almost as if he knew she was upset. His warmth and undemanding presence comforted her.

Jaz was sitting on the wall between Bel's house and Patsy's when Bel came up from the beach after an evening swim.

'Could I come in for a minute?' the teenager asked shyly.

Bel smiled and ushered her inside. 'Cuppa? I could do with one myself – the sea's still pretty nippy.'

Jaz, hovering near the door, grinned. 'I don't go in till the temperature goes above sixteen.' She waved her phone at Bel. 'I've got the app. I can show you.'

Bel laughed. 'Thanks, but I think I'll pass. I'd never get in if I knew how bloody freezing it was.'

Jaz was silent as Bel put the kettle with the wonky lid onto the hob and waited for it to boil.

'I often used to drop in here when I got home from school.' The girl smiled at the memory. 'Lenny would always be sitting in that stinky old chair of his with the TV blaring. But he kept this plate ready with biscuits or cake – covered with a page from a magazine – especially for me.'

It was a touching image that made Bel's heart constrict. 'I'm afraid I haven't got around to cake yet.' She remembered when Tally had been that age, how ravenous she'd always been on her visits.

'Oh, no worries. Nonna's made me terrified of sugar,

these days. It was just so sweet of him, though. I couldn't refuse.'

Bel handed Jaz her tea in one of the petrol-station mugs Lenny had left, with the faded yellow and green BP shield on the side. 'So how was school?'

Jaz shrugged. 'Pretty crap.' Then her face lit up. 'But this is my last term. I'm leaving after GCSEs. Can't wait.'

'Leaving school?' Bel was aghast. She seemed so young. 'I'm sixteen in August.'

'Heavens . . . What will you do?' She'd tried to keep the disapproval out of her voice.

'Well, that's what I needed to talk to you about. I want to be a chef.' The girl glanced at Bel nervously, as if to gauge her reaction. 'You said your partner was one, and I wondered . . . Do you have any advice?'

Bel thought for a minute, a bit blindsided by the question. 'Umm, I don't think Louis had any proper training. He just worked his way up in kitchens, got experience that way. But it was really hard, Jaz, I do know that.'

The girl seemed undeterred. 'I'm going to open my own organic café when I'm older. I'll serve food like Nonna's and have my own veg patch.'

Bel smiled. 'That sounds great.'

'Could you ask him for me? I mean, if you're in touch with him still.' She looked so awkward and so young that Bel wanted to hug her. But the question forced her thoughts to return, unwillingly, to Louis and his baby. Or *not* his baby.

Was this upheaval in my life, in his, in Tally's, in Dad's, all for nothing? She was surprised to find that although the thought was frustrating, it did not disturb her to the extent it might have done, even a few weeks back. Because if Louis hadn't gone chasing a phantom, Bel would not have been in Cornwall right now. And that, she realized, would have been a terrible shame.

She brought her focus back to the girl in front of her. 'Listen, I'll find out what I can,' she promised cautiously.

21

'That's where I used to have the office for my cleaning business,' Patsy said, the following day, pointing to a small industrial estate on the outskirts of Penzance as she drove Dora towards the town on her way to meet a friend. She'd passed Bel standing at the bus stop and offered her a lift. 'The girls and I did holiday lets. Went in like the cavalry on change-over day and whipped the places into shape for the next lot.'

'Do you miss it?' Bel asked.

'Nah. I'm glad I packed it in before Covid. One of my old team told me it's a nightmare, these days. They're chronically short-staffed and incredibly busy ... Seems the season's been extended too, to accommodate the older lot who still aren't travelling abroad.'

They drove in silence for a while.

'Jaz told me she's leaving school,' Bel said.

'Over my dead body,' Patsy declared stoutly.

'Can you stop her?'

Her friend sighed. 'Probably not. If that useless daughter of mine would get her head out of her backside, take some responsibility for a change ... Not that Jaz really sees her these days. Doesn't want to.'

'Where exactly is her mother?' It was a question Bel had often been on the verge of asking Patsy, but something had always stopped her.

'Ruby? In St Austell, I imagine, shooting up as much smack as she can lay her hands on.' Her normally steady voice was shrill and bitter, echoing harshly under the van roof.

'Oh my God. I'm so sorry, Patsy. I didn't know.'

'Yeah, well.'

They were both silent.

'It used to torment me. All the various attempts at rehab, the hope. But I've had to learn to step away or go nuts. Nothing I can do.' She coughed. 'Except try to make sure the same thing doesn't happen to Jazzy.'

'That's not nothing, Patsy,' Bel said quietly.

Patsy shot her a sad smile. 'We might live in a magic place, Bel, but we're just as screwed up and crazy as everyone else on the planet. Remember, it's never all icing and no cake.'

Bel noted what sounded like a warning bell. She glanced at her neighbour, but Patsy had her eyes firmly on the road. *Is she just talking about her daughter?* she wondered. Or had she intuited the degree to which Bel was viewing her new life through impossibly rose-tinted spectacles?

She felt her pulse quicken. Now that her father was threatening to intrude, her promising future no longer seemed limitless. She had the sense she was running against the clock, needing to make herself and her life in Cornwall bulletproof before the onslaught of Dennis Carnegie.

Bel took the white toilet seat out of its box later and scrutinized the instructions. She eyed the plastic bag of fixing screws warily. *How hard can it be?* she asked herself, carefully spilling the contents into the plugged basin so she wouldn't lose anything. At first glance, the instructions were baffling, but her mother had always told her that if you read anything often enough, you'd end up understanding. And in this case her mum was proved right.

With Patsy's borrowed screwdriver, she managed, within a very short time, to secure the seat to the bowl. Standing up and admiring her handiwork – raising and lowering the lid, like a child with a new toy – she had the first pee since she'd arrived without freezing her butt off on the porcelain. *Solid as a rock.* She was ridiculously proud of herself and cheered out loud. *Shower curtain next.* The new one was white with a blue mosaic pattern. 'Mildew resistant', the sticker on the wrapper declared.

Her DIY efforts were interrupted by an incoming text buzzing in her back pocket. *Fancy a little light sex on the beach tonight? It's going to be hot x*, JJ was asking.

Bel laughed. *Does he mean the sex or the weather?* Although it was true that the temperature was set to rise to twenty-five degrees over the weekend.

The Zumba class – women pounding the sand in the setting sun to what sounded, to Bel, like salsa music – had packed up and gone, the dog-walkers and their pets had pottered back for their supper, the girl kayaking across the bay had lugged her craft up the hard. It was getting dark and Bel and JJ had the beach to themselves as the tide slowly crept up over the sand.

'We've got an hour and a half,' JJ said, consulting his tide app.

He'd lit the wood in the firepit he'd carried down from the van and laid a metal grille on top. A row of chipolatas was currently wriggling and hissing above the flames. Bel had brought beer – both had an open bottle wedged into the sand beside them – and a punnet of strawberries. She was sitting proudly on her newly purchased acid-green dry robe – the only colour on sale at the Co-op, but she rather liked it.

It was still hot, even with a gentle sea breeze, and Bel was revelling in the moment. If she'd been in love with JJ, it would have been incredibly romantic. As it was, it was just relaxed and fun, the prospect of perhaps making love in the open air on the cool sand giving her a pleasurable tingle in her groin.

JJ sliced open a fresh white bap and forked a pile of charred sausages inside, handing it to Bel with the ketchup bottle. The bun was delectable and they munched quietly in the glow of the logs, dark waves creeping ever closer, the smoke from the fire occasionally blowing in their faces and making their eyes water.

'Do you speak Cantonese or Mandarin?' she asked, remembering his heritage as she gazed at his profile in the fading light.

'Neither. I can only say things like "bedtime", "eat up", "stop fighting".' He grinned and said something in Chinese. 'That's "clean your teeth". Mum spoke Cantonese, but Dad never bothered to learn. It was only when we were young that Mum talked to me and my brother in her own language. Shame, really.'

'Where's your brother now?'

She saw JJ swallow hard. After a moment's hesitation he said softly, 'Dead.' Then he took a deep breath. 'He hit a deer with his Suzuki doing the North Coast 500 – that's a scenic route round the north coast of Scotland – three years ago, smashed into a tree. Never made it to hospital alive.' His voice was barely above a whisper.

Bel gasped. 'Oh my God. That's awful, JJ. I'm so sorry.'

He gave a shuddering sigh. 'It's why I'm here. Life may be short, Bel. We have to enjoy every single second.'

They were silent for a long time, leaning back on their elbows, knees bent, toes mining the sand, gazing into the fire. Then JJ sat up. 'OK, try this.'

She watched as he drew up his legs and lifted each bare, sandy foot onto the opposite thigh, wriggling on the towel to settle himself. Then he tucked his index fingers into his thumbs to form a circle, other fingers outstretched, palms face up, backs of his hands resting on his knees. '*Chin mudra*,' he said. 'Helps you connect to your higher self.'

He waited while she tried to copy him. She had spent many hours cross-legged following her skiing accident because the physio said it opened her damaged hip, but her feet refused point blank to sit on her thighs.

'Now, back straight and breathe in deeply,' JJ instructed, ignoring her failed efforts to achieve the lotus position. 'Then make a tiny constriction in your throat for the long out-breath . . . Like this.' He demonstrated. 'It's called "ocean breath". Close your eyes and try it.'

216

Bel breathed. The fire was warm on her closed eyes, her body lazy and unwound by the beer and food. Everything faded except the sound of the sea and her breath, in and out.

The next thing she was aware of was JJ's hot breath against her cheek as he dropped a flutter of soft kisses around her mouth. Then he was pushing her gently back onto the sand.

Bel woke on Monday morning with her belly twitching with nerves about her first day at the farm shop. She'd bought Patsy a mega-pack of washing powder and taken up her offer to use her machine over the weekend, so at least her jeans and sweatshirt were clean.

She'd spent Sunday afternoon washing the new pans and oven trays, the bowls and bundle of wooden spoons, spatulas and knives she'd bought on her Penzance shopping trip. It made such a difference, having the wherewithal to cook, to see the array of shiny new equipment in the tiny, scarred kitchen, even if she hadn't yet got around to making a proper meal for herself, lured nightly, as she was, to another of Patsy's delicious spreads.

At least now she would be able to return the favour. She was already hatching plans to cook for Patsy, Jaz and the guys maybe the following weekend – even if they had to eat it in Patsy's kitchen because of the lack of space and chairs in the cottage.

It was bright and fresh, the wind off the sea strong, as Bel biked up the hill and across the main road, arriving at the farm shop twenty minutes early. She wanted to get the hang of some of the prices on the fruit and vegetables, poke around to see what was on the shelves before the first customers arrived.

Mr Ajax was in the back, hugging a mug of something to his chest. He looked pinched and tired, she thought, and just grunted in response to her greeting. He pointed silently to the flowered plastic tray next to the kettle on which stood an array of mugs – one of which held teaspoons sticking upright – a catering tin of instant coffee, a round canister Bel assumed must contain teabags and a red and white striped Cornish-ware sugar bowl. 'Milk's in the fridge,' he said.

Bel was determined to be friendly. 'This looks professional in here,' she said, waving her hand around the kitchen, with its shiny stainless-steel counters. 'Do you ever cook stuff for the shop?'

'Nope,' he snapped, dumping his mug in the sink with unnecessary force. He hustled her out of the room. 'I'll show you how the till works. We prefer cash – unlike the rest of the world – but since the bloody virus, everyone wants to use their card.'

Bel sat on the ladderback chair – padded with a threadbare blue cushion tied to the base – at the wooden table, nervously surveying her new domain. Mr Ajax had wandered off outside with a broom and she could hear the clanking of crates. She checked the cork board above the till. It was pinned with the usual cards advertising items for sale, yoga classes, babysitters, cleaners, ukulele lessons and times of church services. She didn't have time to read many before a middle-aged woman in leggings and a fleece walked in.

'Hi,' the woman said. 'Lena gone back to Poland, has she?'

'Um, I think so.'

She pulled a face. ''Bout time. She was ginormous. Thought she'd drop the baby right here on this dodgy floor.' Lowering her voice, she grinned as she whispered, 'Mr A would probably have stepped right over it.'

Bel, nervous that her boss would hear, didn't know what to say, so she gave what she hoped was an understanding grin in response. The woman complained about the wind and the people from the caravan park blocking her lane as she paid for a white farmhouse loaf, a pot of chicken paste and a lettuce. She gave Bel cash – which was stored in the locked drawer of the table, the key around Bel's neck. *Very nineteenth century*, she thought, as the woman creaked away across the boards.

The shop was never full but there was a steady stream of customers throughout the morning. Bel got flustered on many occasions, when she couldn't find the price of something or the card machine wouldn't work and she had to shout for Mr Ajax. But on the whole the customers were chatty and tolerant, many of them on holiday and in a relaxed mood.

Just after ten, exhausted from the unfamiliarity, she nipped into the back to get a drink. While she made herself a cup of instant coffee, she kept darting out to make sure no one was waiting. Mr Ajax was busy unpacking crates of vegetables and cardboard boxes of produce, but he didn't ask for her help. Holding her cup before her, she hurried from the kitchen, and bumped smack into Harris, the wildlife artist, splashing dots of coffee over her T-shirt.

'Oh, Christ, I'm so sorry,' he said, his handsome face a picture of distress.

'It's OK. My fault,' she said, through clenched teeth – it hardly looked professional, having coffee down her front on her first day.

'Quick, rinse it off,' Harris was saying, taking her cup from her. 'It'll stain.'

He came into the kitchen with her. 'I'm so sorry.'

She smiled. 'Honestly, it wasn't your fault. I was rushing – I'm a bag of nerves today.'

He watched as she scrubbed the marks vigorously with a wet dishcloth. 'Can I do anything?'

She shook her head. 'I hope no one's waiting.' She cast an anxious glance towards the till.

'You'll hear them creaking across the floorboards from a mile off.'

When he'd made his own tea and was seated on his usual chair, long legs crossed, Harris said, 'Don't let Ron bully you.' Mr Ajax had just left in his van to pick something up, but the remark still made Bel twitch, as if the walls had ears.

'He's not really a bully, just a bit crabby. He's obviously not a happy man.'

Harris shook his head. 'Never been the same since his wife legged it with Charlie, the beekeeper with the smouldering eyes. They live over in Wadebridge.'

'How incredibly humiliating,' Bel said, wincing at the unconscious intensity in her words as she noticed Harris's eyes widen. 'Poor man.'

'She was lovely, Elowen. Baked bread, cakes, quiches, that sort of thing. Now he's given up stocking everything except the bread, which he outsources.'

'Oops. I asked him this morning if he ever cooked, because the kitchen looks professional standard. I was only being friendly.'

Harris laughed, his normally serious face lighting up. 'Bit your head off, did he?'

Bel raised her eyebrows in agreement and turned to deal with another basket of shopping. She was beginning to feel almost at ease and was reminded she'd been on the front line with customers, bills and tills – albeit computerized – for years at 83.

When they had the shop to themselves again for a minute, she said, 'I hear you're a very talented artist.'

He bowed his head. 'It's nice people say so.'

'Do you have a website?'

'I have, but it's rubbish. You must come up and see my etchings sometime,' he intoned mock-suggestively, then grinned.

Bel couldn't help laughing. But Mr Ajax interrupted her reply. 'Shouldn't you get on with that pretend work of yours, Harris, stop distracting my staff?' he queried, not unpleasantly. It was clear he liked the artist. 'Here, what's-your-name, can you unpack that box of olive oil? I'll show you how the tagging-gun works.'

By the time midday came round, Bel felt as if she'd been in the shop for a year. She cycled tiredly home and flopped down on the bed for a nap, only to be woken half an hour later by Zid's whiskers tickling her cheek. When she went downstairs, she saw there were three missed calls from Tally and one text, which read: *Where are you? Pls call me asap. It's Dad. xxx*

Bel's heart somersaulted. Tally's voice messages sounded increasingly frantic. *Is he ill . . . dead?* The painful thought flashed through her mind as she pressed on her step-daughter's number.

'Oh, Bel, thank goodness,' Tally sounded breathless. 'Hang on a sec while I get rid of this email . . .'

Then she was back. 'You – will – never – guess – what,' she began, emphasizing each word. 'That father of mine has done a runner, *again*.'

'Wait! He's walked out on his two-week-old baby?' Bel was aghast.

'*Not* his baby, apparently. He was actually in the van on the autoroute when he called.'

'What on earth . . . ?'

'"Not mine", he kept repeating. He was so het up, Bel, not making any sense at all. He rambled on about Valérie, Trinny's mum, being a Nazi or something. Said she never liked him from the moment he suggested she use red onions instead of brown in her onion soup.'

Bel couldn't suppress a smile. It was almost comical, the notion of the Frenchwoman and Louis going head to head over something as trivial as soup. *Not trivial to Louis.*

Then the reality of the situation hit her. 'What's he going to do?' She remembered his ludicrously pompous letter about his new life with Trinny and nearly felt sorry for him again.

'He's coming home.'

'Home? But he hasn't got a home. It's a vape shop now.' Tally sighed. 'Yeah . . .'

'He's not going to land on you, is he? You can't let him do that, Tally.' She took a breath, tried to calm herself. She was infuriated. 'I know he's your dad, and I know you love him, sweetheart, but this mess is all his doing. You can't disrupt your life because he's being such a useless flake.'

'What can I do, though, if he asks to stay?'

'He can sleep in the van. He's done it before. Let him work it out. He's got mates.' She did a quick run-through of his friends. 'Maybe Jason'll put him up on the sofa.' She was clutching at straws, unable to see the uncompromising Tina – Jason's wife – going along with that. The pair ran a café near 83 and, unlike Louis with his duck liver parfait, Essex lamb sweetbreads and walnut bread in an area better suited to fusion, modern European, Caribbean, had made a real success of not moving with the times. You wouldn't find ricotta hotcakes or chorizo and cavolo nero hash at Jason's, but the bacon sandwiches, with thick, heavily buttered and unashamedly white sliced bread, washed down with a proper cup of builder's, brought daily queues.

'It's like I'm the adult, these days,' Tally said, in a small voice, 'and Dad's the gap-year kid having to be rescued from dodgy foreign adventures.'

'You don't have to rescue him. He's a grown man.'

Her stepdaughter was silent and Bel could understand the pressure she was feeling. 'He's broke, too.'

'Oh, God, of course he is,' Bel said bitterly. She tried not to criticize Louis to his daughter, but it was getting increasingly difficult.

'I can't see him destitute, Bel.'

Bel groaned. 'That won't happen. He's a chef. He'll have job offers coming out of his ears.' From the ensuing silence, she could tell Tally was not convinced. 'Listen, let's just wait. He might have a plan, once he calms down and begins to think rationally. He's very resourceful, your dad.' She wasn't sure this was true, but she wanted to reassure Tally somehow.

'OK,' Tally said doubtfully. 'I suppose I could lend him a bit, just to tide him over.'

You won't see it again, Bel almost said, but managed to hold her tongue. 'Be very careful, sweetheart. That's your hard-earned cash.' She hoped Louis would have more self-respect than to sponge off his young daughter, remembering with shame the much more substantial sum she and Louis had borrowed from her own father – which she intended to keep chipping away at, even on her current low wage.

After they'd said goodbye, Bel leaned back in her chair, aware of the same vague feeling of threat that she'd experienced when her father had said he was planning a visit. She felt a prickle run up her spine. *Thank God he doesn't know I'm in Cornwall.*

22

'Jaz has important exams for the next couple of weeks,' Patsy told Bel, as they sat on Patsy's bench with a cup of tea the following Thursday, sixteen days since Bel had arrived in Cornwall. 'So I won't be doing any suppers for a bit. It's too distracting.'

'You've done way more than your fair share, Patsy. Let me cook for you. It's my turn and I'd love that. I wouldn't stay, just deliver the food, and you two can eat in peace.' Bel had finally begun to christen her new kitchen equipment with some basic cooking, which also tested the stove's capabilities. The shabby, falling-apart kitchen depressed her, though: it seemed impossible to make it clean.

Patsy smiled. 'That's very kind. But save it till she's finished and we can all celebrate together.' She sighed. 'Not that I think much will come of the exams. She's done the work, but her heart's not in it.'

'She might surprise you,' Bel said.

'Yeah, she might. But she hates school, and she's not going to change her mind about staying.' She took a sip of tea. 'The kids there are so pig-ignorant. Her father – long gone now – is from Colombia, so the witless fools call her "Gyppo", tease her he's a cocaine smuggler. They're merciless about her mum, too, of course.'

Bel shook her head. 'Poor Jaz.'

They lapsed into a thoughtful silence, enjoying the warm afternoon sun.

Bel had just finished at the farm shop for the week and was feeling relaxed, aware of a small sense of achievement. There had been no more news of Louis to wind her up. According to a very relieved Tally, he was staying with an old friend in Portsmouth – Louis had mates all around the country, people he'd bonded with in kitchens over the years. This particular one he'd bumped into coming over on the Le Havre ferry.

She was also looking forward to having a break from Mr Ajax. He was the sort of boss who only criticized, never praised. It was wearing, trying to keep ahead of him. She had come to rely on Harris's almost daily presence in the shop – his injection of humour and teasing seemed temporarily to improve her boss's mood.

But, aside from the money, there was an advantage to working there that outweighed her problems with Mr Ajax. Every evening he left out a green plastic crate in the kitchen with all the stock past its sell-by date that he couldn't pass on to his customers. It was mostly fruit and veg, bread, some dairy, but still perfectly edible. Bel hadn't had to buy food all week.

'I'm thinking of getting back to baking,' she told Patsy now. 'I used to be good. Not sure I've got a sufficient handle on the Rayburn yet, but it's worth a go.'

And if that 'go' succeeds . . . Bel thought, hardly daring to focus on the germ of an idea that the empty kitchen at the farm shop and Harris's tale of Mrs Ajax's abrupt departure with the beekeeper had given her, if things went according to plan.

Sitting in the sunshine with her friend, she recalled the pleasure of baking: the dough, cool, slippery and elastic under her fingers as she kneaded. Her ridiculous excitement when she lifted the cloth to find the pillowed puff, risen and ready for the next stage. The yeasty tang filling the warm room as the bread baked, the hollow tap that told her it was cooked. Then good butter melting on a fresh slice . . . the crisp, crusty bite on her tongue. Even contemplating it made her mouth water.

Patsy laughed. 'That old thing! I went electric years ago. Got bored having to tend it like a baby all the time.'

'It is a bit like a baby,' Bel admitted. The stove had gone out on her a few times because she'd put in too much wood or not enough or not the right sort at the right time or the wind was in the wrong direction – she never quite knew what she'd done wrong. But she didn't mind the hassle. It was integral to her romantic enjoyment of her little stone cottage. 'I should get the kitchen sorted first, I suppose. I don't want to ask the guys. They won't charge me enough and they've done so much for me already.'

The prospect was daunting. Lenny's scorched laminate counters and rickety, rotting wooden cupboards needed stripping out, and new shelves and worktops installed around the Rayburn and sink. She knew it would be costly – even if she did take advantage of Micky and JJ's mates' rates. Money would have to be spent on the bathroom, too, with the mouldy grout and broken shower attachment, poor water pressure, curling lino tiles. Getting the place vaguely habitable had been her primary goal. But now she realized she wanted more. She longed to transform the place into somewhere really lovely . . . a home.

'Talk to Logan at the pub,' Patsy was saying. 'His brother does kitchens. Can't remember his name. Something stirring and Scottish. Angus, Stuart . . . *Hamish*, that's it.'

'Won't he be expensive?'

'No idea. Apart from the cooker, my kitchen hasn't been touched since the Methodists built it in 1797.'

Bel laughed. 'Well, they did a bloody good job. It's gorgeous.'

Both women watched as the plump figure of Rhian Parry hurried down the lane. Patsy sat up straighter and smiled in welcome.

'Have either of you seen Zid? He hasn't been home all day and I'm getting worried,' Rhian said, as she approached, slightly breathless. 'I mean, I know he's a bit of a tart and spends more time in your houses than he does with me, but he's always home for his tea.'

Bel shook her head. 'I'll go and check. I might have shut him in by mistake this morning.' As she walked the short distance to her house, she sensed a sudden lift around her heart. This was a proper life she was living. She loved caring about the cat and Jaz's exams, witnessing the love on Patsy's face for the vicar. She looked forward to every day now. *I'll make a big orange, beetroot and courgette salad for supper, bake Yarg croutons with that stale bread*, she thought. She'd drop some in to Patsy, despite her neighbour insisting she was sorted. An evening swim was also on the cards. She might even meet up with JJ . . . When she opened the cottage door, she spied Zid curled up in the chair, fast asleep.

It was more than a week later that Hamish was standing in her small living room late on Saturday afternoon, sucking his teeth. He was a broad, sandy-haired Scotsman with a statement orange beard – which seemed to arrive before he did – and a winning smile. He was very like his brother. Patsy had introduced Bel to Logan Spieth, the Queen Bess's landlord, when they'd dropped in at the pub for a drink one evening. She kept meaning to drop in again, find out if Logan had a room free for her father, but so far, to her shame, had failed to do so.

'It's not a big job,' he said, his accent soft from the Borders, 'but I'm afraid I'll not get around to it till September, soonest.' He must have seen her face fall. 'I'd like to help, seeing as you're a pal of Logie's Patsy, but it's crazy out there. Everyone wants to renovate. I'm still having a tricky time getting timber.'

Bel thanked him. 'I'm not going to wait till September,' she muttered resolutely, as she watched Hamish, face bowed to his phone screen, amble slowly past the window and onto the lane, where his truck was parked. She sighed, turning back to the kitchen, glaring at the offending units. Then, without thinking, in a rush of uncharacteristic irritation and fervour, she yanked hard on one of the cupboard doors. To her great surprise, it came away in her hand, the wood around the hinges clearly rotten. She dropped it, as if it had bitten her, letting it thump to the stone floor.

Hmm, she thought, her body buzzing as she reached for

the other door. That proved more resistant, but it wasn't long before both were lying at her feet. Her blood was up now and she set about the cupboards themselves, first removing the few items she'd stored in them and piling them on the counter out of harm's way. It took a bit of leverage with the stout iron tool she raked the stove with before the flimsy plywood pulled away from the wall with a loud crack.

Bit by bit, Bel worked to tear away the crumbling units. She was red-faced and sweating in the hot June evening, using every ounce of strength, her muscles toned now, from almost a month of daily swims back and forth across the bay. After a while the room was full of choking dust, the floor covered with a pile of rubble.

'Whoa.' A voice stopped her in her tracks. JJ was hovering in the doorway, grinning. 'Was it something it said?'

She stood back, hands on hips, breathless, almost unable to believe what she saw. 'Oh, God,' she said, eyes wide as she surveyed her handiwork. 'What have I done?' The adrenalin was slowly draining away and she felt exhausted and not a little dismayed. 'I just couldn't wait.'

JJ's eyes were alight with amusement. 'Remind me not to upset you.'

'Hamish, Logan's kitchen-fitter brother, said it would be September,' she said, almost apologetically.

'You're taking charge. I like that,' he said. 'Although you could have asked us.'

Bel shook her head. 'I know, and thanks. But you've done so much for me and you won't charge the going rate. It's not fair on you.'

JJ's shrug implied that he didn't agree.

'What do I do now?' she asked, almost to herself.

JJ swept a considering glance over what had been the kitchen. 'Think about it in the morning. Micky and I are on the way to pick up a Chinese. Join us?' He laughed. 'You definitely can't eat here.'

Bel, wiping her dusty face with the back of her hand, nodded. 'Great.'

The three of them sat in folding chairs round the firepit on the headland, passing plastic boxes between them containing spring rolls, chicken in black bean sauce, crispy shredded beef, salt and pepper king prawns, rice and Singapore noodles. It was exactly what Bel needed. She was starving after her exertions.

'You should have seen her,' JJ was telling Micky. 'Magnificent. Like Superwoman.'

'Mad woman, more like,' Bel retorted, although now she realized she was quite proud of what she'd done. It felt cathartic. 'I'll borrow Dora tomorrow, if Patsy's OK with that, clear away the rubble.'

Micky raised an eyebrow, obviously amused. 'With your current superpower, I expect you can manage that single-handed. But if you'd like some help?'

'I can do it, but thanks for the offer.' Bel grinned around a mouthful of noodles. 'Then all I need is shelves, and a worktop that isn't covered with scorch marks.' She munched in silence for a moment. 'I'd love to do it myself.' It was a novel idea and she wasn't sure she meant it.

JJ looked sceptical. 'You've done DIY before?'

She laughed. 'No.'

'O-*kaay*,' Micky said. 'Well, if you want to do it your-self, I'm up for showing you.'

They sat around the fire long into the warm summer night, Micky, a good raconteur, entertaining them with stories of his surfing exploits, his previous life as a nerd working for a social-media site, and the adventures he was planning in the future. 'I'm thinking of doing Peru this winter.' He interrupted a comfortable silence, during which the three of them had been gazing sleepily into the fire. 'Met a guy last week who said Máncora is the place. Has a perfect left-hand reef break with an epic ride, he says. Their summer's the time to go: October to March.'

'Will you come back here?' Bel asked. JJ had gone very quiet as his friend rambled on.

Micky dropped the corners of his mouth, glancing at JJ, whose head was bowed in the firelight, dark hair cur-taining his face. 'JJ is good with just hanging, getting to grips with all that spiritual shit Patsy feeds him. But I'm getting bored. You can't live in a van for ever.'

Bel saw JJ's eyes spark with irritation but he said nothing.

'Sorry, mate. Not "shit", that's the wrong word.' Micky gave his friend a beseeching smile. 'Come with? Warm water, sun, rideable waves . . .'

JJ shrugged, but didn't reply.

Later, when Micky had stumbled off to his van, JJ moved his chair closer to Bel's and reached his arm across her shoulders.

'Might you go to Peru with Micky?' she asked noncha-lantly. She knew that what she had with JJ wouldn't last, told herself she'd accepted it for what it was, although she'd never before had such a casual sexual friendship to compare it with. But he – Micky, too – were so much part and parcel of her new life, she didn't want either of them to go.

JJ didn't answer her question. Instead, he asked one of his own: 'How about a night in the van? New experience?' He waited for her to decide, and when she didn't immediately do so, went on, 'Or I can walk you home. But there's rubble all over the floor and the stove'll probably be out.'

Bel didn't take much persuading. Her arms and shoulders were throbbing from the destruction of the kitchen and she was chilly now, despite the fire. She wasn't sure she could even make it to the van, let alone up the dark lane.

It was cosy inside, and she was glad of the warmth. JJ stripped to his boxers and threw back the duvet. 'Come,' he said, as she stood uncertainly at the foot of the bed area, wondering if this was such a good idea after all. She was too tired for sex.

JJ spooned into her, laying his arm across her body. It felt good to be held and she closed her eyes, beginning to relax. A few moments later when he began to drop gentle kisses on her naked back, she let him, too sleepy to respond. But her body had other ideas and she felt her nipples harden under his fingers, her groin stir to life. All her physical aches and pains fell away as she turned to him and they began to make love.

The next thing she knew, JJ was nudging her awake, a small espresso cup in his hand. 'Up you get. It's a glorious day. Swim-time!'

23

'Hi, Dad,' Bel said, surprised to hear her father's voice, as he seldom called her, these days. She hadn't stopped worrying about him and still phoned and texted him regularly, communications he often chose to ignore. But she'd been so busy recently that he no longer occupied centre stage on her radar. If she'd had time to think about this, it might have felt good. But she hadn't.

Between shifts at the farm shop Bel had been wrangling unforgiving chunks of wood, sawdust on every surface, terrifying drills and hacksaws, nails and screws, blistered palms and bruised knuckles, all of which had resulted in such aching muscles it was painful for her to lift even one of Mr A's crates. She was, in all areas of her life, on a steep learning curve. It was the third week of June – she'd been in Cornwall more than five weeks now – and her kitchen was all but ready. It just needed a lick of paint, once the plaster behind the stove had dried.

Micky and JJ, despite her protestations that she could do it herself, had helped clear the debris from her wrecking-ball moment. Then Micky had steered her towards a salvage place that sold reclaimed wood. It was more expensive, but because of that, not as popular as the new timber that was currently in such short supply – and she didn't need much.

Bel had insisted on paying him to show her how to render the wall behind the stove and put up shelves, paid him, too, for fashioning the worktop, which Micky crafted in wide planks of reclaimed ash. Bel didn't do all the work by a long chalk, but she'd measured and sawn wood, mixed plaster, sanded and drilled, levelled brackets – although Micky wouldn't let her near his SDS drill – done enough to feel a real satisfaction in the open shelves and pale-wood worktop that fitted snugly around the Rayburn and sink, giving the place a lighter, airier, more rustic feel.

The room felt properly hers, now, the last vestiges of Lenny finally drifting away. And his absence seemed to leave room for the warmth of Agnes's spirit to return. Bel was more and more conscious of her mum, sensing her loving aura all around her in the little cottage that had meant so much to her. She felt closer to her now, in fact, than at any time since she'd died. It was almost as if her father's overbearing presence in the flat had kept her spirit away. Bel didn't find this notion far-fetched or fanciful, didn't question it at all, just welcomed her mother back into her life with open arms and began a comforting dialogue.

Chuck it, or repair it? Bel asked her mum one evening, for instance, as she eyed the stained teak coffee table, although she already knew the answer. 'Repair it, of course,' would have been Agnes's reproving reply: her mum had never thrown anything away. So Bel set about sanding the table, removing all the seventies varnish until the teak was light and unmarked. It was much harder than she'd anticipated, especially around the legs, the tips of her fingers rubbed raw by the sandpaper, the task taking till late into a couple of nights before she was satisfied and could rub Danish oil – recommended by Micky – into the wood with a soft cloth, to protect it. But it did look lovely by the time she'd finished.

Now, her father was speaking and she forced her tired brain to concentrate.

'I'm coming down on the seventh of July,' he declared. 'You were doing sod all about it, so I booked myself in with that Scottish fella at the pub. Says he knows you. Seemed to approve.'

It was true that Logan and Bel had got to know each other a bit these last weeks. As the summer took hold, she would sometimes sit with Patsy and friends at one of the pub's outside tables, with a beer and boxes of triple-cooked chips. The chef's speciality.

'Everyone knows everyone round here,' Bel said, feeling a strong twinge of guilt. It wasn't that she'd forgotten to arrange her father's visit. She'd just kept putting it off. 'Great, Dad,' she added, not really focusing as she realized the loaf she was baking in her new, almost finished kitchen was nearly ready, the timer telling her three minutes. She was already enjoying the tempting waft of warm toasty smells leaking from the oven. 'How long are you staying?'

'Ten days. He was fully booked after that.'

'Sounds good,' she said. *I can cope with ten days*, she told herself. *How bad can it be?*

'You'd better get rid of that chap you've got hidden away down there. No room for two men in your life, girl.' Her father snorted, obviously in a high old mood.

236

'OK, will do,' she said, with equal cheer. 'Listen, I've got to go. I've been baking and the bread's nearly ready. I'll call later.'

The moment of truth, she thought excitedly, as she put her phone down and reached for the cracked Bakelite oven handle. She'd waited for an age to get the Rayburn up to temperature, but she wasn't sure the gauge was even vaguely accurate any more.

She opened the door to a cloud of steam, and sighed with disappointment. The bread had not risen above the rim of the tin. It looked dense and a little burned around the edges. Discouraged, she tipped the loaf into her oven-gloved hand and inspected the bottom, tapping it with her finger. It responded dully and seemed to weigh a ton. *More brick than bread. Almost as bad as last time in Dad's oven*, she thought, setting it on its end – because she didn't have a cooling rack – with a wry smile. But, after the moment of let-down had passed, Bel was undeterred. She hadn't really expected to get it right first time in another unfamiliar oven.

Leaving the loaf to cool – she might just be able to eat it later – she hurried out of the cottage in her swimsuit and dry robe. JJ and Micky were taking her and Jaz – who had just finished her exams – windsurfing at Praa Sands, where their mate ran a surfing school. The wind was just right, JJ insisted, the swell perfect. Jaz was quite an accomplished windsurfer, so it was only Bel who was nervous as they piled into the van.

As they drove up the lane to the main road, a vehicle coming in the opposite direction took the corner too fast and JJ had to swerve. 'Arse,' he shouted, out of the open window. Bel was turned, chatting to Jaz on the back seat about her last exam the day before, and hadn't seen what happened. When she heard JJ curse, she checked the side mirror and saw the back of a red van careering down the lane and out of sight.

Bel, as it turned out, was not as useless as she'd feared. It took a mighty heave to get the sail upright, and the strain on her arms as she held it in place, at the same time balancing on the surfboard, knees cracking, thighs screaming, took up every ounce of concentration. She fell off more than once. But the thrill as the sail filled and she began gliding along the shore was worth the effort. Afterwards, they stopped at a pasty pop-up along the main road and had their supper, all of them damp, sandy, salty, exhilarated, lined up on a bench against the shack wall as the sun went down.

It was after nine when JJ dropped off Bel and Jaz.

'That was brilliant,' Jaz said, as they parted at the gate. Her eyes were bright and she seemed happy and relaxed, not the depressed teenager Bel was more familiar with. It was lovely to see.

'Let's do lots more over the summer,' JJ said, as they waved goodnight.

The cottage, in its new guise, always made her smile when she walked in. It smelt of *her* now, of baked bread and damp, salty beach towels, pine cleaning spray and burning logs. There was sand underfoot and cat hairs on the orange chair, a pile of books she'd bought from Anne – an old lady who lived in the centre of the village and sold second-hand knick-knacks and junk from her garage for charity – decorating the rejuven-ated coffee table.

Settling down with a cup of tea, delicious warmth com-ing from the stove, she felt her limbs tingling, her skin pleasantly tight and salt-dried by the sea and sun, and closed her eyes. *You should have seen me windsurfing, Mum,* she whispered silently.

Bel had no idea how long she'd slept when she was awak-ened by a cautious knock at the door. *JJ?* she wondered. But he would rap cheerful and loud and just walk in, not wait for a response. She stumbled sleepily to her feet and cautiously pulled open the door.

She was instantly jolted awake. *Louis?* Her ex was stand-ing hesitantly in the porch. But when he saw her, his face broke into a wan smile. 'I wasn't sure this one was yours . . . I've been prowling along the lane for hours.'

Her instinct was to slam the door in his face. But he looked so haggard, despite his South of France tan, his normally immaculate appearance marred by black smudges under his dark eyes, creased, grubby jeans and sweatshirt, his hair – forever tied back in a pristine ponytail – now hanging lank around his face. The look he gave her was hopeless and beseeching. Bel, naturally soft-hearted, had received much kindness lately when she had been in a bad way . . . So she hesitated, and the moment was lost.

Dazed, she regarded the man who had caused her so much pain and heartache.

'May I come in?' Louis asked softly, glancing around

and shivering. It was not a particularly cold night, but it was late, the sky a deep navy towards the horizon.

Bel felt completely discombobulated. It seemed beyond her to do anything but stand back, allowing Louis to step past her, over the threshold and into her little sanctuary.

As soon as the door was shut, he turned to her, arms wrapped around his thin body. 'God, Bel, I'm so, so sorry.'

She watched him in silence, her whole body tense. *Make him go away*, she begged the universe.

Blinking tiredly, he looked around distractedly. 'This is nice.'

'What are you doing here, Louis?' She managed to speak at last and was surprised to hear how detached she sounded.

He exhaled loudly. 'Would it be possible to have a cup of tea?' He coughed pathetically. 'Things have been a bit tight and I haven't had anything all day.'

What can I do? she asked herself. Refuse the man she'd loved – and with whom she'd shared her life for almost two decades – a cup of tea? Reluctantly she went over to the sink and filled the kettle, lifted the stove top and put the water on to boil. Louis, standing stock still behind her, remained silent.

She handed him the mug, but didn't offer him either chair – the orange one or the wooden upright. They stood propped against the new ash counter top in silence as she watched him sip the tea, hearing his stomach rumbling loudly. The failed loaf sat between them, still on the wire rack. 'Do you want a slice of bread?' she offered.

He nodded. 'Please, if that's OK.'

None of this is OK, she wanted to shout. But she wasn't going to have a starving man on her conscience. She sliced three thick chunks from the solid loaf. 'It's probably disgusting. My first attempt in this stove,' she apologized, feeling a horribly familiar sense of inadequacy in the face of Louis's culinary prowess. Then she was immediately angry with herself for minding. She pushed the plate towards him, followed by butter in the yellow pottery dish she'd found, like so much else, in the treasure trove that was Anne's garage.

'Not kneaded enough?' Louis couldn't help himself. But he was chomping the bread with relish, clearly ravenous. 'It's not so bad,' he said, maybe feeling he had to be generous in the circumstances.

'What are you doing here?' she repeated doggedly.

He seemed almost to ignore her insistence. Swallowing a mouthful, he took his time to lay the remains of the bread on the plate and say, 'I know I've done a terrible thing, Bel. I can't even imagine how much I've hurt you. It was a disastrous mistake on my part –'

'I don't want to hear any of this, Louis,' Bel interrupted him briskly. 'I asked, why are you here, in this village, in my house?'

He gulped, his Adam's apple leaping in his thin neck. 'Because I realize what a fool I've been. I threw away everything that was precious to me –'

'Oh, OK,' said Bel, her voice bright with sarcasm. 'So when you said in your letter you hadn't been "happy for a long while", that things seemed to have "fizzled out" between us, that wasn't true?' She held up her fingers in quote marks as she spoke, remembering every word of the devastating script.

Louis had the grace to look shamefaced. 'All I can say is that I was completely nuts back then, Bel. I wasn't thinking straight. Maybe it was Covid, or a full-on midlife crisis – call it what you will – but I was drinking too much, as you know, and destroyed by the failure of the restaurant. Things just came together in a perfect storm in my head and I took off.' He reached out for her hand, but she stepped away. 'I'm so, so sorry.'

Bel inhaled sharply but said nothing.

Louis gazed at her, clearly disappointed by her reaction. *What did he expect?* she wondered angrily. 'I'd like you to go,' she said.

He held up his hands, palms outward. 'OK, OK, I understand you're angry with me. Of course you are. I just desperately wanted to apologize for the way I've treated you.'

'You've done that,' she stated.

Louis bowed his head. 'Thing is . . . God, this is hard . . . I'm totally broke. I spent my last penny on petrol for the van. Is there any chance you could lend me something? Just to see me through until I get a job?' He must have seen the incredulity in her face because he hurried on. 'Which, in this current climate . . . There's a pub on the main road advertising for a chef, for instance. The Lantern? I saw it when I passed. So it shouldn't take long, not with my skills.'

Bel was horrified, her throat choked with bile even at the *idea* he might be gunning for a job up the road. She cringed, too, noticing the tiny spark of pride in his voice, pained to see the man she had so admired fall to these depths. *Is he sleeping in the van?* She wasn't going to ask him. There was no sofa in the cottage he might crash on. And he certainly wasn't going to share her bed. Reluctantly, she asked, 'How much do you need?'

He hesitated, obviously calculating how to calibrate his request, but she detected immediate relief in his eyes. 'A hundred and fifty? Can you afford that much? I'll pay you back, obviously, as soon as I'm employed.'

Bemused he had the nerve even to ask her, she replied, after a moment's thought, 'I could run to a hundred. There's a cash machine at the Co-op. I'll cycle up tomorrow morning.'

She watched in dismay as weary tears formed in his eyes. 'Oh, God, thank you, thank you, Bel. I don't deserve your help, of course, but I didn't know who else to turn to. I couldn't ask Tally.'

She nodded briefly. *Go*, she whispered silently. *Just go.*

As if she'd spoken out loud, Louis gulped down the remains of his tea and bread. 'I suppose I'd better be off.'

'Where's the van?'

'In the car park down by the beach, the one with the honesty box.'

'I'll bring the cash in the morning.'

Louis, clearly disinclined to leave the cosy warmth of the cottage for the cold, unwelcoming van, hovered a moment longer, perhaps hoping against hope that Bel would relent and ask him to stay. But when he read the implacable expression on her face, he gave a resigned nod.

'Thank you again,' he muttered, as she showed him out into the chilly darkness.

After he'd gone, Bel slumped into the chair. She felt exhausted. Louis seemed, in a short space of time, to have sucked the lifeblood out of her. *A job at the Lantern? Seriously?* The pub, which she'd never set foot in, was a slightly down-at-heel joint only five minutes from her cottage. She rode past it on her bike every morning on her way to the farm shop. *How could he do this? How could he?* she kept asking herself. Setting up his life within spitting distance of where she lived, when she'd gone to such lengths to find her own path ... to be free. The thought made her groan out loud.

Bel tossed and turned all night, still stunned by Louis's sudden appearance and unable to stop thinking of him sleeping only a few minutes' walk from her front door. *He's not going to ruin things*, she kept telling herself. But sleep wouldn't come.

She gave up at five and went for a swim, holding her breath as she crept past the red Berlingo, not even looking inside. Powering through the chilly dawn water, back and forth, she slapped her hands through the waves, taking out her anger and her sleepless night on the cold sea. As she slipped into her dry robe and wrapped it across her body she at least felt fresh and awake as she stared out towards the horizon, taking in the soft, hazy beauty of the summer morning. But calm, like sleep last night, eluded her. All she could think about was Louis, huddled in the dank confines of his van at the top of the steps.

'Your dad's here.' Bel called Tally before she left for the Co-op. 'Banged on the door late last night looking like something the cat dragged in, begging for food and money.'

'Oh, shit.' There was a pause. 'Sorry, Bel, that might be on me. He asked about you, and I told him you were having a great time in Cornwall. I didn't . . . He was safe in France back then. I never thought . . .'

'Oh, don't worry about that, sweetheart. He'd have found me soon enough.'

'Is he OK?'

Bel heard the understandable concern for her father in her stepdaughter's voice. 'He's bedraggled and feeling sorry for himself, but fundamentally all right, I think.' She sighed. 'Problem is, he's threatening to apply for a job in one of the local pubs.'

Tally groaned. 'Oh my God. What are you going to do?'

'I honestly don't think I can do anything. He's obviously desperate. It's grim, seeing him like this.'

'He's not staying with you, is he?'

'Certainly not. He's sleeping in the van. I know it's hard-hearted, but I really can't handle him being in the house.'

'It's not hard-hearted, Bel. Have you agreed to lend him money?'

'Didn't feel I had much choice.' She sighed. 'Anyway, he'll charm his way into a job in no time, the way things are.'

'But he'll be round the corner!'

'Yeah, well, you know your dad. He's not going to settle for some crummy job in a rundown pub in the furthest reaches of the country, is he? Not for long, anyway. He'll

245

be off as soon as he has a bit of cash and a better offer, I imagine.' Bel was almost a hundred per cent sure she was right about this. But she said it to make them both feel better. Hard enough for her to see Louis like that. How much harder for poor Tally to hear about it?

It was still early as Bel mounted her bike. Turning to check for traffic, she caught sight of Patsy striding up the lane from the beach. Bel waved and Patsy came over, tanned face glowing from her walk, breathing hard, tendrils of grey hair wild around her head. She seemed indignant.

'I just saw this dodgy guy climbing out of a red van in the beach car park. He must have slept there, because he looks really grubby and rough.' She shook her head. 'No one checks the place since Bert died.' Bert had lived in the cottage next to the car park and made it his daily duty to run off anyone who looked as if they might be settling for the duration and clogging up the limited parking area with their mobile homes and attendant rubbish.

Bel felt her cheeks flush. 'My fault, I'm afraid. It's Louis . . . my ex.'

Patsy's eyes widened.

'Turned up on my doorstep last night. Long story.'

Her neighbour gave her a concerned look. 'You asked him to come?'

'*No*. God, no.' Bel shook her head vehemently. 'I haven't slept for worrying and now I can't think straight.'

Patsy laid a gentle hand over Bel's, as she clutched the handlebars. 'Don't panic, love. Take a breath. Whatever this is, we can sort it out together.'

Letting go of the bike, she clutched Patsy's warm hand but couldn't speak the thanks she felt, or acknowledge the comfort brought by her words. *It's the sort of thing Mum might have said*, she thought.

'Where are you going?'

Almost ashamed to admit it, Bel replied, 'Up to the Co-op to get him some cash.'

Patsy nodded slowly. 'OK. Well, I'll see you later, anyway. We can talk then.'

Bel looked blankly at her friend. In her shock at seeing Louis on her doorstep, she'd momentarily forgotten it was tonight that Patsy was throwing a supper for Jaz and her friends, to celebrate the end of GCSEs. She'd promised to help and was making the broad bean and mint couscous, the salads.

'Are you sure you're OK?' Patsy was asking.

Bel tried to focus and managed a weak smile. 'I'm fine,' she said unconvincingly.

'And I'm a Dutchman,' her friend declared, with a sympathetic grin.

24

Louis was leaning against the side of the van, arms crossed, gazing towards the sea, when Bel slid to a halt in the car park. The place had filled up in the time it had taken her to get the cash: people arriving for a day at the beach. It was a warm, sunny June Saturday and later it would be packed on the sand.

Seeing him again, realizing he was actually here, Bel still found it vaguely shocking. Like a bad dream where people and places are all muddled up.

Propping her bike against the van, she took the wad of twenties out of the back pocket of her jeans, handing it to him in silence, genuinely not knowing what to say to him.

He stood to attention, smiling tightly, and thrust the notes into the pouch at the front of his sweatshirt. '*Thank you*. Really, thank you, Bel.' His voice was heavy with relief.

She moved aside to let a Dacia with surfboards tied to the roof rack reverse slowly into a slot by the hedge. 'What are you going to do now?' she asked.

Louis shuffled his feet, didn't look at her. 'Umm, one more small favour? Could I have a quick shower at yours? I want to present myself at the pub before it gets busy. But if I go like this they'll take one look and tell me to fuck off.'

Bel knew this was probably true, but she felt a sudden spurt of resentment. Louis was dragging her into his mess: making this *her* problem. 'OK,' she said shortly, then reached for her bike.

Louis grabbed her arm. 'Please, don't walk away. We can talk, can't we?'

Shaking him off, she inhaled slowly, so as not to shout at him. Then she squared up to him. 'Listen, Louis. Your apology may mean something to you, but it means almost nothing to me. You nearly destroyed me. I'm trying to build a life for myself down here, now. And that life does not include you.'

Louis's tired face registered immediate shock. He jerked back as if she'd hit him. 'Whoa, Bel. That's a bit harsh.' Then his face fell, his expression no longer indignant. He added, 'I realize I deserve it, of course, but . . .'

She stared at him. 'But what? I hope you're not looking for sympathy from *me*.'

Louis seemed suddenly defeated. 'No, no, of course not. I'm sorry. I know this whole thing is totally my fault, but I'm in a dreadful state right now and saying all the wrong things . . .'

She took a breath and felt the anger drain away. Speaking more gently, she said, 'Stop talking then and get yourself cleaned up. Go and find a job. The front door's open.'

She didn't know where she was going, but it wasn't to stand around in her house while Louis had a shower and tried to inveigle her into more conversations about how incredibly sorry he was.

'Do you want to ask Louis to the party tonight?' Patsy asked later, when Bel was sitting in her neighbour's kitchen, pinching off the tops of blanched broad beans and

249

sliding the bright green inside out of the wrinkled, waxy skin for the couscous, which would accompany Patsy's spicy harissa chicken.

Bel stopped what she was doing and stared at her friend, astonished: she'd spent the last half-hour explaining how shocked and depressed she was by Louis's presence in the village.

Patsy, having turned the chicken pieces with a pair of tongs, slid the tray back into the oven. Then she came over and sat opposite Bel at the table, hands clasped. 'I heard you, Bel,' she said, 'but you can't stop him being here. If you're going to be in a perpetual state of anger and irritation that he is, it's *you* who's going to suffer.'

Bel bridled. 'So you're suggesting I just open my arms and forgive him?'

Patsy raised an eyebrow at her tone. 'I'm saying you don't have to be frightened of him, love. He can't control you. So he comes to live nearby. So what? You see him here and there, you wave, you move on.'

'You don't understand,' Bel wailed. 'Maybe he wants to get back with me . . . I looked after him too well before. I don't want the pressure. I just want to be left alone.'

Patsy shrugged as if she didn't understand the problem. 'Just be very clear.' She smiled kindly. 'If you're clear, he'll hear you, I promise.'

Bel knew Patsy was right. So why did it feel threatening to have him in her space? What was she afraid of? *My own weakness?* Louis wasn't a thug: he wouldn't insist if she told him to leave her alone. 'Please don't ask him for supper, Patsy,' she begged.

'Of course I won't, if you don't want me to. It was only a suggestion . . . I've always found schmoozing the enemy works better for everyone than lining up the tanks.'

'Yeah, OK. But can we schmooze Louis another night?'

Patsy grinned. 'Finish those beans, sweetheart, then go and lie down. Or have a swim. Or a nice warm bath. You're traumatized. Give yourself a break.'

Later, Patsy's kitchen was buzzing, the room filled with fragrant cooking smells, music, laughter and noise as the joyous teenagers joshed each other and swigged beers, crammed crisps into their mouths.

Bel had been for a soothing swim and had calmed down somewhat. She'd listened to Patsy. Now she and Rhian were laying the bowls, cutlery and napkins on the table. Supper was ready. They would start as soon as Micky and JJ arrived – both five minutes away, according to a text from JJ.

'This is so lovely,' Bel said, surveying the scene.

Rhian smiled. 'Patsy has a way of making her kitchen feel like home to everyone who walks through the door. It's quite a gift.'

Patsy, her back to them both, harrumphed. 'I just like the place full of people.'

The side door was pushed open and JJ's tall figure, followed by Micky's curly blond head, appeared. They stood side by side, tanned and grinning – Bel noticed they'd even put on tidy shorts for the occasion. Then Micky stood back, revealing someone immediately behind them.

'Look who we found lurking in the lane,' Micky said,

holding out his hand with a loud ta-dah, like a magician producing a rabbit out of a hat. 'He says he's a friend of Bel's, which is good enough for me.'

Louis's eyes immediately sought Bel's. He looked beyond sheepish. 'Listen, I don't want to gatecrash. But Micky said I should come and at least say hello.'

Patsy hesitated, then waved her wooden spoon in the air. 'You're here now. Stay. There's plenty for everyone . . . It's Louis, right?'

Bel was silent, feeling her cheeks flame with annoyance as introductions were made. Louis was at his most charming, self-effacing best. Even Jaz, as soon as she heard he was the chef who used to live with Bel, came over all wide-eyed and eager, the shy looks she usually reserved for Micky now solely for the new arrival.

JJ sidled up to her, as everyone began to help themselves to food, and nudged her shoulder. 'The ex, I take it,' he whispered, swishing his eyes towards where Louis was making the teenagers laugh about something. 'You OK?'

'Not really.'

'Micky insisted,' he said apologetically.

'Not his fault,' she replied.

The teenagers sloped off with their bowls to drape themselves on the sofas at the other end of the long room. The adults sat on benches round the laden table. Bel gazed at her food, but suddenly didn't have an appetite. She noticed Louis kept his distance, planting himself between Micky and JJ, as if for protection. It didn't take long, though, for him to regain his usual confidence and begin to hold court. As always, it related to food.

'You should see the kitchen,' he said, of the Lantern. 'It's disgusting, totally chaotic. I'll have quite a task licking it into shape. The fridge is so full of mouldy food it could walk to the bus stop.'

Amid the general laughter, Bel caught his veiled glance: he was checking her reaction. *So he got the job,* she thought, torn between relief that he wouldn't be borrowing any more money, and despair that he was clearly staying. She stared back at him blankly, without smiling or acknowledging the news, and he quickly turned away. As with earlier, she thought she sensed his disappointment. And it was that which depressed her still further. *He wants me to forgive him.* Such an unfair emotional pressure.

When, much later, the party broke up, Bel stood at her front door and watched Micky and JJ, Louis between them, saunter off down the lane into the night, laughing and chatting like old friends. She shut herself inside the cottage, jealousy twisting viciously at her gut as she hunched in her chair, feeling quite sick from too much wine and too little to eat. *Louis's the charismatic one. Louis's the brilliant chef and raconteur. Louis's the person everyone's drawn to.* And herself? A 'genderless lump' who'd lost her spark, according to her father. The painful feelings of inadequacy – held back in recent weeks as she basked in her life-affirming new friendships and freedom from Dennis's put-downs – now came flooding back. *Bastard, bastard, bastard,* she muttered, not clear whether she was referring to Louis or her father. Or both.

25

It was raining when Bel woke, still curled stiffly in the orange chair, her cardigan pulled around her shoulders. The room was chilly – she could hear the wind whistling around the door – the stove, which she'd forgotten to feed in her misery last night, now gone out. She felt creaky, bone-cold and old, as she set about raking the ash, then collecting kindling and logs from the outside store by the porch. It would be hours before the water was hot enough for a shower. Her instinct was to fetch a nice warming coffee and a bacon roll from Martine's, but she was concerned Louis would be doing the same thing. And it was also an expensive habit she knew she had to break.

Standing watching the flames take hold, and enjoying the heat spreading across her face, she felt a sudden pang for his situation. It was all very well sleeping in the van when the weather was clement, the sun shining, but today would be very bleak. *Stop it.* She shook herself and went upstairs to put on some warmer clothes.

Later, she made herself a strong cup of coffee and a thick slice of buttered bread and honey from the farm shop. *I'll stay in and bake today*, she decided. Even if the result was rubbish, like last time, the process would be one in which she might lose herself for a while, forget what was going on down the lane.

Pressing, pulling, rotating the soft, claggy dough under her hands on the ash worktop, she slipped into a soothing rhythm. Thoughts fell away, until there was nothing but the smooth doughball against the heel of her hand, the hiss of the stove, the quiet puttering of the radio, the soft grey coastal light of morning struggling through the casement.

She'd just set the bread to rise in a large oiled bowl covered with a tea towel – she would normally have used cling film but she didn't have any – and placed it on the side of the Rayburn to prove for a while, when there was a knock at the door.

She wasn't surprised to find Louis standing there, damp and hopping from foot to foot, a beseeching look in his eyes, wet hair poking out from beneath his sodden anorak hood.

Resigned, Bel beckoned him inside.

Carefully wiping his trainers on the mat, he went over to the stove and stood against it, rubbing his hands together, then fanning them above the hotplate lid. 'I'm bloody freezing,' he complained, glancing around. 'Any coffee going?'

Seeing her look, he added, 'I'm sorry about all this, Bel. I know I've no right to be here. You've been so kind.' He let out a long sigh. 'Ben at the pub says I can rent one of his rooms from Monday – which is when I start the job. So you'll be shot of me soon.'

'Great,' she said unenthusiastically, thinking, *This mess wasn't thrust unfairly upon your delicate shoulders, Louis*. But his old sense of entitlement was flexing its muscle again.

'By the way, I gave him your name and address for the reference,' Louis went on. 'Hope you don't mind? I don't imagine he'll follow it up. He's pretty desperate. But you're the only person who could possibly vouch for my cheffing skills.' He gave her a charming grin.

I loved this man once, Bel thought. *He was my whole life*. It seemed like an odd notion now. But under the glow of his smile, she felt the edges of her resentment melt, just a fraction.

When he came down from the shower he'd requested, he looked clean again, his hair scraped back off his face and secured in the usual ponytail, although his clothes were still crumpled and none too fresh. Wandering over to the proving bowl, he lifted the cloth. Without asking, he poked his index finger into the dough, then shook his head. 'Not ready yet.'

'Leave it alone. It's *my* bread,' she said, regretting the childish outburst as soon as she saw Louis's eyes widen.

He came over to where she was sitting, pretending to read. Perching on the wooden chair, he said earnestly, 'Talk to me, Bel. Please. Tell me how you're feeling. Let it out. I can take it.'

Bel slowly lowered her book to her lap, trying to stay calm. 'I honestly don't see the point,' she said tiredly. And she didn't. But she felt the anger rising, like the dough. 'What exactly are you after, Louis? Chapter and verse about how I coped when you took off with the girl you'd been fucking under my nose for months . . . taking the van and every last cent?' She saw him flinch and was perversely pleased. 'But if that wasn't bad enough, now I have to listen to your justifications and *take pity*?' She shook her head, and intoned with heavy sarcasm, 'Let me see . . . You weren't yourself, you had a mad moment, it didn't work out as planned, and now things are hard and you're truly sorry. Have I forgotten anything?'

'No. I'm ashamed to say you're right on the money.' He met her eye, his expression craven. 'Look, I realize you're angry, Bel, but please . . .'

He didn't continue and she wasn't sure what he was asking of her.

Silence fell. Bel's heart was thumping with rage.

'I don't want your pity,' he said quietly. 'And I don't expect you to forgive me right now. I know I've behaved like an arse, but I'm not a complete idiot.' He was staring at her intently, his expression so yearning it was her turn to flinch. Then he added fervently, his voice rising, 'What can I say, Bel? What can I do to convince you?'

Surprised, she asked, 'Convince me? Of what?'

There was a long pause. He seemed to be struggling with something in his mind, his eyes blinking fast. Then he said, 'You know I still love you.'

Bel could not have expressed in that moment – either to herself or others – her emotions when she heard Louis's words. They were bouncing around in her head, creating a jumble of disbelief, sadness, anger, doubt . . . But overriding all of these there was *confusion*.

Stumbling over her thoughts, heart pounding, she

remembered Patsy's advice for just this situation. 'I . . .' She faltered before she'd even begun, finding herself quite unable to be 'clear'.

Louis held up his hand. 'OK, OK, I shouldn't have said anything so soon. I'm sorry. I'm such a fuck-up at the moment. Things come out of my mouth when I don't mean them to.' He gave her a searching look. 'But it's God's honest truth, Bel.'

She looked away, wanting to avoid his craven expression. *Do I still love him?* The question took root in her brain. But she ignored it. This was not the time. Now all she wanted was for him to leave her alone.

Finally summoning a modicum of Patsy's clear-headed strength, she said, 'Please, Louis. I can't deal with this. Just go.'

He looked resigned, as if he'd expected this response, but not defeated, as his next remark implied: 'My bad. I knew I should have waited.'

There was silence, the air between them flat and dead, as if they'd both run out of steam.

'You know we owe Dad a ton of money.' Bel finally spoke – the debt, she felt, the one issue between them she was confident in addressing. 'I emailed you about it in France, but you never replied.'

Louis gave a despondent sigh. 'Yeah. I know. Sorry. There's not much I can do about it at the moment. But I *promise* I will, Bel. I totally *promise*. Half of the debt is mine, of course. More than half. I can start paying it back as soon as I'm earning what I should be.'

Which isn't right now, thought Bel, glumly.

She held her breath as he thanked her politely for the shower – she'd never got around to giving him coffee – and opened the front door onto the miserable Sunday. 'Sorry,' he muttered again, as he trudged off down the path.

She exhaled, found she was suddenly really cold, almost shaking. Getting up, she went over and stood, as Louis had done earlier, against the stove for warmth and comfort. Remembering the bread, she lifted the cloth and poked it. The dent made by her finger stayed and she knew it was ready to be knocked back and put into the tin for the second proving.

Bel curled in the chair as the loaf cooked. She loved this waiting time, almost soporific, the place filled with warmth and the promise of a slice of fresh, crusty bread. She was trying to focus her thoughts on what Louis had said. *I still love you.* His words rang in her ears. She tried, for a moment, to imagine being his partner again: making love to him, waking up to his face on the pillow, watching him cook, dealing with his intensity and passion. *Do I still love him?* She returned to the question – aware the switch from loving to not loving wasn't so easily flicked off. No clear answer presented itself. As she rose from the chair to rescue the bread, she did know one thing, though, for absolute certain: *I don't trust him.*

26

Monday morning found Bel in the farm shop again. The bread had been a success. Not perfect, but with a good, even texture, a crisp crust and very edible buttered, with a sliced tomato, anchovies and a drizzle of olive oil for supper. She felt calmer today and the sun was out, the air warmer again.

When the shop was momentarily empty Harris walked in. It had been a busy morning – Mondays often were – with Mr A in an exacting mood. But now he'd gone out for an hour and they had the place to themselves. Bel was pleased to see the artist. He seemed like the only friend she'd made who wasn't tainted by Louis. He organized tea for them both and she relayed to him the events of the weekend as she unpacked the box of goat's cheese that had just arrived from the farm up the road.

'Hmm, what would I think if my wife – or ex-wife – made a sudden comeback?' He pulled a face. 'Not that she ever would.'

'When did you split up?'

'Oh, aeons ago. Twelve years it must be, at least. Alexa couldn't hack being buried in the middle of a field with a work obsessive.' He smiled. 'Fair enough. I was hurt at the time, but I understood. She's married to a Florida real-estate guy now, who literally never takes a day off.' He took a sip of tea. 'Sorry, this isn't about me.'

Bel waited for him to go on. He was someone who seemed to choose his words carefully. 'If you're not sure of your feelings for this man, you could give it some time, maybe, see how it goes with him being around.'

She sighed. She'd spent all weekend wanting to do exactly the opposite, slam the door on the whole Louis saga, once and for all. 'That doesn't feel very comfortable,' she replied.

'Because?'

She threw her hands into the air, her voice rising as she said, 'I don't know! I don't trust him, I suppose. I don't want him here. I don't . . .' She didn't know quite what else she didn't want about Louis – pretty much everything, she was sure – and ground to a halt.

Harris gazed at her with his calm grey-green eyes, said nothing.

'He'll take over,' she added into the silence.

'He's controlling?'

'Not exactly,' she began, using her father as the gold-standard controller and realizing that Louis was only a pale imitation. 'He's just very good at making sure everything's exactly as *he* wants it, regardless.'

A customer walked into the shop and Bel greeted her. After the woman had left with her purchases, Harris said bluntly, 'Not the best basis for a relationship, I'd say.'

Bel heard real conviction in his voice and found herself storing his words – just as she had Patsy's – like a piece of armour she might need to call upon in the future.

'I'm having an open day on Sunday.' Harris pulled a

slightly squashed flier from his back pocket and handed it to her. 'Ron said he'd put it up on your board there.'

The photograph was of a beautiful line-drawing of a Sandwich tern – so the caption told her – with its shaggy black crest, white neck and long, yellow-tipped beak. She smoothed it out with an appreciative smile, impressed by his unquestionable talent. 'Really lovely. Pity about the creases.' She was struck by Harris's obvious equivocation when it came to marketing himself. He looked at her and they both laughed. It was an oddly intimate moment and she felt a sudden warmth for the artist. He made her feel heard.

That afternoon, buoyed by her success with her latest loaf, Bel was reading through online croissant recipes on her laptop when her phone rang. She'd had a sudden yearning for the croissants she remembered eating in France with Bruno – who had faded in her consciousness somewhat since her arrival in Cornwall, his life in the snowy Alps feeling very far from her current mindset. The sort of pastry you could never, ever find in Britain. The ones Martine served, like so many others, were chewy and bland – none of the buttery crispness she longed for. And they left a too-sweet, synthetic aftertaste. *How hard can it be to make a proper one?* she asked herself.

'Hi, Dad.'

'Crap weather here. Hope it's going to cheer up for next week.'

Next week? In all the furore over Louis, she'd forgotten his visit was imminent.

'What have you got planned for your old dad, then?'

'Umm, what would you like to do?' She hadn't told him about Louis, dreading his reaction. *Is it better to wait until he arrives? Or tell him now and get the inevitable rant over with?* But she couldn't face the latter. She would wait. For all she knew – miracles did happen – Louis might up sticks and disappear in the next week. It had been known . . .

'Is it warm enough to swim?'

'It's not the Med, Dad, but I've been in every day.'

He chuckled. 'You were such a water baby when you were young. Couldn't get you out of the pool. Your mum used to try to frighten you by saying you'd dissolve like a sugar lump, but you paid her no heed.'

She laughed, remembering. 'I did sort of believe her.'

'So, have you finished the clear-out yet? Even a hovel should sell well at the moment, with all these namby-pamby eejits droning on about a *better quality of life* out of town.' His tone was scathing.

'Well, it is better.'

'Don't get too cosy down there, Bella.' Dennis sounded amused, as if he didn't even consider that she might. 'I need you back home.'

Home, she thought, looking around her little space with affection. 'So what time will you arrive?' she asked.

'I'm planning to leave crack of sparrow next Thursday. Get ahead of the traffic. Should be there by lunchtime.'

Bel knew this was unrealistic. Her father was always notoriously late – he expected others to wait – and she suspected the drive would be much more arduous at his age than he anticipated. But she didn't quibble. 'Well, text me when you're close. I get off work at twelve.'

'*Work?*' His voice was sharp and Bel remembered, too late, that she hadn't mentioned the job to her father. 'What work?'

'I do mornings at the local farm shop,' she said, reluctantly. 'Just for a bit of cash.'

Her father started a rumbling mutter, but Bel rushed on: 'Sorry, Dad. Just realized the time. Got to go. Talk soon.' She said a hasty goodbye and clicked off, staring nervously at the phone in her hand, hoping everything wasn't going to explode in her face when her father finally arrived on her turf.

JJ looked a little sheepish as he stood in the porch late that night. Bel hadn't seen or heard from him since Saturday, when he'd walked off into the darkness, laughing with Louis. Not that she'd contacted him, either. She wasn't entirely sure how this sex-buddy thing worked, or how Louis's arrival changed things. By rights, it shouldn't make any difference. But JJ's van had been up on the headland all week, so he hadn't been away surfing.

The red Berlingo, on the other hand, had disappeared. Although Louis hadn't been in touch since their spat at the weekend, she assumed that he was now ensconced in the Lantern, with a job and a room.

'OK if I come in?' JJ asked now.

She ushered him inside. It was after nine, but she'd been enthralled by video after video on YouTube, demonstrating how to make the perfect croissant. 'Tea?' she asked.

'Yeah, thanks, that'd be nice,' he said. 'I saw your light on as I was going past.' He hesitated. 'I wasn't sure, with your ex in town, what you'd want to do . . . about the sex?' His question was delivered with the usual frankness.

Bel laughed. 'Put like that.' She made them tea and set their cups on the coffee table, then sat down, indicating he should squeeze into the orange chair too. She slung her legs over his thighs as she had that first time. It was good to have him there.

'So, you and Louis . . . ?' He paused.

'No,' she answered quickly, pleased at how firm she sounded.

JJ cocked an eyebrow. 'He told me and Micky he adores you.'

Bel pursed her lips in irritation that Louis had had the cheek to involve her friends in their relationship.

Stroking her thigh, JJ asked, 'If things have changed for you, now Louis's here . . .'

'Louis has nothing to do with anything.'

He nodded slowly. 'Seems like an OK guy.'

'I thought so.'

They fell silent as they drank their tea. Putting his mug down, JJ turned to her, wrapping her in his arms and dropping a soft kiss on her cheek. Bel hesitated, then turned her mouth to his.

Later, as they lay sleepily in the darkness, JJ warm against her back, Bel knew her heart had not fully been into the sex tonight. It was good between them, as usual. But despite her determination that Louis's presence in her life wouldn't affect her choices, something – as JJ had suggested – had changed. Now, with JJ's soft breath on her neck, she came to the realization that this casual-sex thing wasn't for her – fun as it had been. She wasn't scared of Louis finding out – in fact, she almost relished the thought of telling him. This was about her own feelings.

She knew she'd been a bit wound up that she hadn't seen JJ all week, knew that she was in danger of investing too much in their liaison – while at the same time being aware it wasn't going anywhere. JJ could pick it up with her or not, as the mood took him. Bel was not that cool – Patsy had warned her. *This was the last time*, she told herself regretfully, as she dropped off to sleep. She hoped, though, that they'd be able to keep their friendship.

When she told JJ in the morning, over a coffee and some of her home-baked loaf, he pulled a sad face. 'That's a shame. But fair enough, I get it,' he said, then smiled. 'I'll really miss it. You're a gorgeous woman to make love to.'

Bel blushed. No one had ever told her that before.

'So you're thinking you might give Louis another chance?'

'No, I'm definitely not,' she replied. 'But I need a clear run at things.' She touched her hand to his arm. 'You're a gorgeous man to make love to, as well, JJ. I shall definitely miss it.'

'Well, if you change your mind . . .' JJ winked at her, making her laugh.

27

On Sunday Bel biked through the lanes to Harris's open day, intrigued to see where the artist lived, what his work would be like. She felt she was beginning to know him quite well, although the time they spent together was limited to the random forty-five minutes he took to drink his cup of tea of a morning.

Riding along the rutted lane behind the shop now, she passed Mr Ajax's brick farmhouse on the right and rounded another bend. The cottage sat directly on the lane, a white-painted stone cottage with a slate roof and what looked like a newer extension tacked onto the left-hand side of the building.

Bel felt a little nervous as she knocked on the door, which was ajar. 'Harris?' she called.

The neat, well-appointed farmhouse-style kitchen she spied through the doorway – which looked onto fields at the back – was empty, although the kettle was steaming on the countertop. She called again. This time the wooden latched door that led to the extension opened and Harris appeared. His curly hair was even wilder than usual and he appeared distracted. But when he saw Bel, his face broke into a smile.

'Oh, good, it's only you.'

Bel wasn't sure if this was a compliment or not. 'Am

I too early?' It was gone ten thirty and she'd thought the flier said 10 a.m. to 5 p.m.

'No, no. It's great you're here.' He sighed, rumpling his hair. 'I dread these things. People in my space, judging my work . . . never knowing what they really think.' He hovered, clearly at a loss as to what to do with himself or her.

'Do you have to do it?' Bel asked reasonably.

He shrugged. 'It's expected, I suppose. Though most of my sales are online or at exhibitions.'

The insecure, harassed side of him was new to her. He always seemed so calm and confident when he visited the shop.

'Tea?' he asked.

'If you're doing some.'

His face relaxed into a smile. 'We'll have to be quick, get one in before the hordes arrive. I'm not making everyone a cuppa.'

Mug in hand, he finally ushered Bel into his studio. It was a light, airy room with a skylight and big windows wide open, a breeze coming in across the fields. Around the space, on the slanted drawing table where he worked, on the window ledges and the walls, stacked on the floor, was his artwork: pencil sketches, some pen and ink, like the one on the flier, some watercolour, but all exquisitely detailed representations of local wildlife, flora and fauna – many birds, but also lizards, dragonflies, field mice, brown trout, a roe deer, fungi.

Bel walked slowly round the room, Harris watching her nervously from his seat on his drawing stool. She stopped at an image of a majestic falcon perched on the side of a hill. 'This is wonderful,' she said, indicating the print. 'They're all really beautiful.'

He gave her a broad smile.

'As soon as I can afford to, I'll buy one. My cottage is crying out for something like this.'

'Thank you. I'm delighted you like them.' She noted a flush colouring his tanned cheek at her praise. 'How's the renovating going, by the way?'

'Slowly. I got caught up in baking – my one true love – when I should have been painting the walls.' She sighed. 'And my father's due on Thursday for ten days.'

Reading her expression, he said, 'Not looking forward to it?'

Before she could answer, they heard someone calling, and a middle-aged man poked his head around the door of the studio, followed by a woman, both wearing shorts and T-shirts, fleeces tied round their waists.

Bel did another slow round of the room, looking more closely at the drawings and marvelling at their intricacy while Harris chatted to the couple. She thought she ought to go, but she didn't want to interrupt or just walk out without saying goodbye.

The couple left with Harris's website details, promising to order one of his prints when they got home to Manchester.

'If they don't buy here and now, the moment tends to pass,' Harris said, when they were safely out of earshot.

'Do you think you'll sell many today?'

'A few, maybe. I've got a fair number of fans round here,' he said, with a self-deprecatory grin.

'Listen, I'm going to leave you to it, let you bond with your admirers. Thanks. I've loved seeing your work.' She held out her hand. Harris took it, his shake firm, then he pulled her into a quick, unexpected hug. She picked up the clean tang of lavender detergent from his grey T-shirt, a hint of coal-tar soap from his skin.

As she mounted her bike she saw Brigid coming towards her on the path. She sometimes took over from Bel at lunchtime, but she hadn't seen her much since that first time.

'You're leaving?' Brigid asked, in her gravelly voice. Before Bel had a chance to reply, she went on, 'I've seen it all before, of course. But I thought I'd drop by to give him moral support. I know how he dreads these open days.' She spoke airily, as if she was marking Bel's card. *I know him better than you*, she seemed to imply.

Are she and Harris still having a thing? Bel wondered, as she pedalled away, surprised to find she hoped they were not.

In the run-up to her father's visit, Bel was like a small tornado. She barely slept, so keen was she to paint the kitchen and sitting room, make the place so pretty – downstairs at least, the bathroom was another story – that her father would understand why she loved it and wanted to live there.

She was also desperate to make a start on the croissants before her father interrupted her life. They were burning a hole in her patience, like an excruciating itch that needed to be scratched. It was almost as if she perceived the baking of a successful croissant as a kind of talisman. *If I can get it right, my life here will be assured.*

She'd done as much research online as she could handle. There were hundreds of recipes, none of them entirely agreeing with each other. She'd had to pick and choose which elements she thought would work in her limited space – she didn't have a dough mixer, for instance, or a freezer for the butter. There was something all recipes agreed upon, though: croissant-making was a palaver, a delicate, touch-and-go process, where any tiny element, such as the temperature of the air in the room, could ruin things. But Bel was not daunted: she loved the challenge.

On the Tuesday evening before D-day – as she termed Dennis's arrival – she set about her first attempt. She'd assembled a baking sheet and baking parchment, rolling pin, scales, tape measure – the last two borrowed from Patsy – good-quality strong white flour and butter from the Co-op, active dried yeast. She was ready to go.

Mixing and proving the dough was the easy part. But then she was instructed to bash the butter into an exact rectangle between two sheets of greaseproof paper, measuring it to precisely 20 x 15 centimetres before chilling. But the butter was soft from sitting beside the Rayburn and splodged about untidily, making it hard to trim the edges. She went on to roll the dough into another centimetre-perfect rectangle, only bigger: 40 x 20. It took her ages to get the exact size for both.

It was rather satisfying, later, to lay the now cold sheet of butter on the dough and fold the bottom half up, the top half down, until the two edges met and enclosed the butter, like a letter in an envelope, then roll it, double the whole thing over as if it were a book and put it back in the fridge. After the requisite chilling time, she went through the meticulous process of rolling and folding another six times – three to six was the recommended number, and Bel went for broke. It was nearly midnight now, and she was exhausted as she wrapped the dough in cling film and put it to chill overnight.

On Wednesday morning, she jumped out of bed at five and hurried excitedly down to the kitchen in her T-shirt and knickers, stoking the Rayburn to max, then tenderly lifting the rectangle of dough from the fridge and laying it on the ash worktop with reverence. This seemed like the fun bit, rolling the dough and cutting it in half, dividing the two strips into isosceles triangles – precisely measured – and gently coiling each one with the tips of her fingers into a croissant shape.

Bel finally completed the meticulous process in the quiet of the early-morning kitchen, and twelve perfect little crescents of pale dough sat in an orderly row on the metal trays. She gazed at them in awe, a small smile on her lips, feeling the utmost sense of satisfaction. Covering the croissants with oiled cling film, she laid the trays on the side for the final proving and hurried off for a swim – almost loath to leave her precious little parcels unattended. She should just have time to complete the baking before setting off for her shift at the farm shop.

*

Fifteen to eighteen minutes, she read from the detailed guide she'd written in her notebook – an amalgam of countless online pages of advice, warnings, common pitfalls, must-haves and more. Would the Rayburn come through? She'd set the dial to 'bake', but did this mean anything with the ancient stove?

After lightly egg-washing the now beautifully risen, puffy dough coils, she opened the oven door and slid the trays inside. Then she sat on the orange chair, clutching her new timer, almost holding her breath as she stared fixedly at the stove – willing it to perform – for the longest quarter-hour of her life. By the time the pinger went, she was fizzing with anticipation, the room filled with a warm, sweet, intoxicating aroma that was making her mouth water and her empty stomach rumble.

The moment of truth . . . Biting her lip, Bel slipped her hands into the oven gloves and very cautiously pulled open the oven door on the sixteenth minute. Steam gusted in her face, making her blink . . . but, miracle of miracles, there they were, two trays of perfectly puffed, shiny, golden brown pastries.

Bel laughed, patting the Rayburn appreciatively. 'Beginner's luck,' she told the empty room, marvelling at the result of her labours. Although the diligence, the enthusiasm, the *love* she'd put into the process was worthy of a good marriage.

She didn't have a wire rack, so she propped the croissants in pyramids on the worktop to cool while she made some coffee – she'd bought a cafetière at the weekend, knowing her father would sack her if she offered him instant. Then she laid a croissant reverently on a plate, her mug of coffee beside it on the table, sat down in her chair and took a deep breath. Tearing the end off the pastry – admiring the many dough-layers as she did so, she put it slowly into her mouth, prolonging the moment, then bit down. Warm, crisp, buttery, flaky sweetness flooded her senses. *It's gorgeous*, she thought, although she said so herself.

She didn't have much time, but Bel sat for a short while and finished the croissant with relish, savouring every single morsel. She remembered her mum adoring croissants on their holidays in France, her pretty face, with the kind eyes and neat brown bob, lighting up at the sight of a basketful in the local café, and wished she was here now, to celebrate her daughter's baking success.

On a high, she wrapped four of the pastries in greaseproof paper and left them on the ledge outside Patsy's kitchen, sending a text to tell her friend they were there in case Zid swung by and nabbed the lot. Then she put another couple in an old paper bread bag and stored it in her backpack for Mr Ajax and Harris – if he turned up today.

Bel waited in eager anticipation for her artist friend to appear, praying he'd be in – it wasn't a given. Around ten, she saw his tall figure step onto the outside platform of fruit and vegetables and smiled to herself. When he was settled with his cup of tea, she held out the bag. Mr Ajax, when she'd done the same earlier, had merely raised an eyebrow and muttered a thank-you, but had not even looked at her offering.

She watched as Harris bit into the croissant. 'Wow,' he said, after he'd swallowed his first mouthful. 'That is absolutely delicious, Bel.' His face was alive with pleasure. 'Such a talent! Worth making the kitchen wait for its paint-job, I'd say.'

She laughed. 'Oh, I did that too. I'm on a mission.'

'To do what?' he asked curiously.

'Umm . . .' *Answering the question with the truth will sound ridiculous*, she thought. How could she say she was scared of her father's presence in her life again, so was trying to nail her future with a croissant? Instead, she said, 'I needed to get the place in shape to start baking.'

'Well, here's to the next time,' Harris said, through another mouthful.

'Oh, it probably won't work so well next time. The stars were just perfectly aligned today.' As she said it, she almost believed herself. The moment when she'd opened the oven door had felt magic. More significant by a mile than a mere row of pastries.

28

Bel was hovering outside the Queen Bess when her father staggered stiffly out of the sleek green Jaguar just after five on Thursday, sunglasses askew, brushing his mane of white hair off his face. It was a hot day and he was red-faced and sweating. Bel went to hug him, then settled for a quick peck on the cheek, knowing her father wasn't one for physical contact.

'Bloody fan system's kaput,' he complained, breathing heavily. 'But the old girl still gives me a good ride.' He patted the Jaguar's bonnet fondly, as if it were a beloved lady-friend.

Bel had been extremely tense in the run-up to his arrival.

'He's not staying in your house, Bel,' Patsy had encouraged, when she noted Bel's anxiety. 'Logan will take care of him. And he's only here for a short while.' She'd nudged her as they'd walked along the beach earlier. 'How bad can it be?'

Bel honestly didn't know. She couldn't explain her fears. It seemed too pathetic to imply that she, a woman in her late fifties, was in any way nervous of, or in thrall to, her aged father.

Her new friends had told her they'd be happy to help entertain Dennis: Patsy said he was invited to supper any time, JJ offered to take him paddleboarding if he was up for it, Rhian to show him around the church – parts of which dated back to the fourteenth century – and Micky wondered if he liked snooker. She'd been grateful: it was essential to keep him busy. What was winding her up, though, wasn't how her father might spend his days in Cornwall as much as how he would treat her – what he would expect from her.

Now he stood, arms akimbo, breathing in the fresh Cornish air. Shading his eyes against the sun, he eyed her up and down. 'You're looking good, girl. Lost weight at last? A tan always helps.'

Bel tried to smile at the backhanded compliment. 'Let's get you up to your room, Dad.'

As she spoke, the landlord emerged beaming from the low door of the old coaching inn and went over to Dennis, vigorously shaking his hand, his red destination beard – like his brother Hamish's – glowing in the evening sun.

'Welcome to Cornwall, sir. Come in, come in. You'll no doubt be wanting a wee glass of something after all that driving.'

Her father perked up. 'Man after my own heart,' he said, trotting obediently behind Logan as they turned and disappeared into the pub.

She went to the boot and heaved out her father's old brown canvas suitcase. *Maybe this isn't going to be so bad, after all*, she thought, immensely grateful for Logan's kindness in finding her father a room at the pub's busiest time. Then she remembered Louis.

There had been no sign of him in the previous

week – Bel cycled a different route to the farm shop, just in case – and she had tentatively begun to think she might cope, being in such close proximity. Chefs, after all, work excruciatingly long hours.

Then Patsy had told her she'd invited him over for supper last Monday, when the pub was closed, so that Jaz could chat to him about becoming a chef. She'd asked Bel to join them, but Bel had declined, then sat nursing her resentment all evening as she heard the shouts of laughter coming through the open window on the warm summer night: *Louis at his entertaining best.*

He'd knocked on her door after the meal. Dismayed to realize she'd have been disappointed if he hadn't, Bel knew she both wanted to see Louis, and didn't want to, in a tangled mesh of feelings.

'Thought I'd check on you,' he said. From his slightly glassy stare, she could tell he was a little tipsy.

'I'm fine,' she said, not inviting him in. He gave her a puzzled look and she felt childish, suddenly, and stood back to let him pass.

'Patsy cooks like an angel,' he said, throwing himself into the orange chair as if he owned the place. Then he began to recount every detail of the meal of roast chicken and anchovy butter, crisp chunks of sourdough bread and chilli-roasted vegetables from the garden. Bel realized she was bored. *Food is all this man ever talks about*, she thought, making no attempt to offer him tea.

Then Louis had sat up, his gaze intense. 'Bel, I know I shouldn't be asking you this, but I really need your advice . . . about Apollinaire.'

278

She resisted the urge to give a sardonic eye roll and waited for him to go on.

'Tally told you he might not be mine?'

She nodded.

Louis wiped his hands across his face – a gesture with which Bel was very familiar. 'I've only Trinny's word. She never said a single thing until that witch of a mother started kicking off. Then one day, when she's watched me fall in love with the little guy – encouraged it, even – she springs it on me that she was screwing this Turkish low-life . . . and that the baby's most likely his.' He sighed. 'But she could be lying, obviously . . . to get rid of me.'

Bel stopped trying to be nice and gave an impatient sigh. 'Don't you think you should have stuck around and sorted this out with Trinny, instead of running away, Louis?'

He gave her one of his beguiling looks, which she'd always found hard to resist. But the magic wasn't quite working tonight.

'*You don't understand.* Valérie made life hell for me. She wanted me gone. What was the point of staying when Trinny was telling me I wasn't the father?' Louis's head drooped. When he raised it again she saw anguish in his eyes. 'I loved him, you know.'

Bel was speechless. She felt for him, how could she not? But she couldn't help remembering how he had *never wanted another baby* . . . how he had tried with every ounce of sympathy and charm to make her have a termination.

She watched as he began to drag himself upright. 'I'm sorry. I really shouldn't be involving you in this. Too many

279

glasses of Patsy's Beaujolais.' He gave her a wan smile. 'It's just you're so good at working things out. You always know what to do. I took you completely for granted, of course.'

Holding herself very still, she'd waited as he ambled towards the door. When he drew level, he'd turned and, head on one side, taken her face in his hands, his palms warm and slightly sweaty against her cheeks. He stared at her, his dark eyes soft with wine and sentiment. She thought for an uncomfortable moment that he might try to kiss her. She twitched her head, just fractionally, and he dropped his hands.

'Night, sweetheart,' he'd said, his expression unreadable.

He hasn't called me sweetheart in such a long time, she'd thought, as she closed the door.

It had all made her sad. Everything about Louis made her sad, or angry, or resentful. Because she would have to tell her father about him. Dennis would suspect the worst, of course, crow about how right he had been about Bel being up to something, having a secret 'fella', rant on and on.

Now, lugging her father's case up the narrow inn stairs, she felt she could hardly bear the impending drama.

Later that evening, Bel and her father sat outside the Queen Bess, eating the pub's fish and chips and mushy peas. Dennis was obviously exhausted from the drive, and not a little stewed from the 'wee glass' – which had turned into more like three neat whiskies – that Logan had administered earlier. But he was in a mellow mood and clearly enjoying the summer evening, which was lovely, the sun a misty pink in the sky, the air cool and fresh.

She knew it was now or never. 'You'll never guess who pitched up here a couple of weeks ago.'

Her father's eyes narrowed as he thought, but he shook his head.

After another beat, during which her stomach flipped uncomfortably, she muttered, 'Louis.'

He stared at her blankly for a moment. 'Louis? You mean, *your* Louis?'

She nodded, holding her breath, waiting for the onset of the tsunami of bile.

But Dennis just looked puzzled. 'I thought he was in France with the totty. What the hell's he doing here?'

'I honestly don't know, Dad.'

Her father narrowed his eyes. 'He wouldn't have come unless you asked him.'

'I *didn't* ask him.' She tried to keep her tone even.

Continuing to regard her with a degree of scepticism, Dennis was silent for a moment. Then he declared fiercely, 'That thieving wee scrote owes me a lot of money.' He pointed a finger at Bel. 'So that's what you've been hiding, girl. I knew there was something!' He gave a low whistle. 'You've taken him back, haven't you? He's shacked up with you in the hovel *right now*.'

'No,' she said, with teeth-grinding patience. 'He just found a job in a pub on the main road. *They* are putting him up.'

Shaking his head back and forth as if he was befuddled Dennis, completely ignoring her denial, said, 'I don't understand you, Bella. Why would you take that shite back after all he's done to you? Are you that spineless?' He threw his hands into the air. 'Christ, I've warned you enough.'

'Dad, *listen to me*, will you? I have *not* taken Louis back. *We're not together.* I never asked him to come.' She sighed. 'I absolutely hate him being here, if you want the honest truth.'

Her father sat back suddenly on the bench, obviously forgetting he wasn't in a chair, and nearly toppled onto the ground, only saving himself by clutching the edge of the table with one hand. Recovering, he stated, 'Won't be a problem when you're back home, sweetheart. The bastard can't bother you there, not on my turf he can't.' He sounded like a possessive husband seeing off his wife's lover.

I'm not coming back. Bel wanted to stand up and throw her arms wide, shout from the rooftops. *I'm never coming back.* But this was not the moment, when her father was tired and harbouring an unfounded paranoia about Louis. She wasn't even sure her silent declaration was completely true, despite her desperately wanting it to be so. Instead she said, 'Pudding? The sticky toffee's not bad.'

Dennis brushed off her question. Instead he muttered, 'I need to see him. I need to see that Louis de-flaming-Courcy. He owes me money.'

'Listen, Louis and I are both very aware of our debt to you, Dad, really we are,' she replied soothingly. 'I know it's been slow, but you will get your money, I promise. I'm working on it from my side, putting away what I can to give you.' The meagre savings were squashed into a jam jar in her bedside table. It was an almost pointlessly small amount. It just made her feel she was doing something, at least, towards getting the debt off her back. 'And Louis is fully committed too. But he's not in a good place, financially, at the moment.' She didn't add that he was currently borrowing money from her, as well.

'I need to see him,' her father reiterated, disregarding what she'd just said. It was clear that alcohol and tiredness were beginning to take their toll: Dennis's words were now slurring, his gaze unfocused, eyes blinking tiredly. 'I want to have it out with him *right now*.' He attempted to stumble up from the bench.

Bel rose, too, and grabbed her father's arm to steady him. 'OK, Dad. OK. We'll go up tomorrow, if you like. But you're not in a fit state tonight. You can't drive after all those whiskies.'

Dennis gazed vacantly up at her for a second. 'Help me find my room, girl. I can't remember where it is . . . I need to lie down.'

After she'd seen her father safely into his room, Bel walked slowly down the lane to her cottage with a heavy heart. She felt beleaguered, dreading the inevitable confrontation between Louis and her father in the morning but helpless to alter the course of Dennis's will.

29

True to his word, the first thing her stubborn father said to Bel when she met him outside the pub the following morning was 'Where's this place Louis works? Take me there now.'

Bel stood her ground. 'Honestly, Dad, this is pointless. What are you going to gain by it? He's totally skint right now. And you can't tear strips off him in front of his new boss. He needs this job.' *I need him to have it, too.* She didn't want his share of the debt sliding onto her shoulders . . . or her ex-partner sleeping in the van on her doorstep again, either. 'Let me talk to him.'

But Dennis was already moving towards the car, parked in one of the few gravelled slots reserved for guests at the inn.

Bel followed him. 'Dad, stop.'

He took no notice of her as he opened the car door and got in.

So, she climbed in beside him, resigned. *If they fight, they fight*, she told herself. Louis was a grown-up . . . mostly.

Louis was obviously surprised to see them. *He doesn't look as worried as he should*, she thought grimly, as he greeted her taciturn father without much enthusiasm. His puffy eyes and untidy ponytail gave him the appearance of someone just out of bed – he would have been working late, she knew.

'Do you want coffee?'

Both shook their heads. Louis pointed to one of the rickety picnic tables out front – like the pub itself, in need of an upgrade – indicating they should sit. But Dennis just crossed his arms.

'Bel didn't tell me you were coming down,' Louis said to her father, adopting a conversational tone.

'Aye, well, she didn't tell me you were already here,' Dennis parried curtly. He seemed to have revived from the previous night, and looked dapper this morning, Bel thought. Not the frail old man she'd helped up to bed. 'But then that's Bella for you.'

Louis, swaying from foot to foot uneasily, looked as if he wasn't sure what this meant. 'Are you staying –'

'I'm not here for small-talk,' Dennis interrupted him brusquely. 'You owe me money. A lot. Don't think you can wriggle out of your responsibility, son. I need a contribution from you. A down payment. *Now.*'

Louis recoiled. He glanced at Bel, but she couldn't help. 'Listen, Dennis, I know I've fucked up. I'm really sorry you had to step in –'

'I don't want snivelling apologies. I just want my money.'

Louis took a breath. 'I'm afraid I'm literally flat broke at the moment.'

Her father, who'd known this all along, of course, regarded Louis with utter contempt. 'So what's your plan?'

'Umm . . .' Louis hesitated, casting a glance towards the pub as he lowered his voice. 'I'm not making much here,

285

and there's rent . . . But of course I'll start paying you back as soon as I can, Dennis.' Bel could tell Louis was trying to sound convincing, but her father wasn't impressed.

'I'll need more than vague promises, ya slippery wee shite.' Dennis raised his eyebrows, cocked his head at Louis. 'Don't you get it? I want *cash*.'

Bel was so wound up she had a strong desire to laugh. This scene was like something from a TV drama, where the heavy comes round – complete with Glaswegian accent, which was getting stronger the angrier her father became – and threatens to kneecap some unfortunate wretch, unless he does what's required. Nobody, though, was laughing.

'I'll pay it all back, of course,' said Louis, drawing himself up in an attempt to restore some dignity to the situation. 'But on my current salary, it may take some time.'

The air went still. Then Dennis moved forward with a menacing calm until he was standing so close to Louis that the chef reared back. It made Bel shudder, reminding her of that night over the backgammon board, his violence in the hall after she'd been to see Nathan Riker. Now Dennis and Louis were nose to nose.

'You cocky little prick,' her father growled softly into his face. 'Never give a rat's arse about anyone but yourself, do you?' Breathing heavily, he stepped back, shaking his head wearily as if Louis suddenly wasn't worth the trouble. 'No fucking respect, that's your problem.'

Louis looked shaken and cowed. She sympathized, knowing how it felt to be on the receiving end of her father's anger. He straightened his shirt and shook himself.

Casting an anguished look at Bel – as if she could help him – he stood for a moment, looking a bit dazed, then spun on his heel and disappeared back into the pub slamming the door behind him.

'That went well, Dad,' she said tightly.

He didn't speak until they were in the car again, but it was clear Dennis was still quietly incandescent, his cheeks almost purple with rage. He turned to face her. 'This is your fault, girl,' he spat. 'You picked him. You pandered to him, handing over every penny for that useless gaff of his. I'm sick of waiting around while he laughs in my face and does what he likes.' He stamped his foot on the brake as he turned on the ignition, yanking his seatbelt so fiercely that it locked and he was left tugging helplessly on the thing, each jerk only increasing his fury. 'Dribbling cash my way isn't good enough any more, girl. If the pair of you can't do better, you'll have to sell that hovel you're so proud of and stump up the full amount ASAP.' He shot her a pained look. 'Because you don't understand. *I need that money.*'

Bel sat in trembling silence. She was shocked. She had no idea about the state of her father's finances, and if she'd asked, Dennis would have told her to mind her own business. *Surely he owns the flat*, she thought, *that must be worth a few bob*. He frequently referred to his 'millions', too, although that could all be bluster. She had no way of knowing if he'd borrowed against the flat, or made some unwise investment decisions recently. He'd been something of a gambler in his younger days.

Her father had seemed satisfied – although she appreciated he didn't have much choice – when she'd made a promise to pay back the loan bit by bit. 'I'm not gagging for it,' he'd told her back then. *Has something changed?* Bel wondered, nerves jangling with anxiety. She was doing everything she could towards reducing the debt, with proceeds of the sale of stuff from the Walthamstow flat, her mother's watch, a portion of her wages. If things had, indeed, changed maybe he was now desperate for all of the cash. *Seeing as Louis's flat broke* . . . She would have no option but to sell the cottage. The knowledge made her feel utterly sick.

Staying silent as Dennis roared dangerously back to the village through the narrow lanes, she realized she couldn't even be sure if her father was telling her the truth. Did he actually need the money for himself or was it the principle of the thing? He had, after all, every right to want the money back. *How serious is he?*

Then another, less comfortable question began to pick at her brain. *Is he devious enough to use the debt as leverage to force me back to London?* Holding her feet to the fire like an old-fashioned school bully? There was no way of knowing.

When they arrived at the Queen Bess, she said in a subdued voice, 'I've got some things to do at the house, Dad. Will you be OK for an hour or so?' She just needed to get away from him.

Her father's face fell. He'd calmed down now, always quick to snap out of a mood if he chose. 'Can't I come too, sweetheart? You haven't shown me the cottage yet.'

'I won't be long,' she replied, biting her lip. She hurried away before he could persuade her otherwise. As she walked home, her phone rang. Tally.

'You must be telepathic ... Or maybe you heard our dads shouting at each other from Canary Wharf,' Bel joked bitterly, then filled her stepdaughter in about Louis and the contretemps between him and her own father.

Tally groaned. 'Nightmare, poor you. So humiliating. Is Dad OK, apart from just now? What's the place like? He's not replied to my last two texts.'

'I don't think he's particularly OK, to be honest, sweetheart. When I saw him earlier in the week, he was obviously very cut up about the baby. And that rubbish job won't last a fortnight.'

'So you two are talking ... getting on?'

Bel had been about to scoff at the suggestion. But she'd heard the hopeful note in Tally's voice and held back. 'We're ... It's hard to say what we are. He's not all bad, your dad.'

She heard Tally laugh. 'Well, that's a relief. Get him to call me, will you? I worry when he goes quiet.'

'I'm way too old for this malarkey,' her father grumbled, when he and Bel reached the beach that evening, on JJ's invitation. He was eyeing JJ's paddleboard with considerable misgivings.

'Yeah, and I'm totally too old to be a surfer dude,' JJ said cheerfully, 'but that's never stopped me.'

Her father narrowed his eyes, hearing the challenge. 'Oh, go on, then. Show me.'

The sea was almost calm and JJ made it simple for her father – as he had for Bel – holding the board steady, helping him climb on, guiding him along until he'd got his balance. 'Terrific,' Dennis kept repeating between curses, clearly nervous, but loving every minute. Bel found she was proud of him for being so game at his age.

Now she and her father were sitting side by side on her open dry robe, legs outstretched. She felt more relaxed, the dramas of the morning fading under the rays of the warm evening sun.

'That JJ fella fancies you,' her father said, eyeing JJ as he pulled the paddleboards up onto the sand and unfastened the ankle leads.

Bel winced. Her father's hyper-vigilance for anything related to his daughter never ceased to amaze her. JJ hadn't been overtly flirting, had he? Perhaps he'd stood a little close as he helped her onto the board. Maybe his smile had been quite intimate when she fell off. She'd enjoyed the game. 'He's been a good friend,' she said, noncommittally.

'He's OK,' her father announced, to Bel's amazement – she hadn't expected surfer dudes to come high on Dennis's approval list. She watched as her father rolled awkwardly onto his side, then leaned heavily on his knee to push himself upright – all with a fair amount of grunts and moans. 'Right. Come on, girl. Time to show me the hovel. I don't know what you're hiding, but you seem very reluctant to let me inside.'

Bel forced a laugh, but didn't get up. It was true, she had hustled him past the cottage on the way down to the beach. Part of her didn't want him anywhere near the place. 'You only got here yesterday evening, Dad.'

JJ, flopping down beside Bel, interrupted their conversation. 'You guys coming to Patsy's tonight?'

'The pink-haired hippie next door?' Dennis demanded rudely.

'You know her?' JJ asked.

'Met her when Bella's mother was still alive. She didn't take to me back then,' Dennis replied, with a sly grin. 'Reckon men aren't her thing.'

'She likes me and Micky,' JJ mused in response. 'And Logan . . . Louis.'

Her father snorted. 'I hope she hasn't asked that bloody eejit to dinner. I'm not sitting down with him.'

'Dad,' Bel implored, 'can you stop being so grumpy? It's very kind of Patsy to have us round. She's a brilliant cook.'

Before he could protest further, JJ said, 'Take you surfing next time there are waves, Dennis?' And her father's tetchy frown dissolved.

Holding her breath, Bel pushed open the front door. They had walked up the lane in silence, as Dennis, quite reasonably worn out from his exertions, was breathless and taking his time. Each step seemed agony to Bel as he crept closer to entering her private domain. She knew she was being ridiculous, but the thought of him in her space was actually making her feel sick – her churning stomach made worse by the real fear, now, that she might be forced to sell the cottage.

Stumbling over the threshold, Dennis stood there in silence, casting a beady eye around the room. Bel had made it as pretty as she could, with blush-pink roses from the bush in the back garden on the coffee table, everything tidy, the windows open to let in the smell of summer. She thought it looked lovely.

'Christ, it's even pokier than I remember,' her father pronounced dismissively. 'Although I suppose it looks better than it did in your mother's day.' His expression implied there was a bad smell under his nose. 'What do you think it'll sell for?' he asked, as he settled himself in the orange chair. 'No point in your doing any more to the place. Whoever takes it on will rip it all out and start again.'

'Tea?' Bel pretended not to hear his question while silently asking one of her own: *What did I expect?*

'That old crock runs to a cuppa, does it?' he asked, casting a scathing glance at poor Ray.

Seeing the cottage for the first time through her dad's jaundiced eye, Bel didn't know how to respond to his disparagement. OK, it was small. And not elegant or remotely smart with her bodged-together DIY renovations. *But is it 'poky'? Am I fooling myself that I can be happy here?* This was why she'd been reluctant to let him past the front door. As usual, when in her father's company even for a short time, she found all confidence in herself and her decisions draining slowly away.

30

Dennis had been in Cornwall a week. *Two more days*, Bel counted, her spirits soaring as she set off for the farm shop on Thursday morning. As the week passed, so Dennis's mood had mellowed – he seemed to be having a great time, everyone being so kind, putting themselves out to entertain him. He gradually stopped ranting about Louis – who sensibly stayed out of sight – appearing more cheerful than Bel had seen him in a long while.

After his initial depressing visit, Bel kept him away from the cottage as much as possible. It was clear he found the place distasteful and there was no proper table at which they could have their meals. So they mostly ate at the Queen Bess or Martine's – Dennis declaring he was on holiday and wanted to eat out. And one night they took Patsy to the Chinese on the main road – a small thank-you for her insistence on cooking for Dennis and the others.

Her father had, from his first encounter with Bel's friend and neighbour, been on a serious charm offensive, despite his snippy remarks. He minded being disliked. And Patsy – although Bel was certain she saw through Dennis – played along, sparring with him, taking no nonsense, even teasing him on occasion, sending Bel's heart bursting through her chest when she saw her father join in the laughter. He loved it when someone stood up to him . . . as long as it wasn't Bel.

He even attempted a bit of tipsy flirting with Rhian, who simply appeared not to notice. 'She's a nice wee thing, the vicar,' her father had said, walking up the lane to the pub after supper at the chapel. 'Didn't seem interested in me, though. Maybe she bats for the other side, too.'

'So if she doesn't laugh at your jokes, she must be gay?' Bel had said, with an incredulous snort. She wasn't going to explain Rhian and Patsy's love for each other. She was pretty certain her father wouldn't understand loving someone and not wanting to go to bed with them. Bel wasn't sure she did, either, although there was no denying the strength of feeling between the two women.

Now, as she rode up the hill out of the village on her way to work, she realized she was hanging on by a thread, aching for the moment when her father would climb into the Jaguar, start the engine and drive back to London.

She'd been in a blind panic since the conversation about selling the cottage. Throughout his stay, Dennis had made constant reference to the sale. His tone was mostly light-hearted and confident – as if it were a given, he and Bel happily on the same page.

His conversations frequently began with the prefix 'When you've sold the hovel . . .' or 'When you're back home . . .' followed by various suggestions about their life together in the London flat. He wanted to get the place painted, he said. He thought it might be nice to book theatre tickets and have some meals out in the restaurants – like Wilton's – he'd frequented before the pandemic. Bel didn't know how to respond to these suggestions, so she fudged her replies or changed the subject. It was so wearing, the threat hovering over their exchanges, like a hawk preparing to swoop. She knew she should challenge him about it all, she just didn't feel she had any satisfactory alternative to offer.

Mr Ajax was in the kitchen when she arrived, his usual cup clutched to his chest, a faraway look in his eye.

'Those croissants,' he said, when she greeted him. 'I've been having a think . . . You do them a lot?'

She shook her head. 'First time. But I'm starting some more today.' Sensing the opening she'd imagined when she'd first seen the farm-shop kitchen, she added quickly, 'I used to bake professionally for a London restaurant. I can do bread, cakes, pies, anything, really.' She listed the things she remembered Harris saying that Elowen had baked.

There was a long pause. Then Mr Ajax said, 'We can always sell baked goods here, you know.' The look he gave her was uncharacteristically engaged. As if her croissant had broken through some barrier. He wasn't exactly smiling, but it was close.

Bel took a huge breath, pushing her shoulders back. 'I would absolutely love to bake in this kitchen,' she said, her voice unwavering. This was the moment she'd been waiting for.

Her boss nodded, perhaps a bit surprised by her enthusiasm. 'You would? Well, then,' he said, wandering over to the sink and turning on the tap to rinse out his mug.

Bel held her breath. He slowly spun to face her. She thought she saw resignation, as if he was finally accepting something he'd been resisting. 'Maybe we could have a chat about it.' He carefully set his mug upside down on the draining-board. 'Early Monday? Before your shift?'

Bel smiled. 'Great. Yes, I'll do that. Thanks, Mr Ajax,' she said, hardly able to suppress her excitement. If this worked out, not only would she be doing a job she loved, it would boost her earnings considerably. *Maybe I can persuade Dad to go back to his original arrangement, if I can prove I've got more money coming in*, she thought, as she settled, breathless, behind the till.

When Harris appeared late morning, she was busy, but she had one ear open for the sound of his leather boots creaking over the shop floorboards, anticipating the smile of greeting that always lit up his serious face.

'How's it going with your father?' he asked, in a lull between customers.

Bel shook her head wearily. 'I think *he*'s enjoyed himself. Can't say I'm not relieved he's off on Saturday.' Another basket thudded onto the table and she turned back to the till before Harris had the chance to reply. She longed to tell him about Mr Ajax's offer, but nothing had been decided and she didn't want to jinx it before she'd had a proper discussion with her boss.

It was busy, and it was only when her father was standing right in front of her that she looked up and jumped. 'Dad!'

'Thought I'd come by and find out what you get up to in here,' Dennis said cheerfully. She had offered to show him the farm shop on a number of occasions when they'd driven past, but he'd declined, as if he didn't want to acknowledge she had a job at all.

'Nice wee place,' he went on, checking out the nearby shelves. 'If it wasn't for the rip-off prices.'

Bel glanced anxiously round to see if Mr Ajax was in earshot. Luckily he was busy in the lean-to, freshening the vegetable display. 'Please, keep your voice down,' she begged, not keen to upset her boss, just when she'd persuaded him to open up his kitchen to her.

Dennis's eyes widened in mock alarm. 'Not wrong, though, eh?' he said, with a wicked grin.

To distract him, Bel indicated her friend and said, 'Dad, this is Harris. He's the wildlife artist Patsy was talking about the other night. Harris, this is my father, Dennis.'

'Oh?' Her father turned, interest piqued. 'Those women raved on about your work. I might take a look while I'm here.'

Harris got to his feet. 'Good to meet you, Dennis,' he said politely, but making no move to shake his hand. 'I'd be happy to show you, anytime.' He sounded formal, almost wary of her father, and Bel remembered what she'd said about him in the past.

Dennis nodded. 'Well, I did plan to leave on Saturday. But now I'm thinking I might stay on for a while. The city's shite at this time of year. And my disloyal daughter here seems reluctant to shift her arse back to London yet.'

Bel felt the breath go out of her lungs. Harris, maybe sensing her distress, looked uneasy and did not share in Dennis's caustic laughter. He shot her a sympathetic glance, but Mr Ajax, lugging a large box of lettuces in from the lane, interrupted them with a shout: 'This isn't a social club, you lot. If you're not buying, then take your chatter outside. There's people waiting to be served, Bel.'

Her father frowned at being addressed in a manner not dissimilar to the one he regularly meted out. 'Nice way to treat your customers,' he grumbled, crossing his arms but not moving.

'Sorry, Ron. Just off,' Harris said good-naturedly, taking his mug back to the kitchen. As he went past, he reached out a hand and gave Bel's arm a supportive pat.

'I'll see you back at the pub in an hour,' Bel said to her father, silently pleading with him not to upset her employer further.

Harrumphing quietly, Dennis, lips pursed, stomped away, giving Mr Ajax a dirty look as the two men passed each other in the narrow aisle between the vegetables.

Bel cycled back to the village at the end of her shift, her mind in turmoil now she had the chance to focus on her father's most recent bombshell. *He can't stay*, she kept telling herself firmly. *Logan's fully booked all summer and so is everywhere else.*

The green Jaguar was nowhere to be seen as Bel rode past the pub. She wondered where her father had gone. But when she drew level with Martine's café, she caught sight of Louis and Jaz, sitting opposite each other with takeaway cups at one of the picnic tables. Distracted from her thoughts for a second, she braked to a stop, dismounting and propping her bike against the hedge.

'Hi, you two.'

Jaz greeted her with a wave and a broad grin. 'Hey, Bel. Come and join us. Louis's filling me in on the horrors of the professional kitchen.'

Louis also smiled, but warily, clearly still unsure what to expect from her. Bel was too upset, though, to remember she was no longer his friend. She plonked herself down on the wooden bench, leaned on the table and dropped her head onto her arms with a despairing groan.

'Dad's threatening to stay on,' she wailed.

Jaz looked puzzled by her outburst. But Louis got it. 'Shit,' he said, then cast an apologetic glance at Jaz. 'Sorry.'

The teenager laughed. 'Heard much worse.'

'He can't stay with me,' Bel went on, as if someone had suggested he should. 'There's only one bed and one chair.'

It was clear that neither Louis nor Jaz knew what to say.

'Jazzy!' A yell came from the lane. Bel turned to see two teenage girls – long hair, long legs, short shorts, phones held out in front of them, like talismans to ward off evil, beach bags slung over their shoulders. 'You coming?' shouted the taller of the two.

Jaz waved. 'In a minute. You go on.' She hesitated as her friends moved off towards the beach. 'Better go,' she said to Louis. 'Can we talk another time, please?'

'Good kid,' he said, when Jaz was out of sight. 'Reminds me of Tally.'

'Me too,' Bel agreed. They shared a certain vulnerability, an honesty, and a wry sense of humour. 'So, why aren't you at work?'

'Leak in the kitchen ceiling. The place was ankle-deep

299

in brown water when I went down this morning.' He frowned. 'What can we do about your dad?' It was not an unfamiliar question, and took her back to many similar conversations in the past when Dennis had been playing up. 'I mean about the money,' Louis went on. 'Not sure I can help with him staying on.'

'I don't know. He insists he really needs it.' Bel sighed. 'Demanded I sell the cottage right now and pay him the lot.'

'For fuck's sake.' Louis looked horrified, then immediately pensive. 'I'm not much use. I'm so sorry, Bel. I've literally got peanuts left at the end of the week at the moment. But I reckon I can get a better job soon, and then I promise I'll start contributing.' He paused. 'But there's no way I can raise a lump sum . . . if he genuinely is desperate for it.'

Bel caught the note of scepticism in his voice. But she knew that Louis's attitude tended to be that people who owed him money were crooks, while those to whom he was indebted didn't really need it and could wait. 'Could you borrow some?' he added, raising an enquiring eyebrow at her.

Resenting the implication that it was her responsibility to do so, she spoke more sharply than she intended. 'Who from, Louis? The banks and mortgage companies would laugh in my face at my age, with a part-time job on minimum wage. Especially these days.' Even if Mr Ajax agreed to the baking venture, she doubted it would even be worth asking.

'Aunt Phyllis?'

Bel shook her head firmly. 'I wouldn't dream of it. Why

300

should she lend me cash to pay off a brother who's shunned her for decades?'

There was a tense silence.

'So what did you tell him?'

'I didn't tell him anything,' she said miserably. Articulating to Louis the prospect of losing her home made it suddenly so horribly real. All the hope she'd invested in her new life, only to find herself imprisoned back in the London flat . . . 'I can't sell.' She heard the tremulous bravado in her voice, but she knew she might not have a choice. 'I should have a better job soon,' she added, still not wanting to take anything for granted. 'I'm going to try to persuade Dad to give us more time.' She thought for a moment. 'Maybe he'll agree to leaving it another year before deciding to sell.' *Anything could have happened by then*, she told herself.

'I'll definitely start contributing as soon as I can,' Louis assured her.

Neither spoke for a few minutes, both lost in thought.

'What's happening with the baby?' she asked eventually. Any subject, even Apollinaire, was better than focusing on her uncertain future in Cornwall.

'Trinny's agreed to a test.' Louis raised his hands, dropped them again in a resigned gesture. 'We'll see.'

'Will you go back? If he is yours?'

He hesitated for a long moment. 'I don't know how I could. Trinny and I, it'd never work.' Then leaning forward, his gaze suddenly intense, he asked, 'Would it matter to you, Bel, that I have a relationship with him?'

She was taken aback. *Oh, shit*, she thought, light slowly

dawning. She knew she was staring at him like the proverbial rabbit in the oncoming headlights but couldn't find anything to say in reply.

Another silence.

Then Louis gave a heavy sigh. 'You and me, don't you feel there's still something there?' He held up his hand. 'I know, I know. Obviously I'm not expecting you to forgive me right now. I just wondered . . . if we take it slowly over the summer . . . get to know each other again?' He gave her a winning smile. 'We made such a great team, Bel.'

It felt as if the bottom had fallen out of Bel's stomach. *Don't*, she thought. *Don't do this, Louis.* During the time she'd been in Cornwall, the shadow he'd cast over her life by leaving her had begun to fade in her consciousness – as if from a pulsing dark red to the softest of pinks.

She felt bewildered. Despite his gross betrayal, seeing Louis again reminded her, too, of the good times – the life they'd shared, the love she'd once felt for him. She took a breath, unsure if she had the strength or clarity to know her own mind.

Louis reached for her hand, stroking her skin gently with his thumb. He had chef's hands: scrubbed pale, nails short, various nicks and scars dotting the surface.

Bel let him, his touch involuntarily triggering a deep-seated longing to stop struggling against the seemingly uphill task to find independence. *So much easier . . . so much easier*, the voice murmured softly in her ear. She was tired. She was getting nowhere. Louis would help her stand up to her father. *They were a team.*

'I mean, maybe – just a thought – we could look for a

place that needs both of us: chef *and* front-of-house? Someone who'd kill for our dream team – because we were good together, no?' He squeezed her hand encouragingly, gave her a tentative smile. Then his face fell to something more serious. 'Look, I know I've hurt you very badly, Bel. And I'm so, so sorry.' He sat up straighter. 'But you have no idea how much I miss having you in my life. I want to make it up to you, if only you'll let me.'

Bel, throughout his speech, had found her heart turning somersaults. *What he's suggesting isn't such a stupid idea, in principle* . . . In principle. She wished he would stop talking, stop setting up bumps in a road Bel felt she had been negotiating just fine until he had pitched up.

'Do you still love me?' He interrupted her thoughts, an edge of doubt creeping into his voice. 'You know my feelings for you . . .' His hand was still clasped around hers, as if he didn't dare let go, but in the sunshine it felt sweaty and uncomfortable. Very gently, she extricated herself, putting her hands in her lap, out of reach.

Louis was eyeing her nervously. 'Say something, Bel. You haven't said a word. What are you thinking?'

Bel shook herself. *How would I feel,* right now, *if I say yes?* she asked herself urgently. A montage of the imaginary life Louis was describing for them flashed briefly across her vision. She blinked . . . But all she could see was *him*, centre stage once more, herself in the background, his willing acolyte, drowned out by his manic energy, his obsession, the exacting demands of his work. *Do I want to be a spare part in that drama again?*

Heart exploding in her chest, she felt as if she'd been

running full tilt, then screeched to a halt right on the very edge of a deep abyss. *No*, she decided. The word slotted neatly into place, as if it had only been waiting for her permission. NO.

Taking a deep breath she spoke gently. 'I'm sorry, Louis. This isn't about me still being angry with you. I'm just really loving doing my own thing.' She watched his eyes cloud. 'And I need to be by myself to do that . . . if my father will let me,' she joked, to take the sting out of the tail.

Louis didn't speak for a minute, maybe wondering how he could pitch again, and better. He wasn't someone to give in easily.

'Do you still love me, Bel?' he asked again, softly but insistently.

She felt her cheeks flush. 'I . . . I . . .' No clear answer came to her. When eventually she replied, her tone was kind but surprisingly resolute. 'It's not the same, Louis. Nothing's the same. *I'm* different. Or, at least, I want different things for myself now.'

Looking puzzled, he asked, 'What things?'

She threw her hands wide into the air. 'This! My cottage – if I'm allowed to keep it – the village, the people . . .' She was going to add 'baking' to the list but feared he would scoff.

'You could still have that with me.'

There was a fragile silence as their eyes met.

'No, Louis. *I couldn't*,' Bel said, with a finality he couldn't fail to hear. There was no need to explain further.

Louis's mouth tightened. After a long moment he said simply, 'OK. Right.'

'I'm sorry.'

'Yeah, me too. Although I realize I deserve it.'

She didn't reply.

'I only came here for you, Bel,' he said forlornly. 'If that's not happening, I'll start looking for a better job somewhere else. Get out of your hair.' It didn't sound like a threat so much as him applying a final test of her feelings. But to Bel it felt as if a huge stone had been rolled away from the path in front of her. So much so that she was almost lightheaded.

'I should get on,' she said, trying not to show how his words made her feel. 'I baked some croissants last week – thought I'd give it another go.'

Louis sucked his teeth. 'Ooh, tricky one. If you need any help, I'd be happy to show you.'

It was a genuine offer, but all Bel heard was the echo of his slightly patronizing attitude to her cooking in the past. 'Thanks,' she said. 'In fact, the last lot turned out brilliantly.'

As she rose from the bench, Louis did too. After a moment of hesitation, he put his arms round her and hugged her. His hug felt so familiar on one level, but now also awkward and strange. Bel tried to respond with her heart, but found she could not.

Wheeling her bike the short distance to her door, she felt her lungs inhaling the warm sweetness of summer with trembling relief. Her feelings for Louis, she knew, were still muddled – it wasn't even a year since they'd separated. But she also understood that the bonds that tied them together had been irrevocably broken the day he'd walked out on her.

As she pulled the bag of strong floor off the smooth ash-wood shelf and watched the soft white cascade pile up in the scales pan, she realized she was almost shocked at how strong, how clear she'd been with Louis. But, most of all, she was thankful that she felt so sure.

Patsy dropped by just as Bel finished the final folding of butter into pastry and laid the square reverently in the fridge till the morning. Her friend looked uncharacteristically tense.

'Make me a cuppa, love,' she said, leaning on the worktop and dropping her head. 'Had a bit of a shit day.'

Patsy didn't say another word while Bel made her tea and handed her the mug. She indicated the chair for her friend to sit, but Patsy didn't seem to notice, remaining standing with her back against the stove rail.

'What's up?'

Patsy's eyebrows twitched and she shook her head. 'I took Jaz into Truro this morning, to meet her mum for a coffee.' There was a pause. 'She didn't want to come, but I insisted . . . I told her it would be good to see her.'

Bel waited.

'But that dear, reliable daughter of mine – who promised on Jaz's life that she was now clean – was a sodding no-show.'

'Oh, shit. I'm so sorry. I just saw Jaz with Louis and she seemed OK.'

Patsy gave a harsh laugh. 'Yeah, well, that's Jaz for you.

Good at hiding it.' She shrugged. 'Although, unlike me, she seems to have given up on any expectations from that quarter . . . very sensibly.'

Bel winced. 'Maybe something happened that meant Ruby couldn't make it.'

'Oh, yeah, I'm sure "something" happened. Like, another hit of whatever poison she's currently shooting into her veins.'

Bel put an arm around Patsy's shoulders.

'We waited nearly an hour because I still hoped. Then we came home. It was fucking awful.'

'Maybe it was worth a try, though?' Bel asked, not knowing if she was right.

Patsy jerked around, her face a picture of bewilderment. 'Was it? Really? What's that saying about doing the same thing and expecting a different outcome? Some people just don't give a fuck what effect they have on others . . . because they *only ever think about themselves*.'

Bel thought she knew exactly what her friend meant.

Bel and her father sat on the wooden bench at the head of the beach, overlooking the sands. It was eight thirty and they'd already eaten their favourite fish and chips at the Queen Bess. During supper Dennis had told her about the museum-gallery he'd visited in Penzance earlier, and Laura Knight, the twentieth-century British artist exhibited there. He waffled on about war art and some bloke in a four-by-four who had cut him up at the roundabout, then about the cheese scone he'd had for lunch.

Bel listened with half an ear, but she was only looking for a break in the conversation in order to put her question. She hadn't yet brought up Dennis's comment to Harris about extending his visit, because she hadn't wanted to spoil supper. But it had bugged her all afternoon and now she needed to know. She also realized this was almost her last chance, if he did go home as planned, to have the conversation about the debt – to plead with him for more time.

'Were you serious about not leaving, Dad? It's not going to be easy finding somewhere else to stay.'

Her father turned to her on the bench, his face lit by the sun setting radiantly over the cliff to the western side of the bay. But he didn't answer her question. Instead, he gave a contented sigh. 'You know what? I really like this place, Bella. And I'm thinking, *You could live around here, Dennis, old chap.'*

Bel stared at him.

'Listen, sweetheart, I'm not stupid,' he went on enthusiastically. 'I know you don't want to come back to London. And I can see why. So I've come up with this great wee plan.'

She waited, heart thumping, while he shifted about on the hard bench. 'You sell the hovel, as planned, and pay me back. I sell Earls Court. And we buy a nice, roomy place down here. Live in it together.' His smile was triumphant.

Bel could not prevent a small gasp escaping her lips. She was almost used to – although not compliant with – his repeated affirmation that she would sell the cottage. But this new attack on her ever-dwindling hopes of freedom horrified her. 'Dad, you love London. It's where all your friends are . . .'

'Ha! Friends? My only mate is Reg, and he's on his last legs by the look of him. The rest I don't much care for.'

'What about Pauline?'

Dennis shrugged. 'There'll be the equivalent down here.'

Bel frowned, a bit shocked at his casual dismissal of a friend. Although there probably were plenty of older women in the area who would welcome her father's company.

Her father was eyeing her questioningly. 'You do realize she's a tart, don't you?' He waved a hand and hurried on, 'Anyway. This is the perfect plan, don't you think?' When she didn't immediately respond with whoops of joy, he added, 'It'll take the financial burden off you. Security for life . . . And you won't have to do that ridiculous job any more.'

'I like my job,' she muttered weakly. It was all she could think of to say – the smallest bite she could take from the massive, indigestible meal he'd thrown down in front of her. 'And, anyway, I'm getting a better one soon – baking at the farm shop.'

Dennis did not seem to hear her. He leaned forward and nudged her arm. 'How about it, girl? Think how much fun we could have. It's a good crowd you've hooked up with – apart from that grumpy old sod in the farm shop. I could be part of that, too.'

'I love Mum's cottage, Dad, you know I do.' Bel's breath caught in her throat. 'Listen, when I'm earning more money, is there any way we could stick to our original arrangement?' she pleaded, seizing the moment. 'Unless you really, really need the cash . . .' Her father was watching her, but she couldn't read the expression in his dark eyes. 'With this new job – and with Louis pitching in soon – between us we should be able manage a reasonable amount every month.'

Her mind was whirring. She had no idea what Mr Ajax would offer her financially. He was famous for being stingy with his workforce. But she thought he needed her as much as she needed him. And it would be way better than her current income.

'Oh, come now.' Her father's voice interrupted her thoughts. 'You're saying you'd rather slum it in the hovel, where you can touch all four walls at once, than enjoy a proper bit of space, maybe even a sea view?'

He's not listening, not taking me seriously, she thought despairingly. Trying a different tack, since he didn't seem willing to respond to the debt issue, she adopted a cheery tone as she said, 'Dad, come on. You've been in Cornwall a week and suddenly you're moving here?'

Dennis laughed. 'Well, you did exactly that,' he pointed out reasonably, 'and you seem to love it.'

'You have no idea what it's like living in a village,' she said, her voice strident with suppressed panic. 'It's parochial, small-minded. You'd hate it. You're a total townie. And it's summer now, but the winters are bleak, so Patsy says.'

Her father's face seemed set and determined. Taking her hand – which he never did – he stared into her eyes. 'Bella, sweetheart. Please. I'm nearly eighty. I've not got long. I need you . . . You're my only family. Don't be stubborn. You can lead your own life, do whatever job you like. I won't stop you. You know your mum would have wanted it.'

Bel's heart contracted. He was, indeed, very much alone without her. *A man like Dad doesn't make many close friends*, she thought. And at his age the ones he did have were dying off or getting too frail for socializing, like Reg. But the prospect of him living even close by in *her* village – as she'd come to think of it – sent her into a funk. And, unlike with Louis, she couldn't just walk away: he was her flesh and blood, her father. *Would it be so terrible, to share a house . . . if it was big enough?* she found herself asking silently. But her pounding heart provided the answer.

'Why don't you go home as planned, Dad? We need time to think this all through properly. See how you feel in a couple of weeks.' Getting him back to London was her prime concern right now.

Dennis nodded, a small smile on his face. 'So you think it's a sound idea? Good girl.'

She squirmed inwardly. 'Come on, I'll walk you home. It's getting chilly now.' They linked arms and began the ascent through the village to the pub, Dennis breathing heavily, even at the slow pace he chose, and stopping frequently. It was as if he were deliberately advertising the extent of his frailty to her.

Once her father was safely ensconced in his bedroom at the Queen Bess, Bel walked disconsolately back down the lane to the cottage, tense and furious with herself. *Nothing's been agreed*, she kept repeating silently. But it was hard noticing the hope engendered in her father's face by her cowardly lack of resistance to his new plan.

As she turned onto the path leading to her front door, she glanced across to the headland and JJ's van. The lights were on. She hesitated for a moment, then walked back to the lane.

'Hey, you.' JJ's smile was broad and welcoming. 'Nice surprise. Come in, come in.'

'I need a drink,' she said grimly.

Later, after the consumption of a bottle of Rioja – during which JJ listened to her impassioned ranting with admirable patience – they ended up in bed. Bel was too weak for principles tonight . . . and he didn't seem to mind.

It was only when she got back to the cottage the following morning that she remembered the croissant dough, chilling in the fridge. It was Friday, she didn't have to work, so she set about fashioning the pastries, stoking the Rayburn, leaving them for the final prove, then sliding them into the oven.

But she was sure, as she did so, that this batch was doomed. She was feeling none of the pleasure and calm she usually experienced in the baking process. The threat from her father to move down here, too much wine and sex, lack of sleep: none of these made her mood conducive. She felt tired and rough around the edges. Her croissants would sense it and rebel.

When, with trepidation, she opened the oven later that morning, she was depressed to find she was right. The row of pastries looked dismal: shrivelled, burned round the edges and solid to the touch. She told herself it was the oven heat, or the room was over-warm for the second prove, or she'd sloshed on too much egg-wash and sealed the layers. But she knew the problem went deeper than a mere technical misstep.

Bel walked up to the pub to find her father after she'd binned the offending croissants. She hoped he'd have forgotten his crazy idea of the previous evening – aware he'd had quite a bit to drink at supper. Hoped, too, he would be packed and all set to leave for London tomorrow.

But she was met by the landlord at the door, looking harassed. 'I was just about to come and fetch you. Your dad's back's crooked. He's still in bed, says he's been trying to ring you. You'd best go up.'

Bel checked her phone, which she'd put on silent mode

during the night and hadn't switched back – and found six missed calls from her father. She cursed silently as she mounted the stairs and knocked on his door. Hearing a grunt, she went in. Dennis was flat on his back, knees tented under the covers, groaning. When she came nearer, he peered up at her, his small eyes full of reproach.

'It's gone again. You insisted we sit on that damn bench in the cold. That's what's done it.'

Protest rose in Bel's throat. But she held back. 'Poor you. What can I do to help?'

'I need Holly. She's the only one who can fix it.'

'I'm sure there's someone round here. I'll go and ask Logan. Do you want coffee or something to eat?'

'Help me up,' her father demanded, ignoring her question. 'I need to sit up.'

She managed to settle him half propped on the pillows, amid a lot of moaning and cursing. He looked terrible, his hair wild, chin unshaven, gaze befuddled and dark with discomfort.

'Coffee,' he growled, closing his eyes.

As Logan made a double-shot espresso at the machine, he seemed uneasy, not his usual jolly-landlord self. 'Look, Bel, I hate doing this to your dad when he's sick, but I will need the room tomorrow morning. We're chock-full now, till September.'

Bel tried not to panic. 'I'm sure he'll be OK by then. He often gets these spasms. Do you know of any physios?'

Logan looked as if he wasn't sure what a physio was. 'I've got the doc's number.' He pulled a face. 'Not that you get much joy from that lot these days.'

She thanked him. *Patsy will know*, she thought, as she took the coffee upstairs to her father, then went into the corridor to call her neighbour.

Amber, Patsy's friend and reiki master, wafted into Dennis's room on Friday evening in an ankle-length soft green caftan, grey hair sweeping down her back like a sheet, silver bangles jingling softly. Bel thought her father would have a conniption, knowing his opinion of anything vaguely alternative. But her gentle voice and general air of calm seemed to soothe him and he gave in to her ministrations without fuss. *It probably helps she's so beautiful*, Bel thought, wryly.

Afterwards Dennis was in a daze. 'Bloody hell. That woman's a wonder. Hardly touched me. But the heat coming off her hands was like a blow torch.' He'd grinned up at Bel from the bed. 'She pinpointed every ache and pain without asking. Never felt so relaxed in my life.'

His back wasn't completely better, but the crippling spasms had eased a little, leaving aching and stiffness in their wake – the anti-inflammatories Bel had given him were probably kicking in too. Amber promised to return the following day but Bel knew the writing was on the wall. Dennis would not be sliding onto the pale leather seats of his green Jaguar in the morning, and driving away. There was not a chance in hell.

It was just before ten on Saturday morning when Dennis hobbled from the pub, leaning heavily on Micky's arm. Bel had packed for him and his bag was stowed in the boot of the Jaguar.

'You're not driving my car, girl,' her father objected, when he saw her opening the driver's door. 'I can get it as far as the hovel, for Christ's sake.'

'Yeah, but you'll need to put it in the car park, Dennis,' Micky pointed out. The two men had bonded over a couple of evenings of snooker with Micky's friend down the coast. 'And it's a long walk up.'

Dennis frowned at him. 'You drive, then.'

Micky shot Bel a questioning glance, his round blue eyes full of amusement. She just shrugged. No use arguing about the relative competency of women drivers when her father was in this state.

In anticipation of Dennis's stay in Bel's cottage, Logan had loaned her an airbed, Jaz her pink beanbag, JJ a sleeping bag – he'd invited Bel to stay with him in the van, but she knew that was a bad idea and, anyway, her father might need her: those narrow stairs were a death trap to a wobbly old man. *Only a couple of nights*, she kept telling herself.

Later, Bel and Patsy finished pumping up the black, flocked airbed, which, when laid flat, took up a good proportion of the sitting area. Dennis was upstairs in Bel's bed, snoozing.

Patsy stood staring at her. 'Hey, come on, sweetheart,' she said, giving Bel a hug. 'It's not for long. You'll be fine.'

'Will I?'

'Amber's coming later. She'll sort him out and he can be on his way in no time.'

Patsy was trying to comfort her and Bel made an effort to look as if she was succeeding. But she knew her father's back wasn't the real issue here. His last bout of back pain had mysteriously appeared a couple of days before she was due to leave for Cornwall. This was his response when he felt Bel was slipping out of his control. It was as if she were a fish who'd swallowed an angler's fly. She hadn't been reeled in yet, but she had the sensation she was already doomed.

After her friend had gone, Bel climbed the stairs with a cup of tea for her father. When she entered he was propped up in bed, looking thoroughly uncomfortable. He hadn't shaved or brushed his hair today, and appeared derelict.

'How's the back?' she asked, putting his mug down on the bedside table.

'Shite,' came the predictable reply. 'This bed's hard as nails.'

'Well, it's only for a couple of nights,' she said briskly, hovering uncertainly in the doorway.

Her father raised an eyebrow. 'You might at least pretend I'm welcome in your house.'

Bel was stricken. *Is it that obvious?*

'You said it yourself, Dad. "Poky", I think you called it.' She kept her tone light, trying not to sound defensive. '*I* barely fit, so it's hardly ideal for us both.'

'I don't want to be here either, believe me.'

'Hey, come on, Dad.' She suddenly regretted the rancorous atmosphere – for which she felt responsible – and went over and perched on the end of the bed, patting her father's legs through the duvet. 'I've got pasties for lunch. Do you think you'll be able to make it downstairs?'

She could see him struggling to put aside his crabbiness, his mouth twisting as if he were trying actually to swallow it. 'Amber said I should move around, so I suppose I'd better get up. But those stairs are treacherous, I'll need help.'

Once safely downstairs and settled in the orange chair, Bel saw her father eyeing the mattress. 'You're sleeping on that?'

'It'll be fine.'

His features softened. 'I do appreciate you giving up your bed for me, Bella. I've been a bit of an old grump, I know, but this back thing drives me mad. It reminds me of my age, makes me feel like such an old crock.'

'Poor you. It must be horrible.'

'But I suppose I am getting old . . .'

She felt him watching her as she pulled the pasties out of the oven and put them on two small plates. He was about to say something serious, she could tell from his tone, and she wasn't sure she wanted to hear it. 'I haven't got any tomato ketchup, I'm afraid,' she said, as she handed her father his lunch.

He put the plate in his lap. Smiling charmingly at her, he said, 'Me moving here . . . You've had some time to think about it?'

'Umm . . .'

'We used to get on so well, you and me, back in the day. My life ran like clockwork with you in charge. Do you remember when I was supposed to pitch up on that radio show? I'd been on the sauce the night before and you had to rescue me?' He shook his head in admiration. 'You knew as much about those wines as I did.'

Bel did indeed remember. She remembered having to wrangle her father into a clean shirt, turning her head aside to avoid the stale reek of whisky-breath, then bundling him into a taxi, pressing the notes she'd scribbled out at the last minute into his hand when they arrived at the studio building. She'd hardly dared listen to the broadcast, in case he stumbled and bumbled and made a fool of himself. But Dennis rose to the occasion, of course, and put in a lively, convincing performance.

In those years before Louis, when Bel had worked for her father – running the wine workshops, organizing trips abroad, doing the admin for his business and his life – he was exacting, controlling, but showed few signs of his violent temper. He hadn't needed to, because he had his daughter where he wanted her and loved it. When she moved in with Louis, the various people who replaced her as administrator of Carnegie Wines never lasted and he'd sold his business five years later. He was in his late sixties by then, and quite ready to retire, but he always blamed Louis for stealing Bel.

She knew she was being schmoozed by her father now. 'Let's talk about it when you're better, Dad,' she said lightly. 'Amber will be here in a minute.'

Dennis pursed his lips, his expression tinged with suspicion. 'Is this about that bawbag chef? He wagged a finger at her. 'You're holding out on me, girl. Why is that?'

Bel inhaled slowly. *Even if I have to sell my beloved cottage, I'm not going to live with you.* She framed the words, but when it came to it, she just couldn't speak them. She caught a flash of peacock blue passing the open cottage window and sighed with relief: Amber was at the door.

32

By Monday morning Bel was frazzled. She couldn't sleep properly on the blow-up bed. The cold from the stone – even in the summer heat – seeped up through the mattress, and each time she turned over, trussed like a sausage in the sleeping bag, the thing threatened to tip her out onto the unforgiving, uncarpeted floor. There was no successful way to lie, except very still, flat on her back, like a corpse: she'd never been able to sleep properly on her back. And today she had to be on her best form for her interview with Mr Ajax.

Leaving her father to sleep, she crept out for an early swim, which woke her up and gave her the energy to face the day.

'Hmm. So you can do savoury tarts as well as bread?' Mr Ajax asked, continuing to peruse the handwritten list Bel had given him, which lay on the worktop between them.

Bel nodded nervously. 'I thought I could start with two types of loaf – white sourdough and seeded wholemeal – which I know are both popular. Plus maybe muffins and individual quiches, a vegetarian option.' She pointed to the plan. 'Do croissants at the weekend, because they're too time-consuming for every day.'

Mr Ajax, head bowed, said nothing. He seemed to be

tussling with something in his mind. *Maybe giving over to me the place his wife had cooked in is hard*, she thought. But then she saw him take a deep breath. Leaning his palms on the counter, he finally looked up and met her eye. 'We'll need to work out the finances.'

Bel nodded, trying not to smile yet.

'You'll be able to do this on your own?'

She'd thought about it. 'I think so. If it takes off, I might need help. But your kitchen is really well set up.'

Mr Ajax sighed. 'Elowen managed, of course.'

'Harris said she was a first-class cook,' Bel ventured, hoping this wasn't the wrong thing to say.

But her employer only nodded, a faint smile on his lips. 'She was, indeed.'

'Right,' Ron Ajax said, standing up straight and looking relieved, almost happy for once, as if he'd just success-fully hurdled a high barrier. 'It'll be good for the shop. The customers aren't big fans of the bread we currently sell. Come and find me when your shift's over and we can discuss the nitty-gritty.'

Bel did as he asked. He wanted her to start as soon as possible, to get the best of the summer trade. Her mind was whirring with all that she had to put in place – working out the supplies she'd need, checking out the kitchen equipment, finding recipes – as she cycled home later. She felt hamstrung by her father, though, her joy slightly tar-nished by his continued presence in her house. It was hard to have a clear enough head to plan as she didn't know when he was leaving. And there was no sign of that.

*

A couple of days later, Dennis, despite appearing to be moving with a lot more freedom than he had at the weekend, still claimed to be unable even to contemplate the long drive home. He was cosy, she could tell, getting his feet firmly under the proverbial table.

'This is nice,' he'd said, on more than one occasion, cocooned comfortably in his orange throne, when the two of them had been eating supper in the sitting room, bowls on their knees, chatting because there was no TV and she hadn't got Wi-Fi yet. Or he would stand in the warm sunshine on one of the walks she insisted he do every day and close his eyes, breathe deeply with pleasure. 'This is nice,' he'd say again.

In fact, he was behaving so astonishingly well, Bel might have begun to relax, if she hadn't been well aware of the rock-solid purpose behind Dennis's effort to keep his temper, hold back from his usual tormenting behaviour. Her father was nothing if not strategic – wilful, even – in pursuit of a goal. Harassing her, he must have realized, wasn't working this time. Instead he was adopting Patsy's softly-softly approach that favoured chatting up the enemy rather than sending in the tanks.

Patsy was firm in the face of Bel's anxiety. Although she could see why Bel had issues with her father, she still maintained the way forward was to stand up to him. 'He's the sort that likes it if you do,' Patsy stated, when Bel escaped her father's company for half an hour to go for a swim with her friend. Bel, who attributed much wisdom to her, did not correct her. Dennis relished sparring with Patsy, maybe. He did not appreciate doing so with his daughter.

Micky and JJ – who'd both clearly enjoyed their respective snooker and paddleboarding sessions with her father before his back went – paid daily court to Dennis while he was laid up at Bel's, taking it in turns to pop in and see how things were going. They would settle down on Jaz's beanbag with a beer and engage in long, meandering conversations together. Even Zid padded in and took up residence on Dennis's knee as if he'd known him all his life. *It's a man thing,* her father seemed to be saying, as he tacitly excluded Bel.

She was grateful, of course, relieved to be able to share the burden of entertaining her physically compromised father in the confined space. Although she couldn't help feeling a little peeved at Dennis's seduction of her friends. He could be charming, of course, a man who'd travelled widely and was a good raconteur, who'd lived a lively social life before the pandemic, when age and solitude soured his mood.

Right now, though, she felt isolated in her historical fear of him, the eggshells she seemed perpetually to walk on in his presence, the memory of the crushing feeling of worthlessness his put-downs engendered in her soul. She even began to wonder if she was exaggerating his unkindness. It made her question herself. Louis was the only person who would understand, and she couldn't seek his help without giving entirely the wrong signal.

Work was her only reprieve. She had agreed with Mr Ajax that she would prepare the kitchen over the next week, get the supplies in, then swap her job on the till for five days of baking – starting very early each morning. Meanwhile, she was still not sleeping, exhausted, on edge with anxiety about her father and her new role in the farm shop.

Today, as ten o'clock approached, she was eagerly listening for Harris's footfall. She hadn't seen him all week and realized how dull the farm shop was without his morning visits. He was also the only one of her friends who didn't seem to have fallen under either Louis's or her father's spell.

'I've missed you,' she told him, when he did eventually appear, trying for a bright grin and a light delivery, not entirely managing either.

'Sorry, I was going to tell you, then your father arrived and Ron booted me out. I was in Falmouth for an artist's retreat thing. I shared the sessions with this other wildlife artist, Glenda Wynne. Have you heard of her?'

Bel shook her head. Now he was here, she wanted to pour her heart out to him about all that was happening in her life, the shop being momentarily empty. But, overcome with tiredness, she suddenly felt like crying instead.

Harris, eyeing her, looked concerned. 'Are you OK?'

She replied softly, 'Not really.' Then explained what was going on as succinctly as possible. This was not the moment to break down, although she sensed the sleepless nights were making her slightly out of control.

'You poor thing.' His eyes searched her face. 'Good news about the baking, but is your father being a nightmare?'

Bel gave a short laugh. 'No. The opposite, in fact. I just never know when he'll flip.'

'He's not violent, is he?' Harris asked.

She bit her lip but didn't reply. *I don't want to be this person*, she railed silently. *I just want to get on with my life*. Her last words were a silent scream.

'You know you can always escape, come round to mine any time.' A thought seemed to strike him. 'You could even stay in my shed while he's here, if you want.'

A shed? She was touched by his offer, but couldn't help wondering. Bel's face must have betrayed her, because Harris hurried on: 'It's more of a summerhouse, really. It's got a proper bed and shower and hob and everything. My sister happily camps out there for three weeks every summer.' He looked a bit sheepish. 'I'm not great at guests in the house.'

She laughed. 'Thank you, Harris. That's incredibly kind.' *Is he serious?* 'I probably shouldn't leave Dad alone but if he stays much longer . . .' She was half joking, not quite able to imagine treading all over Harris's space – he was, by his own admission, such a private man.

'I mean it. You'd be very welcome,' Harris said sincerely. 'Gill's a head teacher. She isn't due till August, after she's put the school into mothballs for the summer.'

'Bel?' Mr Ajax shouted from the lane. 'Stop rabbiting with old Leonardo there and help with these spuds, will you?'

That night, Bel and Dennis were at Patsy's for supper, although Bel had cooked this time. There was no room in the cottage for them all, but she was determined to take her turn at the stove, despite Patsy's protests. Rhian was there, but Jaz had gone for a sleepover with a friend in Penzance. Bel's supper was lightly fried goujons of haddock – which she'd bought from the pop-up fish truck by the beach – with nutty, buttery brown rice and Mr Ajax's tomatoes, slow-roasted, rocket and black olives.

'How's the new baking project coming along?' Rhian asked, as Patsy placed a large bowl of strawberries on the table, sticking a dessertspoon into the tub of creamy Cornish vanilla ice cream Bel had bought. 'Those croissants you made were so yummy.' She kissed her fingertips in appreciation.

'What croissants? You haven't made me any,' her father said reproachfully. 'Although if your lockdown bread was anything to go by . . .' He gave her a patronizing grin.

Replying to Rhian, Bel said, 'I'm setting up the kitchen, getting stuff organized. But I must make another batch.' Despite her impending job, though, she realized she had no real heart for baking at the moment. She should have been trying out bread, tart and muffin recipes, but she kept putting it off. She just couldn't settle with her father taking up all the space in her house and her head, her fate hanging in the balance.

Shortly, though, she would need to be very much on point – she couldn't afford to mess up this golden opportunity. *I'll be all right when Dad leaves*, she kept repeating to herself.

Now, she made a show of offering strawberries to her father in an attempt to dispel her thoughts.

Rhian was talking. She had just been to visit her mother in Plymouth again. 'She's the only family I've got left,' she said sadly. 'There's an uncle in Porthmadog, but we don't speak. He and Mum never got on.'

'I haven't spoken to my sister in twenty years,' Dennis said surprisingly – he never talked about Phyllis. He turned to Bel, giving her a wistful smile. 'That's why I want to move here, be close to my daughter. She's all I've got, too.'

In that moment, Bel felt a strange mixture of love for her father – fundamental, but so often obscured – along with pity and a weary dread.

'She's resisting me,' she heard him say. 'She doesn't want me anywhere near her. Other fish to fry, I suspect.' He shot a woebegone smile at the two women.

Bel, who watched Patsy and Rhian's faces become still with uncertainty about how to react, was about to object when Dennis added, his tone turned steely, 'Bella, here, would rather live alone in her pea-sized hovel than throw in her lot with her poor old dad in a proper house by the sea.' He raised his eyebrows at her, just a brief, angry flick, as if throwing down the gauntlet. The mask was slipping.

Patsy said, 'This is all a bit sudden, Dennis, your moving here.'

'I don't have time to hang about at my age, do I?' he muttered pathetically.

No one spoke until her father went on, 'I've no doubt you'd have your mother living with you like a shot, Rhian, if she wasn't demented and you weren't a vicar with commitments.'

The vicar, looking a little shocked by his callous assessment of her situation, hesitated just long enough to make clear that he was right.

'Aha!' he jumped in, triumphant. Turning to Bel, he said, 'See?'

She didn't know what to say. She was beyond reiterating for the umpteenth time that she loved her cottage and wanted to live there, *alone* – if her father would agree to the debt being paid back more slowly – however selfish that might sound. It was a week, now, since Bel, sitting with her father on the bench by the beach in the sunset, had last raised the question about the debt. He'd ignored her pleas then, and had not mentioned it since. And Bel felt too shattered – with all the pressures – to face a confrontation with him that might result in renewed demands for her to sell her home.

Patsy got up and began to clear the bowls. 'You can't always make people do what you want, Dennis,' she stated emphatically.

Her father narrowed his eyes at her, but Patsy didn't flinch. 'If it's not working for Bel . . .'

Dennis waved a dismissive hand. 'What neither of you realize, because you haven't known my daughter very long, is that Bella doesn't always know her own mind.'

Bel felt the familiar twisting in her gut.

'Hmm,' said Patsy, with a slight raise of the eyebrows. 'She seems to me like a woman who very much knows her own mind. If I were you, Dennis, I'd try to respect that.'

Her father's face fell. He'd obviously counted on Patsy and Rhian to back him in the cause of family.

Bel wanted to hug Patsy, despite the potentially dire consequences. She was ashamed it hadn't been her who'd stood up to her father.

'Well, I see I'm not getting much support around here,' Dennis grumbled, getting up abruptly and throwing his napkin onto the table. Without another word – and with no sign of back pain or stiffness in his gait – he stalked out of the kitchen, leaving the door open behind him.

Bel sighed. 'Thanks, Patsy.'

Patsy said, 'Plant your feet firmly on the ground, love. He's trying to uproot you.' She came over and gave Bel a long hug.

When she got in later, having helped Patsy clear the supper, her father, thank goodness, had already gone up to bed, his door closed. Another miserable night on the airbed lay ahead, but she felt something had shifted tonight. *My friends are with me*, she thought. They didn't think her mad or bad for wanting to live her own life.

By the following morning a switch had been thrown, her father reverting to his old modus vivendi: curmudgeonly sniping. There was no sign of the urbane, charming man who had seduced the whole village.

'How's your back?' Bel asked tentatively, when he appeared back downstairs mid-morning. He looked spruce, she noticed, in a clean white shirt and jeans, his chin shaved, his hair brushed. But the expression on his face was ominous.

'Now why would my dear daughter want to know about the state of my back?' he mused sardonically. He took the mug of coffee Bel held out to him without thanks and glared at her over the rim as he took a large gulp. 'So you can tell me to bugger off back to London with a clear conscience, eh?'

'Dad, please. Can't I ask how you are without you biting my head off?'

He didn't answer, appearing suddenly to remember something, his face losing its peevishness as he checked the time on his watch. 'Why aren't you at work?'

'It's Friday. I don't work on a Friday.'

Her father seemed a bit nonplussed. 'Oh. So what are you up to this morning? Don't feel you need to look after me.'

Bel was puzzled by the sudden volte-face. 'Umm, it's gorgeous out there. Do you want to go for a walk? Maybe your back's better enough for a swim.'

'No, no,' Dennis said, too quickly. 'I'll stay here.' He forced a smile. 'You go and have a swim. Don't hurry back, I'm fine.' He was almost shooing her out of the door.

What's he up to? she wondered, as she got into her swimsuit in the bathroom – it was the only place she could dress in peace – and collected her dry robe from the hook beside the front door. But it was a beautiful warm summer morning as she walked past the gardens bordering the lane, thick with fragrant blooms and the gentle drone of honey bees. She couldn't think of many things her father could get up to, alone in the cottage, after all. *Unless he's planning a Pauline-type visit.* Bel shuddered at the thought.

She sat on the beach and FaceTimed Tally after her swim, twirling the phone round to take in the golden sands, the sunshine and the shimmering water.

'So you were right. Dad's on the move again,' her step-daughter stated, after she'd groaned with envy at the slide show.

'What do you mean?' Bel hadn't seen or talked to Louis, she realized, since the awkward encounter in Martine's garden. In fact, she'd barely given him a thought, enmeshed as she was in her father's manipulative and confusing web.

'He says he's been contacted by some woman who owns a chain of gastro-pubs in the Oxford area. Wife of a mate of a guy he used to work with – something like that. She wants Dad to come and see her about a head-chef job.'

'Wow.' Bel didn't know what to think. She was surprised to feel a small pang of sadness at the knowledge that Louis was leaving.

'He said . . .' Tally paused. 'He said he was pretty sure you didn't want him around any more.' She was trying, unsuccessfully, to sound neutral, Bel could tell.

There was a short silence.

'I'm sorry, Tally.'

'You were the best thing that ever happened to him,' her stepdaughter said sadly.

'It just wouldn't have worked . . .'

'No. I know.'

'Has he left already?' Bel asked.

'In the morning. The landlord's gutted, obviously.'

More like incandescent with fury, Bel thought, knowing the devastation Louis's midnight flits left in their wake.

'I'm so glad we've survived Dad behaving badly, Bel.

I don't know what I'd do without you,' Tally said, sounding infinitely weary.

'Oh, sweetheart, I'm glad too. You know how much you mean to me.'

'Can I come and visit you in Cornwall?'

'Once I get rid of my dear father, absolutely. It's a blow-up bed, I'm afraid. Hideously uncomfortable.'

Tally laughed. 'I don't care. The beach looks divine.'

There was another moment's silence.

'I'll bike up later, check on your dad, make sure he's OK.'

'Thanks.' Tally sighed. 'I suppose Oxford's a lot nearer than Cornwall. Every cloud . . .'

A shiny blue Golf was parked outside the cottage when Bel got home around lunchtime. She wondered who it belonged to. *Maybe Patsy has guests*, she thought, as she pushed open the front door.

Her father was standing, arms crossed, talking earnestly to a slim blonde in a navy pencil-skirt, flimsy cream blouse with a Peter Pan collar and pumps, her pretty face and tanned limbs setting off the simple outfit to perfection. She had a clipboard in her hand, on which balanced a phone. When Dennis saw Bel, he jumped, his face a picture of guilt.

'You're home,' he said, blinking fast. Collecting himself, he went on, 'This is my daughter, Bella.'

The blonde smiled professionally and bowed her head, still using the greeting favoured during the past pandemic. 'Lucy Cutler-Jones,' she said. 'Miller Countrywide,' she

333

added, as if this might mean something to Bel, which it did not.

She waited for someone to explain. After a moment of awkward silence, her father said, 'Lucy has been kind enough to come round and give us a valuation for the cottage.' He spoke defiantly, cocking his head as if daring her to object.

Bel, almost too stunned to speak, managed to croak, '*Valuation?*'

The agent – for that was clearly what she was – must have seen Bel's expression, because she faltered. 'I . . . Your father . . .'

Bel pulled herself up and took a deep breath. She didn't look at her father. 'Thank you, that's very kind, Lucy,' she said, trying for her most dignified – not made easy by the wet hair and bare, sandy legs. 'But this cottage belongs to me. And I will decide if and when it's for sale.'

'Oh.' Lucy blushed, as if caught out in something underhand – although it was not she who was in the wrong. 'I'm so sorry. Mr Carnegie said –'

'My father was mistaken,' Bel cut across her apology. 'I'll see you out,' she added grandly, although the door was only a long step away.

Lucy grabbed her bag from the worktop and meekly followed Bel, giving an embarrassed wave in Dennis's direction.

Bel waited until she heard the slam of the Golf's door, the ignition firing, waited some more until the sound of the car's engine had faded up the lane. She stood stock still, as did her father. There was not a sound in the small

334

room except the soft hissing of the stove. As she turned to him, she could feel her body – recently so relaxed on the warm summer sand – becoming stiff with anger.

'Listen, it's not what you think,' her father began, seeing her expression and reaching out to lay a placating hand on her arm. 'I bumped into the girl in the village and we got talking, and I thought, since she was here, she might as well pop in and take a look.'

Don't take me for a fool, Bel thought, shaking him off, her breath coming in controlled gasps.

Dennis attempted an urbane smile. 'I thought it was a good idea. Get things moving while the market's hot.' A pause. 'You said you were up for it.'

But Bel could see that for a change it was he who was nervous of her mood, not the other way around.

'I think it's best if you start getting your stuff together, Dad, plan on going home tomorrow.' Her insides felt solid as iron. It was difficult to speak. 'I'll help you.' She moved briskly towards the stairs.

Dennis panted after her. 'Don't be snippy, sweetheart. My back's still crooked. I can't manage that journey, not yet.' He sounded frightened, and she was ashamed to realize that she was glad.

'You should have thought of that before you tried to sell my house from under me.' She began to climb the stairs, but Dennis grabbed at her arm, pulling her back.

His expression hardened and, for a second, they eyeballed each other in silence, neither willing to concede.

'Can we stop all this nonsense?' he said coldly. 'Just sell the fucking place, pay me the money you owe me and come back to London, where you belong.' Then he sighed heavily, his beady eyes looking suddenly weary and old. 'I'm just trying to help, make you see sense, girl. Your mother always claimed you were stubborn.' He gave a sad laugh. 'But, bless her, she saw it as a sign of character . . .'

As she stood there, face to face with her difficult father, Bel felt overcome by a sense of hopelessness. The conflict between them was never going to end. It was like trying to struggle out of a closed trunk. And each time she reached the rim, poked her head out into the sunshine of freedom, the lid was slammed firmly shut again. *I can't go on doing this*, she thought. The battle between a sense of duty to her father – exacerbated by the money she owed him – and the independence she craved seemed impossible to resolve.

'I'm going out,' Bel said, turning away from him and mounting the stairs again. Pulling open the drawers in her bedroom, she hurriedly gathered a T-shirt and a pair of knickers, collected her toothbrush and face cream from the bathroom, all of which she stuffed into her backpack, hanging on the bedroom door. With no space in her head to know what she was doing or where she was going, she only knew she had to escape: the atmosphere in the cottage was threatening to choke her.

Coward. The word rang loudly through her brain as she packed. *This is your home, your inheritance. Stand up for your rights, for God's sake. Talk to him. Persuade him to change his mind.* But she didn't think she knew how. Her father always bested her in any argument . . . *Always got his way.*

When she went back downstairs, Dennis was sitting

tense in the chair, arms crossed. 'Running away?' he questioned, as she passed him on the way to the front door, his tone contemptuous. 'Remind dear Louis, as you climb into his bed tonight, that I'm still waiting for the fucking money he owes me.'

'I'll be back to see you off,' she said, through clamped teeth.

33

Bel mounted her bike, suddenly knowing where she was heading. She rode fast, breathing deeply, but even in the fresh air with the wind in her face, she still felt stifled and choked. Words she knew she should have spoken to her father were collected in her throat, like a thick hairball in a cat.

Passing the Lantern, she spotted the red Berlingo, back doors open, Louis hurling his leather holdall into it. For a split second, she contemplated riding on past, unwilling to engage with his no-doubt chaotic agenda. But she slowed, nonetheless.

'You're leaving,' she said, breathless as she dismounted.

'Thought I'd better, before I get stabbed up,' Louis muttered, casting a nervous glance towards the pub door, as if he genuinely thought Ben, the landlord, might emerge brandishing a carving knife. He gave her a rueful grin. 'Tally told you?'

'Yes. Oxford.'

'You remember Asif? The guy I worked with in Mayfair before 83? Well, his friend's wife has just opened this high-end gaff, part of a group, in a converted church in Kidlington.' He paused. 'I put the feelers out when you said ... when I knew things weren't going to work out here.' He gazed at her wistfully.

Bel tried to ignore the look. 'Not sure I remember meeting Asif,' she said.

Louis was eyeing her. 'You OK?'

'Fine,' she said. 'Just Dad.'

He frowned. 'You know I'll pay the bastard back, don't you? I'll get proper money for this Oxford job. As soon as I'm paid, I'll set up a standing order every month, chip away at the debt.' He reached over and laid a palm briefly to her cheek. 'Promise.'

'Thank you,' she said, at the same time not entirely sure, despite all Louis's genuine assurances, that he would. *He believes he will*, she thought. But she worried his money would never be deemed quite 'proper' enough to consider sending any to her father. *Maybe he'll surprise me*, she thought. *If it isn't too late by then.*

'I'd better get going,' she said, as if she needed to be somewhere. 'Hope things go well for you.'

Louis was staring at her, his gaze suddenly intense. He moved forward until he was standing right up close, laying his hand over hers, which rested on the handlebars. 'Hey, Bel. Come with me. Leave the bastard to his own devices. Oxford's great. Think what an adventure we could have.' His eyes, recently so lifeless and careworn, were briefly sparkling again, and an image of him when they first met flashed across her brain. He'd been so charismatic, so enthusiastic, so driven . . . just bursting with hope. 'Jump in,' he was urging, steering her bike towards the Berlingo. 'I'll drive you down and you can pick up your things.'

For one mad moment, a single second when the world stood still, Bel actually considered Louis's offer. She pictured her father's outrage as they swept in and grabbed her stuff from under his nose, told him their plan – *It would almost be worth it just to see his face*, she thought. But she knew she'd regret it even before they reached Truro.

She looked up at Louis and smiled. 'I can't,' she said softly.

He gave her a rueful grin and took his hand off the handlebars. 'Worth a try.' He pulled her into an awkward embrace, the bike wobbling against her body. 'Offer's still there if you change your mind.'

Bel felt the warmth of someone she'd loved in his hug, breathed in his familiar scent, felt a brief tightening around her heart that was mostly sadness . . . and pity for a man who had made one too many mistakes. But it felt right that he was leaving.

'Did you hear? About the baby?' she asked, as they stood hesitantly, neither wanting to be the one to walk away.

Louis looked towards the sea, but not before she'd noticed his eyes mist up. 'Definitely not mine,' he mumbled, roughly brushing his hand across his face.

'I'm sorry.' And she was. He looked so beaten down, so pale and defeated in the hot afternoon sun, his clothes shabby, his hair greying. *Not my problem any more*, she told herself, pushing away her default desire to rescue him. She mounted her bike and waved goodbye. Just as she was about to join the main road, she heard Louis shouting behind her.

'I got Jaz a pot-wash gig in a gastro-bar in Marazion,' he called. 'Let me know how she gets on.'

Smiling her thanks, Bel rode away towards the farm shop, then bumped past Mr Ajax's red-brick house on the uneven track and round the bend, until Harris's cottage came into view. Nearing the place, she suddenly felt an uncomfortable fluttering in her gut. *Did Harris mean what he said?* she wondered anxiously.

It was only when Bel pulled up outside the dove-grey front door that she noticed Harris's black Peugeot wasn't parked outside. *He's not home.* She stifled a sigh of disappointment, realizing just how much she had been counting on being able to sit in his neat kitchen with a cup of tea, his calm green-grey eyes soothing her battered spirit.

Slumping onto the stone step, she considered what to do next. *Maybe he'll be gone overnight, all weekend?* She felt at a loss. *Where can I go?* All she knew was that she would rather sleep under a hedge than go back to her father to be further humiliated. Sitting there, she began to sense a sort of lethargy creeping over her. She felt quite incapable of moving. The sun was still warm on her face, and it was so peaceful, so quiet . . . Leaning her reeling head against the warm wood of Harris's front door, she closed her eyes.

The next thing she was aware of was a hand gently nudging her shoulder and a voice speaking her name. She opened her eyes. Harris looked down at her, puzzlement on his face. Quickly stumbling to her feet, she felt dizzy and disoriented. 'Sorry . . . I'm so sorry.'

Harris put out a hand to steady her. 'Hey, what's up?'

'I . . . Just another set-to with my father.' It sounded so pathetic from a woman her age. She stammered out a brief explanation about the double-barrelled estate agent, the valuation. 'I couldn't stand another minute in his company.' She stopped, out of breath, feeling weak and stupid under the concerned gaze of her friend. She wished she'd never come.

But Harris was taking her arm. 'Come on. Looks like you could do with a cuppa.'

Bel did not protest, allowing him to lead her inside and sit her down in a kitchen chair as if she were unwell. He made tea and found some chocolate digestives in a tin – only a little stale. She sensed her whole body letting go as she sipped her tea in the companionable silence.

'Do you want to talk about it?' Harris enquired.

She shook her head. 'If I start, I'll never stop.'

He smiled. 'I've got the time.'

'I'd rather talk about something else,' she said.

The artist, after a moment's thought, obliged, telling her about a wonderful walk he'd just done at Sennen Cove, the seal he'd seen basking and preening in the shallow water, how it had seemed almost human, enjoying the attention from tourists on the beach as if it was putting on a show. He pulled out a small sketchbook, opened it and pushed it towards Bel. The pencil drawing was beautiful.

'Stay here tonight, if you want?' he said, when their conversation lapsed.

'No, really,' she said wearily. 'Thanks . . . I was thinking I might, if you were OK with it, but it's stupid, running away. I should probably go back.' Staying here would only put off the inevitable. She needed to sort things out with her father, once and for all. Make a firm decision about the cottage . . . about her life.

He regarded her for a moment, his gaze so sympathetic she found herself blushing. 'Stay,' he said, as if this was his final word on the subject.

Bel inhaled slowly. There was nothing, she realized, that she would like more. Just to rest, take a breather, a break from her bullying father . . . and the fickle blow-up mattress.

'It's completely up to you, of course.'

She hesitated. 'I genuinely don't know what to do,' she said, unable to keep her moiling thoughts to herself any longer. 'Should I move in with my father? Look after him? It's what he's pressuring me to do.'

'Does he need looking after?'

'Not physically. Not yet.'

Harris's eyebrows twitched. 'Do you want to?'

Sighing, she replied, 'No. I can think of nothing worse.'

'Well, there's your answer.'

She stared at him as if he'd said the earth was flat. 'But I owe him money he says he needs. I'm paying him back slowly, but he's holding it over my head, expecting me to sell the cottage.'

'Blackmailing you?'

She didn't reply.

'You've been straight with your dad? About how you feel?' Harris was asking.

Have I? She knew she'd said, time and again, that she wanted to stay in Cornwall, that she didn't want to sell

343

the cottage. But had she ever really been honest about the rest? 'It's not easy.'

'You don't have to yell or be cruel. Just be clear.' Harris rose. 'Help me make up the bed?'

Harris's summerhouse was hot from the sun beating on the shingle roof all day, and smelt pleasantly of cedar. He immediately threw open the windows. *Nice*, Bel thought, glancing round the elegant but cosy space. The wood interior was painted in the same dove grey as the front door, a small double bed against the left-hand wall, with a patchwork quilt in soft blues and greys and a wicker arm-chair with cream cushion-seat, the shower room and toilet taking up the area to the right. The galley kitchen in the middle – with breakfast bar and two stools – fronted the view across the fields. It felt so quiet in there, only the buzzing of insects and the tweeting of birds filtering in from outside, the air almost soporific. All Bel wanted to do was climb under the quilt and sleep.

They made the bed in silence. Harris showed her how everything worked – the shower, the tricky Venetian blind, the window locks – then handed her the key. For a moment he seemed to hesitate. Then he said, 'I was planning on fish and chips tonight, if you fancy joining me?' When she didn't immediately reply, her mind barely functioning, he went on, 'Totally understand if you want to be alone. I've got milk and bread and stuff I can bring over.'

Bel shook herself. 'I'd love fish and chips,' she said.

Harris grinned. 'Have a nap. It's only just after five. I'll go down and collect the fish around seven, if that suits. It's such a lovely evening, we can eat in the garden.'

Taking the key from his hand, Bel felt as if she'd been transported to some magical place, where life ran smoothly and harmoniously, and problems – such as her recalcitrant father, her flaky ex – did not exist. 'I can't tell you how grateful I am for this,' she said, waving a hand around to indicate the summerhouse.

'You're most welcome, Bel,' Harris said seriously, giving a slight bow. 'See you later.'

She sank onto the fresh, lavender-scented sheets with a feeling of utter bliss, the cool pillow soft beneath her sweaty cheek, the duvet cocooning her against the world, the distant birdsong lulling her . . . and closed her eyes. It seemed like the first time she had properly let go since her father had pitched up in Cornwall.

Harris and Bel – still dazed from the deepest sleep she'd had in days – sat side by side on the warm bench against the stone wall of his cottage, eating fish and chips from plates on their knees in contented silence as the sun disappeared behind the trees bordering the field in a soft blur of tangerine.

Bel's haddock was spanking fresh, the golden batter crisply delicious, the fat chips – picked from a mound in the white bag – sprayed liberally with salt and vinegar from a nozzled plastic bottle Harris brought from the kitchen cupboard. On the small glass garden table in front of them stood two bottles of lager.

She sighed as she wiped her fingers on the paper

345

napkin he'd provided. 'Perfect. Thank you. I hadn't eaten properly all day.' She smiled at Harris, who was still diving back into the chips bag for another handful.

'So, what are you going to say to your dad?'

Bel leaned back and closed her eyes against the setting sun. 'I'm going to try to be honest.'

'It's usually the best policy,' he said, with a wry smile.

A confusing set of images confronted her as she thought of her father, the manipulation and menace blending with the love she felt for him, his age and obvious frailty. 'I just don't know if I can.'

Harris didn't respond for a moment. He was looking off across the gently swaying heads of corn in the field, now darkening from pale gold to a sandy grey as the light faded. His face was very still. 'I was always scared of my father,' he eventually said. 'He was sort of a casual sadist. Always had a grin on his face when he whacked me across the back of my head with a heavy book, or clamped me in a head-lock so I couldn't breathe, or held me under the water just too long, or deliberately tripped me up.'

'That's horrible,' Bel said.

'He was really strong, too. A sportsman – swimmer, rugby star, golfer . . .' There was a pause. 'I irritated him so much,' he added.

'Because you weren't sporty?'

He chuckled. 'Oh, I was properly sporty as a kid – I had to be. But I didn't *love* it and Dad never understood that. Sport was his whole life.'

'Did you work it out with him?'

'Not really. But after he died I found a big box of my

drawings in his desk so he must have been proud of me on some level.'

How sad, Bel thought. 'I'm sure he loved you.'

He nodded. 'Likewise your father. But that doesn't mean you have to be a slave to his temper or his whim, Bel.'

She didn't reply as she tipped the scraps on her plate into the chips bag and watched as Harris did the same, scrunching it up and setting it on the flagstones at his feet. But she knew he was right. *It doesn't solve my problem, though,* she thought.

'Tea? I've got chocolate in the fridge.'

Harris returned with two mugs and a cold stick of Toblerone. They munched the rich, crunchy sweetness, sipping their tea as darkness fell and the wind picked up.

'I should get some candles for next time,' Harris said, then shot her an embarrassed glance. 'If there is a next time, of course.'

She laughed. 'I hope there is.'

Their eyes met. His a quiet green-grey, hers a deep violet, both shy, but neither looking away. He gave her the softest of smiles and Bel felt her heartbeat quicken. She didn't move, but was aware of the breeze on her bare arms, a strand of hair blowing across her cheek. Harris reached over and gently guided it back behind her ear. A dog barked in the night and the spell was broken.

'I should get to bed,' Bel said, shivering.

Harris seemed to shake himself. 'Yeah, me too.' He stood up and rolled his shoulders, let out a slow breath. 'I'll leave the back door open, in case you need something.'

She got to her feet. 'Thank you for everything. That was such a perfect evening.'

'It was . . . Goodnight, then, Bel,' Harris said, suddenly awkward.

'Goodnight.'

As she settled into bed, listening to the *shirr* of the cornstalks in the wind, she could still feel the touch of his finger to her cheek. *I* will *be honest with Dad in the morning*, she thought, as she slipped into another deep, comfortable sleep.

34

The noise of Bel's phone jolted her awake in the darkness. 'Patsy?'

She dragged herself upright and turned on the bedside light. Her screen said it was only eleven fifteen, she'd been asleep barely an hour.

'It's your dad,' her neighbour said. 'Banged on the door, breathless and complaining of chest pains. He's on the sofa and seems a bit better now. But I've called an ambulance.'

'Oh my God. I'm so sorry. I'll come straight over.'

'Maybe better if I pick you up. They'll take him to Truro – the Penzance place only does minor burns and stuff.'

Bel tried to focus but failed.

'Listen, I'll see him into the ambulance and text you when I'm on my way.'

But as Bel's head cleared she knew she couldn't wait. Throwing on her clothes, she biked to the main road, where she called Patsy again. The ambulance hadn't arrived so she kept going, riding like a madwoman: legs pumping, hair flying, breath coming in harsh rasps as she shot down the dark lane to the village. It crossed her mind as she rode that this was yet another act in the play of her father's manipulation: using his frailty to garner her sympathy when he knew he'd transgressed. But she couldn't be sure. One of these days – maybe this one – it would be for real.

Her father was lying on his back on Patsy's sofa. His colour was certainly poor and his breathing laboured. She knelt on the floor beside him and took his cold hand in hers. 'Dad?'

His eyelids flickered open but he said nothing, just clutched at her fingers.

'What happened?' she asked gently.

'Couldn't breathe,' he muttered. 'Thought I was a goner.'

'The ambulance is on its way,' she said.

This seemed to galvanize him and he struggled to sit up. 'Christ. Don't let them take me to hospital, Bella. Those places are teeming with bugs. I really will croak.'

'You've got to get checked out, Dad. You look terrible.'

This elicited a peaky smile from her father. 'Thanks, girl. Just what a fella needs to hear.'

'I'm serious.'

Dennis lapsed back against the cushions. 'I had a skinful, that's all. I'm fine now. Don't fuss.'

Bel turned to Patsy, bewildered. Her friend just shrugged.

'Dad . . .' Bel tried again, but he interrupted her.

'I was in a panic.'

'About what?'

'Leaving you.'

Bel barely had time to digest this before a vehicle was braking outside, headlights sweeping the room, doors banging.

At the sight of the masked paramedics, her father sat up straighter and smiled warmly. 'Sorry, gentlemen. Apologies for dragging you out at this time of night on false pretences,' he said, instantly adopting a plummy, imperious tone. 'Had too much to drink, I'm afraid. Worried about having to get up early and go back to London in the morning. Nothing remotely wrong with me.'

Bel reckoned her father's assessment of his condition was pretty close to the mark – he wasn't faking it, exactly, but neither was he having a heart attack. The spruce young guys in their green uniforms, though, did not look convinced. One sat beside Dennis and began to ask him gently probing questions about chest pains and passing out.

Dennis answered them all with a cheery denial. 'I'm getting on. Can't take my drink like I used to,' he assured them, with a cavalier laugh, reiterating, in case they hadn't got the message, 'I'm not going to hospital.' He even refused to climb into the ambulance for an ECG: the test for a suspected coronary. 'You'll shut the doors and drive off with me,' he insisted, paranoid to the last.

In the end, they gave up. 'We can't force him,' the one called Tim told Bel. 'A lot of older people aren't comfortable going to hospital since the virus.' He shrugged. 'See how he is in the morning. If you're still worried, bring him over to A and E and we'll run some tests.'

Bel thanked them both and saw them out, aware of her heart beating too fast, her jaw clenched as she and Patsy helped Dennis to his feet and made their way slowly back to the cottage. Her father appeared much revived once the paramedics had conceded to his wishes. In fact, he seemed jaunty and rather pleased with himself.

'Saw off those over-zealous twelve-year-olds,' he said, as he flopped down in the orange chair.

Bel tried to persuade him upstairs. 'Don't feel like bed yet,' he insisted. 'All the excitement's given me a second wind. Any chance of a cuppa, sweetheart?'

'Well, I'm off to bed, even if you're not, Dennis,' Patsy stated, shooting a sympathetic smile in Bel's direction.

Bel thanked her friend, apologizing again for the disturbance. Her heart was really pounding now, as she turned back to the stove. She felt almost queasy. Handing her father his mug of tea, she retreated to lean against the rail of the Rayburn, the stove warm on her bottom, trying to steady her breath and calm her pulse.

But instead of becoming calmer, she found herself beginning to shake. Yet another pointless, wearying melodrama had dragged her back to her father's side, for the sole purpose of focusing on *him, him, him*. Fury was swelling, swirling, snowballing inside her and there was absolutely nothing she could do to stop it. Nothing, she realized, she wanted to do, even though the sheer power of it was unnerving.

Then Dennis began to laugh. She didn't know what he was laughing about and she never found out. But something in the smug, mocking tone of her father's mirth acted on Bel like the ring pull on a can. And the fury exploded out.

Time seemed suspended. There was silence, except for the loud fizzing of Bel's rage in her head. Then she heard herself begin to speak.

Her voice was absolutely calm, her words sharp and clear as the light on the sea in the morning. Her mother was by her side: she could feel her supporting her, giving her strength. 'I have something to say, Dad,' she began. 'And I need you to listen. I mean *really listen*.'

She saw her father's face fall with a mixture of surprise and incomprehension, but plunged on, sentences piling out of her mouth succinct and fully formed. 'You say you love me. And you bang on about people not respecting you. But you don't respect *me*. You never have, not in my entire life.' A slow, solid breath filled her lungs. 'When I'm with you, I feel bullied – everything's always on your terms. I feel put down – you tease me, tell me I'm fat and wear shit clothes, that I'm weak in the head. You casually call me, *your own daughter*, a "bitch".'

Her father seemed to wince at the word, but she had more to say. 'You're always trying to control me, Dad. You assume I'll do what *you* want, never giving a damn about my own wishes.' She paused, shaking, to take one more deep breath. 'And the worst thing is, I've been so scared of your vicious temper, frightened it'll finally boil over – like it did when you actually hit me – that I can't fight back.'

Bel watched as her father's face darkened and he began to speak. But she thrust out her palm to prevent him. 'This isn't a discussion. I don't want a fight. I don't even need you to agree with me, Dad. In fact, I'm sure you won't.' She levelled her gaze at him, feeling the strength of her words buoying her, like a crowd of hands holding her aloft. 'I just needed you to hear *my* truth, once and for all.'

Her father stood up, blinking rapidly, spluttering in his need to defend himself. 'You're being ridiculous, Bella, I never –'

But she shook her head vehemently. 'One more thing.' He subsided immediately at her tone. 'You know I love you, Dad, but please understand this. I will *never* let you to treat me like that *ever again*.'

Her voice seemed to echo around the dark room, vibrating like cymbals in the warm air. She could hear her mother quietly applauding.

Dennis looked stunned and was clearly speechless. He stumbled backwards, feeling for the orange chair, and slumped into it. His breathing was short in his chest, his cheeks coloured dark red.

Bel picked up her phone from the counter and put it into the pocket of her jeans. Her legs felt as if they would barely carry her as she turned towards the door.

'Where are you going at this time of night? Is it that Louis again? Has he put you up to this?' He was trying to sound threatening, but his voice was reedy and uncertain. It held none of its normal domineering authority.

'He left for Oxford yesterday, Dad.'

Her father took this in as Bel reached the door, his look suddenly alarmed. 'So where are you going?'

Bel waved but didn't answer, because at that precise moment she didn't know.

'Bella . . .'

His voice quavered anxiously behind her, but she kept walking. In the porch, she snatched her dry robe from the hook and shoved her feet into her trainers. She wasn't going to Patsy's or Harris's or even JJ's van tonight. Her friends had borne the brunt of her chaos — very kindly, very patiently – for too long. This was something she would sort out for herself.

She turned right out of the gate towards the beach. It was black as pitch, the houses along the lane long closed up for the night. But Bel liked walking in the dark, once her eyes had adapted. It was warm, even so late, and quite still, the stars bright in the July sky. A light breeze coming off the sea rustled the leaves in the gardens she passed. It was the only sound until she hit the beach and heard the lazy swishing of the waves on a tide far out across the sands.

For a while Bel walked along the shore, wrapped in her robe, playing over in her head her statement of intent. *You don't have to yell*, Harris had said. And she hadn't. *Be clear and you will be heard*, Patsy and JJ and Harris had all said at various times and in various ways. Well, she had been very clear. Whether her father had heard was quite another matter. But she realized his reaction wasn't the point. It was not to change her father that she'd said those things but to change *herself*. Now she sensed a cool, still emptiness in her body, as if a breeze had blown through her, taking with it the piled-up frustration and fear of many years. *If I can just hang on to this feeling*, she thought.

Walking to the place by the rocks where she and JJ had barbecued sausages, she sat down. The sand was cold and she cuddled into her voluminous robe, suddenly feeling excessively tired. Gradually, she sank back, until her head, encased in the hood, rested on the sand. *I'll just lie here for a minute*, she thought, lulled by the distant hum of the sea.

The next thing she knew, the sun was poking its head above the horizon to the east, the calm water, now more than halfway up the beach, a glossy, undulating expanse of silvery-pink. It was a beautiful day. Bel groaned as she uncurled her stiff, cold limbs. Her neck ached, her right toes had cramp, her face felt damp from the night air. She levered herself upright with effort and shook off the sand. Checking her phone, she saw there were no messages, no cry for help from her father – a small mercy.

As she began to climb the rocky steps, breathing hard, the prospect of another day wrangling with Dennis was not a pleasant one. But she knew she'd made peace with herself the night before. She would cope. She would tell him her plan again. He would accept it.

The cottage was quiet when Bel entered, the stove gone out. She stood for a moment, listening to the silence, knowing her father must still be asleep. She longed to rip off her damp clothes, have a shower and lie down in her own bed. But she would have to wait until he was awake before showering, and maybe a lot longer for a night under her own duvet.

She set about riddling the ash box and laying new kindling over a couple of fire-lighters, then went out to the wood store for more logs. The process was so familiar to her now that she did it on autopilot, remembering with a smile how frightened she'd been the first time. As she set a match to the stove now, she had a strange instinct that something felt out of kilter in the house. She looked around as the kindling caught, suddenly nervous, then quickly closed the stove and crept upstairs.

The wooden door of her bedroom door was half ajar. When she peered tentatively inside, she found it was empty. The bed was rumpled, obviously slept in, but there was no sign of her father. Or, on further inspection, his case and clothes.

Bel sat down on the bed, bemused. While she'd been sleeping on the beach, her father had obviously packed and left. She thought back to her walk up the lane just now. She hadn't noticed if the green Jaguar was in its usual space in the car park but, then, she hadn't been looking. Pulling out her phone, she left a text: *Fell asleep on the beach. When I got back you were gone. Let me know you're OK x.*

Is he really attempting the long drive back to London with a hangover and hardly any sleep? she asked herself, knowing she should be worried. But she found she couldn't get worked up about his sudden departure. In fact, shameful as it was, she was feeling a blissful surge of relief, drinking in the silence as she sat there on her own bed, in her own house, all by herself for the first time in what seemed like ever – but was, in fact, only a couple of weeks. The air no longer felt strained and toxic. Her nerves were not primed to defend her. There was peace.

She jumped up and immediately stripped the bed, carrying the armful of linen downstairs to take across to Patsy's washing machine, which sat in a lean-to between their houses, so Bel could use it without bothering her friend. *It's a hot day, they should dry by tonight,* she thought. Then she remembered Harris. He might wonder where she'd gone. She sent him a quick text. *I'll call him later to explain properly.*

Bel needed to be at work by eight. It was Saturday, but she was doing an extra shift, her last before she became the official farm-shop baker. Tracey, who usually did weekends, was off because of childcare problems. But she had time for a tepid shower and change of clothes, maybe a quick coffee and bacon sandwich at Martine's. Bel was suddenly ravenous.

35

Micky and JJ were slumped at their favourite outside table, just as they had been on the day Bel had arrived in Cornwall. Seeing her, they grinned and waved, shifting to accommodate her on the weathered wooden bench.

'Hey, you,' JJ said, pressing a kiss to her cheek as she joined them with her sandwich and coffee. 'Haven't seen you in a while.'

She laughed. 'No, well . . .' Raising an eyebrow wearily, she related the ambulance fiasco. 'Then Dad did a midnight flit when I was asleep on the beach.'

Both men looked taken aback, although she couldn't tell which part of the story surprised them most.

'You slept on the beach?' JJ said. 'Why didn't you bang on my door?'

'I didn't mean to sleep. I just wanted to clear my head . . . Dad and I had words after the paramedics left. Then I just sort of passed out on the sand.'

'So Dennis cut out in the middle of the night?' Micky looked almost impressed by her father's behaviour.

She nodded. 'I assume he's halfway to London by now, although I haven't heard from him.' She bit into her sandwich, butter dripping out between the layers of crisp bacon. She thought nothing had tasted so good in her whole life.

'Aren't you worried?' JJ asked, as he took a gulp of coffee from the bamboo takeaway cup he always brought with him to the café.

Bel felt a prick of shame, unwilling to articulate the relief she felt in case the men thought her a monster. 'You think I should be?'

'He's not in great shape.' Micky pulled a sheepish face. 'I might not have helped. I dropped round yesterday afternoon and we sort of settled in, had a few. He was pretty tanked up when I left.'

'You're not responsible for my father, Micky,' she said. *And neither am I*, she thought, amazed to find that, for a change, her silent assertion was not hedged around with guilt.

Silence fell between them.

'Not sure doing that long drive is such a clever idea,' Micky said, obviously concerned.

'Of course it's not, Micky, but what can I do?' She heard her voice rise with frustration . . . and defensiveness.

'Hey,' JJ said. 'Dennis chose to leave, Bel.'

Tiredness suddenly overwhelmed Bel. 'I told him. For the first time I really told him how he made me feel.' She blinked wearily. 'I just couldn't take the bullying any more.'

JJ put an arm around her shoulders and gave her a squeeze.

Micky nodded sympathetically, fiddling with the corner of the cardboard box that had contained his roll. 'Look, I like the old rogue, but we've all seen how he treats you, what a rude bastard he can be.'

'You did?' Bel asked, surprised. She'd assumed her friends had bought into his outward charm and bonhomie without noticing his darker side.

'Dennis is a tough one. I wouldn't worry about him,' JJ assured her.

Bel felt almost too tired to move from her cosy seat in the sunshine and the warmth of her friends' sympathy, but she knew she would be late if she didn't get going. Saying goodbye to the two men, she hurried back to the cottage to collect her bag.

As she looked around for it, something caught her eye. A folded piece of paper lay on the seat of the orange chair. She hurried over to it, immediately recognizing her father's writing in the single word, 'Bella', scrawled on the outside.

Her heart fluttered. She didn't want to open it, dreading the rage she could imagine burning through the single sheet. Her thoughts went back to the day she'd found Louis's 'Dear John' letter on the doormat, and her fingers shook as she lifted the note, holding it away from herself as if it was contaminated.

I'll read it later, she thought, laying it carefully on the coffee table. But by the time she got to the door she'd changed her mind, admonishing herself for her feebleness. Texting her boss, she said she'd be fifteen minutes late – she was doing him a favour in covering Tracey's shift so he couldn't really complain.

She picked up the note, sat down in the chair and lifted the flap, steeling herself to face the contents.

Sweetheart, I'm sorry [her father had written]. *You're not wrong.
I can be a brute sometimes, I know. I never mean to hurt you. My
temper just gets the better of me sometimes. And I'm not myself
these days, haven't been since the plague.*

You have no idea how much I respect you.

I'll leave you in peace.

Love you, my wee girl. Dad xxx

Tears poured down Bel's cheeks, unchecked. She kept
reading and rereading the note, picking over each phrase
in the short, staccato sentences for hidden meaning, a
hint of condescension or disdain, but she found none. *If
you're clear, you will be heard.*

Bel pressed out a text to her father through her tears.
Thanks for the note. Love you, too, Dad xxx. She kept it short,
no gushing, knowing that by now her father might be
embarrassed by his words, maybe even wanting to forget
he'd ever written them. She was well aware he hadn't
miraculously changed overnight – she wasn't that naïve –
but this at least felt like a small moment of epiphany on
his part: significant for them both. Tiredness and confusion whirring in her brain, she stuffed the paper into her
back pocket, grabbed her bike and set off up the lane for
the farm shop.

'Everything OK with your father?' Harris whispered,
when he arrived later that morning. The shop was full, Mr
Ajax hovering within earshot as the artist dumped a full
basket beside the till.

As she totted up his shopping, Bel filled him in.

Harris's eyes widened. 'You must be shattered.'

'I feel all over the place, to be honest. And a bit worried I haven't heard from him.'

'I don't imagine anything will have happened to him, Bel. People like your father always get the help they need.'

'I hope you're right.'

He paid and picked up his canvas bag. 'If you ever fancy another fish and chips . . .' he muttered, his voice low so as not to draw unwanted jibes from Ron Ajax.

Bel smiled her assent, feeling a warm surge of pleasure at the prospect. 'And thank you for last night. You're so kind. It was lovely.'

When Bel got home from work she hung out the sheets on the whirlybird in the garden – she'd laboriously removed the rust with white vinegar one Sunday afternoon – then tried her father again, phoning him this time, hoping he would hear the ringtone and get back to her. She was now beginning to worry. At that time of the morning, the journey to London shouldn't take more than five hours, six at the outside – especially as Dennis always drove uncomfortably fast. He'd been gone at least eight and must have stopped by now, checked his phone, seen her messages. She knew, of course, that despite his apology he wasn't above leaving her hanging, punishing her for being too honest.

Not knowing who to contact to find out where he might be, she finally remembered Martin Riggs, the porter in the Earls Court block. 'Is Dennis back yet?' she asked him, when he returned her call around two.

'No sign of him,' Riggs told her. 'I'd know, because he always gets me to park the Jag.'

'Could you send me a text when you see him, please? He's not answering his phone.'

Bel dropped round to Patsy's at teatime, not wanting to be alone, her nerves shredded. Her neighbour listened as she said how worried she was, then shook her head. 'Look at you, love. That man controls you even when he's done a voluntary bunk and is hundreds of miles away.' She handed her an opened packet of shortbread.

Bel was taken aback by her friend's casual reaction. By now she had her father under a bus, driven head-first into a concrete overpass, keeled over with a heart attack in a Little Chef, passed out behind the wheel in the fast lane of the M4. 'What if something's happened to him?'

'If it has, we'll deal with it,' Patsy said calmly.

For a moment neither spoke, Bel slightly indignant that Patsy wasn't taking her worry more seriously.

'You and I are the same,' Patsy stated, with a sigh, as she munched a biscuit. 'We're both in thrall to utterly selfish people. We constantly excuse them, allow them to push us around, respond to their manipulations with the usual fear, fall for it every time.'

When Bel didn't reply, she went on, 'Mark my words, Bel. Right this minute, Dennis will be chatting up some waitress somewhere, tucking into a big, juicy steak, discussing motors with someone he met over a whisky in the hotel bar.'

Bel smiled, the scene all too easy to imagine.

Her friend eyed her. 'Let him go, Bel.'

Her father finally deigned to call around ten that night. 'Hi, sweetheart,' he said jauntily. 'Well, I've had quite the adventure since I last saw you.' Without giving her a moment to respond, he raced on. 'You know old Bill Mendy, the fella who used to run that chain of dodgy clubs? We supplied his wine for years.'

'I do,' Bel said. She'd never taken to the man: all hail-fellow-well-met, but cold behind the eyes.

'Well, I remembered he moved to Salisbury when his business went tits up. So I gave him a bell.' There was a breathless pause. 'He was thrilled to hear from me – don't think he has many friends. Even invited me over to lunch and broke out a stonkingly good Zin – and you know I'm not a fan of Californian reds. We jawed away for most of the afternoon, like a couple of old women.'

'You could have let me know, Dad. I was worried.'

'Worried? About what?' He chuckled, clearly buzzing from his encounter with Mendy. 'Most fun I've had in ages.'

Is he deliberately winding me up? she wondered. *Probably not deliberately*, she conceded. He was just doing what Dennis Carnegie always did: exactly what he wanted, when he wanted, with scant regard for anyone else. But her father's potentially recovered independence was worth any amount of irritation. He sounded like a very different person from the morose, sniping patient with whom she'd recently shared her house.

She listened to her father bang on about some lane closure on the M4 and realization slowly dawned. *He doesn't need me.* The thought sank in, took hold. *Let him go.*

When she'd moved into the flat, she'd caught her father at a time when he'd been at rock bottom, of course, isolated and lonely, cut off from everything he loved in the wake of the pandemic. Now Bel felt as if she was shedding a layer of skin as the burden of responsibility for her father fell away.

She reminded herself that Dennis had driven to Cornwall alone, swum, walked, even climbed onto a paddleboard, bonded with a host of new people, and had just survived another massive trip across the country, spontaneously reaching out to an old acquaintance and getting drunk, negotiating traffic chaos. All of which had left him in seemingly high spirits. He wasn't necessarily the frail, broken old man he'd allowed himself to be when he wasn't receiving the attention he thought he deserved. *Is he getting his mojo back?* Bel couldn't help rejoicing at the possibility.

36

August found Bel buzzing. *Am I really allowed this life?* she often asked herself, as she got out of bed every day to another magical dawn and the daily bake.

The debt was still her main worry, although Dennis had remained silent, since his return to London, on the subject of selling the cottage, his immediate need for money or taking up residence in Cornwall with Bel. And she thought it better not to prod the hornets' nest.

Now she was earning better and able to send more substantial amounts to her father – given her frugal lifestyle – she hoped with all her heart that it would be enough to assuage the financial panic Dennis had claimed earlier in the summer. Especially as Louis was finally contributing too, now he was on a good salary. He sounded surprisingly ferocious in his determination to pay off the debt.

But although she felt she and Louis were keeping to their side of the original arrangement, without her father's specific assent the threat still lurked above her head – a constant presence that woke her at night sometimes with a thrashing heart and a cold sweat.

Because her father hadn't fundamentally changed. Bel was well aware of that. His mood might flip. At any time he was quite capable of renewing his demand that she sell the house. But at least the small, sharp shard embedded in her psyche, created and maintained from fear since child-hood, seemed to have faded to a fainter shadow. She would never forget the abuse he had perpetrated on her. It would always be there, saved on the Cloud in her mind, ready to pop up again if the right button was pressed. But, most importantly, she knew she would never let it happen again. By telling him her truth, she had managed to sepa-rate from him, finally let go.

As the summer wore on and she gradually got into a rhythm with her baking – nailing the timings, the quanti-ties, the recipes, what sold and what didn't – she turned her attention back to the cottage. After that first flurry of clearing out, she needed to take it to the next level, as if she were putting her mark on it, securing it as her home, even if it was still under threat.

One Saturday morning, she started to clean every inch of it from top to toe, scrubbing the stone floor, polishing the windows, taking the cotton curtains down and washing every piece of clothing she possessed, and anything else she could lay her hands on until the place was squeaking in protest – Zid gave her a wide berth, she noticed, alarmed that he might be next in the firing line. The process took her a few days – she even pressure-washed the small patio garden and bought some pots in which to grow herbs.

Right now, Bel was vacuuming the bedroom with Patsy's gleaming new, supersonic turbo-charged cleaner. As she ran it over the wooden floor, the nozzle-head sucked up an entire short floorboard against the wall near the window. It was obviously loose, although Bel hadn't noticed before.

As it hung, clamped by the powerful suction to the nozzle, she peered into the hole it had revealed and saw a flash of something. Turning the machine off – the board clunking loudly to the floor as it was released – she knelt down and reached in. Her fingers met cold metal. Wriggling her hand in the constricted space, she took hold of what felt like a tin, and manoeuvred it onto its side until she could slide it out.

Sitting back on her haunches, Bel examined her find. It was, indeed, an old rectangular biscuit tin, scratched and rusty round the edges – *Probably from the sixties, or before*, she thought. And heavy. On the lid and round the sides were painted depictions – now faded with age – of Trooping the Colour, marking the Queen's official birthday. Against the backdrop of Horse Guards Parade and Whitehall in the distance, stood serried ranks of soldiers in their scarlet tunics and bearskins. On the bottom, as Bel turned it over, was a large sticker with photos of the biscuits the tin had once contained, including the famous 'milk and honey' with jam in the middle – her dad's favourite, she remembered – pink wafers and lemon puffs.

The image on the lid was partially obscured by a fraying strip of what looked like white surgical tape – the sort used to hold dressings in place. On it was written, in faded blue biro, the script wobbly copperplate: 'SECRET. rent for the agness lady'.

Bel, taken aback to be confronted by her mother's name out of the blue like this, prised off the lid, stiff with collected rust on the rim. *Money?* She was amazed to find a chaotic mass of notes. Slowly riffling through them, she realized they were all of the ten-pound denomination. There were none of the slippery new polymer ones, which she thought had come into circulation three or four years ago, only the old cotton-paper version, showing either Florence Nightingale's image or Charles Darwin's on the rear.

Stunned by her find, she sat for a moment in silence, then reached for her phone. 'Any chance you could pop round?' she asked Patsy. 'I've got something you need to see.'

Patsy, cradling the tin, gave a sad smile. 'Lord bless the man. Can you believe it? Lenny must have been saving these for ever . . . And on *his* benefits.'

'He never said?'

Patsy shook her head. 'But I know he saw your mum as his guardian angel. I told him she'd passed away at the time, of course, but he never seemed to understand . . . or it made no difference to him. He still thought of her as watching over him.'

Bel's eyes misted, remembering her mother's kindness and the gift she'd made to this vulnerable man. 'What shall I do with it?' she asked, combing her fingers through the notes in the tin, still bowled over by her discovery. 'There must be a good few thousand in here.'

Patsy looked puzzled. 'What do you mean? It belongs to you, love. You and the cottage.' She grinned. 'I'd get that stinky bathroom fixed up if I were you.'

When her friend had gone, Bel carefully counted the money Lenny had left. It amounted to three thousand, eight hundred and ninety pounds. Easily enough to fix the bathroom, as Patsy had suggested. But she had a better idea.

'Dad, listen to what just happened,' she said excitedly, as soon as she got her father on the phone. She told him about the tin and how much it contained. 'It's not enough, of course, but it's a good chunk towards the debt.' She took a deep breath. 'I need to speak to you about that, by the way . . .' Without waiting for him to reply, Bel launched into a prepared speech, reminding him of how much she was now paying each month, how much Louis had agreed to pay towards his half. She quietly begged her father, heart in her mouth, not to make her sell the cottage yet unless his need for cash was more than their joint repayment would total.

When she finished there was dead silence. Bel took a nervous breath. 'Dad?'

'Och, I don't want that poor fella's money, girl,' Dennis said, not responding to the rest of her speech. 'Keep it. Get yourself a new shower . . . and a sofa, for Christ's sake.' He laughed. 'So next time I visit, two of us can sit down comfortably at the same time.'

Bel gulped, wondering what exactly he was saying. *Next time?* He was planning on visiting the cottage in the future? 'But you told me . . . that day in Cornwall . . . You said you were desperate for money.'

' "Desperate"? Did I say that?'

Trying to control the maelstrom of emotions threatening to choke her, Bel could only stammer out, 'You said I had to sell the cottage. You said I had to pay you back the full amount immediately.'

She heard her father chuckle. 'Nah, I was only winding you both up, putting the frighteners on that no-good chef of yours.' Bel heard a wheezy breath. 'And it worked! The fella got my bank details the other week and sent a nice little starter.' He chuckled again. 'Wonders will never cease, eh?'

She gave a relieved smile that her father couldn't see. *Good one, Louis.* But she found herself unable to speak. It seemed like for ever that she'd been beset by the worry she'd have her beloved cottage snatched away.

'So what are you actually saying, Dad?' she asked eventually, her voice pinched with uncertainty. 'Just to be clear, you don't want Lenny's money?'

'If you need to do up the hovel with that fella's cash, go ahead. Good use of it.' Dennis coughed and cleared his throat.

'And the debt? We're going back to the original deal we made?' She knew she sounded insistent and shrill. But she urgently needed to know. Her father's staggering nonchalance, his open admission that he'd been manipulating them about something that sat at the very core of his daughter's heart took her breath away.

'Don't sound so anxious, sweetheart. I'm not an ogre. A deal's a deal.'

By which Bel took to mean her cottage – her *home* – was now *safe*.

Still almost unable to accept her father's volte-face, she didn't immediately reply. Then she said, 'If you're serious . . .' she heard her father's footsteps echoing on the tiled hall floor at the flat '. . . thank you. Thanks, Dad . . . Thank you very much.'

'I'd better get going, sweetheart,' Bel heard him say, ignoring her thanks. 'I'm off to bridge. That lily-livered crew have finally got back on track after all these months claiming it was still too dangerous to meet up.' He snorted derisively. 'I reckoned they'd all snuffed it, but it seems not quite all.'

She laughed shakily. 'Glad to hear it.'

They said goodbye, Bel feeling as if she'd just broken the finishing tape at the end of a double marathon. Sheer relief mixed with anger at the cruelly calculating way her cantankerous old father had played them. But she also marvelled at the transformation in Dennis's mood. It was as if his Salisbury wine-buddy had sprinkled fairy dust on him. Not that she was complaining.

37

By early September, Bel was well ensconced in the farm-shop kitchen. She would arrive on her bike at four in the morning – she had never had a problem getting up early – change into her loose white baker's shirt and immediately set to, preparing the dough for the daily loaves so it had time to prove. The place was utterly peaceful at that time of day, and she was alone, in command of her space, focused and alive.

Next, she would get going on the various cakes and savoury tarts of the day, adding croissants – which sold like the proverbial hot cakes – at the weekend. It was hard work, but she loved every minute.

Now she was getting into her stride, she was adding variety to her weekly repertoire, including treats like apple and cinnamon muffins, chocolate brownies and six-inch-long Parmesan, Cheddar and caraway-seed straws – very popular with the walkers.

Mr Ajax had been watching her progress like a hawk, delivering a daily, pithy critique on her output: 'Tart's not lemony enough'; 'Muffins should be bigger'; 'Orange and polenta cake's too dry.' Bel didn't always agree with him, but she took notice of his comments, tweaked the recipes to his satisfaction. He might not have been the most sociable of men, but he was always honest and treated her with respect now she was delivering what she had promised.

This Sunday morning, Bel was at home. She sat clutching the kitchen timer, almost biting her nails, as she waited for the contents of the oven to finish baking. She could smell the tang of hot pastry emanating from the Rayburn, but didn't dare hope her most recent baking experiment had worked.

The pinger went off, vibrating in her hand, making her jump. She hurried over to the stove. Taking the oven glove, she drew a deep breath and gingerly lifted the Bakelite knob, pulling open the door.

'Oh my God!' she said aloud, to the empty room. The tray she slid from the oven contained two rows of beautifully neat, round almond and raspberry cruffins, the dark pink fruit leaking temptingly from the centre of the woven strands of crisp, golden dough.

They smelt like heaven. She set them on the counter and gazed at them in awe, laughing to herself as she nudged one of the pastries, as if she expected it to speak up and congratulate her. As soon as they were cool enough to handle, she took each in turn and dunked it in the waiting bowl of caster sugar she'd put out in readiness, swirling the little cakes until the tops were drenched in crunchy, melting sweetness.

When, a few minutes later, she tore the cruffin in half and bit into her creation, it was just as puffy and crisp and flaky and full of buttery, fruity sweetness as she could have hoped. 'Here's to you, Mum,' she whispered, raising the pastry into the air. Putting it down and leaning against the warm stove, arms crossed, Bel was aware of a knot of happiness in the pit of her stomach.

Later, balancing a tin on one hand, she lifted the knocker on the dove-grey front door at the end of the lane. There was silence, and Bel suddenly worried Harris was out on one of his rambles, or deeply involved in a drawing and not wanting to be disturbed. She felt a little nervous at her sudden impulse and wished she'd warned him she was coming. This was the first time she'd been here since the night her father had collapsed.

She still bumped into Harris regularly in the farm shop, but now she'd started baking, they had less chance to chat. Bel was no longer sitting behind the till, and had often finished work for the day by the time the artist came in for his cup of tea. Neither had they instigated the fish-and-chips supper he'd tentatively suggested weeks ago, after the debacle with her father – although she knew his head-teacher sister had been visiting during August.

Before Bel had time to lose her nerve, the door flew open. Harris was barefoot, in shorts and a dark T-shirt, his long legs tanned from all the wandering he did in search of subjects to paint, his hair the usual mess of greying curls.

'Hi, Bel.' He looked surprised, but his smile was welcoming and he quickly stepped back to usher her inside.

Suddenly feeling a bit shy, she held out the tin. 'I made raspberry cruffins.'

'Wonderful. I'm not sure what a cruffin is, but I'm sure

it'll be delicious.' He grinned as he took the tin. 'I'll put the coffee on.'

It was a warm, sunny morning, so they took their pastries and coffee outside to the bench overlooking the field. At this time of day, the sun was just peeping round the side of the house, fingering the garden with pale light.

For a while there was an appreciative silence. Then Harris turned to her, holding the remains of his pastry aloft and grinning. 'These are sensational, Bel. I'm hooked.'

She laughed self-consciously. 'Baking is my mood barometer. I can only do it successfully when the needle points to "fair".'

'Seems to me like it's pointing to "fair" pretty regularly these days, if your farm-shop goodies are anything to go by.' There was a pause. 'You're like a different person, Bel. All those dramas with your father . . . It's good to see you enjoying life now.'

'It's taken some getting used to, having a clear run at things,' she replied reflectively.

Harris's eyes lit up. 'I keep expecting Ron to interrupt us, tell me to get back to work, tell you that a customer needs serving . . . or, these days, that a bun needs baking.'

She laughed. 'Our whole friendship, if you think about it, has been based on half-finished sentences.'

'Still, we seem to be managing pretty well.' There was a pause. 'I love our chats,' he said, quietly.

Bel felt a twitch of pleasure. *I really like them, too*, she thought. Now, fumbling for a response that didn't say too much or too little, she finally settled on turning to him with a smile of agreement. Although he was neither physical nor demonstrative with her, she sensed a pull between them, felt the soft stirring sometimes in the way he looked at her. The night of the fish supper, for example, when he'd tucked her hair back behind her ear. *I'm probably imagining it*, she told herself now.

They fell silent, until she said, 'It's Patsy's birthday on Tuesday. I thought I'd do a small party in the garden. Will you come?' She paused. 'And Tally, my stepdaughter, is arriving tonight. I'd love you to meet her.' As she spoke, she wondered if she was coming across too strongly, putting under pressure a man who seemed very private and quite shy. *He can always say no*, she assured herself silently, as she waited for him to reply.

'A yes to both,' he replied immediately.

'Think you got the legs on backwards,' JJ commented, that afternoon, frowning at the wooden garden table that had arrived flat-packed from Amazon the day before. Bel had asked JJ and Micky round to advise on the decorations for Patsy's party. The patio, although now sparkling clean from the pressure-wash, was bare and uninspiring.

Bel groaned in disbelief. 'Seriously?' The bloody thing had taken the good part of two hours to assemble, the so-called instructions like deciphering A-level Finnish.

Micky started to giggle, squatting on his haunches to take a closer look. 'Yup.' He pointed to the crossed wood beneath the slatted top. 'That's why it's wobbling. The feet should sit flush with the ground, not sticking up like this. See?'

Bel did see, now it was pointed out. She shot a

beseeching glance at Micky, who gave her a tolerant smile. 'Get me the Allen key and a screwdriver.'

Later, table properly balanced, the three surveyed the space in silence. The rambling rose was untidy and no longer flowering against the end wall – which gave onto the windowless stone flank of the house behind her own. The lavender in the tub had lost its summer-purple vibrancy. There was only a euphorbia – according to Patsy, as Bel's knowledge of plants could have fitted on a post-age stamp – and some sad sedge grass, turning pale and dry, in the narrow bed along the rickety fence.

'Could hang a pole from one fence to the other and string paper lanterns across,' JJ suggested.

'And bunting?' Micky added. 'Bring the firepit up.'

'I found this old lace tablecloth in Anne's garage,' Bel said. 'It's a bit brown round the edges, but that won't matter. And I've still got a basket of Lenny's jam jars we could put tea-lights in. It won't be quite dark at seven, but getting there.'

'I can bring greenery from Mum's garden to drape over the table and hide the fence. She's been nagging me for weeks to cut stuff back. I'll nip over in the morning.'

'And I'll help you bake the cake, obviously,' said JJ, with a perfectly straight face – it was a joke between them all, his pride in his inability even to boil an egg.

'Very big of you,' she said, laughing. 'Luckily you're off the hook. Jaz is insisting.' She threw her arms around the shoulders of the two men and thanked them for their input. 'Listen, I'd better get going. Patsy's lent me Dora to pick up Tally.'

*

379

Her stepdaughter looked around the little cottage with delight. Turning to Bel, she hugged her close. 'This is gorgeous. I love it.'

Bel laughed. 'It's all a bit bodged together, but we're getting there. You'll be glad to hear I managed to sort out the worst of the grim bathroom before you came – you wouldn't have thanked me for a lukewarm trickle of water and a broken shower fitting.' *Thank you, Lenny*, she thought. When she could find the time, his money would also enable her – with Micky's help – to replace the tiles with a smart tile wall and lay some pretty blue and white laminate she'd seen online. Ray had already had a full service, so now the water was properly hot.

Tally twirled on her toes like an enthusiastic child, her dark hair flying out in a glossy curtain around her head. 'I wouldn't have minded. It's just so great to be here, Bel.'

Bel handed her a mug of tea. 'So, what news from Oxford?'

'Yeah, OK, I think.' Tally gave a slow nod. 'Dad seems to have got stuck in. He's talking the talk about how fantastic it's all going to be. He still looks a bit knackered, if I'm honest. The fiasco with Trinny and the baby really took it out of him.'

Bel sympathized, but Louis now seemed to fall into the same category as her father: part of her life, but no longer an immediate presence in her thoughts. 'I hope he makes it work, sweetheart.' *For your sake as much as his*. Taking a deep breath, she went on, 'I'm afraid the next two days will be a bit chaotic with the party. After that, I'm all yours as soon as I've finished the morning bake. We can swim

380

and hang out, go wherever you fancy. Looks like we're in for an Indian summer, if you believe the forecast.'

Tuesday night was, indeed, warm and still. Bel and Tally had been sweating in the tiny kitchen all day for the fifteen or so guests expected. But now the whole salmon sat beneath its neat rows of sliced cucumber scales in the fridge beside a vat of home-made herb mayonnaise, and on the counter top stood an array of salads: green bean and feta; potato, spring onion and hardboiled egg; tomato and anchovy; mixed lettuce. The patio had been transformed into a magical grotto, the glow from the coloured paper lanterns and tea-lights mingling with the firepit flames to create a bright, cosy cocoon against the fading day. Sprays of the foliage Micky had plucked from his mother's garden decorated the fence, and the lacy linen cloth lay on the table, on which rested an odd assortment of glasses, plates and cutlery. Tally's chilled music selection, sourced from Louis's HomePod mini, pulled it all together.

Patsy had tears in her eyes when she saw what they had achieved. She looked beautiful in her turquoise cotton shirt and white Capri pants, arriving with her hand in Rhian's. 'Blimey, love. This is special. You've really done me proud.'

Fresh from the shower and taking a deep breath of relief that everything was ready in time, Bel beamed. 'It's a small thing, Patsy. I just wanted to thank you for everything you've done for me.' She threw out her arm to indicate the others. 'And I had a ton of help.'

As the evening wore on, Bel found she was waiting for

Harris to appear, looking forward to seeing him. She was pretty sure this wasn't his thing, but she hoped, nonetheless, that he might at least pop in to say hello. He knew Rhian quite well, Patsy and Logan a little. Brigid was here, too, cigarette in hand, blowing smoke over the garden wall, where it lingered like a wraith on the still night air.

'How's it going?' JJ was by her side, swinging a beer by its neck. More bottles, and the white wine, were sitting in a large rubber ice bucket by the fence.

Bel smiled up at him. 'We did it.'

'She looks so happy.'

They both glanced to where Patsy was chatting to a group of people, Micky and Tally among them. 'Think Micky's taken a shine to your beautiful stepdaughter,' he observed.

'He'll have to work hard,' she joked, then found herself stifling a yawn – she'd been up since three thirty to bake. 'Is it too early to do the cake?' Bel, suddenly overcome with exhaustion, longed for her bed. And it was after ten, the salmon and salads long dispatched, the disparate groups mellow with food and wine.

He's not coming, she decided, feeling a little disappointed as she went inside to find Jaz. She stabbed at the unyielding plastic of the candle packet, her mind going back to that moment on the bench, when Harris had told her he loved their chats. But it was hard to know what he was feeling. *Could mean anything*, she thought now.

Jaz appeared from the front garden, where she'd been sitting on the wall with her friend Ellie. 'Time?' she asked. She looked nervous as she took the candles from Bel and placed them in a circle on the glitter-laden chocolate icing, surrounded by raspberries and Patsy's name in flowing silver script. Bel struck a long match and began to light the candles. 'You carry it,' she insisted, to the teenager.

As Bel put the matches away and made to follow the cake outside, she heard a knock behind her. Turning, she saw Harris bending his head at the low door of the cottage. He gave her an apologetic smile. 'Sorry. I'm so sorry, Bel. It's so rude to be this late but I got caught up in work and didn't notice the time.'

She smiled, but cocked an eyebrow sceptically.

Harris seemed to colour under his tan. 'I'm not great at parties,' he confessed.

'Just in time. They're about to cut the cake,' she said.

When the much-admired cake had been handed out on mismatched plates, Bel raised her glass. 'Happy birthday, Patsy!' There was general cheering and clapping, but she held up her hand for silence. Meeting her friend's eye across the crowded patio, she spoke slowly and clearly. 'Since I arrived here, you've given me so much. Support, friendship, practical help . . . endless delicious meals and laughter in your wonderful kitchen.' She took a breath. 'But most of all, you've shown me – someone you barely knew – love.' She swallowed hard. 'All of you have shown me so much love. And I thank you from the bottom of my heart.'

Suddenly embarrassed by all the eyes upon her, by her own emotions, Bel turned her head away as the clapping broke out again. It had been such a journey for her, these last four months, as she'd gradually prised herself away from old habits, old patterns of behaviour that no longer suited her – if, indeed, they ever had. It seemed almost miraculous that she was here at all. And Patsy and the others had been there every step of the way, holding her when it looked as if she might fall.

'Great speech,' Harris, standing beside her, said softly.

But before Bel had a chance to reply, Brigid was upon them, hugging Harris, taking his arm in a proprietorial fashion and pulling him away. 'Something I need to talk to you about,' she muttered. Bel watched as the woman dragged him to a couple of chairs at the far end of the garden and sat him down, leaning towards him in such a confiding way, Bel found herself wincing.

'She's not with him,' JJ, beside her, whispered, following her line of sight. 'Never has been, despite the gossip.'

Bel screwed up her face, mortified at being so transparent.

'Scout's honour,' he added, giving her a friendly nudge.

When the party began to break up, Bel watched Brigid and Harris rise to their feet and make their way through the other guests to thank her and say goodbye.

'Give me a lift?' Brigid asked, smiling beguilingly up at Harris. 'I came on the bike and I'm not sure I can manage the hill. It's dark and I've eaten too much.'

Bel watched as Harris seemed to hesitate for a long moment. 'Umm . . . I think I might stay for a while, help Bel clear up.'

Brigid shot a surprised – and clearly offended – glance at Bel, then looked back at Harris. He shifted from one foot to the other. Brigid's eyebrows rose then sank, in a knowing manner. 'Right, OK.' She reached up to peck Harris on the cheek before turning on her heel, calling over her shoulder, 'See you, then.'

Patsy, weaving across the garden, came over to Bel and pulled her into a fierce hug, swaying with her from side to side, humming to herself. 'That was bliss. The very best. Loved every minute. Thanks, love. Thank you so much.' She lifted her head, smiling woozily. When she let go of Bel, she wobbled violently. But Rhian caught her. 'Best get her home,' the vicar said, with a loving smile.

Eventually it was just her and Harris, alone in the garden. JJ, Micky, Tally, Jaz and Ellie had taken off to the beach for a midnight swim, the September sea still warmed by the summer, Micky with a bottle of wine in each hand. Bel shooed them off, insisting the clearing up could wait till morning. They'd all helped enough.

After a desultory collection of some of the glasses and beer bottles strewn around the garden, she and Harris sat side by side in front of the glowing firepit, each with a mug of tea on the paving stones at their feet.

'Tally's charming,' he said. 'Sorry we didn't get the chance to talk much.'

'I adore her. I worried splitting with Louis would affect our relationship. But so far . . .' She crossed her fingers.

After a long pause, Harris, staring into the ashes of the fire, asked tentatively, 'You don't have regrets about . . . well, Louis, for instance?'

I have plenty of regrets, Bel thought. Some pertained to

Louis, but most to her father. She and Louis had made a good fist of their life together, until the pandemic hit. OK, it wasn't perfect, but she'd been happy enough. *Or maybe*, she considered, now she knew what happiness really was, *busy enough not to question how happy I was*. But she had loved Louis. Patsy always insisted, 'You can only do it when you do it,' but Bel was aware she had wasted too much of her life under someone else's thumb. 'None at all,' she said firmly.

Harris looked at her keenly, then nodded as if reassured.

'You and Brigid . . . ?' Bel found herself enquiring in return, resenting the twinge of jealousy that lingered, despite JJ's assertion, as she pictured the two of them locked in close conversation at the end of the garden.

Harris shook his head. 'We spent some time together over lockdown. Got the tongues wagging.' He turned to Bel. 'I like her. But never in that way. She can be quite intense.'

Bel smiled, also reassured. It was so peaceful in the post-party quiet and warmth of the fire, Zid's silky bulk slinking round her bare calves in search of dropped titbits, the chilly darkness beyond wrapping them in an intimate cloak.

Harris was silent. Then he reached for her cold hand, bringing it to rest in his lap. He covered it with both of his, his grasp both warm and purposeful . . . tender.

Bel gave a soft sigh, but neither spoke. They didn't feel the need to.

Acknowledgements

As usual, I've been surrounded by such a wonderful team at Penguin Michael Joseph. First and foremost my clever editors Clare Bowron, Rebecca Hilsdon and Maxine Hitchcock.

Then there's Hazel Orme, who manages to smooth out a sentence like magic.

Emma Henderson and her sharp-eyed proofreaders, who somehow manage to pull the whole thing together.

Jonathan Lloyd, my ace agent, who has been particularly kind and supportive this year.

And all at Curtis Brown.

Cornwall gets a huge mention – without which there would have been no escape!

And, of course, Don and my gorgeous family.

THANK YOU all so much!

He just wanted a decent book to read ...

Not too much to ask, is it? It was in 1935 when Allen Lane, Managing Director of Bodley Head Publishers, stood on a platform at Exeter railway station looking for something good to read on his journey back to London. His choice was limited to popular magazines and poor-quality paperbacks – the same choice faced every day by the vast majority of readers, few of whom could afford hardbacks. Lane's disappointment and subsequent anger at the range of books generally available led him to found a company – and change the world.

'We believed in the existence in this country of a vast reading public for intelligent books at a low price, and staked everything on it'
Sir Allen Lane, 1902–1970, founder of Penguin Books

The quality paperback had arrived – and not just in bookshops. Lane was adamant that his Penguins should appear in chain stores and tobacconists, and should cost no more than a packet of cigarettes.

Reading habits (and cigarette prices) have changed since 1935, but Penguin still believes in publishing the best books for everybody to enjoy. We still believe that good design costs no more than bad design, and we still believe that quality books published passionately and responsibly make the world a better place.

So wherever you see the little bird – whether it's on a piece of prize-winning literary fiction or a celebrity autobiography, political tour de force or historical masterpiece, a serial-killer thriller, reference book, world classic or a piece of pure escapism – you can bet that it represents the very best that the genre has to offer.

Whatever you like to read – trust Penguin.